Amy Rafferty
AUTHOR

Join me in my VIP reader group to get all my latest updates, newsletters and freebies. I will send you regular pictures of La Jolla Cove, San Diego and the Florida Gulf Beaches where I try to spend as much time as I can. I live in San Diego, my own 'Garden Of Eden' and I am in love with the sea and the beaches in the area. They inspire me to write lots of beachy feel good romance fiction to share with my awesome readers like you. Go to https://landing.mailerlite.com/webforms/landing/y6w2d2to join the group!

SECRETS OF WHITE SANDS COVE

A San Diego Sunset Series - Full Collection

AMY RAFFERTY

© **Copyright 2021 Amy Rafferty — All rights reserved.**

This is a work of fiction. Names, characters, places, and incidents either are products of the author's imagination or are used fictitiously. Any similarity to actual events or locales or persons, living or dead, is entirely coincidental.

All rights reserved. No part of this publication may be reproduced, stored in, or introduced into a retrieval system, or transmitted, in any form, or by any means (electronic, mechanical, photocopying, recording, or otherwise) without the prior written permission of the copyright owner.

The author acknowledges the trademarked status and trademark owners of various products referenced in this work of fiction, which have been used without permission.

The publication / use of the trademarks is not authorized, associated with, or sponsored by the trademark owners.

Formatted by Author Services by Sarah

Cover Design by Primal Studios

CHARACTER LIST

Michael Cooper - Architect, pilot, and part owner of White Sands Cove
Lilly Crowley - Michael's cousin. Business manager and part owner of White Sands Cove
Samantha (Cooper) Green - Michael's oldest sister
Maddison (Cooper) Grant - Michael's second oldest sister. Creator of Maddison Lane

Erin Carnegie - Lawyer
Kelsey Carnegie - Erin's daughter. Studying to be a doctor
Caleb Barnes - Erin's godson. Photographer, videographer, and engineer

Zane McCaid - Guest at White Sands Cove. Honorable discharge from the army after sustaining injuries in the line of duty
Fallon McCaid - Zane McCaid's niece

Sheldon Myers - Erin's ex-husband - deceased
Parker Myers - Sheldon's younger brother

Goose - Male, St. Bernard

Lunar - Female, Golden Retriever

Rafferty - Part Maine Coon

Gretchen Tucker - A local minister

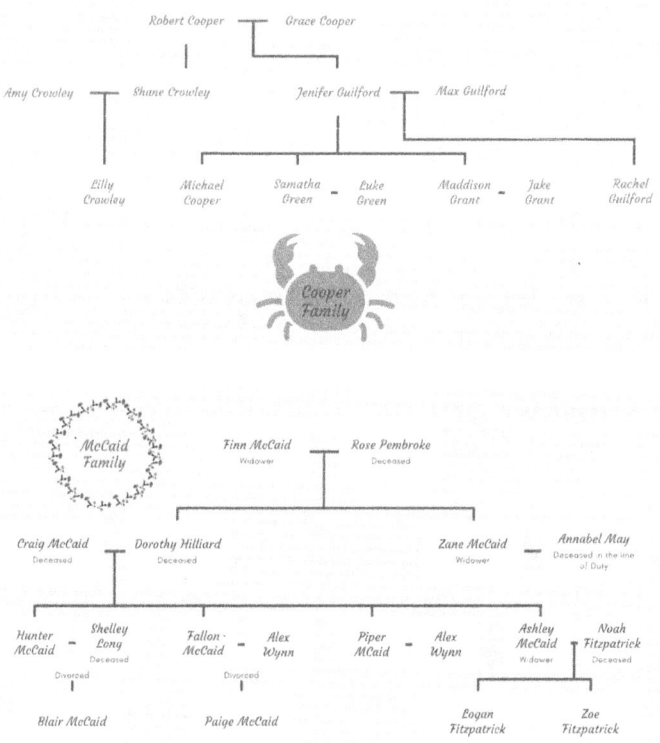

SECRETS OF WHITE SANDS COVE

Book 1

PROLOGUE

*E*rin Carnegie is uprooting her New York life and heading for the warm shores of La Jolla, San Diego to start over. Some might say she's running away but Erin, her daughter, Kelsey, and godson Caleb Barnes, need a fresh start somewhere they can heal and regroup. Thanks to Erin's best friend and former work colleague, their fresh start comes with good weather, white sandy beaches, and people who don't know who they are.

In La Jolla, Michael Cooper and his cousin Lilly Crowley are scrambling to get ready to launch the second part of their White Sands Cove resort project — The White Sands Cove Hotel. As nature and forces they can't control around them conspire against the cousins, their first guests arrive to complicate their lives a little more.

Zane McCaid has sailed with his family to La Jolla for a much-needed vacation and to celebrate his nieces' and nephews' triple wedding. Staying at the White Sands Cove hotel gives Zane and his family the perfect opportunity to go on a treasure hunt and solve a centuries old family mystery.

Join Erin and her family, Zane and his family, and cousins Michael and Lilly as they scramble to sort out their lives, while all getting pulled into an adventure of a lifetime. A treasure hunt and mysterious secret beach caves that get them all trapped in a potentially deadly situation. As they band together to face the dangers ahead, each one learns they may also be in danger of losing their hearts.

Have some fun in the sun on the white sandy beach and get lost in an adventure as the characters try to figure out the secrets of White Sands Cove.

Chapter One
THE REVERSING INCIDENT

"Michael," Lilly ran through their shared bungalow. "Are you going to collect my father and mother from the airport?"

"What's the time?" Michael ran out of his room looking disheveled.

"Time to get to the airport." Lilly rolled her eyes. "If you leave now, you might get there just in time." She shook her head.

"I'm on my way." Michael tucked the tail of his brightly colored cotton Hawaiian shirt into his blue boardshorts. "Do you know where my other shoe is?" He looked beneath the sofa and dining room table.

"Why would I know where your shoe is?" Lilly asked him. "Wear another pair of shoes."

"Fine." Michael ran into his room. "Found it!" He hopped back out of his room pulling his sneaker on.

"Here are your keys," Lilly threw his keys at him, "drive safe."

"Great, just getting a pop-tart." Michael went to grab a pop-tart before running out the front door and to his Jeep.

"Don't forget to stop and pick up those plumbing bits that

9

are waiting to be collected." Lilly ran after him with the invoice. "You're going to need this."

"Thanks, cuz," Michael took the invoice and jumped into his jeep. "Please don't forget to move the two jumps I have today to tomorrow if you can."

"I already have," Lilly waved her cousin off. "They're booked for ten and twelve tomorrow."

Michael waved out the window as he pulled out of the long drive with sandy dunes on the one side and rocky cliffs on the other. He bit into his pop-tart as he bumped along the uneven drive until he got to the main road.

His phone rang and he answered through the car system. It was his oldest sister, Samantha.

"Hi, sis," Michael greeted, "what's up?"

"Hi, Mike," Samantha's voice filled the car. "Can you please fetch me on your way to San Diego? I know you're running late but I'm ready and waiting in the drive for you. I have to get a present for Luke's birthday next week."

"Sure," Michael grinned and took another bite of his pop-tart. "I'll be there in ten minutes."

He hung up the phone and changed direction to head towards his sister's house. It was such a lovely bright sunny summer's day. Michael rolled all the car windows down to let in the fresh morning air as he enjoyed his pop-tart and drove along next to the sparkling blue Pacific Ocean.

Michael couldn't believe it had been almost five years since his family had moved from a big city to La Jolla. Growing up he loved to spend his summers here with his grandfather and great-aunt. Back then, he couldn't think of living anywhere but in the big city he'd grown up in. Then four years ago his mother had packed them all up and moved to La Jolla permanently. Now Michael couldn't think of living anywhere else.

Michael's mother, Jennifer, had inherited White Sands Cove, which once belonged to her great-great-grandfather. Now she'd signed it over to Michael and his cousin Lilly to build it up into a hotel and beach retreat. With the money that the family had inherited five years ago, Michael and Lilly were able to build their beach retreat.

Michael had been studying architecture when he and Lilly started the White Sands Cove project. Together, Michael and Lilly had designed the entire beach retreat. Last summer they'd opened the new White Sands Cove Crab Shack beach restaurant along with the adventure trails side of the business. In three weeks' time they were about to have the grand opening of the White Sands Cove Hotel.

It was a really exciting and really scary time for Michael and Lilly. The weather was being really cooperative this year as well, laying out hot summer days for them. It was going to be the summer vacation period soon and the beach retreat and adventures were booked up. Even their new hotel was nearly fully booked, and it had yet to be opened.

Michael turned onto the street where his eldest sister Samantha lived. She was standing at the end of her drive waiting for him with a small cooler box. Samantha always packed snacks if she came with him to San Diego. She was four months pregnant with her next baby and was so thankful that she wasn't having twins again. His almost four-year-old nephew and niece were cute little handfuls over indulged by their father.

"Hey sister," Michael pulled up to the curb. "I see you have the cooler box."

"Of course." Samantha got into the car so fast it was like she was running away from someone. "Drive, drive, drive." She indicated with her hands.

"What's up with the quick getaway?" Michael asked as he pulled off.

"The twins wanted to come and say hi to you." Samantha sorted out her items at her feet once she'd strapped herself in. "You know where that leads, and I really need a few hours off." She rubbed her belly. "I don't feel like having them bounce around in a car or have to run after them in a store."

"We have to pick up Shane and Amy from the airport first" Michael grinned at the look of excitement on her face.

"I know and I'm so looking forward to mingling in a crowd of nameless faces," Samantha sighed contentedly. "When you have kids, you'll understand that." She grinned at him.

"For now I'm quite content with you and Maddison supplying Mom and Max with grandkids," Michael smiled. "It's really great spending time with the kids but I get to give them back to their parents at the end of the day and sleep through the night in peace."

"Usually hyped on a sugar high when they come back from you." Samantha looked at him accusingly. "Talking about relationships, how is ... Carrie was it?"

"Carly," Michael corrected Samantha, "and that ended months ago." Michael's eyes widened. "Like Lilly said, I had a narrow escape as Carly was really jealous of everyone, even the twins."

"Well then definitely good riddance." Samantha reached into her cooler and pulled out some ginger cookies. "Cookie?"

"Thanks." Michael took the cookie. "I was only able to grab one pop-tart on the way out this morning."

"You must be starving." Samantha reached back into her cooler box. "Luckily, I made a BLT sub for you." She handed it to a grateful Michael.

"You're an angel." Michael took a big bite of the sub. "I don't know if I told you this, but you've always been my favorite sister."

"Uh-huh," Samantha munched on her ginger cookies, "isn't that what you told Maddison last week when she took that yacht cruise out for you?"

"Yeah," Michael shrugged. "But I was still thinking you were my favorite." He grinned.

Twenty minutes later Michael waited for a car to pull out of a parking space at the San Diego airport. The driver's huge car needed more space to back out the parking lot. Michael looked behind him to make sure it was clear before reversing. As he pulled back another car rounded the corner and slammed right into the Jeep.

Samantha jolted forward in the safety belt while Michael swore a blue streak in the car. He switched off the engine and jumped out of the car.

I really don't need this right now! Michael thought angrily as he walked to assess the damage to his car. *Well, there goes a few hundred dollars because that dent wasn't going to be able to be buffed out.*

"Don't you look where you're driving?" a woman yelled through her open car window. "What were you thinking just reversing like that!"

Michael spun around towards the sound of the angry voice. He didn't get angry easily. But when someone rode into him and then made out it was his fault — he got angry.

"Don't *you* look where you're driving?" Michael seethed, glaring at the woman with strawberry blonde hair and overly large sunglasses resting on the bridge of her nose. "My hazard and reverse lights were on and as clear as day." Michael pointed to the lights flickering on his car like a Christmas tree.

"I was turning the corner," the strawberry blonde woman still leaned out her window instead of getting out "and you roared backward in your car from nowhere."

"Michael, what's going on?" Samantha climbed out of the car and walked towards the commotion.

"Now I have to go back to the rental company." The woman finally got out of her car when she saw Samantha. "I hope you're going to pay for any damage to my rental!" She bawled her fists besides her.

"What?" Michael glared at her. "You hit me, lady!"

"You reversed up to a corner!" the haughty princess lifted her chin just enough so she could look down her nose at him. "Who reverses up to a corner when they know this is a throughway for other cars in the parking lot?"

"My car is a jeep!" Michael pointed both hands to his car like he was presenting something. "You can see it over the tops of all five of these sedans parked here."

"Not when you're already rounding the corner and the lunatic in the jeep reverses into you!" She raised her voice.

"Okay," Samantha stepped in. "Michael, it looks like it's just cosmetic damage." She looked at his dented bumper. "And your car also only has a dented bumper." Samantha said to the woman. "So, I think you each pay for your own car's damage and call it quits."

"That sounds reasonable," the woman said and glanced at her wristwatch. "I'm late." She glared up at Michael. "Are we good?" she said impatiently.

"I guess so." Michael's eyes glared down at her.

"Just watch where you're going and don't reverse so fast," she said, climbing into her car.

"Unbelievable!" Michael shook his head and stared at the woman in amazement as she pulled around his car and drove off.

"Let it go." Samantha patted Michael on the back. "Shane and Amy will have disembarked by now." She looked at her watch. "We'd best get parked."

"Can you believe the nerve of that woman?" Michael grumbled still seething from the encounter as he climbed back into his Jeep and parked it.

Chapter Two
TOUCH DOWN IN LA JOLLA

*E*rin Carnegie and her twenty-four-year-old godson, Caleb Barnes, rushed through the airport. Their plane had arrived thirty minutes late. Erin's daughter, Kelsey, had taken an earlier flight. They were also supposed to be on the earlier flight, but it had been overbooked. Erin and Caleb decided to let a mother and her young daughter take their place.

Erin and Caleb had retrieved their bags and were making their way through the airport rush. She was tired and was starting to get a migraine from all the stress of the past few weeks. They had gone by in a blur of packing and getting ready to uproot her, Kelsey, and Caleb's life in New York to move to La Jolla. The last eighteen months since her ex-husband's death had been extremely hard and messy. Even from the grave, Sheldon Myers made her, Erin, and Caleb's lives a living hell. Erin had kept her maiden name for professional reasons throughout her marriage. When she'd finally kicked Sheldon out of their lives for good, Kelsey had her name legally changed to Carnegie.

Erin could remember the look on fourteen-year-old Kelsey's face when her father hadn't even blinked an eye to sign consent for her name change. Never had she wanted to slap a man so badly in all her life as she had on that day. Kelsey hadn't made the decision lightly, but her father's disgraced name was dragging her down.

Poor Caleb had come to live with them after his parents were killed in a car accident when he was twelve. It was the same year Erin had discovered some shocking truths about her late ex-husband. But those truths were nothing compared to the landslide that had hit them upon his death. Two days before Sheldon died, he'd contacted Erin out of the blue after she'd not heard or seen him in eight years.

Erin had known not to take his call or meet with him, but he'd begged her, and she'd gone to the meeting. A decision she was to regret not even eight hours later when the press had hunted Erin and her children down. The Carnegie name had been discovered and linked to that of Sheldon Myers. Once again Kelsey and Caleb had been dragged into the Myers corrupt political shadow. Theirs and Erin's careers had been ruined. Not to mention the fact that they could barely leave their homes thanks to the press constantly hounding them.

Two weeks after Sheldon's death things went from worse to the very worst. After that it had been eighteen months of struggle and fighting for her kids. She'd spent most of her trust fund, sold her house, and even had to borrow money from her parents to keep on fighting and keeping them safe. Her daughter's fiancé had broken off their engagement not long after Sheldon died. Kelsey had been suspended from NYU Grossman Medical School and lost her internship. While Caleb's star tumbled from the sky as his lucrative photographic and videography career was ripped out from under him.

Erin had become obsessed with finding out the truth while defending her kids. All her so-called friends turned their backs on her. All except one, Jennifer Cooper or rather Jennifer Guilford when she remarried four years ago. She'd fought side by side with Erin tirelessly flying across the country whenever she needed to be in New York. Finally, eighteen months after the nightmare Sheldon's death had caused, they'd caught a break.

But when the dust had cleared, and Erin's family had finally won, it was too late. The stain of the past eighteen months would scar them forever. Thank goodness for Erin's mom and dad. Erin's father was one of America's top surgeons and even though he was now retired, he sat on a lot of medical and educational boards. Erin's father had managed to get Kelsey's studies back on track. She'd have to start her fourth year of medical school again and would start at UC, La Jolla with an internship at Jacobs Medical Center in a week's time. It wasn't at her chosen medical school, but it was still a top school.

Erin, Kelsey, and Jacob were getting a new start in a new town almost three-thousand miles away from New York. As soon as that plane had touched down at San Diego airport, Erin had felt like she could breathe again for the first time in almost two years.

It was Jennifer who'd convinced Erin to pack up their lives and move to La Jolla. Erin was going to work at the agency where Jennifer and her husband worked. Until they were settled, Jennifer's son and niece were putting her, Kelsey, and Caleb up in a family bungalow at their new adventure retreat.

"Mom," Kelsey called to Erin, "I'm over here." She waved.

"Hey, honey." Erin walked a little faster towards her daughter, pulling her onboard case behind her.

"Don't worry about me," Caleb called, pushing the trolley piled high with their luggage. "I'll just struggle here with this trolley that seems to find things more fascinating on its left side."

"Sorry, sweetie," Erin stopped and turned towards the tall man she'd come to think of as her son after all these years he'd lived with them. "I'll pull it from the front." Erin switched her small wheelie bag to her other hand so she could steady the trolley for Caleb.

"How do you walk so fast in two-inch heels?" Caleb frowned

at Erin, who he'd started calling mom when he was thirteen years old. Anyone who defended him and looked after him as Erin did deserved to be called mom. She'd even jumped into a well to save his pet frog once.

"Honey," Erin grinned up at him. Even in two and a half inch heels she had to basically crane her neck to look at Caleb's face. His six-foot-three frame towered over her five-foot-four one. "If I didn't wear these heels, I'd get lost in-between the two of you." She pointed from Kelsey to Caleb.

Kelsey had got her height from her father's side of the family and was a good four inches taller than Erin.

"Caleb could always get a purse and put you in it to carry you around." Kelsey gave her mom a cheeky grin. "At least then you'd save your feet from always being shoved into ridiculously high-heels."

"Always the doctor." Erin patted her daughters' cheek while Kelsey took Erin's small case and started to lead the way out of the airport.

"I still have four years residency to go," Kelsey smiled sadly at her mom. "I'm so lucky that Grandad was able to pull a few strings to get me into Jacobs Medical Center and UC, La Jolla."

"We can invite your grandmother and grandfather for a vacation in La Jolla as a thank you when we're settled," Erin smiled encouragingly at her daughter.

One of the worst things to come of the mess Sheldon had caused was how it had derailed Kelsey's medical career and Caleb's photography career. Jennifer's husband, Max, had employed Caleb to be their agency's photographer. It may not be as intense and exciting as his last position but at least he still got to do what he loved. Caleb had even surprised her and offered to do some photos of Jennifer's son's new retreat. As well as the triple wedding highlighted function to be held at the grand opening of their hotel.

Erin shuddered when she thought how close her children had come to a life sentence.

"The car's this way," Kelsey walked towards the parking lot. "I had to get us an SUV because it was all the rental company had available."

"It's cool." Caleb packed all the cases into the trunk of the vehicle. "I'll just go walk the trolley back to the trolley bay."

"Just push it over there and leave it," Kelsey told Caleb impatiently. "Why do you always have to be such a rule follower?" She threw up her hands.

"Why do you always have to look for all the shortcuts?" Caleb slammed the trunk. "I feel sorry for your patients once you become a surgeon." He shook his head as he walked away.

"I hope you two don't plan to bicker the entire trip to La Jolla." Erin hopped into the passenger seat and took out two aspirin for her headache as it raged out of control.

"Are you getting a migraine again, Mom?" Kelsey climbed into the back seat looking over to her mother worriedly.

"I'll be fine now that we're finally here," Erin turned and smiled at her daughter. "How are you holding up, sweetheart?" she asked her daughter.

"I'm getting there." Kelsey smiled at her mother. "I'm worried about Caleb though. He's having night terrors again."

"What?" Erin's head swiveled back towards Kelsey. "How long have they been going on for?"

"They started while we were being held in the FBI secure facility." Kelsey shuddered. "You should've rather let us go to prison."

"I wanted you to be put under house arrest and your grandmother had tried." Erin shook her head and took a deep breath. "But Sheldon's family has powerful connections and he thought it safer for the both of you to be there."

"You mean so that he could make sure you didn't get close to the truth?" Caleb's hazel eyes flashed angrily as he slid into the driver's seat and then cursed. "Kels, couldn't you have moved the seat back?"

"Isn't it enough that I'm letting you drive?" Kelsey raised her eyebrows.

"You're letting me drive because you haven't slept in days and you hate flying." Caleb finished adjusting the seat and then the mirror. "Mom, you and Kels should try to get some sleep on the drive."

"I think I'm going to close my eyes for a few minutes." Erin smiled and leaned back in her seat as Caleb skillfully navigated them out of the airport and onto the motorway.

"How's Rafferty doing?" Caleb asked Kelsey, glancing at her in the rearview mirror.

"He's still groggy," Kelsey put her finger through the cat carrier and scratched her large sleepy cat.

"I'm sure he'll be okay." Caleb gave her an encouraging smile in the mirror. "Mom's asleep." He grinned at Erin who had propped her neck pillow against her window and dozed off.

"She was getting another migraine," Kelsey said worriedly.

"You know she won't go for a scan," Caleb warned Kelsey knowing she was going to try and push Erin to get one again.

"How did things get so messed up for us Cal?" Tears misted her beautiful amber eyes.

"It's going to be okay, Kels," Caleb assured her. "We just have to put that behind us as best we can and stick together while we heal. Like we've always done."

"I hope we can get over this, Cal." Kelsey swallowed the lump in her throat. "Mom has worked so hard to give us a new life. I don't want to let her down by not being able to move on."

"You'd never let her down, Kels," Caleb glanced at the woman who'd come to be his little sister, "and you know I'm always here for you. Don't try and bottle it all up inside."

"I know," Kelsey gave Caleb a watery smile in the mirror,

"and you know I'm always here for you." She put her hand on his shoulder and he covered it with his big warm one.

"As long as we stick to our pact we made in that hell hole," Caleb gave Kelsey's fingers a squeeze, "we can get through anything. We've already proved that haven't we?"

Kelsey gave Caleb a warm smile before putting her head back and drifting off to sleep.

*As the car fell quiet, Erin bit her lip trying to stop the tears from falling down her cheeks and giving her away. She'd heard every word of her children's conversation and her heart ached for them. She knew that she shouldn't think ill of the dead, but she would never forgive Sheldon or his family for what they'd done to her children. The one thing Erin still couldn't figure out or understand was why?

Chapter Three

NOT YOU AGAIN!

"My mom's lawyer friend and her family are arriving soon," Michael told Zane McCaid, who'd been staying at one of the beach bungalows.

"You say they're staying in the bungalow near mine?" Zane helped Michael with the trail sign.

"Yes." Michael drilled the screw through the signboard and into the wood. "It's the only other three-bedroom cabin available."

"You and Lilly have done an amazing job," Zane complimented the young man. "I know my nieces and nephews are loving it here."

"I'm glad they are." Michael grinned. "I can't say that I'm looking forward to all you McCaids going though." He looked out towards the new docks that were being built off to the far side of the cove to open up the beach more. "Fallon has been an absolute savior taking people out on charter tours." He put the drill back in the bag, picked it up, and walked up the trail.

"I'm glad she's actually sailing again." Zane looked towards where Fallon was checking the sails on the small yacht Lilly and Michael owned. "Your sister and cousin seem quite capable sailors."

"Lilly and Maddison have both said how much they've learned from Fallon." Michael and Zane came to the next signpost. "That should do it." He finished the last sign.

"Are you still up for a hike to the cliffs up there?" Zane pointed to the tall wall of rock that enclosed the right side of the cove and jutted out into the Pacific Ocean.

"Of course." Michael looked at the imposing structure. "I've been wanting to get up and look around for over four years."

"Why haven't you?" Zane asked Michael.

"I just never got around to it and I've had no one to go up there with," Michael explained to Zane. "Are you sure you don't mind finishing the docks for us?" he asked Zane as they started walking back towards the sandy cove.

"Not at all. I like to keep busy, and it gets me out of wedding preparations." Zane raised his eyebrows and shook his head. "You know what it's like with a big family."

"Yup." Michael enjoyed Zane's company. The man reminded him of a mix between Michael's late grandfather and his mother's husband, Max. "I think someone's been looking for us." He smiled as the giant Saint Bernard named Goose came barreling towards them.

"He hates missing out on anything." Zane braced himself for a load of excited licks and barks. "Hey boy, where's your new friend?"

"Lunar should be back later this afternoon." Michael laughed as the big dog turned and greeted him the same way he'd greeted Zane. "I still can't believe your family named a dog Goose." He rolled his eyes and continued down the path.

"I'll go check on the electric work before heading back to my cabin." Zane and Michael walked across the long wooden boardwalk towards the hotel. "I really like the way you managed to keep the historical feel of the build and put a modern twist on it."

"I wish that Lilly and my mom would've let me paint it the color called sand, but no they wanted it white with light grey trim," Michael shuddered. "It makes the building lose something."

"I like the way the house integrates a plantation style house with a beach house look," Zane admired the building Michael and Lilly had lovingly restored and built into a hotel.

"Michael," Lilly called to him from the door, "our guests have arrived. Can you please take them to their cabin?"

"Sure." Michael and Zane walked into the hotel lobby together.

A tall extremely good-looking man stepped up to them.

"Hi, I'm Caleb." Caleb turned to introduce Zane and Michael to the rest of his family. "This is my mother Erin and my sister Kelsey."

"YOU!" Zane, Michael, Kelsey, and Erin all said together and the atmosphere in the lobby suddenly became very tense and frosty.

"Uh…" Lilly stopped and looked at the four people glaring at each other. "Do you all know each other?"

"This buffoon likes to man handle women,' Erin hissed.

"Excuse me?" Zane's eyes narrowed in on the petite Erin. "You were barging your way into my niece's hospital room. We didn't know who you were."

"You still had no right to pick me up!" Erin's eyes blazed, and her cheeks stained with an angry red.

"You're the woman that doesn't look when turning corners," Michael's eyes narrowed angrily. "I now have to fork out quite a bit to get my entire bumper replaced."

"She's the woman that hit you?" Zane looked from the daughter to the mother. "Makes sense." He raised an eyebrow before turning to Caleb. "Nice to meet you." He nodded and walked off to go check on the electrics for the function room.

"Does he live here?" Erin looked irritated.

"He's here on an extended vacation." Michael's eyes glittered. "Lilly I just remembered I have to go and help Zane with the electrics. You're going to have to show the guests to their cabin." He gave them a nod and walked off in the direction of Zane.

"You had an accident?" Erin asked Kelsey as soon as Lilly had left them to settle into the beautiful rustic yet modern bungalow.

"It was nothing, just a little fender bender," Kelsey shrugged. "I sorted the car company out and they gave me the SUV."

"That's why you got an SUV and not some sleek sedan." Caleb nodded. "That makes sense."

"I think you should take the main bedroom, Mom," Kelsey suggested. "I'm going to take this one." She ducked into a bedroom facing the sea. "Oh wow!" Caleb and Erin heard her say.

"I guess this is my room then." Caleb kissed Erin on the forehead and walked into the bedroom between Kelsey and Erin. "This is so awesome that every bedroom faces the sea."

"I can't wait to go dip my toes into the water," Erin sighed as she walked into the main bedroom.

"There you go Rafferty." Kelsey stroked her large cat. He was part Maine Coon, part Blue Persian, and part Korat. Rafferty had the sleek more pointed nose of a Korat. His large ears had long sensitive hairs protruding from them. He was not as large as most Maine Coon cats were, but he had their features. His coat was a soft grey with slight stripe markings and his yellow/green eyes slanted elegantly upwards, making him look regal. Rafferty certainly thought he was regal.

Rafferty gave a loud meow and lapped up the water Kelsey had poured before tucking into his special cat meal.

"I see he's up and about again." Caleb walked into the kitchen and pulled open the fridge. "I'm going to the store for Mom." He picked up the car keys from the table. "Do you need anything?"

"I think I'll come with you." Kelsey ran towards her bedroom. "Let me get my sneakers on."

"I'll meet you in the car." Caleb walked out the front door.

"Mom," Kelsey hopped into her sneakers as she headed for the front door, "I'm going with Caleb to the store. Please keep an eye on Rafferty."

Kelsey banged out of the cabin and came to a screeching halt as the biggest dog she'd ever seen was bounding her way.

"Goose!" Michael shouted at the Saint Bernard, who once again couldn't hear him. "Stop!" He ran after the giant dog.

"What the..." Kelsey couldn't step out of the way in time and landed flat on her rump on the ground as Goose couldn't stop in time and skidded into her like a bowling ball.

The big dog called Goose jumped around her excitedly covering her in doggy kisses which Kelsey tried to fend off.

"Not a dog fan?" Michael appeared in front of Kelsey and clicked a leash onto Goose's collar.

"I like dogs just fine," Kelsey hissed, pushing herself back up and glaring at Caleb who was laughing at her. "But that isn't a dog, it's more like some weird pony."

"This is Goose." Michael rubbed the big dog's head.

"I see your dog is just as reckless as you are." Kelsey stepped around Goose and Michael towards the SUV. "If you'll excuse us, we have things to do."

"Of course." Michael stepped aside.

"Did you want to see us?" Caleb asked Michael when he'd finished laughing.

"I was looking for you, Caleb." Michael walked around the car with Goose on the leash. "Max said you're the photographer they've just hired who may be interested in helping with some pictures of the retreat?"

"Yes," Caleb stood next to the open car door, "I would be. Max told me that you wanted me to do shots of the adventure trails and sports as well?"

"I do," Michael grinned, "that's why I'm here. Zane and myself are going to the cliffs tomorrow and I was wondering if you wanted to come with us?"

"The cliff?" Caleb's eyes lit up. "Is there rock climbing involved?"

"We're wanting to go up there." Michael pointed to a large imposing cliff wall jutting out into the sea. "I call it Pirates Wall."

"Sweet," Caleb grinned his eyes shining with excitement, "I'm in. What time?"

"We're going early, around six-thirty in the morning." Michael smiled at Caleb. "We have all the equipment and sustenance."

"Great," Caleb climbed into the SUV, "I'll meet you down at the hotel?"

"Yeah." Michael pulled Goose to one side as Caleb waved and pulled off.

"You didn't waste any time," Kelsey said to Caleb.

"Kels, we've been trapped in four walls for almost two years," Caleb pulled into the far lane of the road, "so, hell yeah I'm not wasting any more time."

"I want to come too." Kelsey looked at him.

"I don't know, Kels." Caleb kept his eyes on the road as he neared the town center. "You'll have to ask Michael." He turned and grinned at her. "From what I've seen, the two of you are a little oil and water."

"He reversed into me," Kelsey defended herself. "Who reverses up to a turning corner?"

"Were you on your phone when you turned the corner?" Caleb glanced at her with raised eyebrows.

"No." Kelsey frowned. "You know I no longer use that thing unless I have to."

"Come on, Kels." Caleb grinned. "I know you. You're normally such a cautious driver that you would've seen the car reversing before you turned that corner."

"It was as stupid mistake," Kelsey said defensively and turned to look out the window at the town they were now calling home. "I'm going to need to go and register with UC and check in at Jacobs Medical Center the day after tomorrow."

"I'll take you." Caleb smiled at Kelsey reassuringly. "It's going to be okay." He pulled into the parking lot of the shopping center Lilly had told him about.

"Thank you, Cal," Kelsey breathed. "What if I've forgotten anything?"

"You haven't." Caleb looked at her with raised brows. "You kept your studies going and helped out in the dungeon with their in-house doctor."

"It doesn't count." Kelsey smiled at how Caleb always defended her. "But Dr. Brown, if that was her real name, was very knowledgeable and helped me a lot."

"There you go." Caleb smiled at her encouragingly. "You should be in your sixth year of medical school already, not repeating your fourth year."

"I'm just lucky I'm not starting all over again," Kelsey breathed. "Thanks to Gramps and some doctor friend of his that knows Dr. Brown."

"Come on, sis," Caleb climbed out of the SUV, "let's go shopping. I know you love to do that."

"Yeah," Kelsey smiled, taking off her seatbelt.

As Kelsey was about to open the car door her phone bleeped. She'd put it face down in one of the compartments between the seats. She turned it over and her face paled as she saw who the message was from. She clicked the phone into sleep mode and put it back down into the compartment where she left it when she went to join Caleb in the store.

He stood on the sidewalk at the edge of the parking lot watching the tall dark-haired man and the blonde woman walk into the convenience store. His hoodie was pulled low over his head, a neck gaiter covered the lower half of his face, and sunglasses covered his eyes. He looked down at his phone and shook his head. He didn't want to have to go to extreme lengths if he didn't have to, as he couldn't afford to draw attention to himself. But there was a debt to be paid and he'd do whatever it took to see that it was cleared.

The man was so busy staring at his phone that he didn't see the woman power walking towards him. She didn't see him either as she tried to figure out the instructions for her fancy watch on her phone's internet. The two of them collided and their phones flew out of their hands hitting the pavement.

"Excuse me," the woman said as the man shoved her, and she fell back hitting her head with a thud against the streetlight.

"Hey," the man hissed, "watch where you're going lady!" The rude man didn't care that the woman had bounced off him and hit her head on the street light pole.

He bent down and scooped up his phone not bothering to pick up hers or ask her if she was okay. He turned and stormed off.

Chapter Four
AN UNFORTUNATE ACCIDENT

Gretchen Tucker, or Gertie as she liked to be called, stood dazed and seeing stars, thinking how rude the man who'd shoved her was. She tried to fend off the woozy feeling as she steadied herself. Her head ached from where it hit the pole and the dots swimming in front of her eyes made it difficult to see. She needed to sit down and knew she couldn't do so on the pavement, so she made her way to the parking lot of the store.

She managed to get to the dark SUV and felt like she was going to pass out. Gertie knew that the owners of the SUV were probably going to have a fit, but she had stopped walking. She didn't want to sit on the hood, she wouldn't have been able to pull herself onto the hood anyway. Instead, she leaned over the hood and put her head down.

"He always leaves his stupid wallet in the car," Kelsey muttered as she stormed towards the SUV. "I'm always the one that has to fetch it!"

As Kelsey drew closer to the car, she stopped, seeing a

woman spread out over the hood of the SUV. She frowned and her heart started beating faster. Her first instinct was to run into the store and get Caleb. But Kelsey knew she couldn't let this fear that had dominated her life for the past two years rule her life. Caleb was right, it was over, in their past: the only thing she had to fear now was fear itself.

What was that saying her mother kept telling her, *Fear is an acronym for false evidence appearing real!* Before all the trouble had started Kelsey would've thought nothing of running straight to the woman to see if she needed help. And everything inside Kelsey was screaming at her that the woman needed help. Kelsey took a deep breath and forced herself to put one foot in front of the other to move towards the car.

"Ex…" Kelsey stammered timidly before pinching her eyes shut and clenching her jaw. *Stop it Kelsey, you're studying medicine and that woman looks like she needs medical help!* She cleared her throat and ignored her hammering heart to get closer. "Do you need help?"

"I need to sit down for a bit." The woman opened her eyes and looked at Kelsey. She saw the keys in Kelsey's hand and tried to stand up. "Sorry, is this your car?" She pinched the bridge of her nose as she swayed.

"Yes," Kelsey immediately stepped up to the woman, her doctor instincts booting her fear of strangers clear out of her system, "but please come sit in my car." She opened the car and led the woman to the back seat.

"What happened?" Kelsey's sharp eyes examined the woman as she helped her into the car. "Your head." She noticed fresh blood matting the back of the women's short light brown slightly greying hair.

"I was power walking and was trying to sort out this watch," the woman showed Kelsey her Smart watch, "it's supposed to count my steps."

"I have one of those." Kelsey gave the woman a warm smile. "They're very confusing."

"They are." The woman rubbed her temple. "There was a strange man standing in the middle of the sidewalk. I ploughed right into him and he pushed me into the street pole."

"How rude!" Anger spurted through Kelsey. She hated hearing stories like this. What the hell was wrong with people these days? There didn't seem to be any decency left in the world. "I'm a doctor," she stopped, "well a med student, but I can help you if you let me have a look at your head. I also think you may be concussed."

"Oh dear," the woman swallowed. "Don't take this wrong but please step aside."

"What?" Kelsey stared at the woman a little shocked at first but was quick to understand when the woman raised her hand to her mouth. "Oh!"

Kelsey managed to jump aside as the woman leaned over and got horribly sick.

"That's it," Kelsey let the woman finish, "I'm taking you to the hospital."

"No, that's so sweet but I'll be …" she leaned over and got sick some more.

"Do you have a headache?" Kelsey asked the woman who she estimated to be in her late fifty's early sixties.

"I do." The woman tried to smile weakly. "I'm so sorry about all this mess I've made by your car."

"Please don't worry about that." Kelsey smiled at her. "Do you mind if I take a look at your head?"

"That's fine." She smiled at Kelsey with glassy eyes. "I'm Gertie," the woman introduced herself.

"Hi, Gertie, I'm Kelsey." Kelsey stepped around the sick and gently turned Gertie's head to the side to examine the bump. "That's quite the bump you have at the back of your head and it's split open." She helped turn Gertie into a sitting position in the car. "I just have to go get my …."

"What's taking you so long?" Caleb popped up next to the

car, frowned and stepped around to see what was going on. "Hello!" He looked at the woman in the backseat of their car.

"Caleb, this is Gertie," Kelsey introduced them. "We need to take her to the emergency room because she's had a bit of an accident."

"Of course." Caleb took the keys from Kelsey. "I'll find the closest hospital." He started typing on his phone.

"My phone!" Gertie said. "When I knocked into the man it fell." She tried to get out of the car to go find her phone.

"I'll get it for you," Caleb stopped her. "Where were you when you dropped it?"

Gertie explained where her phone was, and Caleb took off to go find it for her.

"You and your brother have been so kind," Gertie said as Kelsey closed the door.

"Of course," Kelsey said, sliding into the back seat next to Gertie. "Do you mind if I just do a quick check up?"

Gertie nodded and allowed Kelsey to take her pulse.

"Can you follow my finger?" Kelsey asked her, and did a few other quick tests that she was able to do without equipment. "Lie your head back but don't doze off," she warned Gertie.

"I don't want to sound like a moaner but the pain in my head won't let me sleep," Gertie assured Kelsey.

"Here," Kelsey reached over the seats and pulled her unopened bottle of water from the middle compartments, "sip this." She handed Gertie the bottle of water.

"You're an angel." Gertie took a few sips of the water.

"Is this your phone?" Caleb slid into the driver's seat and handed a phone to Gertie. "I found it lying where you said it was. Luckily there doesn't seem to be much foot traffic today."

"Thank you." Gertie took the phone and as soon as she did, it rang. She frowned when she saw the number calling and turned to Kelsey as Caleb started to pull out of the parking lot. "Can you read that number to me?"

Kelsey read out the number to Gertie.

"I don't think this is my phone," Gertie said.

"Why?" Kelsey asked her.

"Unless my phone can call itself as this is my number calling me." Gertie lifted the phone to her ear.

"You have my phone," a gravelly male voice told her.

"I'm sorry," Gertie said. "Is there somewhere I can drop it off for you?"

"Leave it with the clerk named Betty at the store," the man said. "Tell her Bart will fetch it." He hung up.

"What was that all about?" Caleb asked.

"This must be the phone of the man I knocked into," Gertie said. "He wants me to leave it with the clerk."

"Okay," Caleb turned around and drove back into the store's parking lot. "I can take it for you."

"You and your sister are both angels." She was about to hand the phone to Caleb when she accidently clicked on a message app. "Oh dear what have I done?" She handed the phone to Kelsey.

"Let me look for you," Kelsey took the phone.

Kelsey's face paled as she saw the messages on the phone. Her eyes were filled with fear as she looked at Gertie.

"Did you see what the man looked like?" Kelsey asked Gertie.

"He was wearing a neck gaiter over the lower half of his face, a hoodie, and sunglasses," Gertie explained. "Other than that, all I can tell you is that he was about as tall as Caleb."

Kelsey felt the shock waves prickle through her body like a thousand pins and needles being jabbed into her nerve endings.

"Are you okay?" Caleb's brows drew together as he stared at Kelsey.

"I..." Kelsey looked down at the messages and back up at Caleb who was waiting for the phone. "I'll take it back."

Before Caleb could argue with Kelsey, she was out of the car telling Caleb to keep an eye on Gertie because she had a concussion.

*K*elsey walked into the store. Her heart was pounding in her chest once again and she felt like she was about to have a panic attack, but she pushed herself forward. Her eyes scanned the store as she walked to the first shop assistant she could find.

"Sorry, I'm looking for a store clerk named Betty," Kelsey asked the man.

"You'll find Betty at information," the assistant told Kelsey.

Kelsey thanked the man and walked to the information desk.

"Hi," Kelsey looked at the woman wearing the name tag Betty. "I was told to drop this phone off for Bart."

"Oh, yes." Betty took the phone and handed her an envelope. "The mix up of phones." She smiled, "Bart told me how you'd knocked into each other outside the store."

"Could you tell me what Bart looked like?" Kelsey saw Betty give her a weird look. "I just want to make sure I am giving the phone back to the right person."

"He had sandy brown hair, wore sunglasses, a sweater, and he was very tall," Betty gave Kelsey something to sign. "He had an expensive gold watch on his arm."

Prickles of alarm ran down Kelsey's spine as she stood staring at Betty after signing the form.

"Thank you for your help Betty," Kelsey said as she hurried from the store.

Kelsey's heart was hammering a lot louder than it had when she'd entered the store. The description both Gertie and Betty the store clerk had given her matched the one she knew she'd seen. She'd also seen him a few times in the past eighteen months. No one had believed her, and Kelsey doubted they would now. She somehow needed proof.

"I got it." Kelsey handed Gertie the envelope with her

phone in as she climbed into the car. "Is there anyone we can call for you?"

"No," Gertie shook her head. "My partner isn't here, and I don't want them worried with this."

"Are you sure?" Kelsey asked Gertie who nodded.

"We should be at the hospital in four minutes according to the GPS," Caleb informed them.

Chapter Five
A HIKE TO THE TOP OF PIRATES WALL

"Lilly," Michael shouted through their bungalow, "are you ready?"

"Just tying my hair up," Lilly yelled back from her room. "Have you heard from Zane?"

"Yeah." Michael popped his head into her room. "Are you sure you want to wear those boots again?" He pointed to Lilly's new hiking boots. "They gave you raw blisters last time."

"I can't find my other ones." Lilly plaited her ponytail and tied it off.

"They're in the laundry at the hotel," Michael told her. "I saw them there when I went to fit the new washer." He took her pack for her. "Come on, we can't be late."

"Okay." Lilly shook her head and ran after him. "Zane doesn't mind if we're a minute late."

"Yes," Michael looked at his watch, "but we're already two minutes late."

"Drat." Lilly shoved Michael out the door. "Move. I hate it when he turns all military on us. Reminds me of my entire family!"

"We're going to get the tardy speech again and what it says

about our characters." Michael rolled his eyes as they made their way to the hotel.

"Have you two seen Goose?" Zane was running around the outside of the hotel as Michael and Lilly walked up the front stairs.

"No," Michael frowned, "he was in our bungalow a few minutes ago."

"That damn dog!" Zane muttered, "Why did they have to leave him here with us?"

"Don't worry, Lunar is coming to stay with us this afternoon. She always keeps Goose under control." Lilly ran up the stairs. "I just have to go change my shoes and I help you look for Goose."

"I'll take the east boardwalk." Michael put his and Lilly's backpacks on the stairs.

"I'll take the west boardwalk," Zane looked at his watch, "and you were two minutes late."

"Lilly couldn't find her shoes." Michael threw his cousin under the bus.

"Her comfortable hiking boots?" Zane asked.

"Yes," Michael nodded.

"They're in the laundry," Zane said.

Michael and Zane were about to go looking for Goose when Caleb came walking towards them with Goose walking perfectly next to him.

"I believe he belongs to you," Caleb grinned. "I'm sorry about his face but he was introduced to my sister's monster cat."

"Goose," Michael kneeled down and looked at the scratches on his nose, "those look a little nasty." He eyed out the big dog's scratched up nose. "What is her cat? A tiger?"

"Part Main Coon, Blue Persian, and Korat." Kelsey came walking towards them dressed in her hiking gear.

"Are you going to pay for his vet's bill?" Michael felt his

anger rise the minute he'd heard her voice. She was so cocky and cold!

"He's fine." Zane checked out the dog's face. "Goose here has had much worse. He got shot some months back trying to save one of my nieces."

"Really?" Kelsey asked Zane.

"Yeah." Zane gave the young woman a smile. There was something about Kelsey and Caleb. Like they were walking beneath a black cloud. "He's a hero."

"I'm sorry Rafferty attacked you." Kelsey patted the big dog's head. "He'll come around."

"Are we ready?" Zane looked at the young adults.

"I hope you don't mind," Caleb looked at Zane and Michael, "but my sister and mother asked if they could join us."

"I found my shoes." Lilly rushed out of the front door of the hotel, "Let's go find Goose so we can ..." she stopped and looked from Caleb to Kelsey. "Hi!"

"Hi." Caleb stepped back towards Kelsey. His shoulders stiffening.

"Hi, Lilly," Kelsey greeted Lilly with a smile. "Sorry, I hope you don't mind but myself and my mom wanted to join your hike."

"Uh..." Lilly gave Michael a sideways glance, "I thought it was just the three of us?"

"Didn't I tell you?" Michael frowned, "Sorry. I asked Caleb to come with us to take photos."

"Oh," Lilly said, "the more the merrier." She gave Kelsey a tight smile.

"Where's Mom?" Caleb looked at Kelsey.

"I'm here," Erin walked up behind them. "I had to make sure Rafferty was okay. He was trying to follow the two of you."

"We're all here," Zane looked past Erin. "Let's get going. Fall in line and follow myself and Michael. The trail hasn't been cleared and can get treacherous." He looked at Lilly. "Lilly you take the back of the trail to make sure no one gets left behind and keep Goose with you."

"Yes sir," Lilly saluted Zane. He'd become Michael and Lilly's stand-in father with their parents' blessing.

"Let me guess," Erin said to Lilly with her eyes narrowed, "military!"

"Uh-huh," Lilly put her backpack on.

"Move out!" Zane moved his backpack into a more comfortable position.

"I read in your brochure the trail to Pirates Wall was off limits to guests." Kelsey looked at Lilly. "That's the trail we're doing today?"

"Yes," Lilly smiled at Kelsey. "We're trying to figure out what to do with the trail and how to block it off or have purely as a guide-led trail."

"Nice." Kelsey raised her eyebrows.

"You don't have to come if you're worried," Michael told her as he walked past them.

"I'm good, thanks," Kelsey told Michael coldly, who shrugged and walked off. "Where's his wife?" she asked Lilly as her and Lilly walked behind the rest of their group.

"Wife?" Lilly frowned at Kelsey. "Michael was almost engaged once but he's never been married. Why would you think that?"

"The day he reversed into my car he was with a beautiful pregnant woman," Kelsey explained to Lilly.

"Oh," Lilly grinned. "No, that's Samantha, Michael's oldest sister." She leashed Goose as they got to the start of the trail. "Come on you, you have to stay with me." She patted Goose's big head. "This stretch for about a mile is steep and rather slippery because of the gravel. If you go before me, we can steady each other."

"Good thinking," Kelsey grinned as her foot nearly slipped as she took a step.

"Be careful of the gravel up this incline," Zane called back to them stepping to one side to help make sure everyone got past the slippery path.

As he said that Erin skidded and nearly lost her balance. Zane's hand snaked out and caught her.

"You okay?" Zane asked Erin, releasing her as soon as she nodded. "Michael," he called. "Can you give Erin a hand up to the top?" He looked at Caleb who was taking pictures. "Your son is like a goat." He grinned at Erin. "He walked up this path like he'd done it a million times before."

"He thrives on adventures like this." Erin looked at Caleb. There was something haunting in her eyes. "Thank you for inviting him. He needed this," she said softly to Zane, who looked at her a little shocked.

"Sure," Michael called as he stopped talking to Caleb and hopped back down towards them. "Give me your hand." He smiled at Erin holding out his hand.

"Thank you, Michael." She took Michael's hand. "This steep climb is quite treacherous with those gravel type rocks."

"It is," Michael agreed as he helped Erin. "That's why we don't want to open it to our guests until we manage to make it a little safer."

"It's a breathtaking view though." Erin looked out over the cove, the sea, and miles of beautiful scenery."

"It really is," Michael agreed. "That's why I think this will be one of the most popular trails, but I can't risk guests getting injured on an unguided hike."

"No," Erin shook her head, "that'll just bring a whole lot of legal problems for you."

"I know," Michael laughed. "Mom had to inspect all our adventures."

"Sounds like something Jennifer would do," Erin grinned before trying to look back, nearly falling again.

"Careful." Michael caught her. "Keep looking straight ahead."

"Sorry, I wanted to make sure that Kelsey and Lilly were okay." Erin clutched onto Michael's strong muscular arm.

"Captain Zane's with them," Michael assured her. "He takes his hiking leader duties seriously. Plus, mine and Lilly's parents left Zane as our unofficial guardian while they all went off on their cruise this morning."

"That's right, they went sailing on that big old yacht." Erin snapped her fingers. "What is it called?"

"The Red Mac," Zane came up behind them. "We need to pick up the pace a little." He carefully walked past them.

"We're almost at the top." Michael kept Erin steady as they followed Zane. "The path smooths out a little and there's no more gravel."

They had to climb up onto a rock shelf. Michael jumped up first then helped Erin up.

"Welcome to Pirates Wall." Michael grinned as he saw Erin's eyes widen and her breath catch in her throat.

"Michael, this is beautiful." Erin stood and turned around.

Erin could see for miles out over the sparkling Pacific Ocean. Whichever way she turned the scenery was breathtaking.

"It's awesome." Caleb walked over to join them.

"Don't worry about us," Kelsey called. The rock shelf was a little hard for her to get up onto. She threw her pack up and then picked up Lilly's to throw up.

"I thought Zane was with you." Michael walked over to her, frowning as he looked past Kelsey and Lilly, who was sitting on a rock.

"Goose was growling and nearly pulled Lilly's arm off he was so agitated," Kelsey explained. "Zane took Goose and went to inspect what was upsetting him."

"Here." Michael leaned down and offered Kelsey his hand.

"Thanks." Kelsey reluctantly took his hand and allowed him to pull her up onto the rock shelf.

The minute their hands touched Kelsey felt a zing that woke up the butterflies in her stomach.

"Sorry Kels," Caleb walked over to them, "I got carried away with this view."

"Can you two help Lilly?" Kelsey pointed to Lilly sitting on a rock as soon as she was over the rock shelf, "I need to look at her ankle and those grazes on her leg."

A cold feeling had crept up Caleb's spine when Kelsey had mentioned Goose's agitation. He didn't know what it was, but he couldn't help feeling that their nightmare wasn't yet over. He shook off the feeling as Michael's worried voice caught his attention.

"Lilly," Michael called worriedly to his cousin. He jumped down off the shelf and ran over to where Lilly sat on what she called toadstool rock because it resembled a toadstool.

"I'm fine," Lilly told Michael. "Just a little twist. If Zane wasn't there, I think Goose would've dragged me through the bush."

"Caleb, can you help me get Lilly up onto the ledge?" Michael called up to Caleb.

Caleb watched Michael drop onto his haunches to check out Lilly's ankle.

43

"Sure." Caleb gave Kelsey his camera. "Don't take any pictures," he warned Kelsey who gave him a cheeky smile.

Caleb stopped for a minute, a little floored. He hadn't seen Kelsey's smile touch her eyes for a long, long time.

"Here." Caleb turned away from Kelsey.

Caleb walked to the edge of the ledge and reached down to help Michael lift Lilly. He managed to grab her and pull her up without too much effort. Caleb was solid muscle, fit, and strong.

When she was up, Lilly tried to step away from Caleb but stumbled when she put pressure on her ankle. Caleb reached out and pulled her to him. She landed plastered against his chest. He swallowed as a bolt of electricity jolted his heart. He frowned and took a step back, but was still holding her arms so Lilly didn't fall.

"Thanks," Lilly squeaked. Her cheeks had an appealing red stain across them.

"No problem," Caleb cleared his throat as his voice sounded gruff. "Let me help you over to that rock so Kelsey can look at your injuries."

"Thanks," Lilly gave Caleb a tight smile as he put his arm around her and helped her to the rock. "Kels is an excellent doctor," he said proudly.

"Medical student," Kelsey reminded him as she pulled her first aid kit from her backpack.

"I'll leave you in Kelsey's hands." Caleb gave Lilly a tight smile before walking off and taking his camera from Kelsey.

"I'm going to look for Zane." Michael called up to them.

"Are you ladies okay here?" Caleb looked from Erin, to Lilly, and Kelsey. "I'll go help Michael."

"Go," Erin stepped up to Caleb who towered over Erin without her usual two-inch heels. "But the two of you be careful."

Caleb gave Erin a kiss on the head before taking off after Michael.

Chapter Six
HOLE?

"Zane!" Michael and Caleb called. Michael had been surprised by Caleb's tracking skills.

They heard the anxious sound of Goose's barking.

"This way." Caleb took off through the rough, rocky terrain. "Just be careful, this ground feels a little hollow." He frowned as he stopped and did a test stomp on the ground.

"Did that echo?" Michael stopped as the ground seemed to shudder a little and looked up at Caleb.

"I think we're standing over a cave," Caleb told him.

"If that's the case, there should be an opening around here somewhere." Michael's face paled. "I hope Zane didn't fall into it."

"This way." Caleb followed Goose's frantic barks. "Goose seems rather distressed," he said as they made their way towards the dog and hopefully Zane.

"There he is." Michael and Caleb came over the rise where the rock cliff slanted downward and into the sea. Goose was standing by a small wall of rocks barking his head off.

Goose spotted Michael and Caleb and ran towards them barking excitedly. When the dog reached them, he did a few barking spins before running back to the place where he'd been barking.

"I think he wants us to follow him." Michael frowned and ran after Goose. "What is it boy? Where's Zane?"

"Michael," Caleb cautiously leaned over the small rock wall, "it's Zane."

Michael ran to where Caleb was and looked down into an opening in the rock wall. Zane was lying sprawled out on the shelf. A few inches to Zane's left was a tunnel of darkness.

"I'm going to have to go down there." Michael took off his backpack and started rummaging through it to pull out a climbing rope and a harness which he pulled on. "Are you going to be able to anchor me?" He clipped a side of the rope onto his harness looking over the landscape. "There's that tree." He nodded towards the small oak tree a few meters away from the hole.

"I'll tie the edge." Caleb took the ground peg Michael handed him and walked to the Oak.

Caleb wound the rope around the tree trunk a few times before taking a rock and hammering the ground peg into the ground. As he hit it into the earth, they could hear the echo resound through the hole. Once Caleb had clipped the other side of the rope into the ground peg he went back to Michael and put on the spare gloves Michael had.

"Zane and Lilly always forget to pack gloves." Michael shrugged at the look Caleb gave him when he pulled about four different sized pairs of gloves from his pack. "They have grip on them so you can hold the rope better."

Caleb braced himself against the smaller rock shelf on the sloping side of the hole which was in direct line with the tree the rope was anchored around. It was also directly over the shelf Zane was on.

Michael lowered himself over the lip of the hole and looked up at Caleb who gave him the thumbs up. Michael abseiled down the rock wall until he reached the shelf. He had a spare harness for Zane around his arm.

"I'm down," Michael's voice echoed up to Caleb who cautiously peered over the rim with Goose lying next to him, his head hanging over the edge as he softly wined and watched Michael.

"Zane," Michael felt Zane's neck for a pulse. Michael wasn't a doctor, but he was sure Zane's pulse was still quite strong. "Zane." Michael carefully patted Zane's face. "You've got to wake up so we can get you out of here."

"Michael?" Zane's eyes opened slowly, "Where are we?" He tried to sit up, winced, grabbed his head with one hand and his ribs with the other. "What the hell!"

"Do you remember falling down a hole?" Michael pulled the spare harness off his arms.

"I didn't fall." Zane sat up a little more cautiously this time. "Someone was following us, and Goose and I gave chase."

Zane winced as Michael secured the spare harness around him.

"I came across the hole and was looking in to see if the person had fallen in while Goose sniffed around trying to get the person's scent," Zane continued the story as Michael helped him stand up. "I heard Goose growl and then yelp. When I turned around to see what had happened to the guy we'd been chasing, he came out of nowhere and pushed me."

Michael went cold as he unclipped the rope from his harness and clipped it onto Zane's.

"Did you get a good look at the guy?" Michael asked Zane.

"Not really." Zane gave a tug on the rope to let Caleb know he was coming up. "He was wearing one of those neck gaiter things over his face."

"Are you going to be able to climb up?" Michael asked Zane.

"I think so." Zane gave Michael a reassuring smile. "Do you think Caleb will be able to hold the rope to pull me up?"

47

"Have you seen the guy?" Michael whispered to Zane. "He's a mountain of muscle. I wonder what he bench presses?"

"Let's hope he can lift a full-grown man that is also *solid muscle*," Zane pointed out that he too was fit and in shape with just as much muscle as Caleb.

"Yes, but he has ...." Michael's eyes grew large, and he pursed his lips. "Never mind!" He looked up and called to Caleb that Zane was coming up.

"Good catch.' Zane gave Michael a raised eyebrow look before painfully pulling himself up the rope.

Once Michael had been pulled up, the three men sat for a minute catching their breath and looking out at the ocean while Zane told Caleb what had happened. Caleb's sudden stiffening of his shoulders and look of shock didn't go unnoticed by both Zane and Michael.

Caleb agreed to help get Zane off the trail and get him back to the hotel while Michael went and fetched the rest of their party. They wouldn't be finishing the hike to Pirate Patch Cave today.

"That's where we were hiking to?" Kelsey asked Michael, pointing to the weird looking rock formation that was perched on the side of Pirates Wall. The two of them had fallen into an unspoken truce.

Kelsey, Michael, Caleb, and Lilly sat on the deck of the Crab Shack enjoying a late lunch. Michael and Lilly had bought the old Crab Shack that was once housed at the end of Cave Walk close to Goldfish Point in La Jolla. They had kept its beachy cabana feel about it but added a fine restaurant dining touch to it. The bar was off to one side in what they called the Shack Room. Here you could get a light meal, sit at the bar and they had open mic nights with local artists playing for a fun night out. Their smarter restaurant was closed off from the

Shack bar and soundproofed and was called the Royal Crab Restaurant.

The Crab Shack sat at the end of a long boardwalk that skirted along the flat rock edge just above White Sands Cove beach on the east side of the cove. The restaurant was perched upon a large flat shelf of the cliff that protected the east side of the cove. Both sides of the Crab Shack's lounges opened up onto a deck that jutted out over the Pacific Ocean.

"Yeah," Michael took a sip of his beer, "there's a steep path that leads from the top of Pirates Wall down to that cliff shelf."

"We have a theory that behind that rather odd looking rounded rock is a cave opening," Lilly explained to Kelsey and Caleb.

"The rock looks like it was somehow put there to block the opening to the cave," Michael carried on with the story. "We're not sure how or if our theory is even correct, but we think pirates somehow accessed that cave."

"Zane and his family think there's an entire ship hidden in that part of the cave," Lilly grinned and took a sip of her wine.

"Really?" Caleb stopped mid bite of his burger and turned his head towards the rock wall they were talking about. "If there's no entrance at the front of the rock wall, where do you think an entrance large enough to fit a pirate ship in would be?"

"We're not sure," Michael said. "It's a complete mystery." He leaned forward on the table. "There are a series of tunnels that run beneath the White Sands Cove. We found a bit of our ancestors' treasure in them, but according to our great-great-great grandfather's journal there was supposed to be a lot more treasure than we found."

"There are three entrances above ground to the tunnels that we know of. All the tunnel doors have butterfly symbols on them," Lilly grinned as she saw the questioning looks on Caleb's and Kelsey's faces. "That is another long story. One Michael and I have dubbed *The Sea Breeze Cottage* mystery. We're actually thinking of writing a book about the entire crazy adventure."

"I hope you'll tell us about it some time." Kelsey was genuinely interested. She loved a good mystery.

"Well, you're here for a while so I'm sure we can accommodate that," Lilly grinned, "but back to the tunnels. There's one door inside one of the tunnels we think may lead to a cave in Pirates Wall."

"That's the only door that doesn't have a butterfly on it but a yacht symbol," Michael picked up the story. "That really confused us until the McCaid's docked at our cove. They had another map that also showed a few more tunnels we were not aware of."

"They had the two keys that opened the door." Lilly took another sip of her wine. "You should see the walls in this tunnel. They have a picture story on it about a ship that got lost in this weird storm that sucked the sea up grounding the ship on the sand."

"There was precious cargo on the ship and so all the sailors managed to pull it to safety." Michael leaned back picking up a chip off his plate. "They'd just got it into a safe place when the sea came roaring back with the biggest waves they'd seen that completely covered the cove."

"A lot of the sailors drowned but some made it back onto the boat," Lilly continued, "including the captain and owner of the boat. Captain McCaid."

"I take it that was one of Zane's long-lost relatives?" Caleb took a swallow of his beer.

"Yes." Lilly gave Caleb a shy smile and her cheeks instantly pinkened.

"The rest of the story we only have broken words for and we haven't been able to piece it together yet," Michael told them. "We also came to a dead end and a wall of rocks. We've managed to move quite a lot of them, but it's a lot of hard work lugging them along the tunnel and out through the old boat house."

Michael pointed towards the boat house where they'd built one of the White Sands Cove beaches lifeguard lookout towers.

"Could we see the tunnels?" Kelsey shocked Caleb by asking. "What?" She frowned at the look Caleb gave her.

"Nothing." Caleb gave Kelsey a warm smile. "It's just nice to see the old you come back," he said softly.

"If that rock up there was put there, how do you think it got there?" She looked towards weird rock formation and changed the subject before anyone could question what Caleb meant.

"Thank you for driving me to the hospital, but I was really fine to drive on my own." Zane had refused a wheelchair and insisted on walking out of the emergency room.

"Why can't you just take someone's help without making it sound like you were forced to?" Erin glared up at Zane, wishing she could've put her heels back on. Everyone around her always seemed to tower over her when she was wearing flats or sneakers. "There's no shame in asking for help!" Her green eyes glittered.

"Sorry," Zane sighed, hating feeling weak. "Old habit I guess."

"Let's get you back to the Cove." Erin opened the car and stood back allowing Zane to climb into the passenger seat. "But I'm warning you, if you make one more crack about me looking like an ant driving a tank, you'll soon find out how painful a seatbelt jolt is over a cracked rib," she warned him before slamming his door shut on his grin.

The man was insufferable! Erin stormed around to the driver's side of the SUV.

"You have to admit though," Zane grinned at Erin, "this is a big car for you Smurfette!"

Zane laughed at Erin's exasperated growl.

As they pulled onto the road to head towards Whites Sands Cove a phone rang.

"Is that your phone?" Zane asked Erin.

"No," Erin glanced as Zane, her brows were creased together. "It's not mine. I thought it was yours, although it does sound a bit like Kelsey's phone."

Zane looked towards the sound of the ring and found a phone face down in one of the middle compartments between the front seats. He picked it up and saw it was a blocked number.

"It's a blocked number." Zane turned the phone towards Erin who glanced over at it.

"I wonder who that could be?" A chill gripped Erin's heart, making her shudder.

"Are you okay?" Zane looked at Erin curiously.

"I'm fine," Erin said, not taking her eyes off the road. "I just don't like blocked numbers."

"I don't either." Zane stared at the missed calls on Kelsey's phone. "This blocked number has been phoning her a lot." He couldn't unlock the phone. "Do you have her passcode?"

"No, I think it's her thumbprint." Erin shrugged as she looked at the phone in Zane's hand.

"Is something going on?" Zane asked Erin, not missing the worry and fear in her eyes.

"It's nothing." Erin gave Zane a tight smile.

"This doesn't look like nothing to me." Zane turned the message that had just flashed on Kelsey's phone.

Don't make me have to resort to drastic measures to get you to talk to me! I don't want anyone else getting hurt!

"Why do I have a feeling this has nothing to do with Hope Fields being released two days ago, or the people who are after the missing ship myself and the Coopers are trying to find?" Zane turned and looked at Erin's ashen face.

"Oh my God!" Erin turned and drove them towards Goldfish Point. "Are you hungry?"

"Depends?" Zane looked at Erin with narrowed eyes. "Does this meal come with a story?"

"Considering what happened today," Erin looked at Zane, "yes." She swallowed. "They say that sometimes it helps to talk to a stranger when you can't talk to anyone else."

"So, I take it I'm that stranger?" Zane frowned and then made a face. "Fair enough."

"I was thinking about a takeout and sitting in the car park." Erin glanced at Zane. "This story isn't supposed to be heard, but after what happened today and some incidents I feel it's only fair to tell you." She pulled into the parking lot of a takeaway off Coast Boulevard. "Especially as I know Jennifer and Shane wanted you to keep an eye on Lilly and Michael while they're away."

"Sounds good," Zane nodded, "and I appreciate you being honest with me." He looked at her. "My father always said the only way to protect someone is to be honest with them." Zane grinned at Erin's frown. "I too thought he was crazy because at times the less someone knows the better. But after what happened to my family it turned out he was right."

They climbed out of the car and went to order their food as a sleek black sedan pulled into the parking lot. Erin frowned as the car drove slowly past them her heart started to thud in her chest. But the car pulled into the parking lot of the next takeaway restaurant. Before Erin and Shane walked into the takeaway Erin saw an old man climb out of the sedan and breathed a sigh of relief. She was about to tell Zane the truth about the past two years, so she was being paranoid thinking the sleek sedan had been her ex-father-in-law's.

Chapter Seven
THE CAVE

*L*illy let her mind wander over everything that still had to be done at the hotel before the grand opening. Her early morning runs always cleared her head and gave her time to sort through what she needed to do for the day. She had to admit that she felt comforted having Goose and her cousin Maddison's Golden Retriever, Lunar, with her this morning. Especially when someone had pushed Zane into a hole the day before while they were all on a hike.

As the path changed to a steeper incline Lilly picked up her pace a little while Goose and Lunar ran ahead. Her mind needed to be on the problem of what to do about expanding their cabins. Because since they'd opened, their cabins were always fully booked. Even the hotel had been booked up before it was even open. They already had five upcoming weddings, three of which were taking the full adventure package and honeymoon cruises.

Lilly wished that Fallon McCaid didn't have to get back to her own business in Florida because she was one of the best yacht persons Lilly had ever known. Kelsey had told her last night that Caleb was also an excellent yachtsman but hadn't sailed in a few years. She wondered what was up with the

Carnegies. There was just something about them. They were wonderful people but there was this black cloud that seemed to hang over them and Lilly felt like they were shrouded in secrets.

Lilly gave a soft laugh and mental shake. Writing this new book about the Sea Breeze Cottage was making her see mystery wrapped around everyone. Aunt Jennifer, Michael's mother, had told Lilly and Michael that Erin and her family had had an exceedingly difficult time over the past two years. They were coming to La Jolla to get a fresh start and didn't need people snooping into their past pain. Aunt Jennifer had said the same about the McCaids. Her aunt and uncle seemed to adopt people with a troubled past and help them through the storm.

Aunt Jennifer's and Uncle Max's love story and that of their ancestors is what had sparked Lilly's creative appetite. She'd always loved to write. Even as a girl she kept so many journals, that when they'd found the journals at the Sea Breeze Cottage Lilly had spent months pouring over them. She'd even volunteered to help Aunt Jennifer sort out the attics at both the Sea Breeze Cottage and Seafield house. Lilly had found a wealth of information about White Sands Cove in both attics. The information included what the half-burnt down manor house that stood on the property in the 1800s looked like. It was from that Michael was able to design the hotel to make it a more modern twist on the plantation-style house.

Lilly had almost made it up the steep incline and was proud of herself that she'd gone nearly the entire run without thinking about the incredibly handsome, broody Caleb. She had no idea why the instant she'd met him she'd become all tongue tied and shy. Lilly might have been a little aloof at times and preferred to choose the company she kept, but she wasn't shy. She could speak to anyone and having decided to go into the hotel and tourism industry, she had to be able to talk to people from all walks of life. But for some reason she became a bumbling blushing idiot when Caleb was around.

Lilly picked up her pace once again like she always did to get to the last bit of the hill when Goose appeared on top of the hill with Lunar at his side as they waited for Lilly to catch up.

"I don't have four legs and doggy energy like you two do." Lilly shook her head as she always felt her doggy running companions judged her running prowess at this stage of her run. "But I did do it a lot faster today..."

Goose started barking and came barreling down towards her with Lunar hot on his heels. Lilly's eyes opened wide as the two dogs came straight for her separating around her as they got to her. But Goose didn't judge the distance between him and Lilly quite right and knocked right into her, sending her flying.

Before Lilly hit the ground a strong pair of arms wrapped around her waist and caught her.

"Careful," Caleb's deep voice came from behind her.

Lilly's heart was hammering so hard in her chest it nearly deafened her. She'd got a double fright by being knocked over and then landing in Caleb's arms. When his arms had wrapped around her she didn't know they were Caleb's, and her first thought was that it was the man who'd pushed Zane into the hole.

"Are you okay?" Caleb asked Lilly.

Lilly found herself leaning against Caleb's hard muscular chest with his arm wrapped around her waist. Her throat went dry, and she could feel her cheeks flame as the butterflies started to worry the inside of her stomach once again.

"I..." Lilly squeezed her eyes shut and took a breath. "I'm fine," she managed to croak and reluctantly pulled herself out of Caleb's powerful arms. *He really did have strong arms!* Lilly thought and then berated herself for her wayward thoughts. "Thank you."

"No problem." Caleb gave Lilly a tight smile when she turned around to look at him. "I see you found my running track."

"Actually, Michael recommended this route to me," Caleb

explained. "He said it was quite a challenging route with steep inclines."

"It does have." Lilly nodded. "The path goes down rather rapidly once you're over the rise and then flattens out for a while before you get to run up the next incline which is steeper than this one to bring you back to the retreat." She had no idea why she'd just jabbered on about the path when Michael had obviously already told him.

"Awesome." Caleb clicked his watch. "Mind if I join you and you can show me the rest of the run?"

"Sure." Lilly looked at her watch and reset it. So much for trying to keep track of her time. Goose was like a furry bowling ball at times. "Goose, Lunar," she whistled.

"Wow." Caleb looked at Lilly impressed. "I bet you wouldn't have a problem hailing a cab in New York."

Caleb grinned at Lilly and her heart nearly stopped. She'd seen him smile before, but those smiles were just courtesy smiles, the ones you know people expect or you don't want them to mistake your expression. Caleb was incredibly handsome with chiseled features, hazel eyes, and thick black hair. But when he smiled, his face took on a whole new level of handsome fused with sexy.

"You okay?" Caleb frowned at Lilly, making her realize she was staring, and her cheeks flamed. "It's a long time since I've seen a woman blush," he said softly. "My mom blushes, but that's more an angry red stain." He smiled warmly at Lilly.

"My mom doesn't get an angry red stain on her face, she gets daggers in her eyes." Lilly mentally shook herself out of her daze. "She's ex-military so she has the dagger glare down to a fine art."

"Ouch." Caleb and Lilly set off on their run.

Lunar and Goose ran ahead of them sniffing around the ground, running, and playing with each other while they ran ahead of the humans.

"Michael told me that both your parents are ex-military," Caleb kept up the conversation.

"Yes," Lilly nodded. "Both my parents and my grandparents."

"That must have been great for you?" Caleb smiled.

"You have no idea." Lilly rolled her eyes.

By the time they'd hit the straight patch of the path Lilly felt a little more at ease in Caleb's company and started to relax. They got to the bottom of the incline that would take them back to the retreat when Lunar and Goose started to growl at something in the thicket of trees just in front of them.

"Goose, Lunar," Lilly stopped and called. "I'm so sorry about this, they're not normally so edgy." She swore under breath when the two dogs took off into the wooded area. "Great!"

Without a thought for her own safety, Lilly took off after the two angry dogs.

"Lilly, wait!" Caleb took off after Lilly.

"Goose, Lunar!" Lilly called as she navigated the forest. She didn't really like to stray into the thick-tree studded woods. She was convinced there were all sorts of predators in them. "Where are you two?"

A hand snaked out over her mouth and pulled her behind a large tree. Her first instinct was to bite down hard on the palm of the hand.

"Shh," Caleb whispered in her ear. "Don't make a sound."

Lilly's eyes grew huge, and fear thudded through her. *What could Caleb see that she couldn't? Was it a bear or a mountain lion?*

Caleb removed his hand from Lilly's mouth while he kept his arms around her and hidden behind the tree.

"Caleb, Kelsey," a man called to them. Lilly felt Caleb's shoulders stiffen. "I know you're both here somewhere."

"Do you know him?" Lilly asked Caleb softly.

"I'll explain later." Caleb took Lilly's hand and quietly led her deeper into the woods.

"All I want is to talk," the man called after them. "If you come out willingly no one has to get hurt."

Caleb pulled Lilly quietly through the woods as the man had cut off their path back to the running track.

"Where are you?" The man called and they could hear his footsteps crunching through the foliage behind them.

"Where are Goose and Lunar?" Lilly asked Caleb they ran in what they thought was the direction of the retreat through the woods.

"We can't stop and find out, Lilly," Caleb told her as he stopped to try and figure out which way they were going as they got deeper into the woods that surrounded part of the cove and led into a State forest. "I promise, once we're back at the retreat and the dogs are not home, we'll come back to find them. But with the police."

"Police?" Lilly asked in shock. "Who is that man, Caleb and why does he know you and Kelsey?"

"I'll explain everything once we're safe." Caleb turned and looked at her. "Please Lilly, you have to trust me. That man cannot find us."

"So you do know him?" Lilly continued to question Caleb as he pulled her with him.

"Lilly, please." Caleb looked around them as they heard the man whistling as he followed them like a hunted deer through the woods. "Yes, we do know him, and he's a very dangerous man." His eyes darted around the trees looking for a place to hide. "This way."

Lilly ran behind Caleb. Her hand was still held firmly in his as they came to a wall of rock.

"There," Lilly pointed, "it looks like an opening."

"You're right," Caleb looked behind them. "Go and hide in there." Caleb tore a piece of his t-shirt and emptied his one water bottle.

"Where are you going?" Lilly looked at him in alarm.

59

"To throw him off our trail." Caleb ran back down into the wooded area and disappeared back into the trees.

Panic clawed at Lilly as she was trapped between two places that frightened the life out of her. She was okay in the woods when someone was with her and she was okay with rocky hikes and even caves if someone was with her. But she would never venture into any of those areas alone and now she had the option of entering a cave or facing down a man Caleb had said was extremely dangerous. *What if there were wolves, mountain lions, or bears in the cave?* Lilly thought as she made her way to the opening in the rock wall on jelly legs.

Lilly was cautiously making her way into the cave with her phone's light when a hand once again snaked around her mouth. She was about to go into full blown cat being put into a bathfight type mode when a deep familiar voice whispered.

"Shh, it's me." Caleb told her and let her go.

"Will you stop doing that." Lilly spun around hissing.

Lilly didn't realize how close she was to Caleb and nearly fell over backward. He reached out and caught her.

"I didn't want you to scream in an echoing cave," Caleb said quietly. "I put a piece of my shirt on a thorn branch and dropped my water bottle on the trail."

"You littered?" Lilly's eyes narrowed at him.

"For a good cause and we can pick up the bottle once the madman is caught," Caleb reasoned with Lilly. "I watched him go in the opposite direction."

"What do we do now?" Lilly asked Caleb.

"We call for help." Caleb took out his phone. "I don't have a signal." He looked at Lilly.

"I don't have one either." Lilly looked wide-eyed at Caleb.

"Let's hunker down here for a while and make sure the man is gone." Caleb dusted off a rock and sat.

Lilly stood looking around the cave to make sure they were alone and there weren't some creatures that weren't keen on sharing their cave. Her flashlight fell on something that looked like it had been drawn on the wall.

"Caleb," Lilly called him, "come look at this."

Caleb walked over to where Lilly was running her hand over the rock wall.

"Is that?" Caleb's excited eyes met Lilly's equally excited ones. "Do you think?"

"I'm not sure," Lilly looked up at him, "but I think we should find out." She pointed her phone light towards the dark back chamber of the small cave.

Caleb checked the battery on his phone. It was full and so was Lilly's.

"I'm game," Caleb told Lilly, looking on the ground for two stones. He found what he was looking for and picked them up. "Here," he gave one to Lilly, "we'll mark the walls on both sides as we go. We use your phone until the battery dies and then we turn back and use my phone to get out of the cave."

"You sound like Zane." Lilly looked at him with raised eyebrows. "Please don't tell me you're in the military as well!"

"No," Caleb smiled at Lilly. "I've done many excursion shoots though."

"Okay." Lilly drew an L in a circle on the wall next to one of the pictures she'd found.

Caleb drew a circle with an X in it as they cautiously made their way into the dark cavern.

EPILOGUE

"Zane!" Michael pounded on Zane's cabin door.

"What is it?" Zane's head and ribs ached. He looked at his watch as he opened his cabin door. He couldn't believe he'd slept past eight in the morning.

"Caleb and Lilly are missing," Michael told him. "They went on a run over two hours ago."

"Maybe they're taking in the scenery together." Zane tried to shake the sleep fuzz from his brain.

"I went looking for them," Michael told Zane. "They seemed to have veered into the woods off Lilly's trail."

"Why would they do that?" Zane started walking back into the cabin with Michael following him.

"I'm not sure," Michael stopped and swallowed. "Zane, I found Lunar and Goose, they'd been shot with tranquilizer darts."

Zane stopped and spun around. His eyes narrowed.

"You should've led with that, kid!" Zane ducked into his room. "Get my pack from the spare bedroom," he called to Michael. "Are you ready for a search mission?"

"Yes." Michael walked into the spare room and grabbed Zane's pack. "Should I call the police?"

"Go up to Erin's cabin and let her know what's happening," Zane called to Michael as he got dressed. "Tell her to call the cops and show her where we're going."

"Got it." Michael put Zane's pack on a chair in the lounge. "I'll meet you at Erin's cabin."

"Watch your step here, it's a bit slippery." Caleb helped Lilly climb down the crudely carved steps in the rock.

"It's freezing in here." Lilly shuddered.

Caleb took his sweater from around his waist and handed it to Lilly.

"You'll drown in it, but you'll be warm." Caleb gave her a smile.

"Thank you." Lilly pulled the giant sweater over her head. "This must lead to beneath Pirates' Wall."

"I think so too." Caleb took Lilly's hand again as they carefully made their way through the small passageway they'd come to. "Look there." He shone the light into another chamber that opened up in front of them.

"That looks like tables and chairs." Lilly carefully stepped around Caleb who let her hand go so she could walk ahead while he shone her phone's flashlight in front of her. "Shine the light over there." Lilly pointed to one side of the cavern.

Caleb did what she asked and they both froze at the sight the flashlight lit up. Caleb sucked in a breath in shock while Lilly screamed!

SECRETS OF WHITE SANDS COVE

Book 2

PROLOGUE

Caleb and Lilly have found a mysterious cave in the forested area of White Sands Cove that holds a centuries old secret. While Michael and Lilly set up for their second annual Crab Shack beach game tournament, Caleb seeks Zane's help to catch the dangerous man from his past that is stalking him. Kelsey battles with her secret as she tries to protect her family and someone from Lilly's past once again puts hers and Michael's life in danger.

Take a trip to White Sands Cove as Caleb and Lilly fight their feelings for each other as they fear putting the other's life in danger. Join in the fun and festivities of the Crab Shack beach games and get ready to sit on the edge of your seat as Caleb and Michael are drawn into a trap.

Chapter Eight
THE CAVE OF ALL CAVES

"What the hell!" Caleb rushed into the cavern. His heart was beating in his throat when he thought that something had happened to Lilly.

Caleb stopped next to Lilly and his eyes grew large.

"Is that real?" Lilly asked Caleb. Her finger shook as she pointed to a skeleton sitting next to what looked like a grave.

"I think so." Caleb gave a shudder. "It looks like whoever that skeleton was, lived down here."

Caleb stepped farther into the cavern. The broken rotting boards that leaned against the cavern wall must have been what was used to close the cavern off. There was an old, rusted wood-burning stove. Pots that were rusted from the sea air, crudely made shelving, an old tea kettle, and a table with some chairs were in the middle of the room. On the wall of the room from the side they entered was a dilapidated bed.

"There were rumors that the original owners of White Sands Cove took to the tunnels or caves. They were hiding from smugglers who wanted to use the tunnels and the cove to move their illicit goods," Lilly told Caleb. "They sent their daughter off to live with the Green's when the cove was burnt to the ground in the late 1800s I think." Lilly slowly walked into the cave and looked around. "It was thought they were burnt to death in the fire."

"What an awful story." Caleb frowned at Lilly. "Look at these old things." He picked up a copper urn and tried to wipe the green copper oxide off it.

"Caleb," Lilly walked over to the far wall next to the old wood burning stove, "look at this." She felt around what looked like a carved-out shelf. "I think it pulls out."

Lilly could feel cold air blowing onto her hand.

"Let me see if I can move it." Caleb walked to where Lilly was and felt the opening. "Step back, I'm going to try and pull it."

"Okay." Lilly stepped out of Caleb's way.

With his powerful upper body Lilly had no doubt that Caleb would be able to move it. He wasn't over muscled like bulging bodybuilders; he was more ripped. Lilly gave herself a mental shake.

Good grief she was ogling! No that wasn't the right word, she was gawking! Lilly cleared her throat and looked away. Her eyes landed on the skeleton sitting next to the mound that looked like a grave. There was a stone with something written on it. Lilly moved closer, carefully stepping around the skeleton.

Lilly dusted off the dirt and sucked in her breath. It was a grave that had *Angelique du Bully 1883 - 1912* carved on the large stone that stood at the top of the grave. She jumped up so fast and turned towards the skeleton that she stepped back and fell over the grave. Lilly landed with a thud across the grave. As she righted herself, she saw a yellowed piece of folded parchment paper sticking out from beneath the headstone.

"Lilly," Caleb called to her excitedly, nearly scaring her to death as she was about to reach for the paper. "It's opening."

Lilly looked up and saw the old wooden shelves, which were embedded into the rock, move forward.

"Jus..t... one... more tug!" Caleb grunted and tugged as the rock pulled open.

Lilly tried to pull the paper, but it was stuck beneath the large stone and she didn't want to tear it.

"Caleb," she called him. "Well done on opening the door but do you think you could help me lift this rock?"

"What..." Caleb turned around to see Lilly crouching down beside the grave. "Is there something there?"

"Uh-huh," Lilly nodded distractedly. "And I can't lift this heavy rock."

"Is that a name on the stone you're trying to move?" Caleb frowned as he carefully stepped over the grave.

"Yes." Lilly stood up, not realizing how close Caleb was and nearly bumped him over.

Caleb grabbed Lilly to stabilize her and pulled her against his rock-hard chest. Lilly felt her heart rate speed up and her cheeks heat up.

"I..." Lilly cleared her throat. "I'm so sorry," she said and looked up at Caleb.

Their eyes locked and held. Lilly thought her heart couldn't speed up any more without bursting from her chest. The man was gorgeous, deep, broody, but also had a gallant side. She swallowed and took a step back breaking the spell.

Caleb blinked a few times before clearing his throat and looking away from the incredibly beautiful Lilly. When his family had arrived at White Sands Cove and he'd seen her in the reception he'd been struck by her serene beauty. She had an air around her that drew a person in and made them feel warm and calm. He'd met his fair share of beautiful women but most of them knew how beautiful they were. But not Lilly, she hardly wore any makeup, he'd yet to see her take a selfie or even be on her phone except for business.

Lilly didn't flaunt herself or her beauty. She was just Lilly. As far as Caleb had seen, she was gentle, kind, caring, but fiercely protective when she needed to be. She was also highly intelligent and business savvy which made her such an appealing package. And if he weren't careful, he could find himself doing something he was in no place to do right now. There was no way he could drag someone like Lilly into the world he and his family were currently trying to survive in. If today was any indication, Caleb's family's problems were far from over as they'd hoped. So much for a fresh start in a new city.

"Caleb?" Lilly raised her voice snapping Caleb out of his deep thoughts. "Are you okay?"

"Yes," Caleb shook his head, "sorry I was just wondering if it was bad luck or something to move the head stone."

"We're not going to move it," Lilly reasoned. "You're going to gently lift it and I'm going to grab the parchment paper. You never know, maybe we weren't supposed to open that door. There could be some weird killer alien trapped in there." She grinned as Caleb rolled his eyes at her.

"Okay." Caleb stepped up to the rock and gently lifted.

Lilly had to reach around Caleb to pull the paper out. Their hands brushed and Caleb nearly dropped the rock on her hand as an electric shock zinged through him.

Get a hold of yourself Caleb! Caleb gave himself a talking to. *Nothing can ever happen between you and Lilly.* He had too much baggage and mad men after him and his family. He'd already almost got Zane killed the other day and now Lilly today.

"Got it," Lilly said excitedly as Caleb gently put the stone down and apologized to the skeleton for moving it. "Did you just apologize to the skeleton?" Lilly raised an eyebrow at Caleb.

"Yes," Caleb nodded. "We shouldn't be disturbing the dead," he said softly.

"Look at this." Lilly's eyes shone. "Caleb, it's the missing part of the map." She breathed. "It shows this whole cave, and it seems to be quite large." She frowned and turned the map around. "It also points at the entrance to the cave being in the completely opposite direction to what we thought it was."

"You mean near that weird looking rock that looks like it's been deliberately put there?" Caleb asked Lilly to step up to tower over her so he could look at the map over her shoulder. "If we go through the opening I just opened, it looks like we have to double back on ourselves to get to the main entrance."

"Yes, and it also lists a few caverns as being filled with water?" Lilly frowned. "My French is a little rusty."

"No, you're right." Caleb leaned over Lilly to hold the map with her.

Caleb could feel the warmth of her body and he had the sudden urge to lean over and kiss her. He clenched his jaw and took a deep breath. What the hell was wrong with him? He knew he couldn't have a relationship right now, but his damn body was betraying him and completely ignoring his logic and reasoning it seemed.

"Oh no." Lilly Looked at her phone. "My phone is running out of battery."

"Maybe I should push that covering back and we come back here a lot more prepared to go explore the rest of the cave," Caleb suggested. "We don't want to get stuck having to try and make our way back through that tricky passageway in the dark."

"I agree." Lilly folded the parchment. "I can't wait to show Michael and Zane." She held up the map.

Caleb pushed the cover for the opening closed. As they were about to walk out of the one cavern, Lilly stopped and looked at the skeleton.

"I think we should bring some shovels and give Jacques a proper burial next to his wife as well," Lilly said softly, her eyes glittering with tears. It was in that moment that Caleb knew he was in trouble where Lilly was concerned.

"I agree," Caleb said softly, staring at her. His heart felt two sizes bigger and at that moment he envied the lone tear gently caressing her beautiful cheek. "We'll carve him a headstone just like his wife's."

"Thank you," Lilly wiped another tear away before it could escape. "I'll tell you about their story one day if you want to hear it."

"I can't wait." Caleb smiled at Lilly who smiled back before turning to lead the way out the cave.

"Do you think that man has gone?" Lilly asked over her shoulder.

"I think by now Michael would've got a search party together to look for us," Caleb assured Lilly. "Your cousin and Zane are fiercely protective over you!"

"Tell me about it," Lilly said as she carefully navigated her way through the cave. "My date for the La Jolla Spring Fling nearly dumped me because of them." She sighed.

Caleb felt like someone had clenched his heart at the mention of Lilly's spring fling date and he knew if he was here at the time her date would've been scared off!

"They must be here somewhere." Kelsey stopped and looked at the tree where a piece of cloth was stuck to the branch. "This is part of Caleb's shirt." She pulled it off the branch and showed Michael.

"Is this Caleb's too?" Michael bent down and picked up the water bottle.

"Yes." Kelsey's big eyes looked up at Michael. "They must've come this way."

"Hey boy." Michael kneeled down next to Goose who was still a little groggy and unstable on his feet. "I know you're not feeling too good, but do you think you could find Lilly and Caleb for ..." Before he'd finished his sentence Goose started to bark and run off, falling all over his feet towards the rock shelf that cradled the back part of the cove.

"This way." Michael looked at Kelsey before running after Goose. Lunar had gone with Zane and Erin.

"Let's hope his sense of smell isn't off because of the tranquilizer." Kelsey followed Michael.

"Look!" Michael pointed towards Caleb and Lilly running down the hill to an excited Goose.

"Michael." Lilly waved and laughed as Goose attacked her and Caleb with a million doggie kisses.

"What happened?" Michael ran up to Lilly and grabbed her up into a bear hug. "I was so worried about you and what your father would do to me if anything happened to you." He hugged her again.

"This man was chasing us," Lilly started to tell them while Kelsey ran and hugged her brother. "I thought he'd killed Goose and Lunar." Tears sparkled in Lilly's eyes as she thought that she had to run on and leave the dogs.

"It's okay." Michael put an arm around her and looked at Caleb. "Thank you for taking care of her."

"It was a two-person job." Caleb smiled. "Let's get back to the retreat; I'm starving."

"I am too." Lilly smiled at Caleb. "Oh, look what we found."

Lilly handed the map to Michael who opened it as they walked towards the hotel. He stopped and nearly had Caleb plough right into him.

"Holy cave!" Michael looked up at Lilly then turned to Caleb. "You two found this up there?" He pointed to the rock shelf.

"Yes." Lilly grinned.

Before Michael could ask any more questions, his phone rang. It was Zane. Michael told them that he and Kelsey had found Lilly and Caleb and to meet back at the hotel.

Chapter Nine

THE BEACH BONFIRE AND BBQ KICK OFF

"Thank you both for helping out." Lilly smiled at Kelsey and Caleb. "We started the Crab Shack Annual Beach Games last year and it was an amazing success." She smiled as she directed one of her hotel staff members where to take the tables.

"So this bonfire and BBQ night on the beach kicks off the games for tomorrow?" Caleb picked up a pile of chairs and walked next to Lilly.

"Yes." Lilly smiled up at him trying to not stare as the veins popped up in his arms. "I hope you and Kelsey will sign up for a few of the games."

"You get to choose a partner as they're all two-person team sports." Michael carried some fold out tables. "Luckily my incredibly competitive sister and her husband won't be attending this year as they're off sailing."

"Yes," Lilly rolled her eyes, "Michael's sister Maddison has to win at all costs."

"Last year she sabotaged my oldest sister and her husband Luke." Michael shook his head. "We're actually thinking of banning her from all future games."

"You haven't seen Caleb." Kelsey raised her eyebrows. "Your sister Maddison sounds a lot like him."

"Hey," Caleb bumped Kelsey with his elbow, "you're just a sore loser." He grinned as they walked onto the sand near the old boathouse.

"Yeah, that's what it is." Kelsey rolled her eyes and shook her head. "Caleb once sabotaged my one sneaker at one of our track meets because he might be a six-foot-three hulk, but he's slow." She grinned at Caleb's glare. "And I'm fast."

"Huh, seems you have some competition this year, Lilly." Michael grinned at his cousin. "Lilly is the undefeated sand sprinting champion."

"Only because I love to run on the beach in the evenings at least three times a week," Lilly explained. "So I have a bit of an advantage over everyone else as I have my own beach."

"So, do we get to choose our partners?" Kelsey asked as she unstacked chairs a safe distance from the bonfire and BBQ grills.

"No, we don't, but the ticket holders have to bring a partner." Michael shook his head. "My mom, Aunt Miranda, and Uncle David wrote the rules for the entire function. Just to keep it fair and also because that meant they couldn't compete." He sighed. "As you'll both be considered part of the in-house entrants the judges choose who we partner up with."

"Aunt Jennifer, my father, Uncle David, and Aunt Miranda are usually the judges," Lilly explained. "This year we're wanting to ask your mom, Zane, Piper and Alex." She looked at Caleb and Kelsey.

"Piper... that's Zane's niece who is staying at one of the cabins near us?" Kelsey asked Lilly. "She's pregnant?"

"Yes," Lilly nodded, "that's Piper. She couldn't go on the cruise with the rest of hers and mine and Michael's families because she gets horribly seasick because of the pregnancy."

"I've seen her on the beach with Goose a few times," Kelsey told Lilly. "She seems very nice."

"She really is," Lilly laughed, "but don't let her niceness fool you. She's quick to put a person in their place if they step out of line."

"I'm sure my mother would love to be one of the judges." Kelsey walked back to the hotel to fetch more equipment.

"Your mother would love to do what?" Erin joined them.

"Oh, there you are, Mom." Caleb put an arm around Erin. "I nearly didn't see you without your heels." He laughed when Erin swatted him.

"We were wondering if you'd be one of the four judges for this weekend's beach games?" Kelsey asked Erin.

"Ah, the infamous games that Jennifer created the rules for." Erin smiled. "Of course, I'd love to. What do I have to do?"

"I believe we have to get everyone signed up tonight and then draw names out of a hat to assign the teams." Zane came up behind them.

"Are you also a judge?" Erin turned around to look at Zane.

"I believe so." Zane smiled holding up a folder Lilly had given him earlier. "I have all the rules here."

"Wow, that's quite a set of rules." Erin's eyes widened.

"I'm about to meet with Piper and Alex," Zane told Erin. "Apparently Jennifer took her through what needs to be done for the games and what's required of us."

"Great," Erin smiled at him. "I just need a cup of coffee and I'm ready."

"We have coffee and biscuits." Piper and Alex walked into the foyer. "Hi, I'm Piper and this is my husband, Alex," she introduced herself to Caleb and Kelsey. "I'm Zane's niece."

"Nice to finally meet you," Kelsey said to Piper. "My mom came back from Florida and told us about the McCaid family."

"Mm," Piper grinned, "well I hope your mother told you that I'm the good McCaid!"

"Of course you are, sweetheart." Zane put his arm around Piper and gave her a hug.

"Shall we get this meeting going?" Piper asked. "I'm dying to tuck into Lilly's homemade ginger biscuits."

Zane, Erin, and Alex followed Piper through to one of the hotel's meeting rooms.

"Caleb, would you mind helping me with the bonfire stack?" Michael asked him.

"Sure," Caleb said, his eyes growing wide as Michael showed him the giant crab effigy that was to go on top of the bonfire.

"You can't burn the crab." Kelsey looked at the cute giant red crab with the name Crab Shack on it.

"You must see Lilly light it up," Michael said proudly as he looked at his cousin.

"How do you light it up?" Caleb looked at Lilly who walked behind the reception desk and into the back office.

"With this." Lilly came out with a long bow and special arrow that would be lit.

"Woah," Caleb's eyebrows rose, "I take it you know how to use that?"

"Lilly's an archery champion," Michael bragged. "I think she could even outshoot Robin Hood."

"Michael exaggerates a little." Lilly smiled, her cheeks going pink. "I've been shooting the bow and arrow since I was ten."

"I'd love to learn." Kelsey took Lilly's bow and looked at it. "It's beautiful."

"It was custom made for her," Michael told Kelsey.

"Okay," Lilly took her bow from Kelsey, "we still have a lot to do." She put her longbow away.

"What else can I do?" Kelsey asked Lilly.

"If you'd like to, you can come and help me make sure the food is ready." Lilly led Kelsey through to the hotel's kitchens. "Then we just need to get the cash register and tickets."

"How much are the tickets?" Kelsey asked Lilly.

"Our guests don't pay," Lilly smiled at Kelsey. "The proceeds from the games go to a center for abuse and the children's hospital."

"That's awesome." Kelsey followed Lilly around the impressive hotel kitchen. "Is that cherry pie?"

"Yes." Lilly cut two slices. "My Aunt Miranda makes it. You must have a taste."

"Oh, wow!" Kelsey wiped her lips with a napkin after taking a bite of the confectionary. "That has to be the best cherry pie I've ever tasted."

"I know, right?" Lilly grinned. "I'm going to cut a few pieces for Michael and Caleb."

"Caleb would polish this entire pie off," Kelsey warned Lilly. "So only show him a piece of it."

"Michael's the same," Lilly laughed. "You should see Michael with pop-tarts. He's addicted to them, I swear."

"I love pop-tarts too," Kelsey admitted. "Especially the Chocolatey Salted Caramel flavor."

"Well, don't let him know I told you." Lilly walked over to a cupboard. "This is the families' grocery cupboard." She pulled it open. "You're welcome to come help yourself anytime."

"That's a lot of Pop-Tarts." Kelsey gaped at the two shelves full of Pop-tarts.

"Michael is a Pop-Tart hoarder." Lilly and Kelsey laughed as she pushed the cupboard closed. "Let's go do the tickets and we're done."

While the waves gently rolled onto shore, the evening was clear and warm. Smoke rolled off the BBQs as the hotel chef made BBQ rib, steak, and burgers. A popular local band played on a makeshift stage while people danced on the wooden dance floor that had been placed for the evening. In the distance, patrons of the Crab Shack wandered between the beach and the restaurant. The sound of laughter and merriment could be heard across the designated bonfire night beach area.

As seven rolled near and the last of the game weekend tickets were sold, Michael took to the stage.

"Good evening," Michael's deep voice boomed over the crowd that instantly quietened down.

"Where's Lilly?" Caleb asked Erin when he walked over to get the ticket sales amount from her.

"I believe she'll be here for the lighting of the Crab Effigy and the commencement of the games," Erin laughed dramatically.

"I think she rides in on a horse drawn carriage or something," Zane leaned over and told Caleb.

"I don't think it's a horse drawn carriage, Uncle Zane," Piper frowned. "I think it's a white horse."

"You'd better get the total amount of ticket sales over to Michael." Erin gave the paper to Caleb.

Caleb walked up to the stage and handed the paper over to Michael.

"It looks like we doubled what we made last year," Michael told the crowd, who went into an uproar of applause. "Once again, we'd like to thank you for participating in the second annual Crab Shack Beach Games Tournament. I hope you enjoy the evening bonfire. Please get your plate of the delicious BBQ our hotel chef has prepared."

The crowd applauded and Michael let them clap for a while.

"Now is the part where I have to appear like a party pooper, but in order to make this an annual event we have to enforce a few rules." Michael rattled off all the rules about the areas that were off limits, no alcohol on the beach, it had to be drunk at the Crab Shack, and about littering. Lastly, he let them know they had a bus on stand-by to take people home who couldn't drive.

One of the hotel waiters walked onto the stage and whispered in Michael's ear.

"There you are." Kelsey crept up behind Caleb.

"Where have you ..." Caleb turned around then stopped as

he looked at Kelsey. "Why are you dressed like you're going to a toga party?"

Kelsey was wearing a white one-strap toga. The strap that rested on her shoulder was held there by a red crab pin. A plaited gold and red belt was wrapped around her waist and the toga fell to just above her knee. Her feet had sandals with red laces that laced up her calf to just below her knee. Her sandy blonde hair was in a French braid with a wreath on her head that had small red crabs positioned around it. In her hand she held a small gold staff that had red ribbons entwined around it. On top of the staff was a gold crab.

"I'm part of the lighting of the crab effigy." Kelsey smiled at Caleb. "I'll ride in on the chariot with Lilly. Then I and one of the hotel receptionists will have lit torches. I get to light Lilly's arrow, which she'll shoot at the crab."

"That sounds like a fire hazard." Caleb frowned.

"That's why there are about four fire-fighters here tonight." Kelsey rolled her eyes at Caleb. "For someone, whose whole career has been about chasing adventure, even the dangerous kind, you're being a little bit of a stick in the mud."

"Fire is a whole different type of danger." Caleb raised his eyebrows.

"Look around you," Kelsey pointed towards the beach, "we're surrounded by sand and water."

"Just be careful, okay?" Caleb smiled down at Kelsey and looked at his watch. "Now shouldn't you be going to find your chariot? The bonfire lighting is going to begin soon."

"Yes," Kelsey smiled. "Will you hold my specter for me please?"

"Sure." Caleb shook his head.

Kelsey went up on tiptoes and gave him a kiss on the cheek before running off.

Caleb looked around at the layout of the bonfire night. At the grassy edge of the beach the band was up on the stage that had taken two days to erect. Where the long boardwalk that led to the Crab Shack split for the beach entrance, Erin, Zane, Piper, and Alex sat at the entrance table. From the hotel a long wide wooden path had been set up. Caleb presumed that's where Lilly would be riding in on. The bonfire stood a few feet towards the ocean at the end of that path.

The beach was full of people milling about and having fun. The local band Michael had got to play was really good. They played some of their own music and did a lot of covers of some popular songs. Lilly and Michael had really made something special of White Sands Cove Retreat. The following week Michael was going to take Caleb on some of the adventure trails the retreat offered, as well as show him all the sports and activities that could be found here. One of the activities he was really looking forward to, was the plane ride, as Caleb would get to jump out of a plane again. He loved skydiving but hadn't been for a jump in just over two years.

Caleb was pulled from his thoughts when two of the hotel staff waiters, dressed in the male version of togas, ran down the path and trumpeted.

"Now the moment you've all been waiting for," Michael took the stage once again. "Make way for Queen Crab and the Crab princesses." The waiters trumpeted again as the sound of horses' hooves hitting against the wooden boards could be heard.

A chariot came into view. Kelsey and another woman were standing in front of the chariot next to the chariot driver. The chariot had a small back balcony that was a bit higher than the chariot. Caleb still couldn't see Lilly and his heart felt a bit heavy with disappointment.

The trumpeters lit two long matches on the flaming lanterns that lit the pathway and walked towards Kelsey and the other woman who held out their torches to be lit. They raised the torches up into the sky. Caleb's heart stopped beating as Lilly stepped out from behind the two women and climbed up onto the balcony.

She was breathtaking. Her long golden blonde hair was pulled back into a French braid and topped with a golden crown. Caleb couldn't see the point of the crown properly, but he assumed it had a golden crab on it. Unlike the rest of the crew, Lilly was dressed in a red off-the-shoulder toga adorned with gold trimmings. The belt that cinched in her tiny waist was a plaited rope of gold, as were the laces that hugged her toned tanned calves up to just below her knees. In her hand was her golden longbow and the golden arrow.

As she turned around on the chariot balcony, the crowd went wild, cheering Lilly on. Caleb's heart kicked back into gear and hammered heavily as Lilly's face split into a beautiful smile. As she raised her bow and placed the arrow on it, he noticed that even the bracer on her arm and her finger tab was gold. While the arrow was still pointed down Lilly nodded at Kelsey who lit the arrow.

The crowd started to count down from five. On one Lilly shot the fiery arrow that arched perfectly through the air and hit the crab effigy making it burst into flames. Once again, the crowd cheered as Kelsey and the other woman hopped off the chariot to run around the base of the crab effigy and set the wooden beams alight. Soon the bonfire was blazing, and the party went into full swing as the annual Crab Shack Beach Games tournament had begun.

When the chariot had ridden away Caleb looked around for Lilly. Instead he found Kelsey looking for her specter.

"What did you think?" Kelsey asked Caleb excitedly. "That's the most fun thing I've done in two years." She grinned.

Caleb's heart swelled seeing Kelsey so happy. The haunted shadows that had shaded her beautiful eyes for the past two years had disappeared, replaced by the happy reflection from her genuine smile.

"It was amazing," Caleb grinned down at her. "You look amazing."

"Thank you," Kelsey did a little courtesy. "Now if you'll excuse me, I'm going to join my fellow toga buddies."

"You do that." Caleb gave her a hug. "Where did Lilly go?"

"I think I saw her heading for the Crab Shack," Kelsey shrugged before Michael came to ask her for a dance.

"Sorry Caleb but I'm stealing Kelsey away for a dance." Michael grinned at Caleb.

Caleb found Lilly sitting on the rocks just below the Crab Shack. She was sipping on a soda staring out at the sea.

"Hi," Caleb walked up to her. "Mind if I join you?"

"Sure." Lilly smiled up at Caleb.

"You are quite the archer." Caleb smiled at her.

"Thank you." Lilly pointed to her arm. "I'm so glad that's over. I really hate all the attention, but it creates such a vibe and people really enjoyed it last year."

"So now you have to be the Crab Queen every year?" Caleb laughed.

"Yeah." Lilly laughed with him.

"So why are you sitting out here all on your own?" Caleb looked around a little uneasy at the thought of her being on her own with that madman still on the loose.

"I'm not really big on crowds," Lilly took another sip on her soda, "so I just needed a little alone time to unwind."

"Sorry," Caleb looked up at her, "I'm encroaching on your unwinding." His voice dropped.

"No." Lilly looked at Caleb. Their eyes met and held. "Not at all," she said softly, her cheeks going pink.

"You look beautiful." Caleb's voice was hoarse and low.

Lilly was so close to him he could feel her body heat. Their eyes were locked as their lips slowly drew together. Caleb reached out and put his hand behind Lilly's head and gently drew her to him. She tasted like cherries and her lips were soft as his gently teased her in a soft kiss. He drew back and smiled down at her.

"Lilly," Caleb moaned before he pulled her towards him, and their lips locked once again in a passionate kiss.

Lilly's arms came up around Caleb's neck as she leaned into him. The rest of the world melted away as they got lost in each other's embrace. They were so oblivious of the world around them they didn't see the tide sneaking up on them until they were splashed by the foam of a crashing wave.

The world came tumbling back around them as they sat wet and dazed by what had just happened between them.

"I think I need to go and change." Lilly stood up so quickly she tripped but Caleb caught her.

"I'm sorry, Lilly," Caleb cleared his throat. "I ..."

"Don't apologize," Lilly said shakily. "It was as much me as it was you." She pulled herself out of his powerful arms. "I must go get changed."

"I'll walk you back to your cabin," Caleb offered.

"No," Lilly said a little too quickly. "I'll be fine." With that she turned and fled.

Caleb stood watching her. *What the hell Caleb!* He ran his hand through his hair as he cursed himself.

Chapter Ten

THE CRAB SHACK ANNUAL BEACH GAMES

*L*illy had hardly slept. All she could think of was the feel of Caleb's lips on hers and how it felt to be held in his powerful arms. She knew she'd been a coward running like she had but Lilly wasn't ready to go down that path again. The pain and humiliation of her last break up was still all too real to her. Besides, she had far too much going on in her life right now to get involved with anyone. Especially someone like Caleb. Not only was he extremely good looking, but he seemed to be carrying around a lot of secrets. Lilly couldn't trust someone with secrets and to her trust was everything.

Lilly tied her long golden-blonde hair into a braid, so it didn't get in the way of the sports. She wore a White Sands Cove T-Shirt and matching shorts, along with her white deck shoes that were more like booties as they were waterproof with non-slip soles. She'd given a pair of the same shoes to both Kelsey and the other two ladies on her staff who were representing the retreat. Lilly looked at her watch. Drat! She was going to be late and get another lecture from Zane. He was even worse than her father and mother with their time. She grabbed her sunscreen and White Sands Cove cap as she rushed out the door. She had to go and be paired up with her partner for the sports day.

Lilly rushed up the hotel steps and found she was the last of the eight White Sands Cove representatives to arrive.

"Nice of you to join us, Lilly." Zane looked pointedly at his watch.

"I'm three minutes late." Lilly rolled her eyes at Zane.

"You know what I say about even a minute late." Zane raised his eyebrows.

"Zane." Erin frowned at him. "Ignore him, Lilly." She smiled.

Lilly stepped into line next to Michael.

"What happened to you?" Michael whispered to Lilly. "I'm usually the one running late. I woke you up an hour ago."

"I had a few things to do," Lilly whispered back. "Then time just ran away from me."

"You can leave the spreadsheets for one weekend, Lil," Michael told her. "You're going to burn yourself out. Relax this weekend and have some fun. You deserve it."

"I will." Lilly looked at him, but Michael did not look convinced. "I promise."

"Cousin headbutt promise." Michael's eyes narrowed.

"Fine," Lilly rolled her eyes as they linked pinkies then tapped foreheads together, "I cousin headbutt promise."

"When you two are finished," Zane looked at them.

"We're finished," Michael saluted Zane.

"Zane, Piper, Alex and I have sorted out the teams," Erin started. "Step up and collect your color arm bands from Piper and your water bottle from Alex as we call out your teams."

"I feel like I'm at summer camp." Kelsey leaned over and looked at Lilly with a huge grin on her face.

"I know; wait till you're having fun on the beach," Lilly said, applying sunscreen. "Do you need some?" she offered Kelsey.

"No," Kelsey pulled her sunscreen out of her small backpack, "I'm already all sun screened."

"I need some." Michael took the bottle and put sunscreen on his face. "Thanks." He handed the bottle back to Lilly.

"Can I have some please?" Zane asked and took the bottle Lilly held out for him.

"Blue team," Erin called and looked at Zane.

"That will be Kelsey and Michael." Zane finished putting lotion on his face and handed the bottle back to Lilly before pulling Michael and Kelsey's name tags from a sheet and handing it to them.

Erin called the yellow team and then the purple team. The green team was the only team left which was Lilly and Caleb.

This wasn't going to be awkward at all! Lilly thought as she gave Caleb a tight smile. He hadn't said one word to her, or even looked at her since she'd arrived. In fact, Lilly was convinced Caleb was trying not to catch her eye just like she was trying to avoid him.

"Hi, partner." Caleb gave Lilly a smile. "Are you okay?" he asked her softly while he helped her tie her arm band on.

"I'm great." Lilly gave him a smile. "Let's get your arm band on." She helped tie Caleb's arm band.

Lilly knew the minute she had to touch his lean muscled arm it was a mistake to have offered to help him. Tiny little electric shock waves zinged up her arms aiming straight for her heart. Lilly took a deep silent breath in and tried to fend off the feeling and suffocate the butterflies going wild in her stomach.

"Thank you." Caleb had stiffened at the touch of her on his arm. *He must be regretting the kiss as much as she was,* Lilly thought, and her heart felt like it had become very heavy. *Shake it off, Lilly!* She gave herself a stern talking to.

"Sorry?" Caleb frowned at her. "Did you say something?"

"No," Lilly shook her head. *Oh no! Had she said that out loud?* "We should get going." She turned, picked up her pack with water and snacks in and headed for the beach.

This was going to be a long two days! Lilly sighed as she made her way down to the beach, not bothering to look back and see if Caleb was following her.

Caleb followed Lilly. For the first time in his life he wasn't sure what to say to a woman. The previous night when she'd fled from him, he'd felt like she'd run off with a part of him. Today he'd been excited to see Lilly but at the same time felt he wasn't ready to face her. Caleb knew he had no right to kiss her or feel anything for her, but his emotions and brain were at war with each other over her at the moment. His mind was definitely dead set against any kind of relationship with Lilly.

This terrible chapter of his and his family's life they thought was finally closed wasn't. Zane had contacted some security agency to look into the two incidents that had happened at White Sands Cove over this past week. Caleb's family, Zane's family, and Michael and Lilly had been warned not to go anywhere on their own. Zane had put together a whereabouts board and checklist to ensure everyone was accounted for at all times. It was like another nightmare for Caleb, Erin, and Kelsey, but at least this time Caleb and Kelsey weren't held prisoner in some black ops holding site.

"Is there something going on between you and my cousin?" Michael nearly gave Caleb a heart attack as he'd snuck up on him.

"No," Caleb's eyes narrowed as he looked at Michael, "what makes you ask that?"

"Yesterday you two were getting along fine," Michael looked at Lilly who was walking in front of them back to Caleb, "today she seems to want to put as much distance between the two of you as possible."

"I'm not sure why she's walking so far ahead of us," Caleb lied.

Caleb wasn't ready to open up and talk about what was going on between him and Lilly. He couldn't even admit anything was going on to himself.

"Uh-huh," Michael nodded. "I'm just going to say this to you. Lilly's last relationship ended very badly. She hasn't dated or even looked at another guy in almost two years." He looked at his cousin. "Lilly has a big heart and when she loves someone, she puts her whole heart into it." His eyes flashed with warning. "The man lucky enough to win her heart would have to be someone damn special. Someone she could trust completely and would treasure her because Lilly is a rare gem."

Caleb watched Michael walk off and go on ahead to catch up with Lilly. Caleb already knew everything Michael had just said to him. He also knew he wasn't that special, someone worthy of Lilly's heart. Caleb knew now more than ever he had to pull back and ice over whatever he felt for her. She deserved better.

"Hey," Erin caught up with Caleb, "is something wrong, honey?" She looked up at him with worry shining in her eyes.

"I'm fine," Caleb managed to smile down at Erin even though smiling was the last thing he wanted to do. "Are you looking forward to being the judge and jury of the competition today?" He managed another plastered-on smile.

"I am." Erin linked her arm with his as she walked along with him. "I know it's not my business to pry as you are a grown man now," she made them stop, "but honey, don't throw away a chance at happiness because of your past."

"I don't know what you're talking about, Mom." Caleb frowned.

"Sure you don't." Erin gave him a sad smile. "Honey, we all have eyes. And I've never seen you look at anyone else the way you look at Lilly." She went up on tiptoes and gave him a kiss on the cheek. "Love is about sharing everything, Caleb. True love makes even the heaviest of burdens lighter as you no longer have to haul them about on your own."

Erin walked off to go and find the other judges.

Caleb stood frowning into the distance. His mind was reeling as it screamed at him to stand his ground and stay far away from any emotional entanglement with Lilly. While his heart was egging him to run after her, pull her into his arms, and tell her everything. But he knew he couldn't. It was too dangerous. There were things even his mother and Kelsey didn't know about the past two years. Things he had to keep to himself as they'd already been through so much. He took a deep breath and pinched the bridge of his nose.

Caleb was in two minds about moving here with his mom and Kelsey. But they'd begged him to come and start a new life with them. A new start in a new city far, far away from New York, with a clean slate. Only Caleb's slate was far from clean and now New York was bleeding into their new life. He wanted to move back to New York, but Zane had told him not to and to stay in La Jolla until they'd caught the man that had chased them. When Caleb and Lilly had found that cave, Zane had cornered Caleb and made him tell him what was going on. It had felt good to finally tell someone. Zane had assured him it would go no further than the two of them and had agreed Caleb should keep it to himself for now.

Zane was also someone who could handle himself in danger. Zane also didn't get shocked too easily or make snap judgements, which Caleb was grateful for. At least now someone that wasn't mixed up in Caleb's family's messy life knew the truth. A horn blew in the distance from the beach. Caleb snapped out of his brooding thoughts and hurried towards the beach. Lilly was already giving him the cold shoulder. He didn't want to give her reason to be angry with him as well for missing the first event.

As he rushed towards the beach he wondered about Lilly's messy breakup and how he could find out what had happened without being asked why he was so interested to know.

"Where have you been?" Lilly looked at her watch. "We

have to go and find out who we play beach volleyball against first."

"The first event is beach volleyball?" Caleb smiled. He was really good at beach volleyball and was sure he and Lilly were going to win this event.

The first day of the annual Crab Shack beach games was nearly over. It was a fun filled day of doubles volleyball, doubles frisbee challenge, team swing ball, and beach rounders. Lilly and Caleb had won the volleyball and beach rounders. They were one beach game ahead of the next couple.

Lilly was exhausted and couldn't wait to go home, wash the sand off her, and climb into bed. She had no idea why she'd let Michael and Kelsey talk her into having dinner at the Crab Shack. Lilly was grateful for the dinner though. She would've gone to bed hungry as she really didn't have the energy to cook. She was also enjoying the band they had playing at the Crab Shack this evening.

"Earth to Lilly," Michael snapped his fingers in front of her face, "are you in there?"

"Sorry," Lilly laughed, "I'm exhausted." She took a sip of her soda.

"It's been a really fun filled busy day." Kelsey stifled a yawn. "I'm also looking forward to going home, taking a nice shower and falling into bed."

"Tomorrow is another busy day." Lilly smiled at Kelsey. "I see you two were having a lot of fun today."

"I haven't laughed that much in years," Kelsey admitted. "When are we going on the cave expeditions?" she changed the subject.

"Zane is just getting things together and making plans." Michael ate a chip. "You must know what he's like by now.

Everything has to be mapped out to near perfection before it can be actioned."

"Having been on many expeditions, I can assure you it's better to do it Zane's way than have it end up in a tragedy." Caleb took a sip of his beer.

"Agreed." Michael raised his beer. "I still can't believe what the two of you found." He looked from Lilly to Caleb. "You may have given us a way around the locked tunnel with the yacht in it."

"I was thinking the same thing." Caleb leaned forward on the table. "The other side of that tunnel you said was locked is probably in one of the caverns in that cave."

"I wish we could've studied the map better before Zane took it," Lilly breathed. "Well, that's me for the night." She finished her soda. "I'm sorry but I'm exhausted."

"Stay for one dance." Michael raised his eyebrow. "Then we can all walk back to the retreat together."

"Yes," Kelsey smiled at Lilly, "I promised Michael a dance."

"Okay." Lilly sighed and threw her head back resignedly. "I'll wait."

"Why don't we have a dance too?" Caleb smiled at Lilly.

"Yes," Kelsey pulled Lilly from the chair. "You dance with my brother while I dance with your cousin."

"I ..." Lilly was looking for an excuse but before she could come up with one Caleb's hand closed over hers and gently pulled her onto the dance floor.

The song changed to a slow song. Caleb pulled Lilly into his arms. She stood stiff while they moved to the music.

"Relax, Lilly," Caleb's soft voice teased her ear. "I'm sorry about last night."

"It's okay," Lilly whispered back.

"Lilly," Caleb looked into her eyes, "you are the most beautiful person I've ever met, both inside and out." He smiled. "I'd never deliberately do anything to hurt you." He pulled her closer so he could whisper in her ear. "That's why I have to keep our relationship to friendship only."

"I understand," Lilly surprised him by saying. "You have nothing to apologize for Caleb." She leaned back to look into his eyes. "I was as much to blame for what happened last night as you were." She smiled up at him. "Only I realized I'm still not ready for a relationship other than friendship."

"Does this mean we are friends again?" he asked hopefully.

"Yes, of course." Lilly smiled at him. "Now should we finish this dance?"

"Absolutely." Caleb pulled her close.

Lilly relaxed in his arms and rested her head against his solid chest. She felt so safe and warm encircled in his strong arms. She knew deep down that she'd not been honest with Caleb. But how could she be honest with him when she wasn't ready to be honest with herself about how she felt.

Chapter Eleven
THE MAN AT THE WINDOW

Lilly and Caleb danced another four slow dances together. Neither one of them wanted to let the other go. Kelsey and Michael had left them after their second slow dance. Lilly had offered to close up the Crab Shack for Michael. Caleb offered to stay and help Lilly. Slowly the customers left, and the band started to pack up. When the band was gone Caleb helped Lilly close up.

Before Lilly and Caleb left, he put on one last slow dance for them. He pulled Lilly into his arms and an electric current once again zinged up her spine. She sighed and relaxed in his arms snuggling her head on his chest.

"Lilly," Caleb breathed in the magnolia scent of her before pulling back slightly to look at her.

Lilly looked into Caleb's eyes as they swayed to the music. His head lowered towards hers. Lilly's head lifted towards his, their lips were about to touch when someone started to bang on the closed shutters of the Crab Shack.

"I know you're in there!" the man's voice shouted to them.

Caleb and Lilly lifted their heads and looked towards the side of the shack the noise was coming from. Caleb's arms tightened protectively around Lilly.

"It's him again." Lilly's huge eyes locked with Caleb. Her heart pounded in fear.

"I think so," Caleb said softly. He took Lilly's hand and quietly led them into the kitchen. "Does this door lock?"

"Yes." Lilly quietly pushed the door closed.

Lilly's hand was shaking so badly she couldn't find the right key. Caleb's warm hand closed around hers and took the bunch of keys from her.

"Which one?" Caleb asked.

"The one with the red label." Lilly pointed to it.

Caleb locked the door and took out his phone. He dialed Zane who answered on the third ring. Caleb told him what was happening. Zane told them to stay where they were, he was on his way.

"If you don't come out, I'm going to start shooting my way into this restaurant," the man shouted. "Do you hear me?"

They could barely hear him through the locked door of the kitchen. But they could hear the loud bang of the man trying to kick his way into the restaurant. Caleb pulled Lilly towards the large walk-in freezer. He stopped when he saw the office and noted a bed in it. Caleb ducked into the office and took the blanket from the bed.

"Come on." Caleb pulled Lilly into the big walk-in freezer. "I'm hoping this also locks from the inside and out?" He held up the keys.

Lilly was scared. She didn't know if she was shivering from fear or the cold in the fridge.

"Yes." Lilly felt her jaw start to shake as she shivered. "It's the one with F1 on it."

Caleb locked the fridge door and took them over to a small shelf. He pulled Lilly down on his lap then wrapped them in the blanket.

"We'll keep warmer this way." Caleb pulled her closer to his chest.

"Thank you." Lilly snuggled into Caleb and rested her head

against his shoulder. "I hope Zane hurries up or we'll be human popsicles."

"Lilly, I'm so sorry about this," Caleb said softly. "I never wanted you dragged into my family's troubles."

Lilly lifted her head to look into his eyes. He looked so sad and defeated.

"Now that I am, I think I need to know what's going on." Lilly's brow creased. "I think it's only fair, as this is the second time this man has hunted us down."

"When we're out of here," Caleb gently moved a stray lock from her face, "I'll tell you what I can."

"What do you mean you'll tell me what you can?" Lilly's frown deepened.

"There are still some things I'm trying to work out," Caleb told her honestly, "and some things my mother and sister don't know about yet. I need to protect them for as long as possible."

"I see." Lilly's eyes searched his. "What happened to you and your family?" she asked. "My Aunt Jennifer just said that you all needed a fresh start from a horrible ordeal."

"That was a nice way of putting it." Caleb swallowed as some of the memories of the past two years ran through his mind. "It was a living nightmare straight from hell."

"I know Erin's ex-husband passed away just over two years ago," Lilly breathed, seeing the pain, anger, and torment flash in his eyes. "Was what happened to you and Kelsey related to that?"

"Yes." Caleb's jaw clenched, and his eyes went blank as he masked the emotion ripping through him. "He was never much of a father. He wasn't even a nice man."

"I'm sorry," Lilly said, with feeling. "It must've been so hard for you. I know your parents died when you were young and that's why you went to live with Erin."

"Yes," Caleb gave her a small smile. "She became my mother and in a way she's the only real mother I've ever had. My flesh and blood mother was never the mom type."

"And your real father?" Lilly frowned at the look that flashed in Caleb's eyes.

"I really don't want to talk about him right now."

"Oh." Lilly looked like he'd struck her.

"It's just that it's complicated and brings up issues," Caleb said.

"That's okay." Lilly smiled at Caleb. "It's so cold." She snuggled closer and Caleb tightened his arms around her.

"I think we need to pull the blanket over our head as well." Caleb started to pull the blanket over their head when Lilly lifted hers and their faces brushed.

They both froze and stared at each other. Lilly wasn't sure who moved first but the next thing she knew they were locked in a passionate kiss. Before the cold refrigerator and world around them could fade away there was a loud banging on the refrigerator door.

"Caleb, Lilly," Zane shouted. "I don't have a key for the fridge. I've searched the rest of the restaurant, so I really hope you two are in here."

"Yes, we're in here," Lilly shouted. She was loathed to leave the warm safe haven of Caleb's arms.

"Is it wrong that I want to sit here the whole night with you?" Caleb said softly in her ear.

"I feel the same way," Lilly kissed Caleb on the forehead, "but I think we should remain friends as was agreed earlier and take this, whatever it is, slowly."

"I agree. I have a lot to figure out in my life." Caleb kissed her one more time before she stood up and he followed her.

"I have a lot to work through myself," Lilly admitted to him and took his hand as they walked to the fridge door.

Caleb gave her one last quick kiss before he unlocked the door.

"Are you two okay?" Zane looked them over. "I'm sorry I took so long to get here. I thought it was safer to leave you two locked in the kitchen until we'd secured the area." He led them out of the restaurant. "We boarded up the shutter and window the guy kicked in."

"We?" Lilly asked Zane as Caleb wrapped the blanket around her.

"I called the agency and they sent out some agents right away," Zane explained.

"Did you get the man who broke in?" Lilly asked Zane.

"No," Zane shook his head. "He headed towards the rocky cliffs before we could get him."

"Thank you Zane," Lilly felt exhausted. She was now both physically, emotionally, and mentally drained. "I really need to get to bed now."

"I'll walk you both back to your cabins," Zane told them as they started to walk back towards the retreat. "The agents have taken tracking dogs, but it's much more dangerous to try to track the man on those cliffs during the night."

"He must've been watching us because he knew we were here alone locking up," Lilly told Zane.

"We'll keep an eye out for the man during the games tomorrow," Zane told them. "In the meantime, some of the agents will be staying at the Cove."

"I feel much better knowing that." Lilly stifled a yawn as they came to her bungalow.

Zane and Caleb followed her inside to make sure everything was secure, and she had no unwanted guests.

He stood watching from a safe distance. He would've been able to capture his target if that damn man they call Zane, and his agency friends hadn't interfered. This had dragged on for far too long now and he was tired of hiding in the shadows. But every time he got close to getting what he needed, one of those pesky people from the retreat interfered.

It was time to call in a few favors from some people who

owed him that lived in the San Diego area. He knew it was going to be risky showing his face again, but this mission of his was turning out to be a little more trying than he first thought it would be. Especially now that the family was being protected by some agency, and that Zane person he'd found out was in the special forces.

He wanted this over. He wanted his life back and he was quite willing to tumble the empire who'd set him up to do it. Now that he had most of what he needed, he was well on his way to doing just that. But it looked like he was going to have to get rid of Zane first and he had a good idea how to do that too. It helped that he knew Erin Carnegie very, very well and as such, knew exactly which buttons to press that would help him get rid of Zane.

As Caleb and Zane walked out of the blonde woman's cabin, he faded into the night. There had already been too much of a scene and attention drawn to the Cove for one night. Tomorrow he'd go and get the help he needed and hopefully he'd be able to extract his target without too much fuss.

Chapter Twelve

THE ANNUAL CRAB SHACK BEACH GAMES DAY 2

"Why did Zane have to tell me what happened to you last night?" Michael stormed into the cabin while Lilly was making her breakfast.

"You're up really early this morning," Lilly told him as she made herself some oats. "Would you like a bowl of oats with fresh banana, nuts, and raisins?"

"Don't avoid the subject," Michael sat down at the kitchen counter on one of the high-back chairs, "and, yes please, I'd love a bowl of oats. You make them so nicely."

"It's the fresh fruit, nuts, raisins, a dash of cinnamon, and cayenne pepper that makes it so great." Lilly smiled at Michael as she set about making their breakfast. "There's also a lot of nutrition and energy to get you through the morning."

"I know." Michael poured himself a cup of the freshly brewed coffee from the coffee pot on the counter next to him. "You give me the rundown of your oats every time you make them." He took a sip of his coffee. "Is there any coconut?"

"I'm sorry," Lilly looked up at home and did a sorry frown, "I couldn't find any coconut at the store."

"Aw," Michael moaned. "I love your oats with coconut in it."

"Here you go." Lilly put the bowl in front of him and passed him the warm milk and the honey. "I'll check again when I go to the store next week."

"Okay." Michael poured honey over his oats and added some warm milk. "Now tell me what happened last night." He looked up at Lilly taking a seat with her oats in front of her.

Lilly sighed and told Michael what happened with the man trying to break in. She left out the intimate bit between her and Caleb. Lilly wasn't ready to speak about that just yet. She had a lot to deal with and she really wanted to be able to help Caleb with whatever it was he was battling with. To do that, every instinct in her body was telling her she just had to be his friend for the time being. Once both Caleb and Lilly had worked through their issues they'd know if they wanted more from each other.

"Why is it that this man only ever targets Caleb when the two of you are alone together?" Michael frowned. "Nothing happens when you or Caleb go running off on your own. But as soon as the two of you are together, this man targets the both of you."

Lilly was about to take a spoonful of her oats when what Michael said sank in. She looked at him startled for a moment.

"You're right." Lilly put her spoon down. "It started the day after the hike when Zane got pushed into that hole. The next day we were chased by the man when we were jogging together. Then last night we were alone together at the Crab Shack."

"You and Kelsey have the same height, build, and are both sandy blondes." Michael's brows drew together. "Do you think that maybe this man thinks you're Kelsey and it's actually Caleb and Kelsey he's after?"

"But Kelsey and Caleb have been on a few hikes together with nothing happening." Lilly shook her head. A deep frown creased her brow.

"Maybe the timing wasn't right," Michael said. "Did Caleb say he knows the guy? I know you got a look at his face when he chased you through the woods the other day."

"No," Lilly lied. "I was the one who got a good look at his face." That wasn't a lie.

"Let's hope Max's men find this guy and fast." Michael stood and went to rinse his plate before putting it into the dishwasher. "Until they do, please be careful and stick to Zane's rules." He went over and gave her a brotherly hug.

"I will." Lilly smiled at Michael as she followed him by rinsing off her plate and popping it into the dishwasher. "We'd better get going to make the last few games. I think this year myself and Caleb are going to win."

"I wouldn't count on that." Michael put his backpack on. "The Stevenson's are neck and neck with you two, with me and Kelsey right there nipping at your heels." He grinned as she made a face at him.

Lilly put her backpack on and followed Michael out the door and down to the beach.

"The agents have tracked down Gertie Tucker," Zane told Caleb as they stood off to one side of the beach crowd. "I know she said she didn't see the man's full face, but maybe she could see if there's some likeness to the man that's after you."

"I'm not sure it is the same man," Caleb frowned. "The man who knocked Gertie over and picked up the wrong phone was texting Kelsey," he told Zane, who gave him a black look.

"That would've been handy to know when we had our heart-to-heart the other day," Zane looked at Caleb accusingly. "I need to know these details, Caleb. I told you I can't help you unless I know EVERYTHING!"

"I'm sorry," Caleb held up his hands. "It really did slip my mind until you reminded me about Gertie's phone." He shook his head. "The messages on Kelsey's phone from that phone that Gertie thought was hers seemed more desperate than threatening. If I didn't know better, I'd have thought they were from ..." He stopped and gave Zane a mocking smile.

"Who did you think they were from Caleb?" Zane asked.

"A ghost," Caleb said softly. He leaned over and whispered a name to Zane, bringing a frown to Zane's face. "The guy after me wouldn't send those kinds of messages. His messages are more ominous and vengeful."

"So you're convinced there are two people hunting you and your sister, Kelsey?" Zane asked Caleb.

"Yes," Caleb nodded. "I'm pretty sure the man hunting me isn't the same man shadowing Kelsey."

"What makes you so sure?" Zane rubbed his chin.

"Because the man only comes after me when I'm alone with Lilly," Caleb said softly. "He was showing me he's after revenge."

"You think everything that happened over these past two years comes back around to this man chasing you?" Zane clarified. "If that's the case, why is the person you call the ghost trying to reach out to Lilly?"

"She has something he wants," Caleb told Zane. "We both do. Only, if it is him, he knows I wouldn't give him the time of day."

"The question I have for you," Zane's eyes narrowed, "is why are you still keeping information from me Caleb?" He shook his head. "Once again, I can't help you if I don't know all the details."

"Like I said," Caleb defended his actions, "I wasn't concentrating on the ghost when we had our discussion."

"Okay," Zane nodded. "But tomorrow you and I are going to finish this conversation and you're going to tell me everything. You won't leave out one tiny detail, even if you think it's irrelevant."

"Fine," Caleb ran a hand through his hair, "and thank you Zane." He took a deep breath. "I feel a whole lot better knowing someone else knows my side of the story."

"Well so far, from what I've been able to find out," Zane

assured Caleb, "your side of the story holds up as the truthful account of what happened."

"Fair enough," Caleb nodded. "I have to make a run into the store if you'd like to join me and I'll tell you everything I know. I think you need to talk to Kelsey as well because I think there's something she's been keeping from myself and our mother for a while now."

"I saw those messages on her phone." Zane explained what happened when Erin took him to the hospital. "I have to agree with you that your sister is definitely hiding something."

"Caleb," Lilly smiled at him and waved, "come on. I've chosen us a dinghy."

"I'll be right there," Caleb smiled back at Lilly.

"Just one more thing," Zane stopped Caleb before he left. "Tread carefully with Lilly. Her father left her in my care. She's had a really rough time of it. I really don't want to see her getting hurt and neither does her father." He looked towards Lilly. "If you think I'm harsh, wait until you meet Shane."

"Understood." Caleb gave Zane a tight smile. "I'd better go so we can win this race."

The day had flown by. A couple called the Stevenson's won first place, Kelsey and Michael came in second, while Caleb and Lilly took third place.

"Don't feel bad, cuz," Michael grinned, "there's always next year."

"You're worse than Maddison." Lilly shook her head at Michael. "I know you cheated in the dinghy race and you were the one who tripped me in the beach sprints." She looked at her bruised knee. "Look what you did to my knee! I fell on a stone."

"Ouch." Michael pulled a face as he looked at Lilly's knee.

"I'm going to have a shower and then crawl into bed." Lilly stretched. "We have a full day planned for tomorrow."

"I'm taking Kelsey to start her internship at Jacobs Medical Center at five tomorrow morning," Michael told Lilly, "so I won't be here when you wake up."

"I'll be up by five thirty as Zane is coming on my run with me tomorrow," Lilly rolled her eyes. "He thinks I may also be a target for the guy stalking Caleb."

"I'm glad he's running with you then." Michael grabbed some Pop Tarts.

"I have Goose and Lunar," Lilly shrugged. "He won't let myself and Caleb run together either." She signed. "Until they've caught this man, Zane's going to be glued to my side."

"Well at least I don't have to worry about you running alone," Michael yawned. "Don't take your usual five hours in the shower. I'm beat."

"I won't be long." Lilly ducked into the bathroom.

"Kelsey," Erin called her daughter from downstairs, "can you come downstairs? Zane would like to have a word with all of us."

"Coming," Kelsey called downstairs. She'd just climbed out of the shower. "I'm getting dressed quick."

"Okay honey," Erin called back.

Kelsey ran into her room to go and get changed. While she was brushing her hair, her phone bleeped with a message. She glanced over at it.

We need to talk. I know where he is!

She frowned as she read the message. She was so tired of these messages that came through every day.

Who is this? You know where who is? Kelsey typed.

You know who this is Kels. You also know who I'm talking about. Meet me if you don't want any harm to come to Caleb and his new girlfriend.

You leave Caleb and Lilly alone! Kelsey typed. Her anger made her overlook that she'd just put a name to Caleb's new friend's face.

Lilly is a very pretty name. Does she know why they are being hunted?

She's just a friend and nothing more to Caleb. Leave them alone! Lilly typed. She shouldn't have made contact. Her heart felt like it was beating in her throat. *What do you want?*

I need that evidence you have, Kelsey!

I don't know what you're talking about. Kelsey typed before she switched off her phone regretting her actions of making contact.

Kelsey tied her hair up as she trotted downstairs to go find out what Zane wanted.

Chapter Thirteen

A BAD MEMORY RETURNS WITH A VENGEANCE

"Are you going to be okay for a few hours?" Caleb asked Lilly. "Zane and I are heading into town. He has your order and I have to pick up some things for my mom and Kelsey."

"I'll be fine," Lilly smiled at Caleb. "There's a whole hotel of staff here."

"Please, Lilly, don't go wandering off on your own." Caleb kissed her on the forehead.

"I promise." Lilly smiled at Caleb. "Now go before Zane comes looking for you."

"I'll see you later," Caleb started to walk to the door, "we can go for a hike when I get back."

"Sure." Lilly smiled and waved.

As Caleb walked out of the hotel, a cowboy walked into the hotel. Caleb got a weird vibe from the guy. He shook it off as he rushed out to the car where Zane was waiting impatiently for him.

"Sorry." Caleb slid into the passenger seat of Zane's pickup truck. "Did you see that expensively dressed cowboy."

"No," Zane craned his neck to see into the hotel. "Is he someone we should be worried about?"

"I don't know him." Caleb shook his head.

"Good, then let's go." Zane put the truck into gear and pulled out. "Michael's back from dropping Kelsey at the hospital and Erin's helping Lilly pick out a color scheme for the suits," he reassured Caleb. "She has a lot of people around her."

"It's probably just me being a little paranoid with everything going on." Caleb shook off the bad feeling.

"I'll call Michael when we get to the hardware shop," Zane told Caleb, "and I'll get one of the agents to check up on her."

"Thank you," Caleb breathed. "I should never have come here." He ran a hand over his face. "I've put everyone in danger."

"Don't beat yourself up," Zane told Caleb, "none of this is your fault. Sometimes good intentions go wrong."

"Wrong is putting it mildly," Caleb gave a mocking laugh. "More like an atomic explosion wrong."

"You have to get the truth from Kelsey," Zane said softly. "She was lying to us last night."

"I want to jump down your throat and defend her," Caleb said truthfully, "but I know when my sister is lying, and she wasn't even just bending the truth last night, she was outright lying."

"I think she lied because she's scared of something," Zane said.

"Or scared of someone," Caleb added.

"We need to find out who or what Kelsey is afraid of," Zane breathed, "before she gets in too deep or worse, hurt."

"I know," Caleb breathed, "I'll get the truth from her."

"*L*illy, I like the green with a hint of soft pink..." Erin stopped and frowned as she looked around the empty foyer. "Lilly?" She walked towards the reception desk. "Lilly?" she called again as she walked around to the back office.

Lilly's sweater and cabin keys were on her desk. Erin's heart started to beat a little faster as a bad feeling crept up her spine. She walked out of the office and spotted Lilly's phone on the shelf beneath the reception desk. Her heartbeat picked up even more as she went over and picked it up.

That was strange. It looked like Lilly had created a voice recording ten minutes ago. Erin didn't like snooping on other people's phones but every instinct in her body was screaming at her to listen to it.

"Hello, Lilly," a male voice Erin didn't recognize greeted Lilly.

"What are you doing here?" Lilly didn't greet the man and Erin could swear she heard fear in Lilly's voice.

"Come now babe," the male voice drawled, *"I came to get you back. I've missed you and I'm tired of you playing hard to get, Lilly."*

"I told you nearly two years ago, Adrian, there is no us," Lilly sounded like she was trying to keep the fear from her voice.

"Lilly, my beautiful flower," the man Lilly had called Adrian said, *"that was just a little misunderstanding."* There was a shuffling. *"I forgive you, now come home so we can get married if that's what it takes."*

"I think you should leave, Adrian," Lilly's voice had risen a bit.

"Lilly, why do you have to always do things the hard way?" Adrian hissed. There was more shuffling.

"Let me go," Lilly shouted. *"Michael!"* Lilly screamed. *"Put me down, Adrian."*

"Sorry, sweetheart," Adrian laughed, *"but you're coming with me to my home where your interfering family can't find you. At my home you'll feel differently. You'll see."*

"Put me down, Adrian!" Lilly was shouting.

The phone went dead. Erin swallowed, her face was pale, her hands shook, and her heartbeat pounded in her ears as the shock settled in.

Oh my God, Lilly had been abducted by someone called Adrian. Erin stopped and frowned as she suddenly realized who Adrian was. Her chest rose and fell as her shock was replaced by panic and fear for Lilly. Her hands shook as she pulled out her phone and dialed a number there was no reply. The phone went to voicemail.

"Lilly's been taken, call me as soon as you get this," Erin left the message and hung up.

She ran through to the back looking for Michael. *That was strange, all the staff were missing.* She heard a noise coming from the pool area. She made her way towards the sound on shaky legs. The hotel staff were enjoying a feast of snacks and pizza.

"What's going on?" Erin asked suspiciously. "Why is no one working?"

"Michael and Lilly bought us some pizza and snacks as a thank you for all our hard work," the one man she knew worked in the kitchen told her.

"Where's Michael?" Erin asked the guy.

"Not sure," the man told her before walking off to join another group of hotel staff.

The bad feeling that had crept up Erin's spine turned to chills. *Where was Michael?*

Erin tried his phone but there was no reply. Erin felt like she was in the middle of a horror story. She turned and ran back into the hotel, kicking off her heel as she ran through the foyer, out the front door, and down to Michael and Lilly's cabin.

The front door was ajar. She could hear the frantic barking of Goose and Lunar. Fear propelled Erin forward as she pushed the front door open. Her heart all but stopped as she sucked in a breath when she saw Michael lying unconscious on the floor. Erin ran and slid to her knees next to Michael. She felt his neck for a pulse. He was still alive but had a golf ball size lump on the back of his head.

Michael was going to need a doctor. She had to try and wake him up. Erin gently tapped Michael's face.

"Michael, wake up honey," Erin called to him. "You have to wake up, Michael." She gave him a shake.

Michael's eyes slowly came open and he tried to sit up and grabbed his head.

"What the..." His eye grew large as he felt the lump on the back of his head that made him wince in pain."

"Do you remember what happened?" Erin helped him stand up.

"I heard Goose and Lunar going mad in the cabin." Michael sat down on one of the dining room chairs as Erin got him some water. "As I came into the cabin something hit me at the back of the head and the world went black."

"Oh my God!" Michael took the water Erin gave him as he stared wide-eyed at Erin. "Was it that man that's after Caleb?"

"No," Erin shook her and pulled Lilly's phone from her pocket growing. "Michael did you and Lilly order a pizza and snack feast for the hotel staff?"

"Not that I know of." Michael looked at Erin confused.

"I think someone was clearing the way to abduct Lilly," Erin said softly.

"What?" Michael choked on the water.

"You'd better listen to this?" Erin put Lilly's phone on the dining room table.

"Is that Lilly's phone?" Michael frowned at the phone.

"Yes," Erin nodded. "I think she wanted us to find it because she recorded this."

Erin hit play and Michael's face paled before a red stain of anger replaced the ashen color.

Chapter Fourteen
FINDING LILLY

"Caleb," Zane rushed back into the store where Caleb was at the checkout. "We've got to go."

"Let me just pay for the items," Caleb told Zane as he put his last few items into a bag and handed the women his bank card.

"Hurry it up," Zane said impatiently, "or just leave the stuff and we'll come back later."

"It's all done." Caleb put his card back in wallet which he shoved into his back pocket. "Where's the fire?" He picked up the bags Zane couldn't grab and ran after him.

"We have to get back to White Sands Cove immediately." Zane slammed the trunk once all the grocery bags were stored away.

Caleb's blood went cold as that horrible feeling he'd felt when he'd seen the cowboy walk into the hotel earlier returned.

"What's happened?" Caleb said as he climbed into the passenger seat, closed the door, and pulled on his seatbelt.

The cold started to seep through his entire body giving him a cool feeling of calm.

"Lilly's been abducted," Zane said softly as he glanced at Caleb before pulling out of the store's parking lot.

"I knew I was putting her in danger," Caleb smashed the dash with his fist.

"Hey," Zane said calmly, "take it easy." He looked pointedly at the dash. "No, Erin and Michael are sure it wasn't your stalker."

"Then who took her?" Caleb's brows drew together as she turned to look at Zane.

"It's a long story," Zane told Caleb. "Would you dial a number on my phone for me please?"

Zane gave Caleb the number to look for and he dialed it for Zane.

"Put it on speaker," Zane told Caleb.

"You know you've got Bluetooth right?" Caleb raised his eyebrows and shook his head.

"I haven't set it up yet," Zane shrugged as a voice answered. "This is Zane McCaid, can you put me through to Phillip please?"

A man with a very distinguished voice came on the line and greeted Zane.

"Shane said that if Adrian ever returned to La Jolla and started to harass Lilly, you'd know what to do?" Zane asked Phillip.

"You're talking about Adrian Grey?" Phillip asked for confirmation.

"Yes," Zane said.

"He has a restraining order against him," Phillip advised Zane. "If he's anywhere near Lilly I'll have a team on the way."

"Phillip," Zane said, breathed, "he's abducted Lilly. We don't know how, what car he's driving, but we know roughly when." He paused, "Lilly was smart enough to secretly record their conversation."

"Have you told Shane and Max?" Phillip asked.

"No," Zane shook his head.

"Don't, not until we have more information," Phillip warned. "I'll be at the Cove in ten minutes. In the meantime,

I'll put a bolo out on Adrian." Phillip said his goodbyes and hung up.

"I take it this Adrian guy is the rough time Lilly had not so long ago?" Caleb looked at Zane.

"Yes," Zane nodded, "I believe he is."

By the time Zane and Caleb got back to White Sands Cove, Caleb's mind was reeling. His heart felt heavy, and fear pumped through him for Lilly. He wanted to find that Adrian guy and rip him apart for laying a hand on Lilly.

Zane parked his pickup near Michael's and Lilly's cabin as that was where they'd decided to meet because it was a lot more private.

"Caleb!" Erin ran out of the cabin and hugged her son before turning to Zane. "Thank you for getting back so quickly."

"Let's get inside and you can tell us what happened," Zane ushered Caleb and Erin into the cabin. Michael was lying on the couch with an ice-pack on the bump on his head.

Erin explained what happened to Michael, what happened to the hotel staff, and then played the recording from Lilly. By the time the recording was finished Caleb's jaw ached from being clenched so tight and his hands were balled into fists.

"When is Phillip who you phoned getting here?" Caleb said through clenched teeth. "I take it he's also part of the agency you have looking into our case?"

"Yes, I'm agency, and yes from the agency looking into your case," Phillip Bradford, a tall distinguished looking gentleman walked into the room. He greeted everyone as Zane introduced him. "We have people out looking for Adrian. From what we know he's rather lazy and wouldn't leave for his ranch today." He sounded confident. "So that means he'd need to book into a motel for the night."

"I don't mind visiting every motel in La Jolla." Caleb's eyes glittered.

"Already have men on it," Phillip assured Caleb.

"Can someone please tell me about this Adrian guy?" Caleb hissed.

"During Lilly's final year of college, she met Adrian. He was in one of her classes or something," Michael explained. "He seemed like an okay guy. He was known as the campus cowboy. He was attentive, bought Lilly gifts, flowers, and apparently had fallen head over heels in love with Lilly."

"Lilly had told Adrian many times that she was not wanting a relationship as it was her final year she needed to concentrate on her studies," Phillip continued. "But Adrian was persistent."

"Lilly never kept any of the gifts he sent her as she didn't want to give Adrian the wrong impression," Michael breathed. "One day he asked Lilly to meet him in the park for picnic and asked her to marry him and move to his family's ranch just outside Santa Barbara with him."

"But Lilly told him she didn't feel that way about him and wasn't ready for marriage," Phillip told them. "He insisted that one day she would be so she should keep the ring in the meantime. That's when Lilly had got a little angry and told him please to stay away from her she didn't feel that way about him."

"That's when Adrian showed everyone who he really was," Michael shuddered. "He attacked Lilly one night when her and a friend were studying in the campus library." He closed his eyes as he remembered going to Lilly that night. "The next night the attack on her was even more brutal and luckily two of Lilly's classmates were around to help us."

"Adrian was suspended that night and sent back to Santa Barbara with a restraining order against him," Phillip shook his head. "Lilly hadn't seen or heard from Adrian in months. She'd already graduated and was starting the White Sands Cove project with Michael when Adrian struck again."

"One day when Lilly was walking out of her Pilates class Adrian grabbed Lilly," Michael picked up the story, "and dragged her off to the small local La Jolla church where Adrian forced the vicar to marry them."

"Luckily, the vicar knew Lilly and on the pretense of having to fetch a marriage license escaped to his office and called Shane," Michael explained. "Lilly's well known around La Jolla, so Shane had already got a few calls, including one from the friend that was with Lilly at Pilates that day she was taken."

"When Shane arrived at the church Adrian had Lilly hidden and told Shane if he didn't back off, Shane would never see Lilly again," Phillip went on. "While Shane kept Adrian busy, Lilly's mother was searching the church that was a lot bigger than it looked."

"While Shane was trying to reason with an agitated Adrian Lilly stumbled into the room," Michael swallowed. "Unfortunately, she stumbled right into Adrian's arms." He drew in a ragged breath. "That's when Adrian pulled a gun and warned Shane that if he couldn't have Lilly, no one could."

"Adrian dragged Lilly into a small room and locked the door." Phillip shook his head. "When Shane and his wife managed to bash open the door Adrian flew at them and Lilly was knocked out when she fell against the wall."

"Shane dealt with Adrian while his wife tended to Lilly." Michael cleared his throat. Lilly had a bad concussion and a reaction to the sedative Adrian had given her," "Lilly nearly died," Michael cleared his throat. "She'd had a reaction to the drug Adrian had given her and he didn't even realize it. He just kept giving it to her to keep her subdued."

"Adrian's parents came to La Jolla to plead their son's case." Phillips' eyes glittered, "Apparently Lilly wasn't the first girl he'd become obsessed with." He ran his hand through his hair. "He was taken to a psychiatric facility. We weren't made aware that he'd been let out. I put a call into his parents as the facility won't answer my questions without a warrant."

"What do we do now?" Caleb's voice was gruff with suppressed anger.

"Excuse me a minute," Phillip said as his phone rang.

"I say we go do our own search." Michael banged the table. "How could they let Adrian out of that facility?"

"They didn't," Phillip walked over to them. His brows were drawn into a frown. "Some man claiming to be his lawyer came and signed him out on a court ordered day pass."

"How do you get a court ordered day pass?" Zane looked confused.

"You don't," Phillip shook his head, "but the psychiatric facility said that Adrian's mother was ill and on her deathbed and wanted to see him one last time."

"Is Adrian's mother sick?" Caleb asked Phillip.

"No," Phillip shook his head. "She sounded fit and healthy when I spoke to her a while ago."

"We'll find her," Zane told Michael and Caleb. "Trust me, if I have to scour every hotel, motel, and hostel from here to Santa Barbara, we will find Lilly."

Michael and Caleb looked at each other across the table. A silent plan passed between them.

"In the meantime," Erin said, "I think I'd better get you to the hospital to get that bump looked at," she told Michael.

"It's fine," Michael said ignoring his pounding headache. "I need to be here to hear about Lilly."

Before Caleb could say anything to Michael about his bump, Caleb's phone rang. He frowned as he noted the number. He got up and walked into the kitchen to take the call.

"Hello," Caleb said softly into the phone.

"Is this Caleb?" a familiar voice asked. "I don't know if you remember me. It's Gertie Tucker. You and your sister were kind enough to help me out about a week ago."

"Hi, Gertie," Caleb greeted her, "I remember you."

"Oh good," Gertie sounded relieved. "I don't know if I told you this, but I'm a local minister at a little church in La Jolla."

"I think you did mention that." That cold feeling started to creep up Caleb's spine again.

"There's a young woman here that I think you know," Gertie's voice dropped to a whisper, "I saw you two together at Goldfish pond the other day. I thought she was your sister at first."

"Do you know her name?" Caleb's eyes flew to Michael who frowned back at Caleb. Caleb indicated for Michael to come over to where he was standing.

"Yes," Gertie whispered, "I think it's Lilly. There is a very agitated young man wanting me to marry them!"

Caleb's blood turned to ice before the boiling hot anger erupted like a molten volcano in the pit of his stomach making him see red.

"Can you stall them, Gertie?" Caleb whispered back to her.

"I can. We're waiting on the rushed license I said I had to order," Gertie explained.

"Good thinking," Caleb commended her. "Don't put yourself in any danger though. That man isn't stable."

"Understood," Gertie gave Caleb the address of the church, which he wrote on Lilly's shopping list notepad. Gertie hung up and Caleb pocketed the note.

"Is everything okay?" Michael asked Caleb.

"Yeah," Caleb sighed, "it was Kelsey having some first day rotation jitters."

"My head is in pain." Michael massaged the back of his neck.

"Maybe we should take you to have that looked at?" Caleb suggested to Michael.

"I guess we can," Michael agreed with Caleb. "We don't know how long we have to wait for news, and we have our phones."

"Yes and we'll be closer to the city center if there is any news." Caleb helped Michael up who swayed a bit for added effect.

"That's such a relief," Erin breathed. "Take the SUV." She gave Caleb the keys she had in her pocket. "And let me know what the doctors say."

"Will do Mom," Caleb helped Michael up the path to the hotel where the SUV was parked.

"You've found her," Michael said, getting into the passenger seat and pulling on his seat belt.

"Yes," Caleb took the note out of his pocket and handed it to Michael. "You need to get us to this church."

"No way!" Michael looked up at Caleb in surprise. "This is the same church he took her before."

"We have to hurry." Caleb drove as slowly as he could until they'd cleared Zane, Erin's, and Phillips's line of sight before putting his foot down on the peddle.

EPILOGUE

Two agents pulled up at Michael's cabin a few minutes after Michael and Caleb had left.

"Have you got anything?" Phillip walked up to the men.

"No, we've only two more motels to go to but nothing yet," the one agent updated Phillip.

"Who were the two men speeding out of the driveway?" the second agent asked.

Phillip's brow creased as he looked at Zane whose brow was also creased.

"Son of a ..." Zane stalked into the kitchen and took the notepad Caleb had written on. He scratched over it with the pencil next to it. "Michael and Caleb aren't going to the hospital." He handed Phillip the notepad. "They're going to this church."

"That's the same church Adrian took Lilly to," Phillip hissed. He turned and immediately instructed his agents to get to the church.

Zane pulled up at the church with Erin. Phillip had gone ahead of them and was already there.

"Erin, Zane," Phillip waved them in, "this way."

There were about ten agents scouring the church and the grounds. There were also two ambulances that made both Zane and Erin's heartbeat pickup in fear.

"Did you find them?" Zane noted that Caleb's SUV was still in the parking lot.

"We found Adrian," Phillip told them. "He won't be bothering anyone for an awfully long time as we've taken him into custody. This time he won't be getting out to bother anyone ever again."

"Oh, that's such a relief. I'm sure once Lilly has recovered from this ordeal she'll feel better knowing that" Erin frowned and looked around "Where are Caleb, Michael, and Lilly?" she asked worriedly. "Michael and the vicar, Gertie Tucker, are over at the ambulance getting checked out," Phillip told Erin and Zane.

"Where's Caleb and Lilly?" Zane asked slowly. His eyes filled with worry.

"According to the vicar and Michael, a man wearing a neck gaiter covering the lower half of his face busted into the church as soon as Michael and Caleb arrived." Phillip retold the vicar's story. "He had a gun. He demanded that Caleb and Lilly come with him and said if the two of them did so, no one would be harmed."

"Where are Lilly and Caleb?" Zane asked again.

"The man took them away at gunpoint," Phillip said softly. "We have people out looking for them. Michael ran out after them and got a look at the car and a partial plate number."

"No!" Erin nearly collapsed at Phillip's news. Zane caught her and pulled her against him. Cradling her. "Not again." The tears rolled down her face. "Why is this happening again?" She looked up at Zane with tear-stained cheeks.

Before Zane could answer, Michael ran towards them ignoring the shouts from the paramedics calling him back.

"Erin, Zane," Michael ran towards them, "I'm so sorry." He swallowed and swayed before collapsing to the ground.

"Michael," Erin and Zane rushed to his side. Zane shouted for a medic.

"He's been shot," Zane noted the hole in Michael's shirt on his side. "Michael, can you hear me?"

"His pulse is faint," Erin's eyes were huge as fresh tears fell from them when they looked up at Zane.

SECRETS OF WHITE SANDS COVE

Book 3

PROLOGUE

Caleb and Lilly find themselves trapped in a room after being abducted from the church by a masked gunman. No longer able to deny their feelings for each other after Lilly's terrifying ordeal at the hands of her obsessed ex-boyfriend, they know it's time to share the secrets of their past. Secrets that have held them hostage for the past two years and kept them from being able to move on with their lives.

Caleb knows that if he doesn't tell Lilly his dark secret and explain what he and his family went through over the past two years, the man who abducted them would. Only in the man's version, Caleb is the villain, and the man is out for revenge. A revenge Caleb fears the man tends to use Lilly to exact on him. Caleb has to figure out a plan to save Lilly at all costs even if it means giving up his only leverage to do it.

There is a lot more to Lilly's and Adrian's story than anyone knows. Lilly has lived in fear of getting too close to anyone for two years. That was until Caleb walked into her life. Just as Lilly learns to trust and let someone into her heart again her past comes back to haunt her.

Chapter Fifteen
TRUST AND SECRETS

"Where are we?" Lilly whispered to Caleb as they were pushed into a windowless room.

"I don't think anywhere good," Caleb swallowed.

Caleb's heart hammered in his chest as he looked around the room. There was a single bed in the corner, two wooden chairs, and a round table.

"I'm so thirsty." Lilly cleared her throat.

"What's through that door?" Caleb walked over to a second door in the room and opened it. "It's a small bathroom."

Caleb walked into the bathroom and turned on the sink tap. He let it run for a while and then took a sip of the water before looking at Lilly who'd followed him into the bathroom. "I know it's not ideal, but you can drink this water."

"Thank you." Lilly walked over to the tap and held her hand under it to have a drink of water. "At least that man gave us a bathroom."

"Lilly..." Caleb took her hand and led her through to the bedroom once she'd drunk her fill. "Did you see what happened at the church?"

"No," Lilly frowned at him.

"What's the last thing you remember?" Caleb asked her.

"Adrian was holding a knife to me," Lilly's eyes grew huge with fear. "I can't believe he's back." Her breathing became labored with panic. "Is he the reason we're here?" Her eyes widened even more. "I'm so sorry, Caleb."

"Lilly," Caleb grabbed her by her forearms and bent down to look into her eyes, "this isn't your fault. Do you hear me?"

"It is, Caleb," Lilly shook her head. Her eyes were misting over. "I got you involved in my mess and now you're forced back into what was obviously a nightmare for you."

Caleb's heart melted. She truly was the most precious person he'd ever met.

"No," Caleb shook his head and wiped a stray tear from her cheek. "I fear I've dragged you into my mess." He pulled Lilly to him and wrapped her in his arms cradling her.

"I don't understand?" Lilly sniffed as she wrapped her arms around Caleb's waist.

"Finish telling me what you remember before you passed out." Caleb looked at Lilly.

"Adrian grabbed me and held a knife to my throat when you and Michael arrived at the church," Lilly looked up at Caleb. "A tall man with a gun burst into the church. I felt something sting my upper arm. Within minutes I started to feel a little groggy."

"You started to wobble forcing Adrian to lower the knife as your body started reacting to the tranquilizer," Caleb explained to Lilly why she'd started to feel like that.

"I was tranquilized?" Lilly leaned back and looked up at Caleb in shock.

"Yes, that man had a tranquilizer gun," Caleb told her. "Do you remember the second man bursting into the church?"

"I do," Lilly frowned. "I heard gunshots." Her eyes narrowed. She looked up at him again.

"Yes," Caleb nodded, "as the gunshots started flying, Michael dived at you and the lady minister. Adrian got knocked to the floor."

"I ran at the man with a gun," Caleb told Lilly.

"You ran at the man with a gun?" Lilly's eyes widened as she looked up at Caleb. "Are you insane?"

"He wasn't there to shoot me." Caleb closed his eyes and took a deep breath.

Caleb knew he owed Lilly an explanation. Especially now that she'd been dragged into his family affairs. He looked at her saying, "I wasn't sure he wouldn't hurt you, Michael, or Gertie though."

"That's still a huge risk to take, Caleb." Lilly looked up at him with worry shining in her beautiful blue eyes.

"The third shot you heard was when I tackled him, and the gun went off." Caleb kissed her forehead. "The shot fired towards where you and Michael were. I was so worried he'd hit one of you."

"Is Michael okay?" Lilly's eyes grew large again.

"He seemed fine," Caleb reassured Lilly.

"What happened after I passed out?" Lilly asked Caleb.

"The gunman's weapon toting henchmen rushed into the church," Caleb told Lilly. "One of them went for you. Michael tried to fight the man off but got knocked down for his efforts." He shook his head as anger spurted through him. "The man I'd run at managed to get the better of me when I saw one of his thugs scoop you up into his arms."

"Are you sure Michael is okay?" Lilly asked worriedly. "What about the nice lady vicar and Adrian?"

"Let's sit down." Caleb dropped his arms from around Lilly and took her hand to lead her over to the table. "You still seem a little shaken. I can't believe Adrian abducted you again."

Lilly frowned at Caleb. "How do you know about that?"

"Michael told me when we realized Adrian had abducted you." Caleb took one of her hands in his over the table.

"Oh," Lilly looked at him a little surprised that Michael would have told Caleb. He must've been really worried about her. "I would've told you eventually," she said softly.

"I know." Caleb planted a kiss on her hand.

"Why are we here if this isn't Adrian's doing?" Lilly asked Caleb. "Who was that gunman?"

"He's the same man that pushed Zane into that hole, chased us through the woods, and tried to break into the Crab Shack." Caleb blew out a deep breath.

"You said you knew who he was." Lilly lifted her head to look up at Caleb.

"Yes," Caleb nodded, "I do."

"Who is he then or is that top secret?" Lilly frowned up at him.

"No," Caleb shook his head. "Not top secret, just a little twisted though." He gave her a small smile.

"Oh, well you've heard my twisted story with Adrian," Lilly gave him a sweet smile. "So I guess it's a twisted story for a twisted story."

Caleb gave a resigned sigh. He knew they'd agreed to be friends until they'd sorted themselves out and sorted through the mess of their pasts. But fate had decided that both of their history would not only come back to haunt each of them but would do so in one huge tidal wave. Now they were being forced into making difficult choices neither of them were ready for. It also meant opening up those old wounds and trusting that their feelings for each were strong enough to overcome their sticky pasts.

"Caleb," Lilly raised her hand and touched his cheek, "you can tell me anything."

Caleb took a deep breath and put one of his hands over hers turning his lips into her palm.

"Lilly," Caleb said softly, "after you've heard what I have to say, I fear you'll never look at me the same. So I'm going to tell you something before I tell you my story."

"I don't think anything could change the way I see you," Lilly told him.

"Lilly," Caleb's voice was hoarse as he pulled her chair towards his, so he was close enough to pull her in for a deep passionate, heartfelt kiss. "I'm falling in love with you and every second I spend with you I fall a little deeper," he whispered against her lips and between kisses before pouring all his love into another passionate kiss.

"I thought we agreed to just be friends." Lilly smiled at Caleb when she ended their kiss and leaned her forehead against his.

"I've tried," Caleb swallowed as he looked into her beautiful eyes, "but my heart and fate have other plans."

"I feel the same way about you, Caleb," Lilly smiled shyly at him, "but there are things I feel I need to tell you. Things that you need to know that could change the way you feel about me." Her eyes misted over. "I can't start a relationship with secrets because that feels like I'm lying about who I am. You can't build trust with a heart full of secrets."

"Lilly," Caleb took both her hands in his, "there's nothing you can say that would change the way I feel about you." His voice deepened as it grew hoarse with emotion. "But I would rather you heard my story from me and not from someone else."

Lilly leaned in and kissed Caleb on the lips before he pulled her onto his lap to keep her close to him.

"It means a lot to me that you want to tell me what's been eating away at you," Lilly told him softly. "The haunted look in your eyes was the first thing I noticed about you." She smiled warmly at him. "My heart broke for you because I know that look well and understand the emotions behind it."

"Every time I look at you, I see an angel." Caleb smiled at her. "You deserve so much better than me, Lilly."

"Why don't you tell me your story," Lilly said softly leaning up to kiss his forehead, "and let me decide. I'm no angel Caleb and I have no right to judge you because I too have my secrets."

"I don't believe that you're not an angel," Caleb smiled, "because you're definitely my angel."

Caleb lowered his head and kissed her again.

"I'm so glad you decided to come to La Jolla, with your mother and sister," Lilly smiled at Caleb.

"I am too," Caleb smiled.

They fell silent for a few minutes. Each lost in their thoughts and uncertainty of how the other would react to the shadows that followed them around and trapped them in fear.

Caleb's mind drifted to the first bad break up he'd had. His mother's words had stuck in his head.

Love was a lot like learning how to ride a bike. It could be shaky, hard, and a little scary when you hit bumps too fast or a steep downhill. You'd fall off and land up with a skinned heart many times in your lifetime.

You'd feel like you had bruises that you didn't know how to heal because they were on the inside and made you ache and there was no magic healing balm. The first time was always the worst but only because you don't know any better.

The trick is never to compare one relationship to another because everyone's different. It's like trying to compare apples and oranges. They are two different types of fruit with totally different tastes.

Respect the woman you give your time to and if you find yourself holding back even the slightest part of you, she's not the one. Because believe me, when you do find the one, you'll want to share all you are and all you have with her. And honey I know whoever you give your heart to completely, will be someone incredibly special.

Caleb smiled. His mother had been correct. Not only was Lilly special, but she was also his angel here to save his tormented soul and heal the hurt and pain of his past.

---

*L*illy had never felt this way about anyone before the way she felt about Caleb. She knew her father would tell her she couldn't possibly know that Caleb was the one because she hadn't known him for that long.

Her mother, on the other hand, would tell her that when

you knew you just knew. Her mother basically fell in love with her father the moment their hands had touched when he pulled her out of the sea. When Lilly was fifteen, her mother and father had separated for almost two years. They were both military. Her mother was in the air force and her father was in the marines.

They hit a rough patch when her mother had a miscarriage and blamed herself for it. Lilly still to this day thought her dad also blamed her mother. She'd gone on a rescue mission knowing she was having problems with her pregnancy. But her mother was a hero and as her grandmother said, that's what heroes do — they put the world before themselves and even sometimes family.

Then her father nearly died in the line of duty and retired from the army to become a multi-millionaire. But her mother had refused to leave the military and so they split up. Suddenly Lilly's life became two houses, two birthdays, and there were just too many twos in her life when the only two she wanted was her mom and dad together. It took a misadventure and landing up in danger to bring the two most stubborn people in the world back together again.

Her mom and dad were about Lilly's age when they'd met and were married within six months of meeting each other. Her father's excuse was that they were both fighting a war and whenever they were sent on assignment they didn't know if they'd ever see each other again. Her mother would tell her when you find a diamond in the rough you don't let it go or try to polish it. You love it just like it was and let it sparkle the way it was meant to.

Lilly looked at Caleb. He was her diamond in the rough and a one in a million catch.

"What are you grinning about?" Caleb looked like he'd just snapped out of his own deep thoughts.

"I'm glad you came into my life," Lilly said softly and leaned in to kiss him.

Chapter Sixteen

THE SHADOW OF CALEB'S PAST

"Two years ago, Nadine Myers, Patrick Myers daughter," Caleb started to tell Lilly the truth about New York. "Requested that I go on an assignment with her. She was investigating some fraudulent deal she was accusing her grandparents of."

"They sound like a delightful family," Lilly shook her head. "By grandparents you mean Patrick, her fathers, parents?" Caleb nodded his confirmation.

"That's the day I found out that Sheldon Myers, Erin's, ex-husband, and Patrick Myer's older brother, was my real father," Caleb breathed. "I didn't want to believe it, so I went to confront him." He closed his eyes for a second. "He confirmed it."

"Did Erin know?" Lilly asked him.

"No," Caleb shook his head. "But she soon found out when the tabloids hounded her a few days later after Nadine's car was pushed off the road and she was killed."

"Was her car pushed off the road deliberately or was it an accident?" Lilly looked at him with big eyes.

"At first we were told it was an accident. That is until I was taken to the police station for questioning." Caleb could still feel the shock of being accused of pushing her off the road. "I'd landed an assignment and was going to Greece the next day, so I'd dropped my car at the auto repair shop. Kelsey had put a dent in the door."

"She seems to make a habit of denting cars," Lilly smiled remembering how livid Michael was when Kelsey had driven into him at the airport.

"My car was used to run Nadine off the road," Caleb told Kelsey. "The body shop's cameras were not working that day. The owner is a friend of mine, so I left the keys with one of his staff."

"So you had no proof of when you dropped the car off?" Lilly guessed.

"Correct," Caleb nodded. "The man who took the keys told the police I woke him up in the middle of the night to book my car in. He said that I told him I'd damaged my girlfriend's car and needed it fixed quickly and quietly."

"Why would he say that and how would you know where he lived?" Lilly frowned.

"He lived over the auto-shop," Caleb explained. "The only reason the police looked into Nadine's car being run off the road after originally ruling it an accident was because of her father, Patrick Myers."

"Please tell me he's not the man who abducted us," Lilly knew before Caleb confirmed it with a nod that her suspicions were true.

"Nadine had been taken to the hospital Kelsey worked at and Kelsey had been the one to tend to her," Caleb told Lilly. "Her father was adamant that Kelsey was guilty of medical negligence."

"Oh no," Lilly's eyes widened. "Poor Kelsey."

"She was shocked," Caleb said sadly. "Patrick, made the hospital go over Kelsey and the attending doctor's report with a fine-tooth comb." He shook his head. "Kelsey's entire life was probed into."

"How horrible," Lilly felt for Kelsey. She knew what it was like to feel like your life was under a microscope.

"To cut a long story short, my mom and your Aunt Jennifer found video footage from a shop across the road from the auto shop," Caleb told Lilly. "It showed a time stamp of a man, who was not me, going to auto shop and the man who took my keys letting him in and giving him my car."

"Did they find the man?" Lilly looked at Caleb.

"They didn't get a good look at his face," Caleb's brows raised, "but it proved my story was true and Jennifer found CCTV footage of me where I said I was around the time the man took my car from the garage."

"What about the body shop man?" Lilly asked Caleb. "He must've known who the man was."

"He said he was offered a large sum of money to allow him to take my car." Caleb frowned. "He admitted that I did drop my car off when I said I did and never came back for it."

"So you were no longer a suspect in Nadine's accident?" Lilly frowned. "What about Kelsey?"

"They found that there was no medical negligence on her part." Caleb ran his hand through his hair. "We both had a favorable outcome."

"Why would you think I'd look at you differently over that?" Lilly asked Caleb.

"That was only the beginning of our nightmare," Caleb told Lilly. "A day after we were both off the hook for Nadine, we became accomplices to Sheldon Myers corruption."

"Erin's ex-husband Sheldon Myers?" Lilly looked a little stricken. "He had a heart-attack didn't he?"

"Yes," Caleb nodded. "Sheldon wanted to speak to me and Kelsey about him being my father." He explained. "Kelsey didn't want to go. It was me that made us go. You have no idea how many times over the past eighteen months I wished I hadn't and that I hadn't forced Kelsey to come with me."

"What happened?" Lilly stood up when she saw a knife

beneath the bed. "What's that?" She bent down and picked it up. "I wonder why this is in here?"

"I think that's the knife Adrian had," Caleb frowned.

Lilly brought it over to Caleb and sat down in a chair.

"Yes, that is the knife he had," Caleb examined it and put it down on the table.

"Sorry," Lilly took Caleb's hand. "You were talking about going to Sheldon's place?"

"Kelsey and I got to his apartment, the doorman let us up, and when we got there the door was ajar," Caleb pinched the bridge of his nose with his free hand. "We went inside and found Sheldon lying on the floor."

"Oh no," Lilly's eyes grew huge.

"Kelsey immediately ran off to examine him, but we were too late," Caleb swallowed. "His apartment had been ransacked. We called 9-1-1 and two weeks later Kelsey and I were being accused of being Sheldon's accomplices in his fraudulent children's hospital deal."

"What hospital deal?" Lilly asked. Her eyes were shining with interest in Caleb's story.

"The Governor, Sheldon's father, was accused of misappropriating funds for a children's hospital for low-income parents," Caleb explained to Lilly. "The Governor's wife runs a lot of charities to help struggling parents."

"But the funds for the hospital weren't used for a hospital," Lilly guessed. "The money either went missing or was suspected of being funneled into another more lucrative project."

"Nadine was working on a story about the proceeds that were raised for the hospital," Caleb played with Lilly's soft small hand. "She had evidence to prove there was never any plans for a hospital and the property that was allocated for it was suddenly bought by a new development company."

"And the company somehow connects back to Sheldon Myers!" Lilly guessed once again.

"Not at first," Caleb frowned. "The night of Nadine's accident she called me to meet her at a coffee shop. She sounded scared. That night she told me that she'd found all the evidence she needed. It was about two prominent New York families connecting them to the missing funds and the development company."

"Do you think that's what got her killed?" Lilly's eyes widened.

"I think so," Caleb nodded.

"If someone was trying to frame you for her death they'd obviously seen you meeting at the coffee shop after they realized Nadine had the evidence," Lilly shook her head. "This is why I stay clear of all politics."

"You're right." Caleb looked at her. "I didn't even think about being watched."

"Why else would someone try to set you up like that?" Lilly asked logically. "It seems far too coincidental that the person who took your car would randomly choose your car as a weapon."

"I think I was just so happy to have all the charges against me dropped. I never thought about that." Caleb brought her hand to his lips. "That's something to think about though." His brows drew together as a niggling feeling that there was more to all that happened to them recently than he first thought.

"Why were you and Kelsey drawn into Sheldon Myers' shady dealings?" Kelsey's brows drew together.

"Erin's mother asked us to help her with a charity drive for children in need," Caleb told Lilly. "So we did, and we raised a lot of money over that weekend. There were two a month for over a year after that."

"What did that have to do with the children's hospital that Sheldon was proposing?" Lilly was trying to connect the dots.

"Sheldon was one of our biggest sponsors," Caleb shook his head. "We didn't know."

"Why wasn't Erin's mother accused?" Lilly wanted to know.

"Because she asked us to head up the charity because she

had so many already," Caleb explained. "She didn't know who our sponsors were. We had people helping us with the money side of it. Kelsey and I just came up with ways to raise the money."

"You don't think Erin's mother was involved in anything that happened to you and Kelsey, do you?" Kelsey looked worried.

"No," Caleb shook his head, "most definitely not. Judge Carnegie, Erin's mother, was the one who helped Erin and Jennifer try and prove mine and Kelsey's innocence."

"It seems a little too convenient to pin all the corruption on Sheldon Myers," Lilly's eyes narrowed, "especially when he couldn't defend himself."

"I know," Caleb nodded. "That's what Erin and Jennifer kept coming back to. One minute all fingers were pointing to the Governor and one of his close friends. The evidence against them was pretty solid." His brows drew together, "All of a sudden all the evidence points to Sheldon Myers."

"Why was his apartment ransacked?" Lilly wanted to know.

"No sure," Caleb said, "my mother went to clean up his apartment as he'd not changed his will and everything Sheldon had went to the three of us."

"Oh, wow," Lilly looked surprised.

"I was just as surprised as you are." Caleb smiled. "Mom found pictures of myself and Kelsey through the years. My biological mother had sent Sheldon regular pictures of me."

"Erin must've been gutted to find out her best friend and her husband had had an affair," Lilly felt so bad for Erin. "It must've been bad enough to know her husband was cheating on her but to find out it was with your life long best friend..."

"I know," Caleb said sadly. "If Erin was any other woman than the woman she is she could've resented me, but she didn't. Nor did Kelsey, who was happy that I was her real brother, even though she never thought of me any other way."

"Erin and Kelsey are really special people." Lilly's eyes misted over.

"They are and we were shocked to find that Sheldon had loved us in his own weird way," Caleb smiled.

"Why was he so horrible to Kelsey, cutting her out of his life like he did?" Lilly couldn't understand how a father could do that.

"My mother thinks that he was trying to protect us in his own messed up way," Caleb shrugged. "Just before we left New York Kelsey and I each got a parcel from Sheldon's lawyer. Apparently, Sheldon had given him strict instructions to wait at least fifteen months before delivering it to us."

"What was in it?" Lilly asked.

"Just some stuff he wanted us to have." Caleb smiled and kissed her on the head.

"How did you and Kelsey prove your innocence?" Lilly's eyes grew huge as she looked at him. "Are you hiding from the feds?"

"Nothing that exciting," Caleb shook his head. "We were hounded, questioned, hounded some more, questioned some more, and had our lives turned upside down for close to eighteen months."

"Oh, Caleb," Lilly cupped his face. "I'm sorry."

"You quickly learn who your friends are when you're being torn apart." Caleb's voice dropped. "Kelsey's fiancé, Miles Parker, quickly ended the relationship the moment the news broke about us being connected to Sheldon's corruption."

"Poor, Kelsey," Lilly's compassion shone through. "What a jerk!"

"It's okay," Caleb smiled. "Kelsey was still reeling from the medical negligence that I don't think she even noticed."

"It's amazing how some people are," Lilly shook her head. "I can't believe how fickle they can be."

"Erin decided that it was time to tidy Sheldon's apartment one day during the proceedings," Caleb smiled sadly. "You have no idea what Erin went through during this. She put everything she had into trying to get mine and Kelsey's name cleared."

"Aunty Jennifer was very worried about Erin," Lilly told Caleb. "She never told us, but we heard her talking with Uncle Max about going back to New York to help Erin and her children."

"My mother was obsessed with finding a way to win our battle," Caleb swallowed, he closed his eyes as he felt the burn in his throat. "When she was clearing out Sheldon's apartment, she stumbled on what whoever was ransacking his apartment for."

"What was it?" Lilly looked at Caleb anxiously.

"Sheldon had his entire apartment kitted out with hidden cameras," Caleb told her. "Erin discovered them quite by accident. She took out a weird overcoat that felt really heavy. She found it had something sewn into the inside of it. It was a tablet."

"How weird," Lilly breathed. "What was on it?"

"Sheldon made a video recording for Erin," Caleb's eyebrows rose. "He told her where to find the door to this secret room. In there she found the recording and who was in his apartment when he had his heart attack."

"That's kind of eerie," Lilly shivered. "Like he'd foreseen his own death."

"Apparently he thought he was being poisoned," Caleb shrugged. "It couldn't be proven as he was cremated." He shook his head sadly. "There was, however, clear evidence of someone planting evidence in his apartment."

"Who was it?" Lilly's eyes widened.

"We weren't told," Caleb told her, smiling when he saw the disappointment in her eyes. "We were told it was safer that way." He breathed the relief of that part of his life being overflowing through him again. "We were just happy to have all that ugliness behind us."

"I can imagine," Lilly kissed his forehead.

"By then it was too late for us though," Caleb told her sadly. "Kelsey had lost her internship and had missed so much of her medical training. No one would see me about photography assignments and all those buddies I thought were good friends..." a mask fell over his face.

"It's their loss," Lilly said softly and kissed his lips. "You're the most honorable person I've ever met." She kissed him again before saying, "What happened about the missing money case?"

"It's still on going," Caleb told her. "There are some loose ends that need tying up." Something flashed in his eyes.

"Why do I get the feeling there's more to this?" Lilly's eyes narrowed.

"Nope," Caleb smiled and crushed his lips to hers. "I love you," he whispered.

Chapter Seventeen
LILLY'S TORMENT

"Now you know all my secrets," Caleb kissed her hand before pulling her in to kiss her softly on the lips, "it's your turn."

"Well, you know about the part where Adrian kidnapped me, sedated me, and dragged me off to the church," Lilly swallowed. She hated remembering that day. It still haunted her and gave her nightmares. "I was in my last year of university when I met Adrian. He was in one of my classes. He was new to San Diego and he was called the campus cowboy."

"I believe his family owns a large range near Santa Barbara," Caleb's eyes glittered.

"Adrian had seen me around and obviously I'd bumped into him a few times during my time at university, but I had a long-term boyfriend," Lilly explained. "My boyfriend had graduated the previous year and moved back to Canada just before I started my final year."

"So Adrian saw his chance to get close to you?" Caleb gave Lilly a tight smile.

"He asked me out on a date one day after a lecture," Lilly told him. "I said no, I was still technically seeing my other boyfriend. Then one night I was out with some of my friends at a party when he showed up."

"I enjoyed my college parties," Caleb smiled. "I'm glad to hear you weren't all work and no fun at school."

"When there wasn't an assignment due I would go out," Lilly told him defensively. "I was a rebel when I was in school," Lilly admitted to Caleb. "My parents eventually sent me to boarding school hoping I would settle down to my studies."

"You don't strike me as the rebel type," Caleb teased Lilly. "This is a whole new side of you."

"A friend of mine and I once stole my father's superyacht to go to Hawaii when I was eighteen," Lilly told a shocked Caleb. "That was just one of my exploits but that was my last exploit. I buckled down after that and worked really hard to get into varsity."

"Wow!" Caleb stared at her, impressed. "Your father has a superyacht?"

"Had," Lilly nodded. "It was blown to bits in the middle of the Pacific Ocean."

"What?" Caleb looked astonished. "You're going to have to tell me that story some time."

"Remind me," Lilly smiled. "It was a crazy story."

"Okay, enough going off topic, young lady," Caleb raised his eyebrows at her. "You were telling me about Adrian."

"I'm sorry," Lilly swallowed, "I know it sounds silly but even just speaking about him starts to make me feel panicked."

"It's okay, Lilly," Caleb kissed her, "take your time."

"I wanted to work hard and buckle down at university," Lilly shook her head. "I was doing so well up until Adrian started stalking me." She shuddered and Caleb pulled her to him.

"It's okay," Caleb kissed the top of her head. "I'll make sure he never hurts you again."

"We had a few drinks together and then my friend and I left," Lilly shook her head. "After that night, the flowers and gifts started to arrive at my dorm." She shuddered again. "I sent them back telling him that I wasn't comfortable with receiving them."

"Did he stop sending them?" Caleb asked.

"No," Lilly shook her head. "He promised if I went to dinner with him he'd stop. So I went on one dinner date with him." She swallowed. "He asked if I would go to a friend's party with him. I didn't see the harm, so I went. After that wherever my friend and I went Adrian would show up."

"Stalker," Caleb's eyes flashed.

"He sent me ten to fifteen messages a day." Lilly's eyes darkened with fear, "I made it quite clear to him that I wasn't wanting a relationship." She shook her head. "But he kept persisting and pushing me to go out with him." She looked down at her hands. "It got so bad I changed my phone number, but he somehow found it."

"What a creep," Caleb's voice had an edge of anger to it.

"One day he begged me to meet him in the park." She drew in a breath. "Like an idiot I went. He'd laid out a picnic and that's when he asked me to marry him."

"What?" Caleb shuddered and pulled her closer to him.

"I told him no and that I would never feel that way about him," Lilly said. "His stalking became even worse. He wouldn't leave me alone." Her eyes misted over and became haunted. "It was so scary." She looked at Caleb. Her eyes were filled with fear. "I eventually made a formal complaint and then my parents got involved. Next thing I knew he'd been suspended and moved back to Santa Barbara."

"You thought it was over." Caleb held her a little tighter. "I'm so sorry, my beautiful, Lilly," he said softly.

"Then you know the rest," Lilly cuddled into his broad chest.

Lilly felt safe for the first time in a long time. Even though they were being held by a dangerous man. Lilly felt that everything was going to be okay as long as Caleb was with her.

Caleb held Lilly in his arms. He could feel her shiver when she was telling him about Adrian. Caleb hoped they'd captured the man because if he ever came near Lilly again...

His heart ached for her. A small voice in his head tormented him, telling him he'd not been fully honest with Lilly. He knew she didn't like secrets. She also said she never got involved in politics. This was that dark underbelly of politics that most people knew was there but looked the other way because to become involved was sure to put lives at risk. Caleb had already dragged Lilly into his mess and endangered her life, he wasn't going to endanger it anymore.

It was bad enough that Kelsey was still in danger. The person messaging her knew about Caleb and Kelsey's secret and Caleb was sure the man holding them in this room knew too. He looked at the knife on the table and then at the door.

"Lilly," Caleb gently moved her from his lap. "I think I could use the knife to jimmy the door open."

"I haven't heard any noise outside the room for ages," Lilly put her ear to the door. "I think you should give it a try."

"Step aside," Caleb smiled down at her. "Let's get the hell out of here."

Chapter Eighteen
WATCHING OVER MICHAEL

*E*rin paced back and forth stopping each time she got to the waiting room door to peer out the window for a doctor.

"What's taking so long?" she said for the millionth time and paced back to the windows.

"Erin," Zane stood up and stopped her from pacing. "Come sit down, the doctor will be with us as soon as he can." He led Erin to a chair.

"Where's Kelsey?" Erin dialed her daughter again. "Voicemail again."

"Erin," Zane took her phone away from her. "Calm down. I'm sure Michael is going to be fine."

"What if he's not?" Erin's eyes misted over. "Has there been any word from Phillip about Caleb and Lilly?"

"Phillip got a lead on the man's car," Zane told her. "His name is Patrick Myers."

"Excuse me?" Erin's face paled. "That can't be right." The picture of the sleek black town car pulling into the parking lot a few nights ago flashed through her mind.

"Wait," Zane looked at her, "is he your brother-in-law?"

"Ex-brother-in-law," Erin corrected Zane. "If it is him that has Lilly and Caleb their lives are in great danger."

"It's going to be okay," Zane put an arm around her and pulled her to his side. "Why don't you try and get some sleep?"

"I couldn't sleep now," Erin stifled a yawn. "But if you don't mind, I'd like to sit here just like this for a while." She felt so comforted being close to Zane.

"Of course," Zane moved a little closer to Erin, so she was comfortable.

"Thank you," Erin sighed and closed her eyes for a few minutes.

"Erin,' Zane said softly, "the doctors on his way."

Erin opened her eyes and stretched.

"Did I doze off for a minute?" Erin looked around the room.

"Thirty-five," Zane smiled at her, "but you needed it."

"Oh no," Erin's cheeks went pink, "I seem to have drooled on you."

Zane looked down at his shirt and laughed, "I have a boat load of nieces and nephews that I helped raise. Trust me, I've had a lot worse on me."

Erin was saved from answering when a doctor walked into the room followed by Kelsey.

"Ms. Carnegie and Mr. McCaid?" The Doctor read the chart. "I'm the surgeon that removed the bullet from Michael's abdomen."

"How is he?" Erin jumped up and looked up at the doctor.

"I managed to remove the bullet." The doctor brows drew together. "Has he been complaining about stomach pains?"

"Not that I know of," Zane shook his head and looked at Erin.

"He did feel a little ill the other night after he had dinner with us," Erin told the doctor. "I offered him some stomach medicine, but he said it was probably just indigestion."

"He was having pain after he was hit in the head." Kelsey told the doctor.

"He was hit in the stomach earlier when a fight broke out," Zane informed the doctor.

"I had to remove his appendix because it had ruptured." The doctor typed something on his tablet. "I'll need to keep Michael in the hospital until I'm happy with the bullet wound and that no abscesses develop from his ruptured appendix."

"Thank you, doctor." Erin's eyes misted over. "When can we see him?"

"Dr. Carnegie will take you through in about twenty minutes." The doctor gave them a nod before leaving the room.

"I'll be back soon," Kelsey told her mom and Zane. "Go get some coffee down the hall while you wait." She turned and left the room saying, "Michael's going to be fine. Dr. Barnes is the best."

Erin ran into Zane's arms and let the tears flow.

"Now all we have to do is find Caleb and Lilly." Erin sniffed.

Zane put his arms around her and let her cry. She was so tiny without her ridiculously high heels on.

"We'll find them and they'll be okay."

"*H*ey, there," Kelsey smiled as Michael slowly woke. "You gave us quite a scare."

"Kelsey?" Michael frowned. "Where am ..." His eyes opened wide. "Where's Lilly?" He tried to sit up and groaned in the pain. "What the hell?"

"Keep calm," Kelsey pushed Michael back down on the bed, "you've just had surgery on your stomach."

"What?" Michael looked confused.

"You were shot," Kelsey told Michael. "Dr. Barnes removed a bullet from your stomach and then your appendix ruptured so he removed that too."

"My appendix?" Michael's brows creased.

"Yes," Kelsey nodded. "Turns out that stomach pain you

thought was nothing was actually your appendix filling up with puss from an infection."

"I love your pillow talk," Michael swallowed. "Can I get some water please? My mouth is so dry."

"Of course." Kelsey took one of the bottles of water off the tray next to his bed and opened it for him. "Sip don't gulp. Trust me, you don't want to be getting sick right now."

Kelsey helped Michael take a few sips of his water.

"Thank you." Michael's eyes were drifting closed when something dawned on him again. "Where's Lilly?"

"Phillip and his team are still looking for them," Kelsey told him gently. "I'm going to call Zane and my mom in to see you. They've been really worried about you."

"Okay," Michael smiled.

It was nice to have a mom figure around right now, Michael thought. He was always the first to admit to being a big baby when he was ill. There was nothing better than mom smiles, soft touches, hugs, and love to make a guy feel better.

The room door burst open, and Erin ran up to his bed. The first thing she did was give him a careful hug and kiss on the forehead.

"You feel warm," Erin fussed. "Kelsey," She turned to look at her daughter, "why has Michael got a temperature?"

"He will have Mom," Kelsey told her mother gently. Erin was a typical mother when one of her chicks were sick and with Jennifer away, Michael was now one of her chicks.

"Are you in pain, honey?" Erin took the seat next to Michael that Zane pulled up for her.

"A little," Michael held Erin's hand.

"Kelsey, can't you give Michael something for the pain?" Erin looked at her daughter.

"Mom," Kelsey raised her eyebrows, "Michael's fine for now."

"Hey, son," Zane grinned down at Michael. "How does it feel to have your first war wound?"

"Painful," Michael told Zane. "How's the hunt for Lilly and Caleb going?"

"Phillip had a lead on the man's car that took them," Zane told Michael. "But your doctor, who says he's known you since you were a baby, threatened us with our lives if we upset you in any way."

"Dr. Barnes and I do go way back," Michael grinned sleepily. "Did you tell my mom or sisters I was in hospital?" he asked Erin.

"No," Erin looked shocked and turned to look at Zane. "I can't believe we didn't call Jennifer and Michael's family."

"Please don't," Michael asked her. "They haven't been away in a long time and now that I'm out of the woods there's no need to worry them. Plus, we'd have to explain about Lilly and then the entire United States Air Force and Marine Corp will land on our doorstep."

"That's rather dramatic," Kelsey laughed.

"No," Zane shook his head, "as an ex-marine I can tell you that if one of my kids was in trouble, I'd also call in the troops."

"See," Michael's eyes drifted shut. "Thank you for being here Erin, Zane, and Kelsey." He started to nod off. "It's nice not to wake up in hospital alone." He drifted off to sleep.

Michael woke up hours later. He turned his head to find Gertie, the local minister who'd been at the church where Adrian was trying to get Lilly to marry him. She was sitting reading a book in a recliner next to his bed.

"Reverend?" Michael frowned. "Am I dying?"

"I don't think so?" Gertie smiled at Michael. "Oh," she nodded, "I see. You think I'm here to help you on your way to meet your maker?"

"Are you?" Michael asked her. His head felt like someone was hammering in it.

"No, dear," Gertie said. "I offered to sit with you while your uncle and aunt, lovely couple they are, went to quickly have a shower and change." She put her book down on the table next to the recliner she was sitting in. "They were here with you the whole night."

"They slept here?" Michael pointed to his room. "In my room."

"Uh-hu," Gertie nodded. "In these really comfy recliner chairs that pull out." She hit a button and that chair reclined back and a footrest popped out. "See?"

"Cool," Michael smiled. "So they both slept there in those chairs the entire night?"

"Yes," Gertie frowned. "Is that a problem for you, young man?"

"No," Michael lay back and closed his eyes, "not at all. I was just thinking how nice that was of them."

"It's nice to see a family as close as yours," Gertie gave him a warm smile. "I lost both my parents a while ago." She shook her head. "It's tough being in a new town on your own and you can't even pick up the phone to call your parents."

"I'm sorry." Michael opened his eyes and looked at Gertie. "Are you married?"

"I am, but my other half is currently in another state for a few more months," Gertie told Michael. "You know how it is to leave a job these days. Employers want you to work three months' notice period. So while my partner is in another state working a full three months' notice, I'm here, in La Jolla setting up our new home."

"That must be tough." Michael swallowed and tried to sit up to look for water.

"What do you need?" Gertie aske Michael.

"Some water, please." Michael put his head back down on the pillow. It hurt to move.

"Here you go," Gertie got a bottle of water, opened the cap, and helped Michael have a few sips. "That pretty doctor of yours warned me to only allow you a few sips of water at a time."

"Thank you," Michael lay back down, "and thank you for sitting by me." He smiled, feeling sleepy again.

"You're welcome," Gertie pulled the blanket up over Michael as he started to drift off to sleep again.

"What happened to your wrist?" Michael asked, trying to force his eyes open.

"I sprained it when we hit the floor back at the church," Gertie explained, holding up her arm that had a wrist guard on it.

"I'm so sorry about that," Michael apologized to her. "I didn't mean to push you so hard."

"Don't be," Gertie told him. "You took a bullet for me," she said in awe. "If you hadn't dive tackled me that bullet would've hit me in the chest."

"I'm glad you're okay." Michael was losing the battle trying to keep his eyes open. "You're always welcome to come to White Sands Cove anytime so you won't be alone anymore." He lost the battle with sleep as it took him over once again.

"How's he doing?" Kelsey walked into the room and smiled at Gertie who'd fast become a part of their big crazy ever-expanding new family.

"He woke up for a few minutes," Gertie smiled and yawned. She was feeling a little sleepy herself. "He had some water and tried to chat but I think his body shut him down so it could heal."

"You look like you need some rest yourself," Kelsey smiled warmly at Gertie. She walked to the closet and pulled out a clean blanket that she went and covered Gertie with. "These chairs are comfortable, and they're orthopedic,"

"Thank you, dear," Gertie smiled and snuggled beneath the

blanket. "I can attest to how comfortable these chairs are. I'm thinking of trading in my bed for one."

"We have a few in our staff lounge," Kelsey told Gertie. "You'll be amazed at how many doctors and nurses pass out in them for a couple of hours."

"I love this little tray that pops out like an airplane tray and the light you can position over your head." Gertie stifled another yawn.

"Can I get you a pillow?" Kelsey asked her.

"No thanks, honey," Gertie said. "My head is perfectly comfortable as it is."

"How are your ribs and arms?" Kelsey asked her.

"They're fine." Gertie's eyes started to get heavy.

"You get some rest," Kelsey smiled. "I'll be back to check on both of you a little later."

Chapter Nineteen
A MICHAEL AND KELSEY MOMENT

"Are you sure you don't want to go home?" Erin asked Kelsey who came and curled up in the recliner next to Erin's.

Zane had gone to get them a coffee and Kelsey had just finished a grueling shift. They were short staffed and because Michael was in the hospital, she'd volunteered to take another shift.

"No," Kelsey put her head on her mother's shoulder, "I'm fine right here." She closed her eyes and drifted off.

"Here's your coffee," Zane walked into the room and stopped seeing Kelsey fast asleep on his recliner. He gave Erin her coffee and put his coffee down to go get a blanket for Kelsey. "She's exhausted," he said softly, putting the blanket over her then pulling up another chair next to Erin.

"Kelsey always does this," Erin kissed her daughter's head. "She had this drive to succeed at any cost and her passion has always been medicine. My father bought her first stethoscope when she was eight."

"Wow, that is a young age to know what you want to be when you grow up," Zane took a sip of his coffee. "My niece,

Fallon, loved sailing and yachts. She took her first steps on a yacht."

"Your niece is a truly remarkable woman. She reminds me of a female Caleb," Erin smiled. "Taking the whole world on his shoulders so no one else had to bear the burden."

"Yes, that's definitely Fallon." Zane smiled thinking about his nieces and nephew. He still couldn't believe what amazing adults they had turned out to be. "I spoke to Phillip on my way to get coffee." He took another sip of his brew. "They've tracked down another lead as the car was spotted near Goldfish Point."

"I can't take the wait." Erin put her coffee down. "I think we should go door to door and find them ourselves."

Erin was so frustrated with having to wait and wait. The longer it took to find them ... She didn't want to think about that.

"I don't think that would be a good idea," Zane told her. "That would only spook whoever took them if they knew we were on to them."

"True," Erin took her pillow and gently put it beneath Kelsey's head. "Would you mind putting the chair back for her, please?" she asked Zane.

"Sure," Zane stood up and pressed the button while Erin held Kelsey steady so the opening of the chair wouldn't wake her.

"Did you ever marry, Zane?" Erin asked him.

"No." Something flashed in Zane's eyes and he gave Erin a small smile. "I was engaged once a long time ago."

"Oh, so I take it you don't have any kids either?" Erin took a sip of coffee.

"No, only my nieces, nephew, and great-nieces and great-nephew," Zane said proudly. "They're like my own children."

"I'm actually starving," Erin said. "Do you think we could sneak off and get something to eat?"

"There's a restaurant around the corner," Zane said. "Can I take you for an early dinner?"

"Well, it's more like a lunch/dinner," Erin smiled. "I would love to go to the restaurant with you. We can let these two sleep." She leaned over and kissed Kelsey and then stood and kissed Michael on the forehead. "So he knows he's loved."

Zane gave her a warm smile. He loved the way she took everyone in under her wing. She reminded him of... He wasn't going to think of that now. Zane opened the door for Erin, and they snuck out.

On the way out of the hospital they ran into Dr. Barnes.

"Taking a well-deserved break I see," Dr. Barnes smiled at Erin and Zane.

"I think you deserve one too," Erin told him. "You've been here for hours."

"I'm still here for a few more, I'm afraid." Dr. Barnes shook his head. "There's a stomach bug going around so we're shorthanded."

"We're just going for a quick bite at the restaurant around the corner," Erin explained to the doctor. "I've left Kelsey sleeping in the recliner in Michael's room."

"She must be exhausted," Dr. Barnes smiled warmly. "It's been a tough first day or two for her." His pager went off. "Sorry." He pointed to the device. "Go and enjoy, I'll call you if I need to."

"Thank you, doctor." Zane nodded at the man and herded Erin out the hospital door.

"*K*elsey?" Michael croaked. *Good grief the woman was a deep sleeper,* Michael thought as he tried to call her.

He needed some water. He was so thirsty. It seemed Kelsey wasn't waking up any time soon. Michael turned his head and saw a bottle of water on the bedside table. He tried to sit up, but his stomach burned and when he moved, he felt nauseous. But he was so thirsty. He moved as much as he could with all the drips and contraptions on him. Instead of getting the water he knocked it flying.

The bottle of water banged against the metal cabinet and hit the floor.

"Drat!" Michael hissed.

That didn't go as planned. He'd have to try and wake Kelsey, or he was going to die of thirst.

"Are you okay?" Kelsey's voice was right on top of him and nearly scared him to death.

"Hi." Michael had difficulty swallowing his throat was so dry.

What on earth were you trying to do?" Kelsey stifled a yawn as she checked all the monitors and his drip. "Are you crazy?"

"I was trying to get some water," Michael told her. "I'm so thirsty I feel like I've been drinking sand."

"I'll go fetch you some fresh bottles quickly as you knocked yours down onto the floor," Kelsey shook her head.

"Well it's not my fault you sleep like you're dead," Michael told her.

"It's called power napping," Kelsey explained. "You fall into a deep sleep for short bursts of time to refresh your brain.

"Cool," Michael swallowed again. "I really need some water."

"On it," Kelsey ducked out of the room.

While she was gone a pain sliced through Michael's stomach. He grimaced and couldn't even touch it as he had a bandage on it. His head started to throb. He was probably dehydrated. He clenched his teeth until the pain passed.

He looked around the room wondering where Erin and Zane were. He briefly remembered someone kissing his forehead, so he'd feel loved. He frowned. Whatever drugs they had him on was messing with his brain.

"Here you go," Kelsey put the bottles out of his reach. She popped the cap off the one bottle and took it over to Michael. "Come on." She smiled at him as she put her hand behind his head and put the bottle to his lips. "Small sips."

He took a few sips and winced when the pain sliced through his stomach again.

"Are you okay?" Kelsey put the bottle of water down. "Is it your stomach?"

Michael nodded. "And my head," he told her.

"Do you mind if I have a look at your stomach?" Kelsey asked him.

"Sure," Michael was in too much pain to feel shy at the moment.

"Your stomach is a bit hard." Kelsey's brows drew together. "I'm going to take your temperature." She went to the medicine cupboard and took out a temperature scanner.

"Maybe it's my abs?" Michael tried to make a joke.

"What's your abs?" Kelsey asked him absently, taking his pulse.

"Why is my stomach so hard?" Michael tried to grin, but his head started to get worse. "I don't mean to sound like a baby, Kels, but my head is killing me."

"I'm going to up your pain meds a bit." Kelsey's brows drew together. "Are you feeling nauseous?"

"A little but I feel better now that I've had some water," Michael admitted.

"Your pain meds will kick in in a minute," Kelsey told him. "I just need to feel the glands in your neck."

Kelsey was leaning over Michael feeling his neck when he looked up into her eyes and smiled.

"You're so beautiful," Michael slurred a little as his medication started to work. "I thought so the first day you rammed into my car."

"You reversed into me." Kelsey smiled down at him. He was so cute and was probably not going to remember a word of what he was saying. "I thought you were hot too, but rather rude."

"I was rude," Michael snorted. "You blasted my head off and were so arrogant too."

"I wasn't arrogant," Kelsey defended her actions. "But you were reversing too fast."

"No, no, no," Michael shook his head. He grabbed Kelsey's hand when she moved from his neck. "You have the softest coldest hands ever."

"Thank you?" Kelsey pulled a comical face.

"I was so mad I wanted to pull you from the car and kiss you," Michael grinned as his eyes started to droop. "I think the minute you banged my bumper, cupid shocked me with a bow." He sighed. "Stay with me." He cuddled up to her hand and drifted off to sleep.

Shocked him with his bow! Kelsey smiled down at Michael and gently moved his fringe off his forehead.

"I felt the same way, Michael Cooper," Kelsey said softly and did something she'd never done in her life. She kissed a boy first. Okay she only kissed his forehead.

Kelsey gently removed her hand from Michael's. He moaned. Kelsey lifted the blanket up around him and went to find Dr. Barnes. She was not happy with Michael's stomach.

She was about to leave when Gertie walked in.

"Are you still here?" Gertie greeted Kelsey. "Your mom and Zane asked me if I would come sit and watch over both of you while they quickly went to get some more clothes for Michael."

"I'm glad you're here Gertie," Kelsey smiled at her. "I just want to go call Dr. Barnes to come and check Michael out. He's been a bit restless and having more pain."

"Okay, honey, I'll watch him." Gertie smiled at Kelsey as she rushed out of the room.

"Let's give the new medication a few minutes to work." Dr. Barnes got the nurse to change around the drips. "If he comes around and asks for water try ice chips to wet his mouth."

"Where do I get those?" Gertie looked at Kelsey and Dr. Barnes.

"Just ask the nurse at the station outside," Kelsey told Gertie. "I'm going to help Dr. Barnes," she told Gertie. "Are you sure you don't mind sitting with Michael?"

"Not at all." Gertie smiled.

"Just hit the call button if you need us." Kelsey positioned the button where Gertie had easy access to it. "Thank you."

"How's he doing?" Erin asked Gertie when she slipped quietly back into Michael's room.

"He woke up a few times for some ice chips." Gertie told her as she stretched out. "The doctor came by and was worried about the pain Michael is having in his stomach. They may need to take him for another scan."

"Where's Dr. Barnes?" Erin looked alarmed. "Did he say what he thought the problem with Michael's stomach is?"

"We're worried about an infection." Kelsey smiled at Gertie and gave her mother a kiss on the cheek. "I just need to do some checks." She held her hospital tablet in her hand.

"But surely you need to take him for a scan now if he's in so much pain?" Erin looked at her daughter. "He's been through so much; can't you take him now instead of when something goes wrong?"

"I found parking at last." Zane walked into the room carrying a bag. "Kelsey where can I put some things for Michael?" He noted her raised eyebrows. "Your mother packed them for him."

"Of course she did," Kelsey sighed. Her mother was such a mother hen. "You can put them in the cupboard over there." She showed Zane the locker in the room. "Okay, I have to find Dr. Barnes," she told him. "Don't give Michael anything to drink if he wakes up." She warned her mother.

"Please hurry and get Michael for that scan as soon as you can," Erin told Kelsey. "We need to know what's going on with him before his mother gets here."

"Mom," Kelsey looked at her mother and shook her head. "Did you call his mother?"

"Honey I had to," Erin said. "I kept thinking how upset I'd be if someone didn't call me if anything happened to you or Caleb."

"I called Shane and Amy," Zane admitted. "I too felt guilty about not letting Shane know his daughter was missing when he'd left her in my care."

"You two are going to be in hot water with Michael and Lilly." Kelsey gave Zane a kiss on the cheek. "Thank you though." She smiled at Zane. "I know you're doing everything you can to find my brother and Lilly."

Kelsey left the room.

"It is so nice to see such a close family," Gertie smiled. "I was telling Michael as such."

"Gertie," Zane was perched on the arm of Erin's chair that she kept sitting in and then getting up to fuss over a sleeping Michael, "would you be able to officiate a triple wedding in three weeks' time?" He smiled at Gertie's look of surprise, "Two of my nieces and my nephew all want to get married on the same day at White Sands Cove."

"I'd be delighted," Gertie said without hesitation. Usually she'd have to meet and talk to the bride and groom, or in this case the brides and grooms, and also their families. But this family not only went above and beyond to help a complete stranger, one of them had taken a bullet for her. "I do need to meet the couples first though."

"Fair enough," Zane nodded. "We were trying to get our minister to fly in from Florida, but he's unable to. This is the wedding season, so he's fully booked."

"I have a few weddings on but only nearer to the end of July through to August," Gertie told Zane. "I'm new to town so people are still getting to know me."

"Perfect," Zane breathed a sigh of relief. "I can cross that off my wedding to-do list."

"Are their parents in town?" Gertie asked Zane.

"No," Zane shook his head. "My father and I looked after my brother's four children when he and wife had an accident many years ago," was all Zane offered about the subject.

"I'm sorry," Gertie said. This family really was a strong unit that had gone through so much loss and tragedy.

"It was a long time ago," Zane gave her a tight smile, "but thank you."

"If you can message me the date, time, location, and when I can meet the couples," Gertie told Zane, "I can start making preparations."

"Thank you, Gertie," Zane said. "I'll do that and send you an official invitation to the wedding."

"Erin?" Michael said weakly interrupting the wedding talk.

"I'm here, sweetheart." Erin jumped up and moved to Michael's bedside.

"My head," Michael grimaced, "it feels like it's going to explode." He gripped his stomach, "and my stomach is on fire."

"I'll get Kelsey." Erin looked at Zane. "Please can you call Kelsey?"

"Sure," Zane nodded and went to find her.

"Honey," Erin looked at Michael worriedly, "you're burning up."

Kelsey rushed into the room, did a check of Michael, and hit the call button. A nurse ran in and Kelsey told them to page Dr. Barnes. Michael needed a scan right away.

"Mom, I'm sorry, but you're all going to have to go wait in the waiting room, please," Kelsey went into full doctor mode.

"But I want to be here with him," Erin wouldn't budge.

"Mom," Kelsey looked at her mother, "please don't make me have to get you forcefully removed."

"Come on, Erin." Zane took her by the shoulders and gently moved her out of the room.

As Zane, Erin, and Gertie walked to the waiting room Dr. Barnes flew down the passage and into Michael's room.

The tall man managed to get the window of the cabin open. He climbed in and looked around. He knew no one was home. They were all at the hospital. That fool had accidently shot that kid and taken hostages bringing even more attention to the family. He was right to follow the fool to La Jolla. He'd obviously not got anywhere with his methods.

What he was looking for had to be here somewhere. He'd checked everywhere else. The man went through the whole of the downstairs and there was nothing. A shadow swished past him. He stopped and frowned, looking around the room. He shook his head. He must be seeing things. This whole retreat gave him the creeps. He felt like there were eyes in the hills watching him.

The man ignored his creeped out feeling and climbed the stairs. He heard a low growl he spun around and again all he saw was a flash of a shadow.

What the hell? He thought, craning his neck while he balanced on the stairs. He stood quietly listening and watching but there was nothing. He really was letting this place get to him. Once again, he shook the creepy feeling off and climbed to the top of the stairs. As he got to the top something growled. He turned towards the sound and a large bundle of fur flew at him in an angry hiss.

He fell back holding up his arms to protect his face from the vicious slashing of sharp claws. Before he could move the animal jumped off him and disappeared. He stood up as fast as he could and looked around. There was no sign of the giant fur ball. A flash of memory of another huge fur ball flashed through his mind. *Rafferty!* The biggest cat he'd seen with a bad attitude. Well to people he didn't like, and Rafferty didn't like him.

A meowwwrrrr came from downstairs along with a thump, thump, thump, sound. His brows drew together.

"What now?" The man mumbled.

He hoped no one had come home or to clean the cabin. He wasn't in the mood to have to clean up after himself today. He quietly made his way back down the stairs. He stopped at the kitchen and sitting on the table eyeing him out was Rafferty. Eyeing him out as he swished his long furry tail.

He needed to lock this pesky beast out the cabin, or it would harass him, and he needed to search the upstairs.

"Good boy," he walked slowly towards the huge cat. "Come on kittycat." He reached out to nab Rafferty, but the cat was too fast and used him to leapfrog onto the back of the sofa in the small living room off the kitchen.

"Come here you blasted …." he turned and stopped dead as he heard two low growls. "I see you brought your doggie friends." He hissed through gritted teeth.

A large Saint Bernard and a Golden Labrador stood baring their teeth at him.

He hated dogs!

He slowly backed around the dogs towards the front door hoping he could open it from the inside. As he took two steps back the dogs took a step forward as if they were herding out of the cabin.

"Good dogs," he held up his hands wishing he'd brought his weapon with him. "I'm leaving see."

He didn't take his eyes off the huge dog and his friend nor

the pesky cat that he swore was giving him a smug smile as it sprawled out on the back of the sofa watching him.

The door opened. As he stepped out the dogs started to bark and charged. He slammed the door shut and headed for the parking lot where he'd left his car. Luckily, no one was around. As he got down the hill he heard the barking and saw the dogs and cat all pile out the window he'd left open.

He picked up speed as the three animals barreled towards him. He used his remote to unlock his car and managed to get in and drive away as all three of the animals got close. He was going to have to think of another way. For now, he'd just have to once again fade into the background to watch and wait for another opportunity.

Next time he was bringing a tranquilizer gun. This wasn't the first time those three animals had stopped him doing what he needed to do.

Chapter Twenty
ESCAPE FROM A WINDOWLESS ROOM

"Where do you think the man went?" Lilly asked Caleb. "I really want to get out of here."

"I've nearly got the door." Caleb pounded against it.

Lilly had found a sharp knife lying on the floor near the bed. She'd given it to Caleb to try and jimmy the lock with, but it hadn't worked so he'd gone back to using brute force.

"Be careful." Lilly stood on the other side of the room watching him.

Caleb gave one more thud and the door burst open. He stopped for a moment while he rubbed his shoulder and stood frowning. The house was eerily quiet. It was also quite run down and obviously abandoned or being torn down.

Caleb took Lilly's hand and cautiously moved down the hallway. There was no one in the house. Not even one of the man's thugs that were with him at the church. Caleb found it odd that they would be kidnapped and left alone for no reason. What was the point of doing something like that?

"Didn't you say the man had guards with him?" Lilly asked, walking closely behind Caleb, her hand gripping his tight.

"He did." Caleb nodded looking around the old house. "What is this house?"

"Wait!" Lilly stopped as they got to the stairs. "I know this house." She looked around. "Although I'm pretty sure there wasn't a windowless room before." She frowned.

"Okay," Caleb looked at her. "Does this mean you know where we are?" He asked her hopefully. "Because we have no money or phones with us."

"I do," Lilly smiled excitedly. "We're near Goldfish Point." She took the lead and led Caleb down the long sweeping stairs and to the front door. "Which means we are close to my aunt's house." Lilly put her hand on the door handle but before she turn it the door opened on its own.

"That's odd," Caleb frowned. "The door wasn't closed properly."

"I don't know about you," Lilly looked up at Caleb, "but I don't really care right now all I want to do is get to my aunt's place."

"I'm right behind you," Caleb agreed with Lilly although he couldn't shake the feeling that something wasn't quite right. The escape seemed too easy.

Caleb shook off the feeling and ran after Lilly. She'd been right. They were near Coast Walk, a few houses down from her Aunt Jennifer and Aunt Miranda's houses (they lived next door to each other). When Caleb and Lilly had squeezed through the fence of the old house, he'd noticed that it had been marked to be torn down. A cold feeling crept up his spine when he noted the name of the development company proudly boasting a new townhouse development.

Caleb and Lilly ran down the long sweeping lawn to where it joined the Coast Walk path before running in the direction of the Sea Breeze Cottage Inn. When Lilly flew up the backstairs of the house a woman with dark hair spotted her and opened the glass door.

"Lilly?" Miranda looked at her. "Are you okay?"

"Hi, Aunt Miranda, this is my friend Caleb," Lilly introduced Caleb. "Please can we come in?" She looked over her shoulder worried the man might have come back as they left.

"Of course," Miranda stepped aside. She closed and locked the sliding door drawing the curtains as she ushered them into the lounge. "Don't worry, there aren't any guests here just yet."

"May I use your phone?" Caleb asked Miranda. "I need to phone my mother and Zane."

"Yes," Miranda pulled her phone out of her apron pocket. "I'll make you some tea and you can tell me what's going on." She ushered Lilly into the kitchen.

"That smells delicious." Lilly's stomach growled.

"I'll get you each a plate." Miranda put the kettle on. "Now start talking."

Lilly told Miranda everything while Caleb let Zane and Erin know where they were. Not long after Caleb hung up from Erin and Zane, Phillip called him. Caleb explained where they were. Miranda knew the house Caleb was talking about and gave Phillip the address.

"There are some agents at that old house right now according to Phillip," Miranda told Lilly and Caleb about fifty minutes later. "They've asked me if you're still here with me."

"What did you tell him?" Lilly asked her curiously. "Why does it matter if we're here or not?"

"They found a body in the house where you were being held captive," Miranda told the two of them. "A man named Patrick Myers. He was stabbed." Her brows drew together.

"Patrick's dead?" Caleb asked. "So, it was him!"

"The knife they think was used to stab him was in the room where you said you were being held," Miranda told them. "Did you have a knife in the room?"

"What?" Lilly couldn't believe what she was hearing. "There

was no blood on it. Caleb thinks it's the knife Adrian had in the church. We used it to try and jimmy the door open."

"So you both touched it." Miranda frowned worriedly.

"Yes." Lilly nodded.

"That's why they want to question you both." Miranda shook her head. "Was the knife in the room when you were pushed in there?"

"I don't know," Lilly said honestly. "We'd been in the room for about forty minutes or so when I found it on the floor by the bed."

"No one came in or out from the time we were locked in," Caleb told Miranda. "It must've been there all along."

"And the two of you were together all the time," Miranda asked them.

Caleb was about to say something when Lilly interrupted, "Yes, we were."

Caleb looked at Lilly with narrowed eyes. Lilly reached for his hand beneath the table and gave it a squeeze.

"The one agent said one of the neighbors that was walking past the house told them they saw a fight between two men at the house," Miranda told them. "One of the men matched Caleb's description."

"Son of a ..." Caleb's jaw clenched as he drew in a breath. "I need to get to New York."

"What's going on Caleb?" Miranda's eyes narrowed in on him. "If you want my help, you'll both start telling me the full truth." She leaned back and folded her arms waiting.

Caleb ran his hand through his hair and told them both something not even Erin knew.

When he was finished Miranda and Lilly stared at him. Miranda was assessing the information while Lilly's eyes had slitted angrily.

"Why wouldn't you tell me this?" Lilly hissed.

"I didn't want to put you in any more danger." Caleb let her hand go when she pulled it away. "I'm sorry." He looked at

Miranda. "Now I fear I've put you in danger as well, Miranda."

"Don't you worry about me or Lilly for that matter." Miranda put her hand over Caleb's on the table. "You go to New York on one condition," she told him. "You let me get my cousin Max, Jennifer's husband, to help you."

"I don't know," Caleb shook his head, "I..."

"Trust us," Lilly said. "Uncle Max will help us."

"Us?" Caleb frowned at Lilly. "What do you mean?"

"I'm coming with you," Lilly said stubbornly.

"Lilly," Miranda looked at the young woman. "You don't know what you might be walking into."

"Miranda is right Lilly." Caleb agreed with Miranda. "I'll be a day or two at the most."

"No," Lilly shook her head. "You risked your life to save me, you aren't going to leave me behind."

"Okay," Caleb held up his hands.

"I'm just going to go to Aunt Jennifer's cottage and get a few of my things I left there if that's okay?" Lilly looked at Miranda.

"Of course," Miranda said. "You know where the keys are."

Lilly ran off and when she was out of earshot Caleb turned to Miranda.

"I need a favor." Caleb looked at Miranda.

Miranda listened to what Caleb had to say. She decided then and there that he was a fine young man and Lilly was in good hands.

"But please wait until we've left." Caleb smiled at Miranda.

"Of course," Miranda said. "You and Lilly can take my car to the airport. I'll get my husband to take me to fetch it. We need a date night in San Diego again." She smiled.

"I'm back," Lilly ran inside. "But we'd better move if we're going to get to the airport before the cavalry arrive."

"Thank you for everything, Aunt Miranda," Lilly kissed Miranda on the cheek.

"Call me when you get there," Miranda waved them off.

173

"*I* booked us two first class tickets compliments of my father," Lilly grinned holding up a black credit card, "and I got us two rooms at the Plaza Hotel on my mother's credit card." She held up another black credit card.

"Lilly," Caleb glanced at her while he drove them to the airport.

"Don't worry, I'll pay them back, I always do," Lilly said. "I just thought that you don't want to alert anyone that you are going back to New York. We are travelling as Mr. and Mrs. Crowley. You have a suite under the name of Shane Crowley and I'm his daughter Lilly with my own room."

"Clever, but I'll pay your mother and father back," Caleb insisted.

"I've always wanted to go to New York again," Lilly told Caleb.

"*L*illy," Caleb held her hand as they boarded the airplane, "you didn't have to come with me."

"Where you go, I go," Lilly said stubbornly. "We're in this together now."

Caleb let Lilly take the window seat.

"In case I don't get a chance to say this, because we're about to kick over a hornet's nest," Caleb kissed her hand, "I love you Lilly Crowley with all my heart, my soul, and everything that I am."

"I'm so relieved to hear that, Caleb Barnes," Lilly gave him one of her blinding smiles. "Because I am madly in love with you. You have my heart."

Caleb leaned over and kissed her. They were interrupted by the air steward asking them to put on their seat belts.

"Let's go finish this." Lilly cuddled into Caleb's side. "But as soon as we land. I need to find a clothes shop and store to get some conveniences."

"Likewise." Caleb smiled and kissed her on the top of her head. "I really wish I was taking you to New York under better circumstances."

The airplane started to taxi down the runway. Caleb looked out of the window. This time he was going to end this. Erin had been right — this wasn't their fight. Caleb couldn't protect everyone and holding on to the ghosts of the past was putting people he loved in unnecessary danger.

He swallowed as the airplane lifted into the sky. He hoped that those he loved that would feel the ripple effect of what he was about to do would forgive him. He felt Lilly snuggle into him and relax as she fell asleep. He turned to look down at her and his heart filled up and, in that moment, he had no more doubts that he was doing the right thing.

Chapter Twenty-One
DOING THE RIGHT THING NO MATTER WHAT!

"How is Michael doing?" Phillip walked up to Zane and Erin. He greeted them.

"We don't know yet," Erin said worriedly. "Have you been to fetch Lilly and Caleb from Jennifer's house?" she asked Phillip.

"I have a team there now," Phillip said. "But we have a problem."

"Please don't give me any bad news." Erin's face was pale.

"Lilly and Caleb weren't at Miranda's place when we got there," Phillip told them. "We also found a dead body in the house where Lilly and Caleb were being held captive."

"Do you know who it is?" Zane asked Phillip.

"According to his ID, he is Patrick Myers," Phillip told them.

"No!" Erin's eyes grew huge. "What happened to him?"

"He was stabbed," Phillip said. "We found a knife that could be the murder weapon in the small room where Caleb said he and Lilly were being held."

"Don't even say it," Erin held her hand up to Phillip. "As of this moment you can't go near either Lilly or Caleb without me present."

"We haven't got the ballistics back," Phillip told Erin. "We have witnesses that saw a man matching Patrick's description pushing Caleb and Lilly into the house against their will." He looked at Erin before saying, "He also saw a man matching Caleb's description having a fight with the man."

"Where are Caleb and Lilly now?" Zane asked Phillip.

"Miranda said she had no idea. She gave them something to eat and lent them her car," Phillip said. "We found Miranda's car at the San Diego airport. We believe Lilly and Caleb are heading to New York."

"Oh no." Erin's face was now ashen. "Why would he be going back to New York?"

"I was hoping you could tell me?" Phillip asked Erin.

"I honestly don't know why Caleb would ever want to go back there?" Erin shook her head.

"I best be getting back." Phillip turned to Zane. "We could use your help if you don't mind."

"Of course," Zane looked at Erin. "I'll be back soon."

Erin nodded. She was both shocked about the news of Patrick and confused as to why Caleb was going to New York.

"How is he?" Jennifer Guilford, Michael's mother rushed into the hospital.

"Jennifer," Erin hugged her friend. "They are treating him now. He had an infection, but they've stabilized him."

"Hello, Jennifer." Dr. Barnes walked into the waiting room. "Your son is stable, and you can go see him now."

"Thank you, Dr. Barnes." Jennifer started walking out the room, but Erin sat back down. "Aren't you coming?"

"I thought I'd give the two of you some time." Erin smiled.

"Come on." Jennifer walked over to her friend and pulled her along to Michael's room with her.

"Mom?" Michael looked up and smiled.

"Hi, baby," Jennifer walked over to him and kissed his forehead. "Erin has told me everything."

"Lilly?" Michael looked at Erin.

"I just need to check…" Kelsey stopped as she walked into Michael's room.

"Hello, Kelsey." Jennifer walked over to the young woman to greet her.

"Hi," Kelsey greeted Jennifer. "Sorry, I don't mean to interrupt; I just need to check Michael's drip."

"I was just going to tell Michael that Lilly and Caleb escaped," Erin told them. "They landed up at the Sea Breeze Cottage and Miranda looked after them."

"That's a relief," Michael sighed. "Please tell them to come see me."

"I would," Erin said. "Only they've taken off to New York after their abductor was found dead."

"What?" Kelsey nearly knocked the drip off the stand she got such a fright. "Who was their abductor?" Her eyes were wide with fright.

"Patrick," Erin said softly. "I spoke to Miranda just before Jennifer arrived. She said Caleb was going to New York to put an end to the nightmare once and for all."

"Oh no!" Kelsey's face paled. "I need to talk to Max." She looked at Jennifer.

"Why, honey?" Jennifer asked her.

"Because my brother is going to need his help," Kelsey said softly. "I know what he's up to."

"Then you'd better start talking, young lady," Shane Crowley walked into the room. "Because your brother has my daughter with him."

"Relax, Shane," Jennifer told him in her calm way. She always thought that problems never got solved with a hot head. Although she could do with her bath and tub of ice cream right now. "Max is already on his way to New York."

"*U*ncle Max?" Lilly opened her hotel room door expecting to find Caleb to go and have dinner. "Mom?" Her eyes grew large. "What's going on?" She looked past them. "Where's Caleb?"

"Hello, sweetheart," Amy Crowley stepped into Lilly's hotel room. "Max is here to help Caleb," she smiled at her daughter, "while you and I are going to enjoy New York."

"No," Lilly shook her head stubbornly. "I need to help Caleb, Mom. He saved my life a few times."

"I know," Amy smiled at her stubborn daughter who reminded her so much of her father, "but he asked us here to help him and to keep you safe."

"I like him." Max smiled. "He wants you safe, Lilly, so he and I can sort this mess out once and for all."

"Fine," Lilly said and walked back into her room. "But I'm ordering a very expensive dinner with dessert," she told her mother.

"I agree," Amy said as they said goodbye to Max. "Only we use your father's credit card not mine."

"*H*ello, Caleb," the man's cold blue eyes assessed him. "Max Guilford, we meet again."

"I'm not here to cause trouble," Max told the man. "We just need to get what we came for."

"Did you bring what I asked for?" the man asked Caleb.

"I did." Caleb nodded and handed the man a thick brown envelope.

"You know your father, the real one that is," he jibed, "told me to only give this to both you and your sister."

"Well, she's not here and I don't want her involved in this."

Caleb shook his head. "Why would Sheldon trust you of all people?"

"Let's just say I honor my debts." The man kept his eye on Max. "There's nothing in here of interest to you," he told Max. "Remember I allowed you in here."

"I told you," Max lifted up his hands, "I'm just here with my friend."

The man went into the back room and came back a few minutes later with a safety deposit box.

"I take it you have your sister's key as well?" the man asked.

"Max does," Caleb nodded. "I have my key."

"The bags for free." The man put the box in a leather satchel. "Actually, it belonged to Sheldon. He said I was to put the box in it if his daughter and son ever came to fetch it."

"Thanks," Caleb nodded, he was about to leave but Max stopped him.

"How do we know this is the right box?" Max asked the man.

"Open it," the man shrugged.

Max took the box out the bag. He and Caleb used the two keys to open it.

"Do you mind?" Max looked at the man who hadn't budged and was trying to look into the box.

"Sure." The man turned and walked off to the back of the store.

Max stood over Caleb so if there were any cameras, they wouldn't see what was in the box.

"Oh wow," Caleb breathed. "It's definitely Sheldon's box."

"Let's go." Max closed up the box and shoved it back into the bag. He took the one key and the satchel from Caleb.

"Max," Caleb swallowed, "am I doing the right thing here?" he asked.

"Yes," Max nodded. "Now we need to get you back to the hotel and I need to get this to my contacts."

EPILOGUE

Kelsey, Erin, and Jennifer were back at the White Sands Cove retreat. Kelsey needed to get some rest and so did Erin. They'd left Michael with Zane and Shane to keep him company. They needed to leave Zane behind so he could keep Shane from going to New York.

"I'm going to go back to the cabin and have a shower," Kelsey told Erin and Jennifer who were having a coffee at the White Sands Cove hotel.

"Okay," Erin waved to her daughter.

As Kelsey was walking out of the hotel, she called Zane so she could speak to Michael. She stopped at the door to take her backpack off the hook.

"Hi," Michael's voice came over the phone. "I miss you; these two men are driving me nuts."

"I'll be back in a couple of hours," Kelsey laughed. "I just need a little rest."

"Kelsey?" a familiar voice called her from the hotel door.

Kelsey froze and took the phone away from her ear.

"Miles?" Kelsey looked at her ex-fiancé, her face paling. "What are you doing in La Jolla?"

"I came to see you." He smiled. He had his one hand in his jacket pocket.

"I was just coming to get my bag," Kelsey said and started to back towards where her mother and Jennifer were. "My mother needed an aspirin."

"Kelsey." Miles took two steps towards her.

Kelsey turned and ran.

"Mom, Jennifer," Kelsey yelled. "Run!"

SECRETS OF WHITE SANDS COVE

Book 4

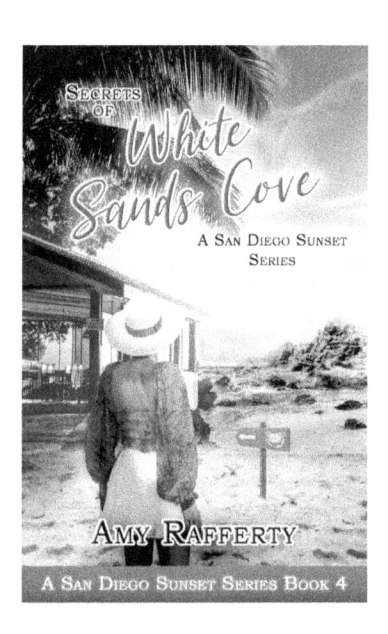

PROLOGUE

It has taken Erin forty-eight years to realize she'd never known what true romantic love was or had ever experienced it. Her whole life up to this point she'd felt like she was missing out on something and now she knew what that something was. Erin also knew that the universe never gave you anything for free. There was always some catch or test to see if you were worthy of its gift. Only she wasn't expecting the test to be quite so challenging and one that may very well rob her of her soul mate and shatter her heart.

Zane had locked away his heart many years ago when he'd tragically lost his fiancé. He'd put her on a pedestal and no woman, up until he'd met Erin, had ever compared to her. For Zane there was no half measure when it came to love. Which meant you gave it your all or you walked away.

Can Erin make Zane see that love is not meant to be easy? It's messy, complicated, and sometimes fate has the worst timing but most of all would he be able to understand her complicated past.

Join the characters at White Sands Cove as they put their past behind them and find a new adventure awaiting them within the rocky walls of Pirates Wall.

Chapter Twenty-Two
NO MORE SHADOWS

Caleb's heart pounded in his chest. He'd just handed in a case full of evidence that was about to cripple two large family empires while clearing Sheldon Myers, his biological father's name. Max had Caleb and Lilly guarded around the clock and they weren't allowed to leave New York until the arrests had been made and all the suspects had been rounded up.

Caleb had put himself and Lilly in grave danger by doing what he'd done. But if they or his family were going to have a chance at a brighter future without the shadow of their past having over them, it was the only way. Caleb felt a bit better having a bodyguard following him and Lilly around. He also suspected there were more than one agent looking after each of them.

Lilly now had three bodyguards towering over her making it almost impossible for them to have any alone time. Especially now that her father had arrived in New York. They'd had Lilly's room upgraded to a suite, so she stayed in the two bedroomed hotel room under the close watch of both her military trained parents.

Caleb fiddled with his hair and his palms felt sweaty as his nerves poked his heartbeat into overdrive. Even handing over all the evidence he had to Max and knowing there could be repercussions for doing so hadn't frightened him as much as what he was about to do. Caleb cleared his throat and was about to knock on the door of doom when a voice came behind him nearly making him have a heart attack.

"I thought you could use a bit of backup," Max grinned when he saw Caleb jump and spin around. Max lobbed forward and caught the bottle of expensive whisky and two bunches of flowers Caleb had in his hands before they hit the floor.

"Are you mad sneaking up on me like that?" Caleb said shakily, taking the items Max had caught.

"I called you from down the hallway," Max looked at him with a half grin on his face, "twice." He held up two fingers.

"Sorry," Caleb gathered his shattered nerves. "I've heard so much about Lilly's father."

"Shane's not that bad," Max raised his eyebrows. "Don't let him intimidate you." Max patted Caleb on the shoulder. "Remember, you're here for Lilly and so stand your ground and fight for her."

"Thanks," Caleb nodded.

"Here," Max knocked on the door, "let me help you rip off the band aid."

"Hello," Shane opened the door.

"Dad," Lilly ran towards her father trying to push him out of the way. "Hi," she smiled at Caleb.

"Hi," Caleb said to Lilly with a warm smile. "Hello, Mr. Crowley." He held out his hand. "I'm Caleb Barnes."

"I know who you are." Shane ignored Lilly and stood blocking the doorway. "I knew your father as well."

"Which one?" Max raised an eyebrow at Shane.

"Both." Shane didn't look at Max, he kept his eyes on Caleb. "How are you, Max?"

"I'd be better if you let us in," Max told Shane. "We're a

little exposed out here as I'm Caleb's bodyguard tonight," he warned Shane.

"Then he's in good hands," Shane grinned at Max. "My daughter tells me that you saved her life from that lunatic cowboy."

"It was a joint effort," Caleb told Shane honestly.

"Did you stab Patrick Myers?" Shane asked Caleb bluntly, watching him closely for his reaction.

"No," Caleb shook his head. "I've only ever stabbed someone once." He shocked Shane and Max by saying. "I was thirteen and Sheldon Myers had just bought me a pocketknife. I was playing around with it when I knew I shouldn't be. Sheldon gave me strict instructions that I could only use it under his supervision. While I was playing around with it, it fell out of my hands and stabbed me in the foot."

Caleb saw Lilly put her hand over her mouth to hide her smile while Shane and Max stared at him in shock before they both burst out laughing.

"That's nothing." Shane stepped back and let them in. "Lilly was inadvertently responsible for blowing up my super yacht."

"Dad," Lilly rolled her eyes at him. "Let it go!"

"It was an expensive top of the line ..." Shane was about to close the door when it was slammed back knocking Shane forward.

Max automatically went for his weapon, while Caleb dived towards Lilly and pulled her behind him protectively backing her away from the danger. Shane immediately went into defensive mode and a few swift moves had the mountain of a man dressed in a black suit on his knees.

"You picked the wrong suit, buddy." Shane held the man in a neck grip.

"You must be the father of Lilly Crowley." Judge Carnegie stepped into the room.

"Gran?" Caleb frowned. "What on earth?"

"Amy, Lilly's mother invited me," the judge said. "Your

grandfather will be up shortly." She looked over at Shane still holding her bodyguard on his knees. "Please don't take out both our bodyguards." She grinned.

Shane let the man up.

"It's rude to barge into someone's hotel suite unannounced," Shane told the bodyguard.

"For goodness sake, Shane," Amy, Lilly's mother, stepped into the room. "You always hit first and ask questions later. I thought we spoke about this?"

"Old habits and ... well, Lilly was in the room," Shane shrugged.

"He once nearly killed one of Lilly's babysitters' boyfriends who was helping the babysitter put up a cot mobile for Lilly," Amy shook her head. She was holding a whole lot of the hotel dining rooms menus in her hand. "Hi, sorry I'm being rude. We spoke on the phone. I'm Amy," she greeted the judge and then introduced everyone.

"I see you weren't joking about my grandson needing backup around your husband," the judge eyed Shane out.

"I think he was holding his own quite well," Max defended Caleb. "Can I pour anyone a drink?" He herded them into the lounge of the suite.

"How are you, Max?" The judge smiled fondly at him.

"I'm well thank you, Judge," Max grinned.

"This is one of the best suites in the hotel," the judge looked around the room as she went over to kiss Caleb hello. "How are you, young man?" She smiled warmly at Caleb. "I heard what you did. I'm so glad you finally decided to come forward," she said proudly.

"Gran," Caleb stopped her from walking into the lounge, "you know this could have some blow back on you and Granddad."

"If it does," the judge smiled warmly at Caleb, "we'll be ready." She gave him a hug. "Don't you worry about us my love.

Your grandfather and I have dealt with our fair share of bullies in our lifetime."

"Your grandmother is quite the bully basher," Dr. Carnegie stepped into the suite. "You really should keep this door closed with everything that's currently going on." His bodyguard closed the door for him.

Caleb greeted his grandfather before introducing him to everyone.

The evening progressed well as the families got to know each other. Lilly learned a lot about Caleb's young life as he learnt a lot about Lilly's. She was right — she was quite the little rebel which only made him fall in love with her more.

He was a bit embarrassed when his grandmother and grandfather told Lilly's family the rest of the pocketknife story. How Kelsey had played doctor, bandaged his foot and the two of them had taken a taxi, then the ferry, to Rhode Island for Caleb's grandfather to stitch his foot up. He didn't want his mother or Sheldon to find out what he'd done and have his pocketknife taken away. It had cost him nearly all his allowance to keep Kelsey quiet and pay for the trip to Rhode Island where their grandparents lived.

The evening went on later than the Carnegies were expecting so Caleb offered his grandparents his suite and would take the couch. By the time they left the Crowley's suite it was nearly midnight.

Chapter Twenty-Three
NO MORE THREATS!

"Who is that man?" Jennifer asked as they locked themselves in Lilly's office. "What does he want?"

"My guess is, it has something to do with the evidence Max and Caleb are handing over," Erin whispered as Kelsey dialed Zane.

"Zane," Kelsey's heart was hammering in her chest, "can you get here, fast?"

"What's wrong, Kelsey?" Zane said, instantly on high alert.

"I think I know who my phone stalker is," Kelsey told him. "He's here in the hotel. Mom, myself, and Jennifer are locked in Lilly's office. I'm afraid he's going to bash down the door."

"Stay where you are," Zane told her. "I'm two minutes away. Do you know who the person is?"

"Yes," Kelsey nodded. "His name's Miles Parker."

"Parker?" Zane asked. "As in Parker Construction and Property Investments?"

"Yes," Kelsey said, jumping when there was a thud against the door. "Hurry."

"Pulling up now," Zane said. "I'll be there in a few seconds. Call Phillip for me." He hung up.

"Zane's here." Kelsey, Jennifer, and Erin were hiding behind Lilly's large old oak desk she'd taken from the attic at Jennifer's house.

"He's going to break through that door," Jennifer breathed and took Kelsey's and Erin's hands. "Zane will get him."

"I have to phone Phillip." Kelsey dialed Phillip's number.

"Hello, Kelsey," Phillip said softly. "I'm here with Zane. I was on my way to come speak to you all about what we've found in the evidence Caleb handed over."

"Thank you." Kelsey jumped again, and Jennifer squeezed her hand reassuringly. "Please hurry, he's trying to bash down the door."

"Kelsey!" Miles rammed the door again, "I just want to talk to you. You know all you had to do was meet with me and hand over the drive."

"What drive?" Jennifer and Erin said together looking at Erin.

"It's not a drive," Kelsey shrugged. She pulled a key chain from a hidden seam in her backpack. "It's a flash drive." She handed it to Jennifer.

"What does it have on it?" Jennifer took the drive. "Why do you have it?"

"Miles and I were engaged," Kelsey explained. "He ended the engagement when Caleb and I were accused of being Sheldon's accomplices."

"Okay," Jennifer frowned.

"There's evidence on this disk that Parker Construction and Land Investments illegally evicted an entire block of residents to put up a high-rise office building for the Myers," Kelsey told them. "In exchange Parker, who's grades were terrible, would get into medical school."

"I didn't think that even a Governor could get that right." Erin frowned.

"Oh he didn't get into college or medical school with his real grades," Kelsey told them. "He miraculously got straight-A's, was a member of a whole lot of school and social clubs that colleges love to see on a student's application form."

"He was never a member?" Jennifer guessed.

"Kelsey!" Miles shouted as he rammed the door again. "You could just come out now. I just want to talk."

"Where are Zane and Phillip?" Kelsey looked around the desk to see the door about to give way.

"We're right here," Zane nearly scared all three woman who screamed as he and Phillip climbed through the large windows in Lilly's office. "I did tell Lilly these windows were a security risk."

"Zane," Kelsey shot up and ran to hug him. "I'm so glad you're here."

"Me too, kid," Zane said. "Now get back down beneath that desk and ...."

"Who let those beasts out?" Miles shouted.

The next thing the five of them heard was the meow and angry roar of a cat followed by a lot of barking and screaming.

Zane and Phillip ran to the door, unlocking it and pulling it open. Erin, Jennifer, and Kelsey ran to where the two men stood.

Miles was backed up into a corner behind the reception desk. He couldn't get over the desk because every time he tried to move Rafferty flew at him spitting and clawing him. Lunar had jumped onto the reception desk to back up Rafferty while Goose stood in front of Miles with his teeth bared and growing warningly.

"I'm so sorry," one of the hotel's staff members looked distraught. "But I heard a commotion going on in one of the cabana houses at the pool and found these three locked in there."

"You did nothing wrong," Erin walked up to the poor girl.

"Kelsey," Miles looked at her, "please call your animals off."

"They don't listen to me," Kelsey's eyes narrowed. "Zane?"

She looked at him. Anger flashed in her eyes. She was so tired of being the victim and being stalked by criminals and the press.

"Don't look at me," Zane put his hands. "Goose only listens when he wants to."

"Lunar," Jennifer called. "Down."

Lunar looked up at Jennifer and gave Miles one last warning growl before hopping off the desk to go sit protectively near Jennifer, Erin, and Kelsey.

"You're the man on the video," the young woman who'd let the animal out of the cabana pointed at Miles.

"What video?" Zane frowned at the woman.

"The security cameras caught him running out of Miss Carnegie's bungalow not so long ago," she pointed to the security system in Lilly's office. "It's all on video in Lilly's office."

"Thank you," Erin told the young woman kindly. "Why don't you go get yourself a nice cup of tea and take a break?"

"Thank you, Miss Carnegie," the young woman smiled and left the reception area.

"Kelsey," Miles called to her. "Please, I just came to talk to you. I've missed you so much and I know I made a mistake ending our engagement," he told her.

"Is that why you broke into Miss Carnegie's cabin?" Zane folded his arms to glare at the man trying his best to keep his distance from Goose and Rafferty.

"I'll tell you whatever you want." Miles tried to move but Goose went for his ankle and Raffety took a swipe at him.

"Can you please take this jungle cat away from me?" Miles pulled back only to be growled at by Goose.

"Goose," Zane said. "Relax." Goose ignored him. "See." He shrugged.

"All I wanted was to see Kelsey," Miles explained. "Please, sir." He looked at Zane.

"Yeah," Zane shook his head, "that's not happening. Because

195

when we got here, we heard you threatening Kelsey and demanding she gives you something she has of yours."

"This," Jennifer handed it to Phillip. "I think he was looking for the evidence which will sink his medical career."

"That's mine." Miles saw the disk and dived at Phillip to catch it.

Zane was about to stop Miles, but Goose jumped on Miles knocking him down as Rafferty walked towards the edge of the counter and sprawled out looking down at him. Rafferty started to lick his paws and swish his tail arrogantly. While Goose decided Miles would make a nice chair and sat on him.

"Wait a minute," Zane looked down at Miles, "you're the man who pushed me into a hole."

"I think he was also the man who rudely pushed Gertie into a pole," Kelsey told them.

"You can't give that disk to anyone Kelsey." Miles tried to move but Goose would not budge. "It will ruin my life." He tried to push Goose off him, but Rafferty gave a low growl and hiss. "Will someone get this mutt off me!"

"After what I saw on this disk," Kelsey looked down at Miles angrily, "you deserve everything that's coming for you." She looked at Erin. "Miles was the one that stole Caleb's car and drove Nadine off the road." Her eyes misted over.

"Goose," Zane clicked his fingers. "Off." He commanded and Goose immediately jumped off Miles. Rafferty jumped onto Goose's back as he went to stand next to Lunar.

"Come on," Phillip pulled Miles to his feet and pulled out a pair of handcuffs to cuff Miles' hands. "I think you're going to be taking a ride with me." He pocketed the disk. "Kelsey you should've come forward with this a long time ago."

"Parker's family were threatening Caleb and I," Kelsey said softly and handed Phillip her phone. "Caleb has a whole lot more on his phone and you can take our laptops with all the emails."

"Honey," Erin stepped up to her daughter, "why didn't you tell me?"

"I wouldn't say anything if I were you," Miles glared at Kelsey.

"I'd keep my mouth shut, if I were you." Zane looked at him warningly. The anger in his voice spurred Goose to bark.

"What exactly did they threaten you with?" Jennifer asked Kelsey.

"The case Erin and Jennifer tried together against Seth Branfield." Phillip was reading through some of Kelsey's messages. "Apparently the person who sent this message warned Kelsey that if she even breathed a word about all she knew they would release evidence they had. It was about Erin, Jennifer, and Judge Carnegie tampering with evidence to swing a guilty verdict."

"That's a lie," Jennifer breathed.

"There's more," Phillip read one. "This was one Caleb got that he forwarded to Kelsey." He frowned and looked up at Erin. "They warned Caleb that it was quite easy to make Kelsey look like the one who'd had her marks tampered with and Dr. Carnegie pulled strings to get her into medical school."

"Rubbish," Erin hissed. "Kelsey was a straight-A student." Her eyes glittered with anger. "She worked really hard to get into medical school."

"Why didn't you come forward with this, Kelsey?" Zane asked her.

"Because of the last text," Phillip handed it to them to all see.

If you don't meet me and bring
the disk people are going to
start being hurt. As a doctor you
know how easy it is to hack
medical equipment these days

and I know your new friend is currently wounded in the hospital.

"You should've told us," Jennifer's face paled. "I have to call Dr. Barnes."

"No," Kelsey shook her head. "I was going to hand the disk over to Phillip later today." She explained.

"I can verify that," Phillip said. "Not about the disk but Kelsey said she had something important to show me."

"I took Michael off all computerized equipment," Kelsey told Jennifer.

"That's why you were being so bossy about having that equipment changed?" Erin nodded.

"Thank you," Jennifer breathed a sigh of relief and then stopped. "If we're all here, who is with Michael?"

"Gertie was taking an hour shift until Miranda got there," Zane smiled at Jennifer.

"I'm going to take Miles here into custody," Phillip got ready to lead Miles out. "There are a lot of people who are going to want to talk to you."

Miles cringed as he walked past the animal trio. The two dogs barked while Rafferty lay sprawled out on Goose's broad back swishing his long tail.

"Why did he run Nadine off the road?" Jennifer asked.

"Because it was Nadine who was working with Sheldon," Kelsey told them. "The night Nadine came into the trauma center she came around for a few minutes. She was the one who asked for me." Her eyes misted over. "When I went to see her, she asked me to keep the disk safe."

"Oh, honey," Erin gave her daughter a hug. "Why didn't you give it to me when you and Caleb were accused of her murder?"

"I didn't know what was on the disk," Kelsey told her mother. "Nadine's heart stopped, and I couldn't revive her. The last thing I was thinking about was the disk." She took a shaky breath. "I put it in the seam in my backpack and forgot about it until after Caleb and I were cleared of Nadine's murder."

"When did the threatening messages start?" Jennifer asked her.

"The day after Caleb was exonerated of all charges in Nadine's murder," Kelsey admitted. "That's when I remembered the disk. Caleb and I watched it together and decided that because the case was over to put it to one side."

"Why come for it now?" Zane frowned. "I mean, Miles Parker and Patrick Myers came here to get that evidence."

"Why would Patrick want that evidence?" Erin asked. "It was about Miles."

"Patrick was the one that did all the dirty work for Myers," Kelsey said. "Nadine, his own daughter, was investigating him as well." She shook her head sadly, "There's an order from Patrick to get rid of Sheldon and Nadine who were investigating the Myers and the Parkers and retrieve all the evidence they'd gathered."

"So Patrick got Miles to ride Nadine off the road?" Erin's face was pale. "His own daughter?"

"Why frame Caleb and then blame you for her death?" Zane asked.

"Caleb was the videographer for Nadine when she went to question the Myers the day she died," Kelsey told them. "She phoned him and asked him to meet her that night a few hours before the accident. I think they knew she was telling Caleb what she'd learned or what she was going to get. That disk she gave me."

"How do people become so corrupt they'd turn against their own children?" Jennifer shuddered.

"Patrick was always a cold fish living under his older brother's shadow," Erin said sadly. "So Sheldon wasn't the one involved in all the Myers schemes?"

"No," Kelsey shook her head. "He was trying to expose

them, but he had to keep close to them to do it. Caleb and I each received a letter from him some months after his death."

"What did it say?" Erin asked her daughter, "If you don't mind telling me?"

"I don't know," Kelsey shrugged, "I never read it."

"Why not?" Zane, Jennifer, and Erin asked at the same time.

"After everything Caleb, my mom, and I'd been through I just wanted to let him stay in the past," Kelsey's eyes misted over. "He just threw us away over eight years ago and even signed off the form without batting an eye for me to change my last name to mom's maiden name."

"Honey," Erin took her daughter's hand, "no matter what you feel, I know your father loved you. He loved Caleb too. He never changed his will for a reason. His lawyer told him he should change it after the divorce and Sheldon had refused. He told his lawyer that everything stays the same as if he was still married to me and the kids were still in his life."

"He cheated on you with your best friend," Kelsey told her mom.

"I know," Erin swallowed. "But even then, the night of Caleb's parents' accident Caleb needed a blood transfusion and your father dropped everything to fly to Olympia with me. I didn't understand at the time, but the hospital needed your father's blood type. I just assumed back then Sheldon shared the same blood type as Caleb's father."

Kelsey fiddled in her bag and pulled out the letter that was at the bottom of it.

"Here it is." She sniffed. "It had the key to that box in it and this."

She poured the contents out and another small SD call fell out.

"What's this?" Erin frowned.

"I don't know." Kelsey shrugged and looked inside the envelope. "Have a look."

Zane took the SD card from Erin and put it into the laptop on the reception desk.

There were a whole lot of pictures of Kelsey on it as she grew up including all her report cards, dance recitals, and more. Tears rolled down her cheeks when she saw that.

"What's on the file?" Zane frowned and clicked on it. "Oh, I think this needs to go to Phillip as well." He stepped aside.

"Those are emails between the Parkers, Governor Myers, and Patrick." Erin stepped closer and her face paled. "Patrick had his own wife killed, Caleb's father killed, and …" She turned and looked at everyone there. "They were threatening Sheldon to get on board and on track to run for mayor."

"I don't understand?" Kelsey frowned.

"Sheldon left us because he didn't want his family to have any more leverage over him." Erin frowned. "His parents had found out about his affair with Joyce and used their accident to manipulate him by threatening us."

"So he cut all ties with you and let Kelsey change her surname to show his parents he didn't care what you or Kelsey did," Jennifer said as she read another email. "He even says in the email that his parents took the only person he cared about, meaning Joyce. "

"In his letter he explains it." Kelsey looked up with wet eyes.

My dearest Angel Kelsey

The moment you were born my entire life changed. There was this tiny little girl with so much spunk even then I knew I could never in my life love anything more. You and your brother were my life, and I did everything I could to protect it. I only wish I could've done more for his mother and baby sister, who was Eric Barnes' child.

I owe you, your mother, and Caleb an explanation and the truth about Joyce and me. Your mother and I were going through a rough patch. We wanted to start a family but were struggling to fall pregnant. We'd taken a break when I went on the campaign tour with my father and Joyce as his campaign manager.

We were two lonely people under a stressful situation and one thing led to another. Caleb was born nine months later, and Joyce let Eric think Caleb was his son because by then me and your mother were expecting you. I was back and forth to Olympia as much as I could, but more to be involved with Caleb than to see Joyce.

Our affair ended the minute I got home to New York after the tour, and she went back to Washington State. My guilt and shame drove a wedge between your mother and me. It had nothing to do with either of you. You were both perfect and I loved you both so much, but my love was toxic, and it got more so after the death of Caleb's parents.

You have no idea how it ripped me apart to leave my family and sign that form giving permission for you to become a Carnegie and letting go of all my rights to you. I already had none to Caleb and he didn't even know I was his father. But you all were a lot better getting out from beneath the shadow of the Myers and everything my family stood for.

The Carnegies stood for everything I wished my family did and that was all I could ever wish for you and Caleb. Miles Parker is not the man for you, he is not who you think he is, and he only got engaged to you so my parents and he could make a point. Please, my baby girl, I know I have no right to ask you to do anything for me so I'm asking you to do this for you. Break off all ties with Miles and the Parkers; they are even more toxic than the Myers.

One day you'll find the right man for you. You'll know without a shadow of a doubt that he's the one when you want to give everything you are to him. Don't settle for less my precious baby girl. You are my princess and deserve a good worthy prince and the full happily-ever-after fairy tale.

I love you always and forever.

Dad

    Kelsey looked up at her mother. Her face was wet with tears. Erin pulled Kelsey to her and they both had a good cry. Even Zane quickly wiped tears from his eyes as he and Jennifer joined in the hug.

Chapter Twenty-Four
MANAGING WHITE SANDS COVE

"How are you feeling today?" Kelsey smiled at Michael as she walked into his hospital room. "I see Zane stayed with you last night." She pointed to the three empty coffee cups.

"He really should cut down on his caffeine." Michael smiled at her. "Can you lift the head of my bed up please?"

"No." Kelsey raised her eyebrows. "One more day lying flat and then when we are happy the infection is gone you can start being more active."

"I'm going to get bed sores lying like this all the time." Michael had always been an active guy. Lying still like this was killing him.

"For the millionth time," Kelsey laughed at him, "you won't get bed sores. The nurses, Dr. Barnes and I check all the time."

"They could pop up during the night and eat away my flesh," Michael told her grumpily.

"Different disease and I doubt you'll come into contact with the bacteria that causes necrotizing fasciitis at the moment." Kelsey shook her head. "You watch way too many medical dramas." She checked his pulse. "The bacteria don't really eat the flesh you know. It releases toxins that destroy body tissue."

"Wonderful," Michael told her, yawning. "I feel much better knowing that."

"Happy I could help," Kelsey grinned at him. "Now try and get some sleep. You can have a little bit of solid food later."

"Yay," Michael said sarcastically, "more damp steamed fish and carrots." Michael's eyes started drifting shut. "Why am I so tired? Did you drug me again?" He gave her a sleepy grin.

"I never drugged you." Kelsey laughed at him. "Dr. Barnes upped your pain medication when your head was bursting and no, I haven't given you anymore pain killers. Your body, however, needs to heal so it shuts you down so it can work on fixing you."

"You make me feel like a road being closed for repairs." Michael's eyes drifted shut.

"Exactly like that." Kelsey smiled down at him.

Something her father always said to her when she was little, ran through her mind for some reason.

Remember princess, there are many, many stars in the sky. So why only reach for one when you can have as many as you can fill your dream pockets with?

Kelsey had thought she'd lost everything when her life was shattered in New York. She'd blamed her father and his horrible family for everything. Her and Caleb hadn't realized that Sheldon Myers had been their Batman watching over them and keeping the dark away.

"Daddy," Kelsey said softly as she looked at Michael sleeping, "I think I've found my prince and my patch of stars in the sky right here in La Jolla."

Tears sprang to Kelsey's eyes as she put her hand in the pocket of her scrubs and felt her father's letter there. She had carried it around unread in her backpack for months. Now she kept it close to her as it was her last link with her father.

She went and sat in one of the recliners next to Michael's bed and pulled out the letter. She'd stapled a picture of Sheldon on it.

"I hope you can hear me, Daddy," Kelsey said to Sheldon's picture.

He was a very handsome man with shadows in his eyes. She'd only realized those shadows were his scars from the pain of having to walk away from his family to protect them.

"I'm so sorry I didn't understand," Kelsey whispered. The tears pushed themselves over her eyelids. "I hope you know that even when I said I hated you or ignored your calls that I always loved you. You were my dad." She held the letter to her heart and let the tears fall. "I just wish I could've told you when you were alive."

"Kelsey?" Michael's hoarse voice made her jump.

"Are you okay?" Kelsey shoved her letter into her pocket and jumped up.

"Are you okay?" Michael smiled up at her, his eyes heavy as he fought off sleep. "I thought I heard you talking to me from far away. Then a white horse was galloping at me and I woke up to see you crying."

"Daddy." Kelsey whispered to herself as she laughed, wiped away more tears, and clutched the letter in her pocket.

"Sorry?" Michael yawned again.

"My father always promised me a pure white horse that I could go riding on in my princess outfit." Kelsey swallowed.

"You had a princess outfit?" Michael smiled at her and reached for her hand. "Why are you so sad?"

"It's about my father and all this mess," Kelsey told him.

"Well I'm not going anywhere." Michael carefully moved over on his bed. "Sit right here next to me and tell me. I know you're on an hour break."

"Okay." Kelsey knew she'd probably get into trouble, but Dr. Barnes was very understanding.

Kelsey hopped onto Michael's bed. Michael took her hand as Kelsey caught him up on everything that was going on while he was in hospital. They laughed about Shane and Caleb. He was so relieved that everything in their past was finally being resolved and he wasn't scared to shed a tear with her when she read him her father's letter.

"It's going to be okay, Kels." Michael squeezed her hand in his. "When I'm out of here, I have someone for you to meet." He yawned again. "I think you're going to fall in love with him." He said before falling asleep. "He's fit for a princess."

Tiny shocks splintered through Kelsey at what Michael had just said. *He wanted her to meet someone else.* She swallowed as she felt her heart fall to her feet. Slowly she untangled their hands and slid off the hospital bed. Kelsey stood looking down at Michael feeling a little bruised.

Something Lilly had told her a little while ago played through her mind.

Michael was badly hurt when he was let down by the girl he thought was his soulmate and one true love. He met her when he was around nineteen years old. They had so much in common and spent the Christmas season on an incredible adventure. After that they went to different universities a few states apart.

Michael did his best to make it work. He'd spend most of his weekends travelling back and forth across the country just to spend a couple of hours with her. The day he graduated he hopped on a plane with a ring in his pocket to propose to the woman he loved. When he got there, he found out that she'd moved on and was about to get engaged to another man she'd been seeing for the past eight months.

Michael blamed himself for her moving on. He put everything he had into getting his degree which meant he could no longer make random trips to see her. He hardly had time to message or call her in his last eight months of college. The thing was, she never even bothered to let Michael know she'd moved on. She told him she just presumed that they'd both moved on. He was shattered! After that Michael just poured his heart into White Sands Cove. It was going to take someone with a lot of patience, love, and persistence to open his heart again.

Kelsey took a deep breath and a picture of a white horse flashed in her mind. She smiled and pulled out her letter. Kelsey knew she'd found the only prince she wanted and took it as a sign from her father that Michael had dreamed of a white horse. She knew what she had to do and for the first time in her life she wanted to fill her dreams pockets with a million stars.

"Thank you, Daddy." Kelsey kissed the letter as she walked out of Michael's room.

Kelsey walked down the hallway of the hospital. The first day she'd walked in here it had felt like she belonged. Dr. Barnes took one look at her face when he met her and told her he'd felt like this was his home the first day he walked through those doors when he was a young intern. He'd never looked back and here he was to this day. Still feeling like he belonged.

Whoever Michael wanted to introduce her to she'd just let down gracefully and keep hammering away at the walk around Michael's heart. As she went to do her rounds Kelsey felt warm, safe, protected, and loved all the shadows of the past had cleared. Her summer had truly begun.

"What do you mean the beach swallowed a few deck chairs?" Erin asked one of the White Sands Cove hotel staff.

Erin had taken over the running of the retreat, with Zane, while Michael and Lilly were away. Her and Zane were finalizing the hotel to ensure the opening wasn't delayed and organizing all the events, tours, hikes, and beach activities went as planned.

While she spent most time with the hotel and retreat, Zane looked after the Crab Shack, airplane rides, and other extreme activities Erin didn't do. She couldn't believe how exhausting it was and felt so proud of what Michael and Lilly had achieved. Erin was also having so much fun even though it was hard work. She felt fulfilled.

"Harry was putting out the deck chairs near the old boathouse when suddenly there was a tremor and a hole opened up on the beach swallowing a few deck chairs," the staff member said with huge eyes.

"Do you know where Zane is?" Erin sighed.

"I think he was on one of the trails," the young man said.

"Can you please get someone to go find him and ask him to meet me on the beach, please?" Erin looked at her watch. "And asked Zane if he has any tape so we can tape off the area of the beach if we need to."

The young man nodded before taking off to do what needed to be done.

The plumber for the suites was going to be here in an hour. Erin didn't need this complication now.

"What do you think this is all about?" Erin looked into the eyes of Rafferty who was sprawled out on the reception desk.

Rafferty had become a little bit more sociable and now followed them around like he was a dog. The cat had become good friends with Lunar and Goose. They played together, went on walks together. Rafferty would usually ride on Goose's back when they went walking, and the three of them even slept curled up in Goose's giant doggie bed.

Erin took off her heels in Lilly's office and slipped on the flip flops she'd left in there for when she went on her walks. Jennifer had told Erin to invest in a pair because they were handy for walking on the hot sand.

As she was about to leave Zane ran into the hotel.

"What's happening at the beach?" Zane asked Erin. "That kid spoke so fast I think I might have whiplash."

"I'm not sure," Erin explained to Zane what she was told about the holes on the beach.

Zane went into Lilly's office and got some warning tape from one of the cupboards before they took off to the beach together. Rafferty idly walked behind them like he was doing them a favor by tagging along.

Chapter Twenty-Five
A CAVE IN AT THE BEACH

Zane taped off the area where a hole in the beach had opened up.

"Didn't Michael say that there's a tunnel that runs from the boathouse?" Erin asked Zane standing a good distance away from the hole.

"Yes," Zane nodded as he directed the hotel staff to move the beach chairs over towards the Crab Shack side of the beach.

"Maybe we should close down the beach and get an engineering team in here?" Erin looked up at Zane.

"I'll check out the structural damage before we decide what to do." Zane gave Erin a smile.

"Shouldn't we get an engineer here for that?" Erin asked Zane.

"My uncle is an engineer," a young voice had Erin spinning around. "Granted he graduated a long, long time ago."

"Zoe!" Zane jumped over the tape and rushed towards his great-niece swinging her around in a big hug. "When did you get in?" He looked at his watch.

"Uncle Daniel hired a car for Chase, Logan, and I." Zoe allowed her uncle to twirl her around. "We got in two hours ago. We would've been here sooner, but Chase and Logan were looking around La Jolla."

"Erin, you remember my great-niece, Zoe Fitzpatrick, my youngest niece, Ashley's daughter?" Zane smiled proudly. "One of our little family geniuses."

"Hey Uncle Zane." Logan, Zoe's twin brother and Chase Goddard walked up to them.

"Hi, Uncle Zane," Chase greeted Zane. "Hello Miss Carnegie," he said politely.

"Of course I remember Zoe, Logan, and Chase." Erin greeted each child with a hug. "Are you all excited about your parents' weddings?"

"Yeah," Chase nodded. "I'm just sad that I'm going to have to go off to university soon."

"That's right. You got accepted into MIT." Erin smiled at the young man.

"I did." Chase smiled. "Thanks to Zoe's tutoring." He smiled at Zoe.

"You were easy to teach," Zoe shrugged it off.

Zane saw the flash in Chase's eyes and sighed. The poor guy had a crush on his great-niece who wasn't very emotionally competent. She was on the super intelligent scale and she saw the world through logic and reasoning. She also had no filter and took everything literally. Her mind was like an amazing supercomputer and sometimes Zane felt she was some sort of android or cyborg.

"What happened here?" Logan peered into the hole.

"Looking at the cave in," Zoe looked down at the hole and then around the beach, "it looks like a shockwave of sorts must've done this." She looked up at Erin then Zane. "Has there been any earth tremors here recently?"

"Maybe it's the ghosts of tunnel pasts warning us to stay away," Logan challenged his sister.

"You're delusional if you think there are such things as ghosts," Zoe stared at her brother. "But I think you're mocking me because I know you're intelligent enough not to allow yourself to believe in such drivel."

"Zoe," Chase stepped in, "why don't we all go put our stuff in the cabin and then go for a ..."

Chase didn't get to finish his sentence when a huge slobbering Goose charged at the three kids excitedly.

"Goose!" Zoe squealed delightedly, plopping onto the sand, laughing as the big dog bounced around with happy barks and slobbering licks.

Goose couldn't decide which teen to greet first and decided on Zoe. "Hey, boy, I missed you." She hugged and kissed the big happy dog.

"I see he's happy," Erin laughed as Zoe was greeted the same way by Lunar. Erin was completely surprised when the cold aloof Rafferty hopped onto Zoe's lap and started to purr.

"Hey Lunar," Zoe stroked Lunar's head before turning her attention to Rafferty. "And who are you Mr. Beautiful?" She giggled when Rafferty rubbed his head lovingly against her.

"Well look at that." Erin frowned. "That cat has never done that to anyone else but Kelsey."

"They say cats can feel kindred souls." Logan lifted an eyebrow.

"That they can." Zane put his arm around his nephew. "He's an intelligent cat. I'll give you kids a hand getting settled and changed so I can get into these tunnels to see what's going on."

"Can I help you with the tunnels Uncle Zane?" Logan asked Zane. "You know I've been dying to get into them."

Logan, Zane, and Chase started walking back towards the hotel.

"Zoe," Erin looked down at the young girl, "I think we should go back to the hotel. Are you hungry?"

"I am," Zoe stood up holding Rafferty in one arm while she dusted herself off with the other.

Lunar and Goose started to bark. Erin frowned wondering why the dogs were barking at Zoe. At first she thought it was because the teen was paying more attention to Raffety. Then Zoe's eyes grow wide. Erin felt a shake. Her eyes fell on Zoe's feet where the sand was moving around them. Zoe threw Rafferty towards the dogs just before she started to sink.

"Zoe," Erin screamed, reaching for the teen as she disappeared. "Zane! Zane!" She screamed on the top of her voice.

Before she could get to the edge of the hole Lunar, Goose, and Rafferty all dove in after Zoe.

"Zane!" Erin stood screaming at the edge of the hole as she fell to her knees trying to see into the dark hole. "Zane!" She felt panic and fear claw at her heart. "Zoe, Zoe!" She tried to see into the tunnel. "Honey can you hear me?"

Erin raised her head to frantically look for Zane. She saw him, Chase, and Logan running back towards them.

"What happened?" Zane's eyes were filled with fear.

"Zoe," Erin pointed to the hole she was kneeling from.

Agitated frantic barking started to come from inside the tunnel.

"Zoe!" Logan started shouting down the tunnel.

"Zoe!" Chase's face was as grey as Logan's was, his eyes were filled with panic and fear. He shone his phone light into the hole. "I can see Goose."

"How deep do you think it is?" Logan looked at Chase.

"Don't you dare," Zane gave the two teenage boys a warning look. "I've called for help and if anyone is dropping down there it's me."

"That's not a good idea, Uncle Zane," Chase told him.

"Chase's right," Logan eyed his uncle up. "Don't take this the wrong way, you're in excellent shape for your age but Chase and I are not as heavy as you. We stand a better chance of not disturbing the tunnel more."

"They have a good point." Erin stood. She felt sick.

"I'm getting a rope," Zane ran off to the boat house.

As soon as his back was turned Logan shone his light into the hole.

"It's quite deep," Logan estimated the drop.

"Six foot? Seven foot?" Chase looked at Logan.

"The dogs can make that jump but I don't think we will," Logan told Chase honestly.

"I'm willing to take that chance," Chase was about to push himself into the tunnel when Erin stopped him.

"No," Erin put her hand on the young man's shoulder. "Don't. Here comes Zane with a rope."

"Zoe's hurt." Chase's eyes were filled with fear. "Listen to the dogs even the cat is meowing like crazy."

"Here," Zane tied the rope around Chase's waist, "Logan, you can help lower Chase down."

"Sure," Logan went to help his uncle.

Erin's phone rang and she answered it.

"Kelsey?" Erin greeted her daughter.

"Mom?" Kelsey's voice came through the receiver, "What's going on?"

"Where are you?" Erin turned around feeling relieved to see her daughter standing waving to her from the hotel. "Please honey bring your kit and get here now. We may need you."

"I'm on my way," Kelsey hung up.

"Kelsey's on her way," Erin swallowed.

"Good." Zane nodded as he and Logan lowered Chase down into the hole.

Erin's heart lurched. She felt responsible for Zoe's accident. She should've tried to catch her.

"Mom!" Kelsey stopped and stared at the holes in the ground. "What the heck?" She looked around. "Is someone down there?" Her eyes grew huge.

"Yes," Erin nodded, "Zane's great-niece got sucked into a sinkhole."

"How far down is it?" Kelsey looked at Zane.

"Around seven to eight foot," Logan told her. His jaw was clenched tight, and his hands shook slightly as he helped Zane lower Chase into the hole.

"Who's on the end of the rope?" Kelsey asked them.

"Chase," Logan answered. "He's my aunt's fiancé's son." He looked at Kelsey, "I'm Logan, Zoe's twin."

"Hi, Logan." Kelsey's eyes softened. "Chase?" She stepped up towards the hole.

"Don't get too close," Erin reached for her daughter as a feeling of vertigo took hold of her.

"It's okay mom." Kelsey smiled at her mom. "Chase?"

"I'm down," Chase called up.

"Can you see ..." Kelsey looked at Logan.

"Zoe," Logan told her.

"Can you see Zoe?" Kelsey called down to Chase. "Can you get the dogs?" She looked up at her mother questioningly with her brows drawn together.

"They jumped in after her," Erin explained.

"They've settled down," Chase called up. "I'm here with Zoe. She's not moving." His voice held a note of panic.

"Chase ...." Zane was about to say something, his voice was filled with the same panic's Chase's held.

"Zane," Kelsey held her hand up to silence and gave him a reassuring smile. "Chase, I'm Kelsey. I'm a doctor," she told the young man. "I need you to do something for me, okay?"

"Okay," Chase called up.

"Do you know how to feel for a pulse against her neck?" Kelsey asked him.

"Yes," Chase called up. "She has a pulse." He sounded relieved.

"What does it look like down there?" Kelsey asked him. "Is there enough room for me?"

"No," both Zane and Erin shouted at once.

Kelsey stopped both of them from arguing with her.

"Yes, if you're not too large and the size of maybe Miss Carnegie or Logan," Chase called up.

"Okay," Kelsey told him. "Can you untie the rope?"

Chase untied the rope and tugged when he had it untied.

"This is a bad idea," Zane warned her. His hands shook as he pulled the rope.

Nothing scared Zane but right now he felt an almost paralyzing fear that had his heart in a vice grip.

"I'll be okay," Kelsey told Zane as he tied the rope around Kelsey. "Chase, you're going to have to guide me down, so I don't land on you or Zoe."

"Okay," Chase called up.

"Mom," Kelsey looked at her mother as she got ready to jump into the tunnel, "please go find flashlights." Erin nodded and took off. Kelsey grabbed her bag. "Chase I'm throwing my bag down. Which side must I toss it to?"

"To your left," Chase shouted, catching her bag as she threw it down. "Got it."

*K*elsey hit the ground in the cold dark tunnel. She took the rope off.

"Hey Chase," Kelsey greeted the teenage boy. "Let's go have a look at Zoe."

"Hi," Chase said, swallowing down the lump in his throat. "Please let her be okay." His voice was hoarse with emotion.

"Let's stay positive," Kelsey said softly. "Can you hold your phone and mine for me." She stopped when she got to Zoe. "Rafferty?" Her brows drew together.

"He took a shine to Zoe," Chase explained.

"He never takes a shine to anyone." Kelsey looked amazed at her cat who was lying protectively next to Zoe's side. "I see she has all her protectors down here." She smiled at the two dogs lying next to the young teenage girl.

Kelsey dropped onto her knees next to Zoe. She passed Chase her phone and took her bag from him.

She started her examination while Chase stood holding the

flashlights giving her the light she needed. A few minutes later Erin called down to them that the rescue team was there.

One of the men called down to Kelsey for their status. Kelsey told them her findings before that passed down a stretcher. Chase helped Kelsey get Zoe onto the stretcher. They helped the rescue team lift Zoe out. As they waited for the harnesses to get the dogs and cat up there was a cracking noise. Chase and Kelsey looked at each other. That's when Kelsey saw the world above them start to crumble.

"Chase," Kelsey grabbed the tall young man and pulled him with her out the way.

The dogs started to bark, and Rafferty hissed while rocks tumbled in on the tunnel cutting off their path to the hole. They could hear Erin, Zane, and Logan screaming from above for them.

"What do we do now?" Chase looked at Kelsey before shining his light down the tunnel. "There's a breeze coming from down there."

"Are you okay?" Kelsey looked at him. She saw her bag lying on its side.

"Yeah," Chase nodded. "Are you?" he asked her.

"I think so," Kelsey smiled at him.

Kelsey's arm felt like it was on fire and her head hurt when she was hit by a rock, but she was still standing. She'd take stock of her injuries later. They needed to try to get out of there.

"Are all the fur people okay?" Kelsey did a quick scan of the animals. "I see Raffety is back on his chariot."

"Is he your cat?" Chase asked her.

"Yes," Kelsey nodded. "I think we need to get through this tunnel as quickly as we can."

"I saw the map of these tunnels," Chase told her. "There should be an opening at this end. I know Michael told us that the door was no longer locked."

"Well that's a bit of good news," Kelsey breathed. "Why would there be doors in tunnels?" She frowned.

Lunar and Goose led the way while Rafferty hitched a ride on Goose's back. Kelsey and Chase used their phones to light the way as they trailed behind the three animals.

Chapter Twenty-Six
OPEN SESAME

"Kelsey!" Erin dropped to the sand and started digging. "Chase!" Tears were streaming down her face.

"Erin," Zane dropped down on his knees next to her on the sand, "the rescue team are going to find them."

Zane was torn. He needed to go with Zoe, but Erin needed him.

"Zane, Erin!" Jennifer ran down the beach. "I came as soon as Phillip called me."

"Kelsey and Caleb," Erin dug through the sand. "They need us to dig them out." She frantically tried to move the sand.

"Erin," Zane swallowed, watching paramedics rush Zoe to the ambulance. He looked up at Jennifer.

"Go," Jennifer told Zane. "I'll stay here with Erin."

"Thank you," Zane kissed Erin on the head. "I'll be back as soon as I can."

"Go," Jennifer told him. "I'll take care of Erin and call you if there's any news."

"Thank you," Zane told Jennifer as he rushed off after Logan towards the ambulance.

"Jen, they're trapped." Erin's eyes were stained with tears

and filled with fear. "Help me!" she said to Jennifer. "Please, please, help me." She started crying as Jennifer pulled Erin to her. "Please help me save my baby and Daniel's baby."

"Hey," Jennifer held her and let her sob as the rescue teams worked to find a way to get through to Kelsey, Caleb, and their three trusty fur guardians. "They're going to be found."

"How did this happen?" Erin sobbed. "When did my world get so crazy?" All the pent-up fear, frustration, anger, and panic of the last few years bubbled up from deep inside her.

"Mom!" Caleb called to his mother as he ran over towards her with Lilly, Shane, and Amy hot on his heels.

Caleb dropped to his knees on the sand next to his mother.

Erin sat up and sifted through the sand again. "Kelsey and Chase are down there in the cold." She looked at Caleb. "She's trapped." Her eyes filled with tears again as her grief burst through her and doubled over her tears wetting the sand.

"Mom," Caleb wrapped his arms around, "we have to move." He looked over his mother's head to Jennifer for help.

"Erin," Jennifer said gently, "we need to move so the rescue team can work."

"No!" Erin shouted at them. "My babies are down there and Chase. No!"

"Mom," Caleb gently lifted her to her feet. "The rescue workers can't get to Kelsey and ..." he frowned at Jennifer.

"Chase," Jennifer told him.

"Chase," Caleb told her.

"Chase was so brave," Erin sniffed. "He was just going to jump right into the dark for Zoe." She wouldn't take her eyes off the sand as she allowed Caleb and Jennifer to walk her out of the way.

"Here you go." Lilly brought a blanket to cover Erin who was shivering from shock.

"Thank you," Caleb smiled at Lilly. "Where do these tunnels go?"

"My father and mother are going to work with the team and go in after them," Lilly told them. "He knows them best."

Erin said nothing but stood staring at the place where the world had collapsed in on her daughter and Chase.

"They were both so brave." Erin stood staring expressionless at the sand. "So brave." She whispered.

"I'm going to go help my parents." Lilly looked at Erin. "We'll find them." She turned to go but Erin grabbed her.

"NO!" Erin shook her head. "Don't Lilly, don't." She looked at Lilly, her eyes huge with fear. "Don't, please don't go down there."

"I'll be okay," Lilly gave Erin a hug. "I've asked my staff to bring some refreshments for you and the crew. They'll bring some sweet tea for Erin."

"Thank you, Lilly." Jennifer smiled at her niece.

"I've got to go help mom and dad." Lilly gave Erin another hug. "I'll find them for you."

"Thank you, Lilly." Erin held onto Lilly's hand. "Please, please, be careful."

"Yes," Caleb stepped past his mother and pulled Lilly to him, "be careful." He didn't care if Shane or the world was watching him as he kissed her. "I love you," he said softly to her.

"I love you." Lilly smiled up at him before going to help her parents.

"It's going to be okay." Caleb went and got some chairs for them.

"So, MIT?" Kelsey said to Chase as they made their way through the cave. "That's awesome."

"Yeah," Chase nodded. "I liked their Bachelor of Science in Mechanical and Ocean Engineering course they offer," Chase explained. "My new mother got the same degree there."

"So your new mother is Zane's oldest niece, Fallon?" Kelsey stepped over the debris in the tunnel.

"Yeah," Chase nodded. "She's awesome," he said. "She's an amazing marine engineer. You should see the Dorothy Rose. It's a yacht she designed."

"I take it you love yachts?" Kelsey grinned.

"I do," Chase smiled. "My father and I sail a lot."

"Look there." Kelsey shone her light on the opening where the dogs and Rafferty were digging and sniffing around. "Does that look like a ..."

"Door?" Chase looked up at it and nodded before glancing down at his phone. There was still a lot of battery but no reception bars. "Do you have any bars on your phone?"

"No," Kelsey shook her head, "nothing."

Kelsey and Chase carefully made their way towards it.

"I thought you said Michael told you the doors were no longer locked," Kelsey and Chase pushed on the door while Goose, Lunar, and even King Rafferty dug at the bottom of it.

"It's moving," Chase told her. "Step back." He gave the door a good karate kick.

The door moved. Chase kicked it again and the door cracked open. Sand started to trickle down from the roof of the tunnel behind them followed by a few rocks.

"Quick!" Kelsey helped Chase heave the stubborn door open. "Why can't anything be as easy as open sesame like in the cartoons?" As she said that the door moved.

Goose, Lunar, and Rafferty pushed their way through the door opening. Kelsey pushed Chase through before grabbing her bag she'd put on the ground and jumping through. Kelsey and Chase pushed the door closed as sand and rock poured down in the tunnel. They managed to push the door shut just in time as they heard the awful sound of a cave in.

"I guess it does work after all." Kelsey breathed a sigh of relief and rested her forehead against the door for a few seconds.

Chase turned and shone his light around the cavern to see where they were.

"Kelsey," Chase turned around and tapped her on the shoulder, "look. We're in some sort of cave."

Kelsey turned around. Lunar, Goose, and Rafferty were all sniffing around the small cavern they were in.

"We must be in Pirates Wall," Kelsey's eyes drew together.

"I was thinking the same thing," Chase said. "If I weren't so worried about how Zoe was doing, I'd be really excited. We weren't able to get that door open before. It unlocked but it was badly stuck."

"I wonder what caused the cave-in?" Kelsey shone her phone light over the wall. "It's really cold in here." She shivered. "Whatever did it must have jolted the door as well, thank goodness."

Chase took off the cotton shirt he had over his T-Shirt. It was a long sleeve shirt with the sleeves rolled up to his biceps.

"Here," Chase handed the shirt to Kelsey. "It's not much but it will help a bit."

"Thank you." Kelsey smiled at the well-mannered young man. "I see your father taught you well."

"My dad has always said be courteous, kind, and mind your manners." Chase smiled.

"He sounds like a great dad." Kelsey swallowed as she pulled the warm cotton shirt on and rolled down the sleeves.

"He's the best. But my new mom's brother, Uncle Zane, and granddad Finn are all great," Chase told her. "I'm really happy my father found Fallon."

"How does Zoe fit into that big heart of yours?" Kelsey gave him a warm smile.

"She's special," Chase told Kelsey, "and brilliant. I mean brilliant on a level that a mere mortal like me couldn't begin to imagine."

"Ah," Kelsey nodded as they walked around the cave looking for a way out. "She's Zane's supercomputer great-niece."

"Yes," Chase gave a laugh. "Her twin brother Logan, I think you met him, the fourteen-year-old giant?"

"Yes," Kelsey nodded. "He was the only one I could get any coherent information from."

"That's Logan," Chase nodded. "He's also super intelligent. But he's more down-to-earth while Zoe's brain is wired differently."

"Does she know how you feel about her?" Kelsey asked him softly.

"We're good friends," Chase shrugged. "I hate that people don't understand her, you know?"

"I get that," Kelsey smiled. "When I was young, all my dolls were my patients, and I collected those medical skeletons?" She grinned as he looked at her with a smile. "While other kids were playing stupid computer games or throwing princess parties, I was dissecting my skeletons and wishing I had a doll that had human insides I could work on."

"I designed Lego ships and used the engines from my Techtronic kits to power them," Chase grinned. "I was never allowed anywhere without at least one bodyguard."

"Oh, that right." Kelsey looked at Chase. "Your father's the billionaire Daniel Goddard?"

"Yeah," Chase sighed. "When we went to Florida and stayed with the McCaids it was the first time in my life I felt my age and could have fun."

"Zane told me the story," Kelsey laughed.

Chase shone his light over the walls of the small cavern to make sure they were stable.

"Look on that wall," Chase walked up to it and ran his hand over a small carving in it.

"It's a carving of a ship." Kelsey's brows drew together.

"Look there's another one." Caleb walked to the next one. There were another six along the wall that faced the door they had come through to get into the small cavern.

"Lilly and my brother Caleb found some more caverns

further back — more towards the forest side." Kelsey followed Chase as she looked at the carvings. "It also had carvings like this in the rock wall."

"Do you think the hidden yacht the Guilford Jewel is in here with all the missing treasure?" Chase's eyes sparkled with excitement.

"It must be." Kelsey felt adrenaline spurt through her as butterflies flapped excitedly in her stomach. "Come on."

They followed the wall until they came across a small opening where the animals were lying waiting for them. Rocks had tumbled down and blocked most of the small entrance that Kelsey could see was another cavern. She couldn't see how big it was without squeezing through the small opening.

"Do you think we could move some of these rocks?" Chase started moving boulders. "You're tiny so I think you might be able to squeeze through. But my shoulders won't get through there and neither will Goose."

Kelsey and Chase grinned as the big dog barked at him as if to say *Hey watch it!* While they could've sworn Rafferty sniggered.

"Your cat is really weird." Chase shook his head when Rafferty jumped up onto one of the rocks that they tossed off the pile blocking their passage.

"He thinks he's a dog." Kelsey pulled a comical face. "He used to always attack my ex-fiancé. Rafferty really didn't like the guy."

"Logan said that animals are a good judge of character." Chase carefully selected another boulder. "Wait!" He stopped Kelsey from taking one of the rocks. "Work with me. We don't want to cause another rockslide."

"Oh, right." Kelsey nodded and moved the rocks Chase pointed out. "Logan is only fourteen?"

"Yeah," Chase nodded. "He is almost six foot."

"That's above average for a teenager of fourteen." Kelsey wiped a stray hair out of her face. "Although you're tall for eighteen as well." She looked at the young man with his lean muscular build that was still developing. "You're about …"

"Six-foot-one," Chase smiled at her, "or just shy of six-two if you want to be exact." He smiled. "Zoe likes to be exact."

"She's going to be alright, Chase." Kelsey patted him on the back. "As soon as we're out of here I'll take you to see her," she promised him. "Dr. Barnes was still on duty when I left and I'm sure as soon as he saw Zane, he'd have taken care of Zoe."

"Thank you," Chase gave Zoe a small smile. "I just wish I knew for sure."

"I know," Kelsey breathed. "My mom and Zane are probably frantic about us."

"I wish my dad was here," Chase said softly.

"Trust me," Kelsey told him, "you may not know this but the minute my mother met your whole family, you became a part of hers. So she's up there right now making sure we're both found."

"Or down there," Chase gave her a cheeky smile. "Sorry, been hanging around with Zoe too much."

Rafferty's fur suddenly stood on end. Luna and Goose shot to their feet and started to growl. Chase and Kelsey stopped moving the rocks and looked around the cavern. A blast echoed off the hollow walls and the entire cave shook. The rocks they were trying to move started to tumble around them.

"Kelsey, watch out," Chase dived at her, pulling her out of the way. Rafferty, Lunar, and Goose managed to jump away just in time as the boulders spewed out into the cavern.

"What in blazes was that?" Kelsey stood up and froze. "Chase." She kneeled next to him.

Chase lay sprawled out on the shingled floor of the cold cavern.

"I'm fine," Chase turned over and rubbed his head. "Sorry about dive tackling you. Are you hurt?"

"Just a scratch." Kelsey noted blood seeping out of a gash on her arm. "Let me take a look at your head."

"I'm fine," Chase tried to stop her from worrying.

"I'm looking anyway and I'm the adult here," Kelsey's eyes widened. "As frightening as that sounds." She smiled and pulled her phone out of her pocket and shone it on Chase's head. "Yeah, that's going to need a stitch or two."

"I think your arms are going to need the same." Chase pointed to the blood dripping from the wound.

"Probably," Kelsey shrugged. "I have some bandages in my bag."

Luckily, she'd left her bag in a safe corner. She picked it up and pulled out some supplies. She poured peroxide on her arm and kept her cussing in her head as the liquid bubbled out anything that may have gotten into the open cut. Kelsey covered it with a bandage and then went to tend to Chase's head.

"I have to disinfect it," Kelsey apologized before swabbing his cut with some disinfectant before putting gauze on it and wrapping a bandage around his head. "Sorry it has to be a bandage that's going to make you look like you had brain surgery." She secured it with a clip. "But we have to keep germs out."

"It's kind of cool." Chase felt the bandage on his head. "Do you have an eye patch?" He grinned.

"Do you have a headache?" Kelsey checked his reactions.

"A bit, but now I'm seeing dots from your light," Chase told her flinching.

"You sit still for a bit and have some water." Kelsey pulled a bottle of water from her bag then noticed three animals' ears perk up as they looked at her. "Are you three thirsty?"

Kelsey pulled a few more bottles of water from her bag.

"Geez," Chase looked at the bag. "Do you have candy in there?"

"As a matter of fact," Kelsey pulled out an energy bar, "here." She threw it at him.

227

Kelsey poured some water into the palm of her hand and gave each animal a chance to have some water.

"Uh..." Chase called Kelsey. "Why is your cat eyeing me out like he wants to eat me?"

"He wants your energy bar," Kelsey told him. "I made the mistake of leaving a few next to my bed for my low blood sugar." She shook her head. "I came home one night and found he'd helped himself to a few of them. It was something I felt awful having to explain to a very condescending vet."

"Weird." Chase took a bite of the energy bar while keeping a vigilant eye on Rafferty who was sneaking up on him.

"I'm going to take a look into that cavern," Kelsey told Chase. "Whatever that blast was, it opened the path."

"Are there excavations somewhere?" Chase asked her. "Because that sounded like a blasting explosion to me."

"Not that I know of." Kelsey frowned as she stepped cautiously into the larger cavern.

Chapter Twenty-Seven
THE SECRET WITHIN PIRATES WALL

"What the heck was that?" Caleb immediately put his hand out to stabilize Erin's chair.

Lilly came running towards them. She had a harness around her like the ones they used to lower people into tunnels.

"Are you all alright?" Lilly asked the three of them.

"What was that?" Jennifer asked Lilly.

"My dad said it felt like an explosion of sorts." Lilly stopped in front of them. "He's called a friend of his to bring my father's helicopter to go and investigate."

"Your father has a helicopter?" Caleb looked at Lilly in amazement.

"Yeah," Lilly nodded distractedly. "I'm just warning you because it's going to land to the left of you on the back grass near the parking lot so there may be some sand spray."

"How are you going to get into the tunnel?" Caleb asked Lilly.

"We're not going in from this side of the tunnels," Lilly told them. "We're going to go in from up there." She pointed to the small platform at the end of Pirates wall with the weird looking boulder that looked like it was blocking the entrance to a cave.

"What are the rescue team doing?" Erin's eyes were a little glazed as she looked at Lilly.

"They're trying to clear away the debris as fast as possible to get in from this side," Lilly explained to Erin. "But that blast didn't help their job."

The noise of a helicopter had all their heads except Erin's turn to see it land.

"That's my ride." Lilly was about to leave when Caleb stood up. "I'm going with you."

"No," Erin grabbed Caleb's hand.

"I'll be alright mom," Caleb said softly and kissed her head. "Jennifer is here with you and I'll keep you updated." He kissed Erin again before following Lilly to the helicopter.

"How is she?" Zane asked as Dr. Barnes came through to the family waiting room nearly knocking over Logan, who'd jumped up at the same time.

"She is one lucky young lady," Dr. Barnes told them. "There are no fractured ribs although they are bruised, but she does have a severely sprained ankle and a fractured wrist."

"And the lump on her head?" Logan asked Dr. Barnes.

"We're keeping an eye on it but so far there's no swelling around the brain." Dr. Barnes gave Logan a warm smile. "You can go in to see her in a few minutes. I'll have the nurse come by and call you. I've put her in the room across from Michael's."

"Thank you, Dr. Barnes." Some color came back into Zane's face.

"Can we go see Michael while we wait to go see Zoe if he's just across the hall from her?" Logan asked Dr. Barnes.

"Of course," Dr. Barnes led the way. "I'm sure Michael will be happy to see you both. He's been ringing the bell ever since he saw us wheel Zoe into the room across from his."

"Thank you once again, Dr. Barnes," Zane breathed and walked into Michael's room.

"Did I just see Zoe being taken into that room?" Michael had been allowed to sit up. "Hey Logan," he greeted the tall teenager.

"Hi," Logan looked at Michael. "I hear you got shot." He lifted his eyebrows.

"I did," Michael nodded. "It's not as fun as you'd think it would be."

Logan laughed at Michael's sarcasm.

"Hello to you too Michael." Zane drawled as he stood looking down at him.

"Sorry," Michael looked up at Zane. "Hi Zane, how are you today and what the heck is going on? Why is Zoe in the hospital?" He looked at Logan. "When did you and sister arrive?"

"We got here earlier today," Logan told him before he launched into what was happening at the Cove. He left off the last bit about Kelsey and Chase being stuck down there.

"Why are the tunnels suddenly collapsing?" Michael frowned. "Where are Chase and Kelsey? I'd thought Chase wouldn't have left Zoe's side at a time like this and I know Kelsey wouldn't leave a patient on their own."

"They're stuck down in the tunnel," Logan blurted out, ignoring the black look from his uncle.

"What?" Michael started trying to pull his drips out, but Zane stopped him.

"What are you doing?" Zane growled at Michael.

"I need to get out of here," Michael hissed. "Kelsey and Chase need me."

"No," Zane pushed Michaels legs back onto the bed. "They need you to stay here and follow Dr. Barnes's orders."

"No one knows the tunnels like I do," Michael told Zane and Logan. "I think there's another way into them from the tunnel that runs from where the old barn used to stand."

"I'll tell Shane and Lilly," Zane promised Michael.

"Lilly's back?" Michael looked at Zane in shock. "Why didn't someone tell me?"

"Because they're under strict orders to keep you calm," Dr. Barnes walked into his room. "Your heart rate has spiked." He looked at Michael.

"Well, I'm agitated with being stuck in this bed while my family and the wo..," Michael stopped, "Chase and Kelsey are stuck in the tunnels."

"You're not going to be much help to them in your condition," Dr. Barnes told Michael. "If you did go there like this, you'd only cause more problems when you collapsed."

"Lilly knows the tunnels just as well as you do," Zane told Michael.

"You can go see Zoe now," Dr. Barnes told Zane and Logan. "You can stay right there in that bed. Your mother has given me permission to strap you down if I have to," he warned Michael before he left his room.

"I'll update you if I hear anything," Logan told Michael. "I'm just shooting over to see my sister."

"Thanks," Michael nodded at Logan. "Tell Zoe hi."

"Will do," Logan nodded and left the room.

🦀

*C*aleb and Shane abseiled down the rocky cliff of Pirates Wall to land on the ledge where Lilly and Amy were waiting for them. While they unclipped their harnesses from the ropes the helicopter took off overhead.

"Shane," the pilot's voice came over the small handheld radio Shane had.

"I'm here," Shane said into the radio.

"I see three men standing on the cliffs on just beyond the reserve. They look like they have some sort of device," the pilot told him. "I'll get Phillip and his men out that way."

"Great," Shane said into the device. "We're about to try and get into the cave."

"Radio when you need me." The pilot took off in the direction of White Sands Cove to fetch Phillip and his team.

"Do you think someone's blasting my Cove?" Lilly said angrily.

"Not sure, sweetheart," Zane told her. "Let's just concentrate on finding Kelsey and Chase."

Zane had no sooner finished talking when another muffled blast shook the cave.

"This isn't a rock." Caleb felt around the structure. "It feels like wood?" He knocked on it.

"Painted very cleverly to look like a rock," Amy frowned as she ran her hands around the one side of it. "It's a large round tree trunk." She looked amazed. "Someone carved it to look like the shape of a rock and painted it."

"It shouldn't be that hard to move then." Shane carefully edged past his wife. "Can you give me a hand, Caleb?"

"Of course," Caleb stepped up to help him.

"Or maybe you both just try to move those stones wedged beneath it that are keeping it in place." Lilly folded her arms and tilted her head.

Lilly knelt in front of the huge door. The bottom of the trunk had groves in it like a cog. There were large rocks wedged between the groove keeping the door in place.

"That's really clever." Shane frowned. "They won't budge." He tried to pull one out.

"Help me dig away some of the sand and dirt," Lilly dug around the one stone with her mother's help. "Try now." She sat back.

Caleb bent down and moved the first rock. It had been carved out to fit into the groove. Once they'd removed the two large stones on eight sides of the door and the four stones wedged in the grooves, Caleb and Shane pushed the door to one side while Lilly and Amy placed the rock back into place to keep the door open.

All four of them stood looking in amazement into the cavern. Shane turned on the flashlight he had on his head and the larger more powerful one he had in his hands. There were crude steps carved out of stone leading down into the belly of the cavern.

"Look," Lilly sucked in her breath. "There are paintings on the walls." She shone her flashlight around it.

"It's a story." Caleb walked up to one of the pictures. "Two ships set sail from France." His light trailed across the wall. "They were ladened with treasure and a ..." He frowned and looked closer. "Is that a king and queen?"

"No," Lilly smiled and shook her head. "It's my great-great-grandparents." She ran her hands over the depiction of them. "Look here; it has something to do with pirates. What does 'cacher le trésor' mean?" She looked at her mother.

"To hide or have to hide the treasure." Amy stepped up next to her daughter.

There was a picture that looked like a giant with a wide chest and thick arms. In each of his hands he held the two ships.

"In the uneven arms of the giant that watches over us," Amy finished translating the rest of the text carved into the wall beneath the picture of the giant.

"Wait," Shane stepped back up onto one of the steps and shone his torch on the wall changing it to a black light. "Look here."

Lilly, Caleb, and Amy rushed up the steps to see what Shane was seeing.

"Holy starfish," Lilly gaped at the wall. "I think we just hit the jackpot."

Before they could say anything else they heard a dog bark that sounded a lot like...

"Goose!" all four of them said together and went as quickly as they could towards the sound.

*G*oose barked to get Chase and Kelsey's attention. They shone their lights to where Goose was standing. There was another opening on the other side of the large cavern they'd just stepped into.

"What is it boy?" Chase walked over to the big dog and patted his head then nearly got knocked over when Lunar ran past him and through the opening. "Lunar." Chase yelled and then ducked as Rafferty flew onto Goose's back as he took off after Lunar.

"What is up with ..." Chase turned towards Kelsey and froze as his light picked up something glinting from another small window type opening on the one side of the wall. "Kelsey, look at this." He walked forward towards the glinting. "There's something through here."

Kelsey turned and looked at Chase as he ducked and climbed through the opening. Kelsey followed him. What they found on the other side made them catch their breath.

"*T*he dogs and that crazy cat of my sisters came from this way." Caleb hurried back the way the animals had come. "Look," he shone his light on the walls. "The picture of the ship on the wall. It's sailing the way we're walking."

The dogs barked excitedly and ran past the four of them to lead them to where they'd left Kelsey and Chase.

"Kelsey, Chase!" Lilly called as she stepped through an opening where the dogs and Rafferty stopped and started to bark.

235

"Lilly?" Chase popped his head out of a small opening in the wall. "Hi Amy and Shane." He squinted at Caleb.

"Caleb," Caleb stepped up to the young man. "You must be a Chase?" The young man nodded. "Where's my sister?"

"I'm in here," Kelsey called. "Come on in."

Caleb turned and looked at the curious expressions and the other three people's faces. Before he shrugged and squeezed himself into the cavern.

"Holy...." Caleb's voice echoed back to the other three.

Lilly popped in next followed by Amy and Shane.

"Oh, my," Amy breathed at the sight in front of her.

"Well I'll be..." Shane whistled as he managed to squeeze himself through the window.

Chapter Twenty-Eight
FIRST DATES

*E*rin, Jennifer, Kelsey, Chase, Lilly, and Caleb walked into the hospital to go find Zane and Logan. They had gifts for both Michael and Zoe. Excitement bubbled inside each of them with the news they had to share with the four people who weren't there to share in the findings at the Cove.

"Do you mind if I go tell Michael?" Kelsey asked.

"Of course," Jennifer smiled at her. "Here take him these Pop-Tarts. That'll sweeten him up a bit. Zane said he was a bit surly because he'd missed all the action."

"Thanks," Kelsey took the Pop-Tarts even knowing there was no way she'd let him eat them at this moment.

"Kelsey," Michael breathed a sigh of relief and held out his arms.

She went to him and he gave her a hug that she felt wasn't the kind of hug she wanted from him.

"Your mom sent you these," Kelsey put on a brave smile, "but as your doctor. I'm telling you can't have them." She grinned and went to put them in a locker out of his reach.

"That's just mean," Michael glared at her. "How are you?"

"I'm fine," Kelsey showed him her arm, "I have stitches in my arm and Chase has them in his head. He's such a nice kid."

"Hey," Michael raised an eyebrow as an emotion Kelsey could not quite make out flashed in his eyes. "He's almost or is nineteen, so he's not that much younger than us. But I'm afraid you've lost out there because he's totally smitten with Zoe the cyborg."

"Come on," Kelsey laughed at him. "First, while Chase is gorgeous, he isn't my type and way too young for me. Second, I'm sure Zoe isn't as bad as everyone makes her out to be."

"Zane said you found something in Pirates Wall." Michael looked both excited and disappointed. "I wish I was there for that discovery."

"Then you would've been both excited and disappointed," Kelsey told him. "It was an awesome discovery, but not the one you were hoping for."

"No treasure?" Michael's face fell.

"Oh, no, there was treasure," Kelsey said. "Well, at least we think there was. Shane, Max, and Zane are going to go explore it."

"But it wasn't the lost treasure we were hoping for?"

"Shane seems to think the treasure may have been there but moved." Kelsey frowned. "They found some old documents your mom and Amy are going to translate."

"Agghhh," Michael put his head back on the pillow. "Not more French!"

"I'm afraid so." Kelsey laughed.

"About what we were speaking about before," Michael smiled at Kelsey. "I'd like to make an official date with you."

Kelsey's heart started to pound in her chest. Was Michael asking her out instead of trying to set her up with his friend?

"Okay?" Kelsey looked at him holding her breath.

"The day I get out of here," Michael smiled at her, "I'm going to introduce you to that someone special I know you are going to fall in love with."

Kelsey's heart once again dropped to her feet. She'd foolishly hoped Michael was going to ask her out on their first official date and had forgotten about him setting her up with his friend. She plastered a smile on her face.

"Sure," Kelsey nodded. *Didn't Michael realize he was the one she wanted to have a first date with, not some friend of his she'd never met?* "What's his name?"

"We call him Phantom," Michael laughed. "I just know you're going to love him. He's everything you've ever wanted."

Kelsey nodded. *What a stupid name. What was this guy a rock star or something?*

Kelsey excused herself and left Michael's room. When she was clear she ran into the ladies' restrooms. Kelsey ran into a stall and burst into tears.

"Kelsey?" Lilly's soft voice came to her as Lilly knocked on the toilet door. "Are you okay?"

"I'm fine," Kelsey lied. "Just a little stressed from everything that's happened."

"I'm here if you need to talk about it," Lilly said.

Michael had convinced Dr. Barnes to let him go to Zoe's room. A nurse had sat Michael in a wheelchair and taken him over there. Before the nurse left, she'd warned Michael not to get out of the chair.

Chase, Logan, Jennifer, Caleb, Kelsey, Lilly, Erin, Michael, and Zane all discussed the happenings and secrets that had been found at the Cove.

"Erin," Zane came up behind and said quietly. "Could I have a word outside?"

Erin looked up at Zane a little worriedly. She was convinced he was going to give her an earful for not protecting Zoe. She didn't know if she could take that at the moment after having a melt down when Kelsey and Chase had been trapped in the tunnel. But she was tough; she could take whatever he had to say.

"Sure," Erin looked at the room. "Does anyone want a snack?" she asked and was bombarded with orders. "Zane and I'll be back with them shortly." She managed a smile.

"Did you get all that?" Zane asked Erin as they walked out of the room.

"Yes," Erin gave Zane a tight smile. "You wanted to have a word?" she said bracing herself.

"Yes," Zane said rather awkwardly. He wasn't good with this type of stuff. "I wanted to know if you'd like to have dinner with me tomorrow night?"

Erin stopped and looked up at him a little stunned. *That's what he wanted to speak to her about?* Relief flooded through her. She didn't know whether to laugh, cry, or throw her arms around his neck and kiss him.

"On a date?" Erin asked him just to make sure she was not misreading the situation.

"Yes," Zane cleared his throat. "Our first official date, of which I'm hoping we'll have many more."

Erin's heart kicked into overdrive and her cheeks went pink as the butterflies danced inside her.

"Yes," Erin smiled.

Erin wasn't sure if she moved towards Zane or Zane moved towards her, but she was soon folded in his strong arms and with his lips crushing hers.

EPILOGUE

Kelsey had left the hospital before everyone else. She needed to be on her own to gather her thoughts and figure out how she could get Michael to notice her the way she noticed him.

Kelsey had gone back to the cabin at White Sands Cove and decided to go for a walk past the small farm that formed part of the retreat. It had horses, donkeys, and Egyptian geese. She hadn't yet had a chance to explore the small farm. Michael had told her they might expand it as they had the land to do so, but that was a project for the future.

She sighed as she walked towards the lake that sprawled out behind the hotel and was shared by the nature reserve behind them. Although the retreat was fenced off the fence ended at the lake. There was a gate you had to go through to get to it. But the warning signs warned people against it and the gate had a huge padlock on it.

Kelsey took a seat on one of the benches that overlooked the lake to soak up the late afternoon sun and enjoy the peace while she sorted out her thoughts.

*B*eautiful big brown eyes watched Kelsey from where he stood. He was also enjoying the peace and quiet while soaking up the last rays of the sun. He was about to amble over to her as she looked a little sad, but the sound of barking stopped him. He turned his head towards the sound. His pure white locks flowed with the movement, glinting like snowflakes in the sun. The two dogs and a large cat rushed over to where Kelsey sat making her laugh. That was his cue to turn and make his way home for the night.

SECRETS OF WHITE SANDS COVE

Book 5

PROLOGUE

After Kelsey and Michael's initial disastrous meeting they'd managed to put their differences aside and become close friends. The more time they spend together the more they come to realize their feelings run a lot deeper than friendship. Kelsey doesn't know if she's ready for another relationship after her last eighteen months of hell.

Michael thought he'd met the one at the age of nineteen. She was everything he'd thought he could ever want in a woman. When college took them in opposite directions Michael soon found out that she didn't feel the same way. After a humiliating experience and having his heart shattered, Michael no longer wears his heart on his sleeve. He keeps it under lock and key. Kelsey deserved someone with a whole heart that wasn't jaded like his.

When Michael and Kelsey find themselves in a dangerous situation, they're forced to face some hard truths as the only way out of the situation is through it. They need to trust and count on each other even if it means facing their worst fears and opening up their hearts.

Chapter Twenty-Nine
REMEMBERING A HERO

It was supposed to have been their fourth date, but Michael was coming home. So Erin and Zane had decided to join Lilly, Caleb, and Kelsey at his welcome home dinner. Zane missed his family terribly. His nieces and nephew had been like his own kids because he and his father had raised them after their parents' accident. After he lost the love of his life, Zane took it as a sign from the universe and concentrated on his immediate family.

There had been a lot of ups and downs, sibling feuds, but Zane wouldn't have changed it for the world. Although his family had gone off and started their own family, there was still a lot of unfinished business within the family unit. A traumatic event had brought the family unit back together. Even though all the McCaids were under the same roof once again, they were still broken. It had taken a dangerous adventure that forced the family to unite and sewed up the ripped seams and healed old wounds.

Now all his adult kids' hearts had found their forever homes. Zane was sure of it and had never seen them happier. They were all off on a one month cruise before their triple wedding. Only his one niece Piper and her husband Alex had stayed behind because she was pregnant, and sailing made her terribly ill. Zane was glad she had because he'd volunteered to plan the weddings and had found that it may not have been the best thing for him to promise. But Piper and Alex had taken over the planning along with Lilly.

The past couple of weeks at White Sands Cove have been a little rocky with everything that had happened to Lilly, Caleb, Kelsey, and Michael, but that was all behind them now. Zane's great-niece and great-nephews had just arrived after having flown in from one of the ports the rest of his family had stopped at. They'd had enough of the high seas and wanted to spend some of the summer at the retreat. Their arrival coincided with the collapse of the old tunnels that ran beneath part of White Sands Cove beach.

Zoe had landed up in hospital while Kelsey and Chase were trapped down in the tunnels. It was Kelsey and Chase that had made an amazing discovery in the caves at the end of the tunnel. While trying to rescue them, Lilly's father Shane had found out the reason the tunnels had collapsed. Some men had overheard Lilly and Michael telling Kelsey and Caleb about the caves that were supposedly within Pirates Wall. After diving to try and find them, the men had decided to try and blast their way into them. A series of explosions had caused parts of the cave and a few of the underground tunnels to collapse.

Zane had hired someone to get the tunnels cleared and closed them up so they wouldn't collapse ever again. He still felt cold inside when he realized that Zoe had been sucked into one of the tunnels. Poor Erin had become near hysterical after Zoe was lifted out and the tunnel caved in trapping Kelsey and Chase. Zane hadn't been there for her because he had to go with Zoe in the ambulance to the hospital.

After all that had gone on, Zane had finally asked Erin out on a date. It had been an amazing first date. They'd gone out for dinner at Seafield House restaurant and then for a walk along Coast Walk. He hadn't felt this way about another woman in twelve years. It had been so great to feel a strong connection like he felt with Erin again. They'd gone out two more times after that on an official date, but they had spent nearly every day together. She'd been helping Zane, Lilly, Piper, and Alex with the wedding preparations.

Being with Erin was also the first time Zane had dated a woman without feeling like he was cheating. Zane swallowed. Even after all these years thinking about what happened made him ache. His family filled up most of his heart. But there was still a big part of it that he'd boxed up and stored away with the rest of his memories of another fiery haired beauty. Then Erin had come along and slowly made him realize he needed to sort out those memories and put them away where they belong. It was time to make space for new memories. Zane may never be able to forgive himself for what happened, but maybe he could make peace with it, with her!

"Zane?" Erin called. "Are you okay?"

"Oh," Zane shook himself from his reverie. He'd been waiting for Erin down by the rocks just below the Crab Shack. He held out the long stem red rose he'd picked from Lilly's garden. "Hi." He grinned and pulled her to him for a kiss.

"Thank you for the rose, it's beautiful." Erin took the rose and smiled up at him.

"Not as beautiful as the woman holding it." Zane kissed her again.

"You are such a sweet talker, Zane McCaid." Erin sighed as she looked past him. "Is this for me?" She looked past Zane to the flat rock with a picnic blanket, a few cushions, and a picnic basket on it.

"It is." Zane grinned and took her hand as he helped her over the few rocks to the picnic. "I figured as our date was cancelled tonight we could have a light picnic lunch instead."

"Who knew that the tough, rugged, Zane McCaid was so romantic?" Erin said breathlessly as Zane helped her onto a cushion.

"I would say more selfishly wanting some alone time with you." Zane grinned, sitting down next to her. "The hotel kitchen made us some cheese, crackers, fruit, and champagne."

"Oh, lovely." Erin took the glass he handed her and watched while he filled it up.

"How did the crockery and cutlery selections for the wedding go this morning?" Zane asked Erin.

"I think your nieces and nephew's fiancé have finally agreed on them." Erin clinked her glass with Zane's.

"You don't know how much I owe you for taking this off my hands," Zane breathed. "I would've just gone with paper plates if not for you, Lilly, and Piper."

"You know, I actually believe that," Erin laughed and took a sip of her drink. "So do you want to tell me what had you staring so wistfully out to sea a few minutes ago?"

"I was just thinking how great these past few weeks have been," Zane smiled. "The tunnels are now sealed. Zoe's okay. So are Kelsey and Chase. Now Michael's coming home, and this weekend we're going to explore the caves." He gave her a big smile. "I've loved spending time with you, and everything seems so right."

"I know what you mean." Erin put her head on his shoulder while they sat and stared out to sea. "I feel the exact same way."

"I guess after all the drama we've both had these past few years I keep expecting the other shoe to drop when we have these perfect moments." Zane put his arm around her shoulders, enjoying the feeling of having her in his arms.

"You know about most of my past, yet I hardly know anything about yours." Erin sat up to take a sip of her bubbly drink.

"What do you want to know?" Zane asked her as he took a few grapes.

"Have you ever been married?" Erin took some cheese and crackers.

"No," Zane swallowed. He knew he'd have to tell her sometime and now seemed as good a time as any. "I was engaged for a few years once."

"Oh," Erin looked a little surprised. "Do you mind me asking what happened?"

"No," Zane shook his head. "I would've told you eventually." He gave her a small smile.

"You don't have to tell me if you don't want to," Erin said quickly, seeing the hurt shadow his eyes.

"It's fine," Zane nodded. "I just haven't spoken about it in a long time."

"What happened?" Erin looked at Zane questioningly. "Why didn't you get married?"

"I got engaged to the most wonderful woman," Zane smiled sadly out to sea. "She had fiery red hair, jewel green eyes, and a heart as big as the ocean."

"She sounds like a princess," Erin smiled.

"My great-niece Blair was three and my other great-niece, Paige, was two when Ria and I got engaged." Zane looked off in the distance. His mind went back to that year. "That was fourteen years ago. Ria loved those two little girls and we got engaged at Disney World in Florida."

"How awesome." Erin took another cheesy cracker. "I've always loved Disney World. I bet the young ones were thrilled."

"I'd like to think so, but their parents insisted the girls were too young to remember." Zane shook his head. "Ria was a firefighter. We were engaged for two years and three months before our wedding ..." He closed his eyes and swallowed. His throat felt dry again.

"Oh, Zane." Erin's eyes misted with tears as she could feel his pain and knew instantly that it wasn't a breakup that ended their engagement.

"We were taking Blair and Paige to visit their aunt in Miami." Zane ran his hands through his hair. "We stopped at a gas station because the girls needed the toilet." He closed his eyes again. "It all happened so fast, but in that moment every second felt like a lifetime."

Erin took Zane's hand in hers and gave him a warm smile.

"Ria thought she could smell gas while they were in the restrooms and wanted to check it out," Zane explained. "She told me to take the girls and park a block away."

"What did you do?" Erin's eyes were huge as she listed to Zane's story.

"In that moment, my heart filled with fear and panic," Zane said. "I had this awful premonition that something wasn't right." He swallowed. "I wanted to yell at her that we all needed to get the hell out of there now. But Ria ..."

"Was a hero, like you," Erin said softly.

"I was no hero that day," Zane closed his eyes and shook his. "I had a split second to make a decision. I knew as soon as Ria opened that door something bad was about to happen." He took a deep breath. "That's when I felt Blair's soft hand in mine and Paige's little arms wrapped trustingly around my neck."

"You made a choice any parent or uncle would make," Erin instinctively knew what he was about to say next.

"I left her," Zane cleared his throat. "I let Ria go through that door alone." Tears glittered in his eyes. "I took Blair and Paige and ran while I phoned emergency services."

"Ria was a firefighter," Erin reasoned. "You know that she wanted you to get the girls to safety. There was nothing you could've said or done that would've stopped her from doing what she was trained to do."

"I know," Zane wiped the tears from his eyes. "We had just cleared a block when she messaged me she'd found the leak. The gas station owner had passed out trying to put off the gas main. Just as relief was flooding me, a blast ripped through the area."

"Oh, no." Tears spilled down Erin's cheeks. No wonder Zane had closed up his heart for so long. Not only did he lose the woman he loved, but he felt guilty for having abandoned her.

"The fire chief said that while Ria was pulling the man to safety a customer, a nineteen-year-old kid, walked into the store smoking a cigarette." Zane swallowed again. "What idiot smokes around a gas station when there are clear warning signs not to?"

"Teenagers always push the boundaries." Erin sniffed and wiped the tears from her cheeks. "I'm so, so sorry, Zane."

"After that, every time I had Blair or Paige in the car, we couldn't go anywhere near a gas station." Zane quickly wiped his eyes. "Since then I haven't really dated much. I had my fair share of romantic flings but nothing serious or anyone I would bring home to meet my family."

"I'm not surprised after you were engaged to someone like Ria." Erin gave Zane a small smile. "Firefighters put their life on the line to ensure the safety of others. It takes a special kind of person to be one. Kind of like a soldier." She wrapped her arms around Zane's neck and hugged him as if she were absorbing some of his pain.

"I'm glad I've told you now." Zane wrapped his arms around her and held her close. "I think I'm falling for you and have been since you first stormed into my niece's hospital room." He kissed her on the head. "You were like a little spitting tiger."

"The moment you lifted me like I was nothing and dropped me outside Fallon's room I had a feeling our paths would meet again one day," Erin admitted. "I was so furious with you it made me forget what my family was going through for a few moments."

"Thank you for telling me about Ria." Erin leaned back and cupped Zane's face with her small hands before giving him a kiss.

"Would you like to go to dinner with me tomorrow night?" Zane asked her.

"I couldn't think of anything else I'd rather do." She sighed as he pulled her to him and got lost in his kiss as the Pacific Ocean gently splashed the rocks around them.

Chapter Thirty
THE FIRST

Michael was enjoying his welcome home dinner, but he was a bit baffled as to why Kelsey was being a little distant. She'd been that way for almost ten days now. When she'd checked on him in the hospital she'd been kind and caring but distant. That's all Michael could describe it as. He'd been so excited to get home and finally spend some time with her without her taking his temperature, pulse, or checking his hospital chart.

Michael had been so sure Kelsey would be more excited about him introducing her to Phantom. He just knew the two of them were going to fall in love with each other. They were kindred spirits. They'd both gone through so much pain, loss, and had people they trusted turn their backs on them. But every time he brought Phantom up Kelsey would get a little frosty or just give him a tight smile. Michael shook his head. Had he read the signal between himself and Kelsey wrong? It wouldn't be the first time that had happened to him.

"Are you feeling okay?" Erin walked over to Michael. "I promised your mother I would keep an eye on you and make sure you didn't overdo things."

"We're going to the main cave tomorrow though, right?" Michael looked at Erin.

"As long as you listen to Kelsey and let us know when you're getting tired," Erin warned him. "There's no reason not to get a bit of exercise. Shane is sending us his helicopter, so we don't have to climb or hike."

"Where's the fun in that?" Michael asked Erin.

"We get to fly in a helicopter and abseil down a cliff and then through a hidden door into a huge cave," Erin grinned at him. "That's going to have to be enough fun for you tomorrow."

"I guess it's a good start," Michael smiled back at her. "Do you think anyone will miss me if I go to bed?" He stifled a yawn. "I'm a bit beat and starting to get a headache."

"Of course not, honey." Erin looked at him worriedly. "Zane and I want to go for an evening walk so we'll walk you home."

"You don't have to," Michael smiled at her.

"Of course I do, and I'll even make you a cup of cocoa for bed." Erin winked at him.

"With marshmallows?" Michael's mouth watered.

"Of course," Erin frowned at him. "Is there any other way to have cocoa?"

"Thanks for the welcome home dinner," Michael felt exhausted, "but I'm going to go to bed now." He looked at his house guests who'd heard Erin was making cocoa and all followed them to Lilly and Michael's cabin. "I'll see you all bright and early to go to the cave."

"Night Michael," Everyone sitting in his living room chorused when he waved and went to his room.

"This is just great." Michael shook his head when he turned on his bedroom light to find three animals had taken over his bed. "It's the three animalteers."

He stripped off his clothes and changed into his pajamas while the three animals didn't budge from his king size bed.

"Come on you three," Michael tried to pull his blanket down so he could get into bed. "At least move a little so I can get into bed."

Goose grumbled but moved. Lunar waited for Michael to turn down the bed before her and Rafferty snuck beneath the covers.

"Of course," Michael shook his head. He was too tired to fight with three animals that insisted on sleeping with him. "Just remember I still have an injury so be careful where you sleep. Especially you two." Michael pointed to Rafferty and Goose that liked to sleep on top of him.

"Goodnight," Michael settled his head into his pillow. It was so good to be in his own bed. It wasn't even a few minutes before he fell asleep under the watchful eye of his three furry roommates.

Goose put his big head on the pillow next to Michael. Rafferty carefully positioned himself near Michael's head while Lunar lay next to him with Michael's arm around her.

"Should we get the animals out of his room?" Erin asked Zane as they went to check on Michael.

"Nah," Zane shook his head. "They seem comfortable, and I bet they'll only come back again. Let them look after him for the night." Zane put his arm around Erin's shoulder as she wrapped hers around his waist.

"He looks so peaceful." Erin smiled.

"I think he'd also be a little creeped out if he knew we were watching him sleep," Zane said softly before dragging Erin out of Michael's room. "I think we'll need to reschedule our walk for tomorrow morning."

"I know," Erin nodded. "I'm sorry. I was looking forward to a moonlight stroll with you down on the beach."

"We have plenty more nights like this one to do that." Zane kissed her.

"You bet we do," Erin sighed and rested her head against his solid chest. It felt so good to be held in his strong arms.

"Are you sure this is okay for Michael?" Erin asked Kelsey as they unhooked their harnesses after having abseiled down the cliff to the cave entrance.

"I'll keep a close eye on him," Kelsey promised her mother.

Kelsey had intended to be Michael's exploration partner today anyway. It made sense with her being a medical student and having looked after him for his weeks in hospital. Kelsey looked over at Caleb helping Michael with his harness. Although he smiled and thanked Caleb for his help, Kelsey could see he hated being vulnerable. Unfortunately, he'd been bed ridden for a couple of weeks now and had had two major operations. It was going to take him time to heal physically. Kelsey was confident she could help him heal his physical wounds. She hoped with all her heart she could try to figure out how to help heal his emotional ones.

"Okay stick with your partner at all times and stay within shouting range of each other," Zane warned them as he and Caleb opened up the cave.

"Yes, sir," Lilly saluted Zane and got a black look from him.

"I don't think that won you any points," Michael whispered to his cousin, Lilly.

"This isn't a competition." Lilly pulled a face at Michael.

"I bet I can find more treasures than you" Michael patted his pack.

"Zane and my dad have already taken out most of what was

on the ship," Lilly reminded Michael. "There's not much left besides a few trunks in some of the passenger rooms."

"Zane did say that there was hardly any treasure on the ship, except for a few trinkets." Kelsey sighed. "You're going to have to face the fact that there may not be any treasure at all."

"That would be so disappointing," Lilly breathed. "We've been hunting for the bulk of the treasure for years. We found the hidden ship's records for the ship called the Guilford Jewel," she explained. "There was more than a small fortune worth of gold and jewels on that ship. We know the ship made it to La Jolla because the original owners of White Sands Cove travelled on it."

"The original owners of the Cove were Jacques and his wife Angelique du Bully, my mother's great-grandparents. They fled France taking all their riches with them," Michael continued the story from Lilly. "Jacques' oldest sister, Alexandria, had left France years ago to run away from an arranged marriage. She was the one who bought this property for Jacques and his wife."

"This was part of La Jolla that wasn't yet populated and was a known hangout for pirates and smugglers," Lilly told them. "Uncle Max, Jennifer's husband's great-grandfather, Gordon Guilford, used some of the well-known tunnel systems on this land to store his pirating wealth."

"Max has pirates in his family?" Caleb looked excitedly at Lilly.

"Yup," Michael laughed walking towards the area where Kelsey and Chase made their amazing discovery.

"My great-grandfather used to build ships for the Guilfords and the du Bullys." Zane shook his head. "We're pretty sure he was a pirate himself."

"That's so cool," Kelsey and Caleb said at the same time then laughed. "Caleb always played pirates with me when I was young."

"When she wasn't trying to push me downstairs or off my bike so she could practice patching me up, that is," Caleb dodged Kelsey's punch. "There were only two things Kelsey loved more than medicine. Pirates and animals."

"Do we have any pirates in our family, Mom?" Kelsey asked Erin.

"No, honey," Erin rubbed her daughter's arm. "But you do have some corrupt politicians on your father's side of the family that could be seen as modern-day pirates, if that helps."

"No," Caleb and Kelsey said together once again.

"It's not the same." Kelsey pouted.

"How did Alexandria find this land?" Erin asked Michael, as she looked fascinatedly around the cavern at the bottom of the entrance steps. She ran her fingers over the drawings on the wall

"Gordon Guilford had been the captain of the ship that brought Alexandria to La Jolla," Michael started to answer Erin's question. "Gordon had lost his wife from a complication during her second pregnancy. He was a widower with a young son. On the voyage from France, Gordon's son befriended Alexandria and she and Gordon fell in love."

"They got married but they never had any children of their own," Lilly continued. "Instead, Alexandria raised Max's grandfather as if he was her own son."

"By the time Jacques and Angelique came over to America, Alexandria had bought and set them up with a whole lot of properties in La Jolla," Lilly said. "I think they were trying to filter some of their wealth into property."

"That's the property where the Sea Breeze Cottage is, right?" Erin guessed.

"Yes," Lilly nodded. "But Jacques and Angelique fell in love with the Cove, and this is where they made their home." She smiled. "The first time I saw the Cove I knew this is where I wanted my home to be too. That's when Michael and I decided when we'd graduated we would turn it into a resort and adventure type retreat."

"My mom and Shane decided to give White Sands Cove to

myself and Lilly," Michael explained. "Neither of my sisters objected to it as they both had their own lives and beautiful houses."

"Don't forget about Ray," Lilly told Michael. "She also has an equal share in the resort."

"Ray likes the farm area and takes in animals in need of special care from the animal shelters." Michael smiled. "When the animals are ready Ray finds them their forever homes."

"Ray's Max's daughter, right?" Kelsey asked Michael. "She's about Zoe and Logan's age?"

"That's right," Michael nodded. "She's a wonderful kid and is currently learning how to sail with Zane's niece Fallon."

"These paintings are amazing," Erin said. "I wonder what this giant holding two boats in his hands is all about." She ran her hands over the inscription at the bottom before reading it. *"May our treasure forever be safe in the uneven arms of the giant that watches over us."*

"My mother read it as *'To hide in the uneven arms of the giant that watches over us'* and we were trying to figure out what it meant." Lilly stood next to Erin. "Look at how the giant is drawn."

"He has some weird hairs on his forearms." Michael frowned. "His eyes look like triangles."

"It's not a giant," Zoe's voice startled them from the entrance to the cave.

All heads turned to the entrance where Zoe, Chase, and Logan stood.

"Zoe, honey," Erin smiled up at her, "how did you three get here?"

"We hiked and used your zip lines to get down here," Logan shrugged as he took the stairs two at a time to join them.

Zoe and Chase followed Logan.

"When Uncle Zane showed me the picture he'd taken of the giant I could see that it was crudely drawn," Zoe took out her flashlight and switched it to a blue light. "Which made me think about the other maps we'd found leading us to the treasure."

Zoe shone the blue light onto the picture of the giant.

"See," Zoe grinned as everyone made an 'Ohhhh' sound. "It's a map of White Sands Cove. The right arm is Pirates Wall, the chest is the Cove itself and the left arm is Crab Shack Cliffs."

"Michael named the cliffs," Lilly made sure everyone knew that. "I had nothing to do with the names."

"I like the names," Kelsey smiled at Michael.

"Thank you." Michael gave Kelsey a little bow. "I rather liked the names myself."

"Zoe is really good at figuring these things out." Chase smiled proudly at Zoe while Logan rolled his eyes.

"Thank you, Chase," Zoe told him before turning back to the wall. "Erin's translation was right about the inscription below it." Before she could launch into why, Logan changed the subject.

"Can we go see the other cavern?" Logan said like an excited puppy. "Chase said it was amazing in there."

"Yes," Zane moved towards the small opening. "But be careful. There's a lot of debris in there," he said, before squeezing himself through the small window.

"Oh wow," Erin breathed as she allowed Zane to help her through the window that led to one of the large main caves. "It's beautiful."

"It must've been a grand ship in its day," Zane said, helping the rest of the family through the window before joining Erin who was standing looking up at the decaying ship.

"It's not the Guilford Jewel though, Uncle Zane." Zoe walked up to Zane and Erin.

"I was really hoping it was, honey." Zane shook his head sadly. "It's a ship called Primus."

Zane looked at the large old sailing ship that landed awkwardly to one side in the rough shingled sand and rocky ground it was stranded on.

"Primus?" Logan frowned as he came to stand next to his uncle and twin sister. He turned to look at Chase who was coming up behind them. "Was there any mention of that ship in my great-great-great-grandfather's shipping ledgers?"

"Not that I recall." Chase's brows drew together. "Although there was that one ship we couldn't quite figure out what the name was because of the smudged ink. I think it was sold to some French Lord or Count."

"I think this was one of our great-great-grandfather's first ships he ever built, or built to sell anyway." Zoe looked up at the railing. "Look, that's the McCaid ship building mark."

"You're right." Zane walked closer and squinted up at what Zoe was pointing out. "But why would you think it was his first?" He looked at his great-niece.

"Primus, the name of the ship is Latin for 'the first'." Erin grinned at Zoe who smiled at Erin and nodded in confirmation.

"Can we climb aboard what's left of it?" Michael asked Zane, getting impatient with all the chit chat, and wanting to explore the old boat.

"Just watch where you step," Zane warned them. "Shane and I haven't been able to fully explore the ship yet."

"Great," Michael said excitedly, and before anyone else could start to talk, he started to climb up the rope ladder Zane and Shane had left on the boat the last time they were in the cave. "This is so freakin cool!" He steadied himself to balance on the lopsided deck.

"Shane and I secured the boat with the ropes as best we could," Zane warned them all. "It should be able to take a few of us at a time. But don't jump, run, or try crazy stuff."

"We're not ten," Michael called down to Zane with a huge boyish grin on his face. He may not be ten anymore, but he really wished he had a pirate hat, sword, and he so wanted to climb up the main mast with a spyglass. "Kelsey," Michael called down from the lopsided deck to her, "you must come up here."

Kelsey didn't need a second invitation. She got up there in

no time. The two of them soon disappeared as they went to explore the ship.

"Whose ship was this if it wasn't the Guilford Jewel that Jacques and his wife arrived on?" Kelsey carefully followed Michael down the passageway the cabins were located in.

"I'm not sure," Michael's eyes lit up when he saw a room that had not yet been cleaned out by Shane and Zane. There was something beneath the sail. He pulled the material back and called Kelsey. "Look in here. There are still some old trunks and stuff."

Chapter Thirty-One

THE MYSTERY BEHIND A SHIP CALLED PRIMUS

"What do you think is in those trunks?" Kelsey asked Michael as they made their way into the cabin on the ship. Her eyes were also shining with excitement.

"Let's open one and find out." Michael grinned.

"How are you going to bust the lock?" Kelsey asked Michael.

Wait here. Michael disappeared for a few minutes before returning with a rock in his hand. He used the rock to split open the lock and they pulled the trunk open together.

"Oh my gosh," Kelsey dropped to her knees in front of the open trunk.

The top of the trunk had a neat shelf laid out on it. A purple velvet cloth covered the top of the shelf. Kelsey gently pulled the cloth back and hissed excitedly, finding around ten velvet bags of various sizes that were neatly laid out in the compartments of the shelf.

"Look at all these velvet bags." Kelsey opened one of the bigger velvet bags and sucked in her breath. "Do you think this is real?" She held up a diamond encrusted tiara.

Michael stopped trying to open the second trunk to sit down besides Kelsey, "That looks real." He took the glittering tiara from Kelsey's hands to look at it before he carefully placed it on her head. "You look like a princess." Something flickered in his eyes but was gone before Kelsey could decipher it.

"This must've been one of Angelique's trunks." Kelsey sorted through the rest of the jewels and trinkets in the other velvet bags before removing the shelf. Below it were some gowns and a journal. "Look at this." She showed Michael opening the book.

"This isn't Angelique's trunk." Michael frowned. "This was Alexandria's trunk." He looked at the name in the front of the journal.

"This was the ship Gordon Guilford sailed Alexandria du Bully out of France on." Kelsey's eyes widened. "That's why there was no treasure other than what Zane and Shane found on it."

"We seem to have found some pretty nice treasures." Michael looked at the jewelry and gold coins that were contained in the velvet bags. "I'm no expert but I'm willing to bet the gold and jewels on their necklaces, broaches, and bracelets are real."

"Fit for French royalty," Kelsey breathed.

Kelsey picked up a beautiful gold broach. The ruby was shaped like a red rose bud, there were a few emeralds as the leaves that were also studded along the gold stem.

"This is beautiful." Kelsey held up the broach.

"Let's get them logged," Michael pulled out the notepad and pen, "then let Zane know we found something. Lilly's going to be so jealous she didn't find it." He grinned.

"You two are more like brother and sister than cousins." Kelsey shook her head thinking how competitive Lilly and Michael were at times.

"We are." Michael nodded.

Michael started to take pictures of everything they found in all three trunks in the cabin that must've been Alexandria's.

"I wonder why she left them here and never took them with

her?" Kelsey frowned. "These clothes are made of fine material." She shook her head.

"I think she was trying to blend in," Michael said. "Remember she was running away from an arranged marriage. I think the last thing she wanted was for her father or betrothed to find her."

"You're probably right," Kelsey smiled. "Maybe she just wanted to leave her past behind her and start again," she said softly.

"Sorry?" Michael looked up at Kelsey, not having heard the last part of her sentence.

"Nothing," Kelsey told him. She went to explore the next trunk he'd opened. "Do you mind if I keep the journal?" she asked him. "I'd like to read it."

"It's in French," Michael pointed out.

"That's okay, my French is pretty decent," Kelsey told him proudly.

"Of course," Michael smiled at her. "As long as you let me know what it says."

"Obviously." Kelsey dipped her hand into the one trunk and pulled out a thick, soft parcel wrapped in tissue paper and tied with a satin ribbon. "Can I open this?" she asked wide eyed like a kid at Christmas time.

"Yeah," Michael nodded just as excited.

"Oh my!" Kelsey stood up and held a white velvet cloak with a hood. "This is stunning."

"It is," Michael stood up next to Kelsey. "Try it on."

"No." Kelsey shook her head. "I couldn't because it's over a hundred years old and probably infected with something."

"Good point, although I don't think anything would've gotten into the trunks — they were covered with those old heavy flax sails," Michael pointed out.

"I know, but still," Kelsey held up the garment, "I don't think I could've left something like this behind."

"I don't think it was left behind," Michael told her. "More like she kept it stored here in the ship in the cave." He grinned.

"How do you think they got this boat into the cave?" Kelsey asked Michael as she packed the cloak away.

"Zane and Shane found another cavern just beyond this one," Michael closed up the trunks after he'd logged and taken photos of the contents. "They think that this cavern and the one beyond it were once a big cave, but a cave-in cut the caverns off from each other."

"Can we see the other part of the cavern?" Kelsey asked Michael excitedly.

"I was just wondering the exact same thing." Michael smiled. "Let's go see what the others are doing and if we can go over to the next cave."

"But we can come back here, right? "Kelsey raised an eyebrow. "We still have some exploring to do on this old boat."

"I was actually wishing I had a pirate hat, sword, and spyglass when I climbed aboard." Michael and Kelsey laughed. "Just as well we never found this ship when I was young. I'd be here every day wanting to play pirates."

"I understand that." Kelsey followed Michael off the boat. "That's the first thing I wanted to do as well when I saw this ship. I'd just been trapped in a tunnel, so I was a little overwhelmed and exhausted."

"I'm so sorry I wasn't here when that happened," Michael said softly.

"Michael you were recovering from a bullet wound and ruptured appendix," Kelsey raised both her eyebrows. "What would you have done?"

"I don't know," Michael looked her in the eyes, "but I would've dug through the tunnels with my hands if I had to, to find you."

Kelsey felt her heart jump when Michael's eyes darkened as they stared into each other's eyes. The moment passed and

Michael seemed to withdraw and went back to treating her like his best friend, much to Kelsey's frustration. But she wasn't disheartened and felt there was hope for them as Kelsey had definitely seen something in his eyes when he'd looked at her a few times that day.

The whooshing and toiling sound of the water filling up the cave echoed around them. Lilly, Michael, Caleb, and Kelsey had only just managed to hoist themselves up onto a shelf they hoped was above the high tide water mark. The four of them had managed to move away enough rock debris to make the small gap between the two caverns big enough to squeeze through.

They'd found another cavern on the other side of the caved-in rock wall. The second cavern dipped into a deep pool that was no more than knee deep during the current Neap tide. Another set of crudely carved out stone steps took them down into the water below. But would probably fill to near the top of the steps connecting to the Primus's cavern. Caleb had checked the tides and confirmed that they had a few hours to explore the cave until high tide rolled in.

Eager to explore how the Primus had ended up where it was, Michael, Lilly, Caleb, and Kelsey had gone into the depth of the second cavern to explore. They found where there must've once been a wide cave opening but it was now closed in by a mesh of fallen boulders. There were small openings at the bottom of the boulders, a few in the middle of the sea facing rock wall, and right at the top. But from the outside they would've looked like nothing more than indentations in the cliff wall.

Then there was the small opening that looked like a small door hole that was just big enough for someone of Caleb's size to squeeze through. Before they'd tried to squeeze through Caleb had done a quick inspection of what they'd find on the other side. To their surprise it was another cove. One that would be underwater during high tide. So, obviously they had to go exploring. They'd been so taken by playing on the small shore and how amazing their discovery was that they'd forgotten about the time. Luckily, Caleb had taken it upon himself to set his watch. What they forgot to factor in was that nature didn't keep exact time and ran on her own schedule. They'd barely made it into the cave and found a place to perch when the sea had come back to cover its secret cove.

They were wet, cold, and stuck on the wrong side of the cave.

"Can you tell me again," Lilly asked Michael, "why you had to climb up the far side of this cavern instead of trying to swim over to the other side before the pool got so full?"

"Because the water was coming in fast," Michael reminded her. "We all made the decision to climb up here."

"We're just lucky we cleared the beach in time," Kelsey shuddered. "I have that nightmare sometimes. The tide is far out and I'm splashing in the shallow water then all of a sudden I'm in the middle of the ocean because the tide has suddenly come in."

"You have issues," Caleb looked at his sister. "There's another ledge up there to my right." He pointed. "There is also a small shelf that runs around the cave and up to that opening over there." He pointed along the cliff wall. "I could climb up and go check out where the opening goes to."

"That's a little dangerous," Lilly looked at Caleb wide-eyed.

"There's no alternative," Caleb smiled down at her.

"Are you four alright?" Zane appeared through the opening on the far side from the other cavern.

"The tide came in so fast," Michael called back. "There's a cove that we went to explore through one of the larger openings in the rock wall that's now covered with water."

"That wall must've been how the ship got in here," Zane called across to them over the noise of the water.

"I think they've actually deepened this cavern so the water wouldn't rise all the way up to that one," Michael explained to Zane. "I think whoever got the Primus in here deliberately sealed the cave's entrance."

"That would make sense," Zane nodded. "So that wall is a type of man-made sea wall?"

"Can we please stop talking about the caves and figure out how we are going to get back to the other side?" Lilly hissed.

"I suppose swimming across is out of the question?" Zane stated the obvious.

"You guessed right," Lilly and Kelsey said together.

"Zane," Caleb called across to him, "I'm going to climb up onto that ledge just above us then shimmy along that ledge to that opening."

"Okay," Zane called back, "be careful." He stood at the ready.

"Please be careful," Lilly went on tiptoes and kissed Caleb. "I love you," she whispered.

"I love you too," Caleb gave her a hug before starting his climb to the higher ledge.

They all stood watching Caleb climb up to the ledge. By the time he managed to pull himself up onto the shelf, Zoe, Logan, Chase, and Erin had joined Zane on the other side.

"Please, honey, be careful," Erin called.

"He's going to be okay," Zane could be heard saying through the echo of the cave.

"Uh," Michael started saying. "I think we need to follow Caleb."

Kelsey and Lilly looked down to see the water rising higher.

"Caleb," Michael called up to him. "Is there room up there for all of us?"

"Should be," Caleb nodded. "I'll wait here to help you all up."

Lilly went first, climbing up the little foothold of rocks until Caleb was able to pull her up. Kelsey came next and by the time

Michael had to climb he was almost knee deep in water which made his climb up to the shelf even more perilous. On the other side of the cavern Zane, Erin, the twins, and Chase had moved all the way up to the small window as the water covered the stairs.

"Well that was just a little bit more excitement than I wanted for one day," Michael admitted.

"We have a little more fun to go, I'm afraid," Caleb said. "I'm going to go across the shelf."

"Be careful," Erin shouted from where she was standing clutching Zane's hand.

"Please, be careful." Lilly swallowed as she eyed the small ledge.

"I will," Caleb assured her.

Caleb carefully inched onto the shelf. He flattened his back against that cold rock wall. Caleb slowly made his way to the opening in the rock wall that would hopefully lead them back to the main cavern. Everyone in the cavern watched as he climbed through the window and disappeared.

"Caleb?" Lilly called after a few minutes. There was no answer.

"Caleb!" Zane yelled louder. "Where are you?" His voice bounced around the cavern.

"I'm right here," Caleb made Erin scream as he popped out the small window on the other side of the cave. "You're going to have to move one at a time along the shelf," Caleb called over to Lilly, Michael, and Kelsey.

"You go first, Lilly," Kelsey told her.

"I'll go around to the cavern window and help you all in." Caleb turned and disappeared again.

"Great," Lilly breathed. "I love heights so much."

"Be careful, Lil," Michael watched with bated breath as Lilly made her way onto the shelf.

Two parts of the shelf crumbled as Lilly moved off of them. Not a noise was heard. Everyone held their breath until Caleb grabbed Lilly as she got to the opening and the last bit of shelf collapsed.

"That's just great," Kelsey's eyes flew to Michael. "How do we get there now?"

"Look above you," Zane called to Michael. "There are three smaller shelves leading up to another window." He pointed above where Michael and Kelsey stood. "Do you think you can reach them?"

"We can try," Michael called back to Zane.

"I'll try to figure out where it leads," Caleb told them through the other rock opening.

"I'll go with Caleb," Lilly could be heard from behind Caleb.

"We'll join you once Kelsey and Michael have made it," Zane called after them.

Chapter Thirty-Two
THE WHITE HORSE

"You can do this, Kelsey," Michael called down to her, holding out his hand. "Just one more foot up and you're here."

"My arms feel like jelly," Kelsey admitted.

They'd managed to climb up two of the shelves. Michael was up on the last shelf and Kelsey was almost there. It had been hard and nerve wracking. Kelsey had thought she was fit and had good upper body strength until she'd tried to pull herself up onto these steep shelves. She was sure she was filled with scrapes, cuts and bruises and she only just realized she still had the diamond tiara on her head. It was well wedged into her hair that was pulled back in a French braid. The sharp prongs where the tiara dug into her hair and pushed against her scalp was starting to give her a headache.

The sole of her one foot throbbed so badly. Kelsey had slipped trying to gain a foothold up to the last shelf and badly bruised it. At that moment she didn't think she could push herself up any further.

"Come on Kelsey," Michael's deep voice called down to her. "I'm right here ready to grab your hand. I know you're tired, scared, and hurting, but it's just one more leg up and you're here."

Kelsey looked up at Michael and nodded. She took a deep breath and forced herself to push up towards the ledge with whatever strength she had left. Like he promised, Michael grabbed her hand and helped pull her up. As she landed on the shelf Michael gathered her into his arms and sat there holding her for a few minutes. It felt so good to be wrapped in his strong warm arms.

"You're okay, princess!" Michael kissed the top of her head as he held her to him. "Are you ready to go see where that hole in the wall takes us?"

"Yes" Kelsey nodded although her body was screaming *'no, I want to stay sitting here wrapped in your arms'*.

Michael helped Kelsey up and she frowned as she noticed him wince.

"Are you okay?" Kelsey's eyes immediately looked at his torso and she sucked in her breath. "You're bleeding." She pointed to his shirt. "I think you've torn your wound open."

"No," Michael waved her off. "It's just a scratch." He smiled at her. "Now let's see where this goes." He pulled his phone out of his pocket and turned on the flashlight.

"Michael," Kelsey took out her phone and turned her light on as well. "You need to let me look at your wound."

"When we're out of here, I promise you I'll let you look at the wound," Michael made a deal with her. "Right now we need to figure out where this small tunnel goes.

Michael shone his light around them. They were in a small tunnel that they couldn't stand up straight in.

"Michael," Kelsey breathed. "Look here." She shone her light on the ceiling. "Carvings of a boat like in the other passage."

"This must lead to somewhere we can get out of the cave from," Michael said excitedly. "Wow, this is quite a cave system."

"Do you think your great-great-grandparents really lived somewhere here?" Kelsey asked him.

"Caleb and Lilly found their graves," Michael reminded her. "So I think for at least a few months when they tried to disappear after their house was burnt down."

"That's such an awful story," Kelsey shuddered. "What criminals won't do to get what they want."

"Come on," Michael pointed to the opening. "I think we're near the end of the tunnel."

"Thank goodness," Kelsey said, relieved. "I was starting to get a sore neck from being crouched like this."

"There's quite a big jump down to the bottom." Michael shone his torch. "Oh, look there are some stairs carved into the rock."

"That's also quite a big step," Kelsey told Michael.

"I'll go first and then help you across," Michael told her.

Before Kelsey could stop him, Michael jumped towards the step and landed without a problem.

"I don't know if I can jump," Kelsey swallowed looking down at the drop below her.

"Come on, Kelsey." Michael shone his light towards her. "You can do this."

Kelsey looked at the gap between where she was and the step where Michael was. The hole was very deep. Her heart hammered in her throat, and she froze. Kelsey's body refused to let her jump. Panic started to claw its way up from her belly to her throat. It's cold fingers spreading paralyzing fear through every fiber of her being.

"No," Kelsey started backing away towards the tunnel. "I can't." Her chest rose and fell as panic got a full hold on her.

"Kelsey," Michael sat down crossed legged on the shelf. "Sit down." He told her. "Where you are. Just sit down and look at me." He shone his light on her.

Kelsey didn't know if her body would even do that.

"Do you remember in hospital, that day I was feeling like I

was going to die of the pain in my head that was so bad?" Michael spoke to her in a calm soothing voice.

Kelsey nodded.

"You told me that whenever you were afraid, felt panicked, or were sick, you and your mom would sing a song?" Michael asked her.

Kelsey nodded, still too afraid to move or breathe too hard.

"What was it called again?" Michael clicked his fingers as he thought about it.

"I..." Kelsey was finding it difficult to swallow.

"I remember it now," Michael smiled. "Wasn't it Wonderful Life by that band or group called Black?" He cleared his throat. "I'll start and see if I can remember the words."

Michael started to sing the song her mother would sing to her, and she sang to him when he was in so much pain.

> *Here I go out to sea again*
> *The sunshine fills my hair*
> *And dreams hang in the air*

Kelsey closed her eyes as his deep voice sang the song to her. Slowly as he got more into the song she started to hum it and slowly sat down while she started to sing softly. Her eyes were still closed as she sang along with him and slowly she started to relax.

Michael smiled at her when she opened her eyes and stared at him while they sang the song together.

"You have a beautiful voice," Michael told her softly. "I was actually thinking of faking a few headaches just to get you to sing to me."

"Thank you," Kelsey smiled as she sat looking across at Michael. "Your voice is not so bad either."

"You promised to tell me why you loved that song so much," Michael reminded her.

"The one night there was a big thunderstorm that ripped

through the sky and rattled my windows," Kelsey told him. "I thought the lighting was trying to get into my room and steal me." She gave a small laugh thinking about it now. "I ran to my mother's room and that song was playing on her bedside radio. She held me in her arms and sang along with it on the radio until I fell asleep."

"Oh wow," Michael smiled. "I never liked lightning either. I still don't to be honest."

"I don't. I still cringe or try to block it out." Kelsey gave a shudder. "But that particular night I felt so safe in my mother's arms as she sang to me. After that, every time I heard that song it gave me a feeling of comfort."

"I love that story," Michael told her. "I can imagine little Kelsey running in her princess pj's to her mother's room."

"More like flew to my mother's room," Kelsey laughed.

"My mother would let all three of us climb into bed with her and she'd tell us stories," Michael shared with Kelsey.

"Moms are amazing people; they're our super girls," Kelsey grinned. "We never really appreciate just how much they do or give up for us."

"I know," Michael nodded. "But let's not forget about the dads like Zane and Chase's dad Daniel."

"You're right," Kelsey looked at him. "My dad was like this on again off again dad. It hurt like hell when he left my mom. Then when he just signed away consent for my mom to change my surname. I thought he was just throwing me away."

"I'm sure that's not true," Michael said softly.

"I only found out recently he never threw me away, and how much it ripped him apart to walk away," Kelsey swallowed. "I understand now that he was protecting myself and Caleb."

"I couldn't imagine having to let go of my child and I don't even have one yet," Michael laughed.

"Then you're going to make a great father," Kelsey told him shyly.

"I'm sorry about everything you went through, Kelsey,"

Michael's voice dropped. "I wish I could take all the pain away from you."

"I've learned to live with it and each day is a step further away from the pain," Kelsey's eyes glistened with tears, "and many tomorrows in the future it'll be years behind me."

"I love your Kelsey quotes," Michael told her.

"You know everything about me." Kelsey eyed Michael sitting across from her.

Kelsey glanced at the divide between them thinking how appropriate it was. They were so close yet there was this big black hole of uncertainty between them. Both of them were trying to sum up the other, wondering if they trusted each other enough to put their lives in the other's hands.

"What do you want to know?" Michael asked her.

"Tell me about April," Kelsey said softly.

Michael went quiet for a few seconds and Kelsey's heart hammered in her throat wondering if she pushed it a little too far by asking him something so personal.

"I was young and thought I was madly in love," Michael told her. "I acted like a silly impulsive fool thinking that she felt the same. Turns out that absence doesn't actually make the heart grow fonder, it makes it wander in another direction."

"Or maybe she wasn't the right one for you," Kelsey swallowed and cleared her throat.

"No, I don't think she was." Michael looked straight into Kelsey's eyes. "I realized that some time ago now." A slow sexy smile spread across his handsome face. "What about you and your ex-fiancé?"

"I don't know why we even got engaged," Kelsey shrugged. "He was from a prominent family and I think on some level I was so desperately trying to win my father's approval..."

"I understand that." Michael nodded. "My father took off when we were young."

"I'm sorry," Kelsey looked up at him.

"It's fine. I was lucky enough to have an amazing mother, grandfather, and great aunt," Michael told her.

"It's getting cold," Kelsey shivered.

"Do you think you can stand up now?" Michael asked her.

"I think so," Kelsey said.

"Just look at me," Michael told her. "Try not to look down, look ahead so you can judge the jump and I'll catch you."

"Okay," Kelsey nodded and swallowed.

Kelsey's heart pounded like it was trying to chisel its way out of her chest. Every nerve ending in her body screamed at her not to jump. She looked into Michael's eyes and he smiled at her. Kelsey knew in that moment without a shadow of a doubt that she trusted him with her life, her heart, and everything she was. She took a deep breath and took the leap.

Michael caught her and wrapped her in his arms holding her tight for a few minutes. As her heart rate slowed down she realized that his heart had been racing as much as hers was. He kissed her head and breathed deeply and Kelsey's resolve to break into his heart grew stronger. She could see it in his eyes and feel it in his touch that he felt for her. When they were out of this mess she was going to tell him she didn't want to meet this Phantom he thought she'd fall madly in love with because she was already madly in love.

Michael and Kelsey made their way through another passageway until they came to a small cavern that opened up into what looked like someone's small apartment.

"This is the room Caleb and Lilly found," Michael said in astonishment. "Look, those are the graves of my great-great-grandparents."

"Wow," Kelsey looked around. "They really did live here."

"It seems so." Michael saw Kelsey shivering. "We'd better get out of here before you catch a cold."

"And I need to take a look at your wound," Kelsey told him, pointing to the blood seeping onto his shirt.

"Okay," Michael rolled his eyes, "Dr. Carnegie." He grinned. "Come on, I think our exit's this way."

Before they came to the entrance of the cave Kelsey stopped.

"Michael," Kelsey looked at him as he turned around looking at her curiously, "I have to say something to you."

"Okay," Michael frowned at her. "Is something wrong?" He looked worried.

"I hope this doesn't affect things between us." Kelsey closed her eyes and shook her head. "What am I saying, of course it's going to affect things between us," she said more to herself.

"Kelsey," Michael stepped up to her and put his hands on her forearms looking down at her. "Nothing you could say would change anything between us," he said softly.

"Okay," Kelsey looked down at their feet and squeezed her eyes shut as she plucked her courage. She'd never confessed her feelings to anyone before. "I don't want to meet your friend Phantom. Because I'm already falling head over heels in love with you."

She kept her eyes shut and wasn't expecting what happened next. Michael pulled her to him and kissed her passionately. Her arms curled around his neck as he lifted her easily off the ground to deepen the kiss.

When Michael ended the kiss he held her with her feet off the floor.

"I'm glad you said that," Michael told her hoarsely, "because, in case you haven't noticed, I've been falling head over heels in love with you since you drove into my car and then yelled at me."

Before she could argue with him his lips covered hers again.

When he drew them apart he put her on the ground and straightened her tiara that was a little lopsided.

"Come on," Michael grinned and took her hand. "We have to go somewhere so we need to get out of the cave. I think I've had enough exploring for one day."

"I have to agree with you about the exploring," Kelsey admitted running after him.

"Where are we going?" Kelsey asked Michael as they ran past the retreat and towards the animal rehabilitation farm that was part of the retreat.

"We're going to meet someone," Michael grinned at her.

"You promised to let me take a look at that wound that's bleeding a little too much for my liking," Kelsey said pointedly.

Kelsey's head was still a little giddy from learning that Michael felt the same way as she did. She felt like she was walking on clouds and a gold light was glowing around her. Michael took them to the middle of an empty field that was surrounded by trees.

"Do you trust me?" Michael asked Kelsey.

"I do," Kelsey said truthfully. "With my life," she said softly.

"Close your eyes," Michael told her. "Don't make any sudden move, keep quiet, and only open your eyes when I tell you to."

"Okay," Kelsey's brows drew together as Michael squeezed her hand encouragingly.

Michael gave a soft whistle and then went quiet. Kelsey kept her eyes closed as butterflies fluttered in her stomach and feelings of such love filled her. She couldn't explain it. She heard a soft noise and in her mind's eyes she saw her father. He blew her a kiss and started to walk away. She wanted to call out to him, but she felt something soft nudge her hand.

"Kelsey," Michael told her softly, "I want you to meet someone. I think the two of you are going to fall in love with each other." He kissed her on the lips, and something nudged her again. "You can open your eyes before he bites me," he laughed.

Confused, Kelsey opened her eyes and turned her head as she heard a soft whine. Her breath caught in her throat.

"Kelsey this is Phantom," Michael grinned. "He needs his forever family. I was hoping you and I could be that family."

"He's beautiful." Tears filled Kelsey's eyes and the most beautiful white horse nuzzled her hand as she reached out to him. "Hello boy."

Kelsey laughed as Phantom's wet nose brushed her cheek.

"Now you're a proper princess," Michael pulled her to him for a deep kiss which was rudely interrupted by a head butt from Phantom. "I think your new friend here wants your attention."

"I think we should find him an apple," Kelsey laughed through her happy tears. "Thank you." She looked up at Michael as she patted a grateful Phantom who was loving her attention.

Michael, Kelsey, and Phantom started to walk towards the stables where they found some carrots.

"I didn't even ask if you ride," Michael suddenly said as he led Phantom into his stable.

"I do," Kelsey nodded. "I love riding."

"That's good," Michael said, trying to dodge the little nips Phantom was giving him wanting more carrots. "Phantom isn't ready to be ridden just yet. But he will be soon."

"Why is he here?" Kelsey asked.

"He was a show horse that, after a car accident, they couldn't use anymore," Michael told her, making Phantom turn to one side.

"Oh no," Kelsey put her hand to her mouth before giving Phantom a hug after seeing the ugly raw scar that ran down his one side. "I'm so sorry for your pain," she said softly to the horse as the tears rolled down her cheeks.

Phantom whined and gently nudged her as if he understood her.

"He's gone through months of treatments and pain. This boy is a fighter with a heart of gold. Ray will be so glad he's found his forever home."

"You poor boy," Kelsey gave Phantom another carrot.

"See," Michael grinned, "I told you you'd fall in love with each other."

Chapter Thirty-Three
THE COLOR OF A ROSE

"You look nice," Lilly told Zane. "Don't listen to Piper and Michael, they're just teasing you."

"Yeah," Piper, Zane's niece, walked up to him and gave him a hug. "I'm teasing you. We're just not used to seeing you in a tuxedo."

"You've seen me in full military dress uniform," Zane shook his head.

Zane's six-foot-three broad shouldered frame filled out his tuxedo magnificently. His dark brown hair was peppered with grey which only made him seem more ruggedly handsome with his jewel green eyes. He was still in excellent shape and looked a lot younger than fifty-five.

"But it's not the same as a suit, Uncle Zane," Zoe said as she, Logan, and Chase walked into the room.

"You must be feeling a little like a duck out of water." Logan grinned at his uncle. "You don't do these formal things."

"You're right, kid." Zane took a deep breath. "This is not my sort of thing."

"You're going to be fine," Michael patted Zane on the shoulder. "Here are the flowers you asked me to pick up from the florist." He handed Zane a bunch of different colored roses.

"Uncle Zane," Piper and Zoe said together.

"What?" Zane looked at his nieces questioningly.

"Remember what mom and gran used to say about roses?" Piper shook her head at her uncle.

"Your mom and gran were a little old fashioned," Zane said defensively. "I'm sure Erin will love all the roses in this bunch. They're her favorite flower."

"Uncle Zane," Zoe shook her head at her great-uncle. "Although there are a few different flowers, their colors have a significant meaning and not a lot of people know about them. But roses," her eyes widened, "nearly everyone, even the younger generation knows about their different meanings."

"I'm going to be late." Zane looked at his watch as Piper took the huge bunch of roses from him.

"What do you think?" Piper looked at Lilly and Zoe.

"I think the red, pink, and yellow ones," Lilly frowned.

"Love, admiration, and friendship," Zoe said, picking out three yellow roses.

"I think you need ten roses," Lilly gave Zane a warm smile.

"Let me guess the number of roses I give her is also significant?" Zane sighed.

"Yes," Zoe's brows drew together, "You don't just give a person one rose unless you tell them it was love at first sight and two roses means a deep shared love." She grinned at her uncle.

"I think these three pink ones," Piper picked out the pink roses. "Three roses means I love you. Six roses means I want to be yours."

"I like these three red roses." Lilly picked out three red roses. "Seven roses mean I'm infatuated with you and nine roses is the symbol of eternal love."

"You're short one rose," Logan tapped his finger to his lips. "What do you think Michael?" Logan looked at Michael.

"White?" Michael frowned.

"No," Logan shook his head and picked one orange rose

from the bunch, "orange roses symbolize passion." He added it to the roses Lilly was collecting from the main bunch. "And ten roses means you're perfect."

"Ah," Zane nodded and shook his head. "I feel like I'm about to go to my prom."

"Well it's kind of like a prom," Michael said. "You're going to some formal dinner ball for Erin's new work. My mom and Max will be there too."

"My mom and dad will also be there," Lilly smiled at Zane. "You and my father can both feel like ducks out of water in your tuxedos."

"Do you want to know the history of the rose's symbolism?" Zoe asked them all.

"Uh..." Logan looked a little taken-aback as he stared at his twin sister.

"What?" Zoe asked Logan.

"Are you sure that falling down into the tunnels didn't bust your brain?" Logan looked at her. "Because you've been doing weird stuff since that day. Like asking us if we want to know the full history of its existence."

"No," Zoe shook her head. "My brain is fine, thank you. I'm trying something new." She shrugged. "You know, trying to be average." She looked around the room. "I'm trying to fit in more."

"Well look at you." Michael gave Zoe a hug and for the first time ever she didn't flinch at human contact. "Even your insults have become a lot better. You made me feel proud of my averageness." He grinned and messed up her hair.

"Thank you," Zoe smiled at Michael.

"She's trying," Chase defended Zoe like he always did.

"Zoe," Lilly looked at the young girl, "you never have to try to be anyone else around us. We love you and that beautiful big brain of yours."

"Really?" Zoe frowned at Lilly. "My brother is a genius, yet he gets all of you and you all get him. I just want to be like that."

"Honey," Zane walked over to his great-niece, "what's brought this on?"

"The other day," Zoe explained, "when Lilly, Michael, Kelsey, and Caleb were trapped in the cave. I saw how all of you were reacting. It was as if you could almost feel what they were going through."

"It's called empathy," Logan frowned at his sister. "You know that."

"I know it," Zoe shrugged. "But while you all feel it, and I think you do, I see the probabilities of them making it or not." Her brows furrowed. "What if what Logan said is true?" Her frown deepened. "What if I'm incapable of feeling like normal people do?"

"Zoe," Piper, Lilly, Zane, and Michael all said at once.

"That's simply not true, squirt." Michael was the first to talk. "Remember when tulip the tortoise got tangled up in all that wire?"

"Yes," Zoe nodded.

"Who spent hours patiently sitting and untangling the wire then tending to him?" Michael smiled down at her.

"Me." Zoe pointed at herself.

"Why did you do that?" Michael asked her softly.

"I didn't want him to be hurt or in pain." Zoe looked at Michael confused.

"What did you feel when you saw him all tangled in the wire?" Michael raised his eyebrows.

"A tightness in my chest that could be attributed to the feeling of fear for the creature." Zoe's frown increased.

"When you knew Chase and Kelsey were stuck in the tunnels," Michael encouraged her to open up, "what did you feel then?"

"I think that would be a panic response?" Zoe's eyes widened. "I see what you're doing."

"Here," Chase gave Zoe one pink rose, one yellow rose, and one white rose. "From me to you." He smiled softly.

"Oh, thank you." Zoe gave Chase a smile as she took the roses and walked off to help Lilly find a home for the rest of Zane's unused roses.

"Don't worry, bud." Michael patted Chase on the shoulder, seeing the look in his eyes. "She's still young. One day she'll realize what the look in those big puppy dogs' eyes of yours means."

"Or" Logan shook his head, "knowing my sister, she probably won't." He shrugged at the black look Michael sent him. "He needs to know that she may have some feelings, but I doubt she has the kind of emotions us average humans do." He grinned and ducked the cushion Piper flung at him.

"Okay," Zane looked at his watch. "Time to go."

"Good luck," Piper gave her uncle one last hug.

"Here," Lilly gave Zane the bouquet of ten roses they had picked out for him, all neatly displayed and wrapped with a ribbon.

"You made the bouquet even better than the original," Zane thanked her and took the flowers. "Don't wait for me," he called over his shoulder before stopping by Michael. "Thanks for helping Zoe. I couldn't have handled that better."

"Of course," Michael smiled.

Zane nodded and left the cabin to walk a few doors down to Erin's. He noticed the limo waiting for them just outside her cabin.

"Hi Zane," Kelsey greeted him as she ran out of Erin's cabin. "You're looking rather dashing."

"Thank you," Zane gave her a tight smile.

Zane was starting to feel a little uncomfortable. It's not like he'd never worn a tuxedo before. He shook his head and sighed. He walked up to the cabin and Caleb walked out.

"Hey, Zane." Caleb looked around Zane. "Did you see Kelsey?"

"Yes," Zane nodded and turned to point, "she went towards my cabin. The rest of the younger generation is there. Piper and Alex are ordering pizza for the game night."

"I know," Caleb rubbed his hands together. "It's going to be so nice to do something normal after all the trouble."

"Enjoy," Zane gave Caleb a smile. "Just please don't make too much of a mess and if there is, get everyone to pitch in to clean it."

"Aye, aye, Captain." Caleb gave Zane a mock salute before heading off to Zane's cabin.

"I thought I heard your voice," Erin's soft tones drew his gaze towards her.

Zane stood mesmerized. Erin's long flaming red hair was piled in a loose flowing bun that allowed some of the soft tendrils to cascade down onto her shoulders. She wore a jewel green dress that matched the startling green color of her eyes that were framed by long black lashes. The shoestrings straps of her dress showed off her golden tan as it dipped into a soft cowl that dipped beneath her collar bone before hugging her petite form to drop down onto her knees. She had long legs for a woman of five-foot-four that were firm, tanned, and ended with her pretty red painted toes in two-inch-heels that matched the color of her dress.

"You look beautiful," Zane said softly. "These are for you." He handed her the roses.

"They're beautiful." Erin smiled and invited him in while she went to put the flowers in a vase of water. "You clean up nicely yourself, soldier." She turned around and smiled at Zane after having put the flowers in water.

"Thank you." Zane gave Erin a slight bow. "Now I think we should go before I pull you into my arms and mess up your lipstick."

Erin smiled up at him while she collected her purse and a light wrap.

The night seemed to drag by. Zane stood to one side with a warm whisky he'd been nursing the entire night, in his hand. Except for dinner, Zane had hardly seen Erin the entire night as her new boss, Phillip, dragged her around introducing her to their clients, potential clients, and other employees. Zane had tagged along at first but then soon had enough before he excused himself and found this nice quiet corner.

Zane was just about to go find Erin and ask for a dance when he saw Phillip introducing her to someone Zane knew only too well. By the look on Erin's face she knew the man quite well too. Zane started to walk towards them, but Phillip stopped him, and Zane's phone beeped at the same time.

"I think we need to give those two a bit of space," Phillip said to Zane.

"Why?" Zane frowned as he looked at his phone message.

"I thought Erin would've told you," Phillip said. "That's ..."

"Trent Wright," Zane said looking from his phone and past Phillip to where Erin was smiling up at Trent. "What's he doing here?"

"He came with his sister who's currently one of our clients," Phillip told Zane. "I know he has a history with Erin, but Trent wants our help." He looked towards Trent and Erin. "He specifically asked for Erin."

"What do you mean about his history with Erin?" Zane felt icy fingers contracting around his heart.

"You know, their engagement?" Phillip's frown grew as he stared at the shocked look on his face. "Isn't that how you know who he is?"

"No," Zane shook his head. "He's the shady lawyer who tried to frame my niece Piper's husband." He looked into Phillips' surprised face. "He's not someone you should be helping. He deserves to be behind bars along with most of his client list."

"I told you the guy was as shady as hell," Shane joined them. "Do you want me to get Trent forcefully removed?" he asked Zane. "I never liked the guy the minute Phillip took us to New York to meet him."

"Ask Shane to get his contacts to look deeper into Trent," Zane advised Phillip. "I would do it for you, but I have to go."

"What about Erin?" Phillip asked Zane.

"Tell her I had to leave." Zane looked towards Erin. "She seems to be enjoying herself."

Zane turned and left before anyone could say anything else and called a cab. Before he went outside he took one last look at Erin talking to Trent. She hadn't told him she'd been engaged. Zane wondered why she hadn't told him about Trent and if she'd left that out what else wasn't she telling him? Erin was so engrossed in conversation with Trent she hadn't even noticed he was leaving. She also hadn't once looked around for him like she'd done up until she was talking to Trent.

When Zane turned and walked away he knew he'd left part of his heart behind him. It was the part of him that stood at five-foot-four inches tall with flaming red hair and jewels for eyes. Zane knew the other shoe was going to drop on his happiness with Erin. He just didn't expect it to hit him like a knife in his chest or hit him with someone who'd tried to destroy his family.

Erin had worked with Jennifer. Surely she knew who Trent Wright was and what he'd done to Zane's family? Is that why she hadn't told him about being engaged to the man? As Zane got into the back of the taxi he wondered if there was a rose that signified betrayal and loss. Because that's how he felt right now. He'd put his trust in Erin and opened up to her as he hadn't done to any other woman in twelve years. He'd thought after everything they had been through she'd been open and honest with him too. What was it that Lilly liked to say? *You can't build trust with a heart full of secrets!*

Zane's phone bleeped again. He looked at the message, frowned, then started to dial.

"Hi," Zane said when his call was answered on the fourth ring. "Do you think you can get me to Mission Bay?"

Chapter Thirty-Four
THE PAINFUL CUT OF SECRETS

"Hi," Logan answered the door to the Cabin he, Chase, and Zoe were sharing with their Uncle Zane. Logan stifled a yawn greeting Erin. He'd just woken up as it was only six in the morning.

"Morning, Logan." Erin held out a basket of muffins she'd baked at four that morning as she hadn't been able to sleep. "I baked some muffins."

"Those smell divine." Logan picked a still warm treat from the basket. "Are they banana muffins?"

"Yes," Erin smiled at him. "I know it's early but is Zane here?"

"No," Logan frowned at Erin. "I thought he'd have told you?"

"Told me what?" Erin asked Logan, looking a little confused.

"Michael flew him to meet up with my mom and Aunt Fallon for the last leg of their journey before returning here for the triple wedding." Logan munched on one of the fresh muffins. "These are so good." He held up the muffin. "Thank you."

"You're welcome." Erin's brow furrowed together. "Do you know when they'll arrive back at the Cove?"

"Four or five days' time," Logan shrugged.

"Thanks, Logan." Erin smiled then turned to leave.

Erin felt like she'd been punched in the stomach. Last night Zane had just left her at the function. When she'd asked Shane he'd been quite frosty to her before shrugging and saying Zane had left. When Erin had asked Shane if he knew why Zane had left, Shane had just shrugged.

Zane wasn't taking any of her calls either. What was going on? She had to find Shane. He knew a lot more than he'd told her last night. Shane was coming to help Lilly with the trellises for the weddings later that day. Erin would ask him when he was at White Sands Cove. In the meantime she had to go into La Jolla and help Phillip with some legal matters for the firm.

Erin walked back into her cabin. The first thing she saw was the ten carefully selected roses from Zane. Her heart jolted as she stopped in her doorway and stared at the bouquet. She'd never felt this way about a man before. It had taken her almost forty-nine years to find her Mr. Right, her soulmate. She was really confused about why Zane had just left not only the ball but White Sands Cove. With no warning, no note, no goodbye, or anything. He was just gone!

"Good morning, Erin." Phillip pulled up at her cabin while she was standing in the doorway staring at her roses. "Are you ready to go?"

"Let me get my purse," Erin turned and gave Phillip a smile.

"Have you seen Zane today?" Phillip asked Erin. He looked a little guilty about something.

"No," Erin's eyes narrowed. "Not since you yanked me away from him at the ball last night."

"Oh right!" Phillip nodded. "I tried to get hold of him this morning and it goes to voicemail." He looked towards Zane's cottage. "Maybe I'll just pop into his cabin quickly to have a word with him."

"He's not there." Erin folded her arms across her chest. "He left early this morning to go meet his nieces and nephew for a week on their yacht."

"He didn't tell me he was going." Phillip shook his head. "We need to reconsider taking on Trent Wright as a client."

"I thought I already told you that?" Erin's eyes narrowed. "What made you suddenly change your mind?"

"Let's just say, I dug a little deeper as Zane suggested I do," Phillip told her. "We're now looking into his connection to the Myers and Parkers."

"Wait," Erin's eyes narrowed. "What did Zane have to do with you changing your mind about Trent?"

"Trent was the one that was making a case against Zane's niece's husband for his crooked client," Phillip told Erin.

"What?" Erin's brows drew together. "Trent was the lawyer on that case?"

"You didn't know?" Phillip asked her. "Turns out he was falsifying evidence against Alex, Piper's husband." He looked at Erin worriedly. "Also, I'm sorry but I may have told Zane you were once engaged to Trent because I honestly thought he knew."

"You did what?" Erin's eyes glittered. *No wonder Zane had left without a word.*

"He knew who Trent was." Phillip told her. "I didn't know it was because of that case. I thought it was because you told Zane who Trent was."

"This is just great," Erin breathed. "Can I ask why you were thinking of helping Trent in the first place?"

"He says he has more evidence against the Myers and the Parkers," Phillip told Erin. "Apparently the information he has will ensure they can't wiggle out of their convictions through some loophole we've not found yet."

"You could've just told me that to begin with, Phillip." Erin looked at him angrily. "I didn't need to have a two hour conversation with him to tell you he was only fishing for information for the Myers and Parkers."

"From what we now know, I understand that," Phillip said apologetically. "This is such a huge case, and it's crippling two of the biggest families in New York." He breathed. "We have to make sure we dot every i and cross every t."

"Like I told you before, you can't trust Trent to help you with that," Erin raised her eyebrows, "because he's the one stealing the dots and heads off the t's."

"He won't be stealing anymore though," Phillip told Erin. "He had a security breach early this morning." He glanced at Erin as he drove. "Trent was caught trying to access some of the files Caleb gave us."

"While you have Trent on those charges you should get a warrant to search his office and home before he has a chance to contact anyone," Erin advised Phillip.

"We're already on that." Phillip nodded while he pulled into his parking space at his office building. "Let's go check out your new corner office with a view of the Pacific Ocean."

"Great." Erin gave Phillip a tight smile.

Erin's head was reeling, and her heart felt like it was being squeezed in a vice grip. On one hand, she was annoyed with Zane for walking out and leaving her without even asking her about Trent. On the other hand, she knew she'd had numerous opportunities to tell Zane about Trent. Now that Erin knew how Zane knew Trent she knew how bad her not telling him about her engagement must've looked to Zane.

But still he could've let her explain, not just walk... not run away! Erin thought, allowing herself to be annoyed and upset at his behavior.

Chapter Thirty-Five
YOU'VE NEVER SEEN THE PARENT TRAP?

"I've been thinking about the Giant that watches over the cove," Zoe told Lilly as she held the lace up to the trellis for Lilly to glue in place.

"Okay." Lilly glued a spot of the lace before tying it off with a sparkling gold ribbon.

"What if the treasure isn't in Pirates Wall at all?" Zoe positioned the next part of the lace.

"You think there's another hidden cave?" Lilly stopped what she was doing and looked at Zoe. "You could be right." She tied the next gold ribbon. "But we've been through the entire cave system of Pirates Wall and we've found nothing." She sighed.

"If you were hiding the wealth that we know was hidden, would you make it that easy to find the treasure?" Zoe asked. "I know I wouldn't, and I've read all the journals Aunt Jennifer has with regards to the treasure and White Sands Cove."

"Of course you have," Lilly grinned. "I've not even got through the first shelf yet."

"I'm a speed reader," Zoe shrugged. "I've been going over that picture in my head. What if there is a hidden cave system in Crab Shack Cliffs?"

"I don't think there is," Lilly told Zoe as she finished off the lace decoration around the trellis Shane had built. "I tell you what, after the weddings are over, we can go explore Crab Shack Cliffs."

"Really?" Zoe looked at Lilly excitedly.

"Yes, really," Lilly grinned. "That'll give you a few more days to do more research."

"Thank you." Zoe did something she never did — she gave Lilly an exuberant hug.

"In the meantime, we need to work on getting Erin and Uncle Zane back together," Zoe surprised Lilly by saying.

"What do you mean?" Lilly frowned. "I thought things were going great with them?"

"Nope," Zoe shook her head. "I overheard your father telling your mother that my uncle walked out on Erin at the ball and then left White Sands Cove."

"I thought he was with your mom, aunt, and uncle for the last leg of the cruise back to La Jolla?" Lilly was a little confused and saddened by the news about Erin and Zane.

"He is," Zoe nodded then told Lilly what she'd heard.

"I think you're right, Zoe." Lilly shook her head. "This definitely needs a little parent trapping."

"What?" Zoe's brows creased together.

"Parent trapping?" Lilly raised her eyebrows. "As in the moving The Parent Trap?"

"Haven't seen it." Zoe shook her head.

"There are a few." Lilly shook her head. "Come on, we're finished here for the day. Looks like we need to get the rest of the gang together to formulate a plan." She looked at Zoe. "And you need to watch at least one of The Parent Trap movies."

"Okay," Zoe shrugged and followed Lilly.

EPILOGUE

Zane wasn't a saint by any means. He'd seen and done things in battle that still haunted him, but he was also a man of honor and integrity. His family and those he cared for meant the world to him and he'd die for them. What he didn't tolerate were half-truths, harmful secrets, lies, and betrayal. When it came to relationships he believed that you had to trust your partner with your whole heart. There was no half measure to love. It was all or nothing for Zane.

Zane ran his hands over his eyes. He was so tired. He'd been up all night — first on a flight to Santa Barbara, and now he sat in a waiting room once again waiting for news about his niece, Fallon.

"Thank you for coming Uncle Zane." Hunter, Zane's nephew, gave him a cup of coffee. "We really appreciate it. But you didn't have to come all the way here."

"Of course I'm going to be here." Zane took a sip of the bitter brew. "What happened?"

"Fallon went riding with Ashley and Cam," Hunter explained. "I still can't get used to having to call my father Cam." He shook his head.

"I know, I keep wanting to call him Craig." Zane smiled.

"Sorry, getting off the subject," Hunter said. "The horse Fallon was on got spooked, reared up and then bucked her off. She hit her head on a rock and now has stitches in her head and is concussed."

"That's not going to look good in her wedding pictures," Hunter breathed.

"Are you okay?" Hunter asked Zane.

"I'm fine," Zane lied. "I'm glad you called. I needed to get out of White Sands Cove for a bit and I missed my family."

"Okay." Hunter's eyes narrowed on Zane. He knew there was something else going on, but Hunter knew better than to push Zane. "I suppose you know that this means you're going to have to sail The Dorothy Rose back to La Jolla?"

"I do." Zane nodded. "I also think it would be best for Fallon and Daniel to fly back to White Sands Cove with Michael."

Zane looked over to where Michael was curled up on a few hospital chairs fast asleep.

"I think that's a great idea and I know the only other person Fallon trusts to sail her yacht is you, Uncle Zane."

Zane was really glad to find out that Fallon, his oldest niece, was okay after being thrown from a horse. Fallon and her fiancé were flying back to La Jolla with Michael in a few hours' time. Zane, along with his nephew, niece, their fiancés, his two great-nieces, and Michael's youngest sister Ray, were setting sail to La Jolla.

Hunter was going to take the first leg to give Zane some time to get a bit of sleep before he took over sailing the large yacht. Zane had taken over Fallon's cabin for the journey. The cabin he usually used had been taken over by three teenage girls. Zane didn't have the energy to argue his way back into his cabin.

It had been a while since he'd been lulled to sleep by the gentle bob of the ocean as The Dorothy Rose sliced through the water en-route to her destination. Even though Zane was exhausted he couldn't sleep. Instead he was lying in a darkened cabin playing with Zoe's multi-purpose flashlight he'd found in Fallon's cabin. He switched the flashlight from normal to blue-light and was flickering it on and off the ceiling and walls of the cabin when he saw something.

Zane frowned and sat up on the bed. He shone the light over the ceiling and down the wall. His eyes widened and his heart jolted when an image he'd seen before was illuminated on the wall.

SECRETS OF WHITE SANDS COVE

Book 6

PROLOGUE

The first wedding to be held at the new White Sands Cove Hotel is the McCaid family's triple wedding. While Lilly puts her heart into making sure everything is perfect for the big day, Erin and Zane each realize they may have been too hasty in misjudging each other.

Can Erin and Zane make their way back to each other? Join the McCaids, Coopers, and Carnegies as they navigate their way through a hellish past into a bright future. A future full of warm sunny days next to the lazy Pacific Ocean while they find true love and adventure.

Chapter Thirty-Six
THE WAY FORWARD

*E*rin's children were finally happy and that cloud they were hoping to leave behind in New York when they moved to La Jolla had finally disappeared altogether. Through the pain and torment of their past her children had soldiered on. Along the way they'd each found their soul mates. So far, it had been a summer full of emotion, fear, new beginnings, and hauntings from the past. What Erin had learned this summer was that no matter how far or fast you ran there was no escaping your past.

Erin had learned the hard way that putting the past behind you didn't mean sweeping it under the rug and then trying to run away from the hidden debris. It meant having to sort through it, every painful bit by painful bit, until it was cleared away or at least put in place. Erin sighed and took another sip of her cocktail as she lounged on the deck chair on the beach. She was going to miss the retreat when she finally moved. Even though it was a ten-minute drive from her new home, she'd loved the Cove and being able to walk to the beach each morning.

Erin had bought the house next to the point house on Ocean Walk. Kelsey and Caleb were worried it had been an impulse buy. Maybe it had been, but the house was close to Jennifer's house and next to Jennifer's and Miranda's Seafield Boutique Hotel. Erin was going into business with Miranda and Jennifer by turning the house she'd bought into an Inn. Over the past four days she'd been spending time with Jennifer and Miranda when she wasn't helping Lilly and Piper with wedding arrangements.

Investing in La Jolla was the right thing to do as it was a popular holiday destination no matter the time of year. The location of the town and its good weather nearly all year around had managed to get Jennifer and Miranda to sway Erin's decision to join them in the hotel trade. Erin would still be working at the agency on a consulting basis like Jennifer and Max did. That way she got to practice law and still be able to concentrate on her new venture. She was extremely excited about her new start in La Jolla. Especially as the nightmare of New York was practically over.

While Erin was staying at the White Sands Cove retreat, she'd helped Michael and Lilly get their hotel ready for the opening. She'd helped plan and organize events, choose color swatches and furniture for the rooms, and helped with implementation of various accommodation systems. Erin had found she'd love it. After the ordeal her family had been through in New York, practicing law didn't give her the satisfaction it once did. Of course, every lawyer knew there were many facets to the law. But every case Erin had won over the years was a step in making sure the judicial system worked. When you find yourself on the other side of the line you're used to fighting for, all the flaws in the legal system become glaringly obvious. Erin's fighting to make things right and matter suddenly started to feel like she'd been pushing a large boulder up the highest mountain.

When Erin had decided to take Jennifer's job offer in La Jolla, she wasn't sure she wanted to practice law anymore. She was looking for something that made her feel good about herself again. Erin wanted to do something that made people happy and made her feel content. When she came to White Sands Cove, the moment she'd stepped out the car and heard the whisper of the Pacific Ocean and smelt its fresh salty scent, she knew she was home. She'd loved the cabin her family had moved into that was perched on a small hill cradled between the arms of the imposing cove cliffs.

Every morning since arriving at the Cove Erin had woken up to the song of the birds, the lulling greeting of the rolling waves, and the crisp fresh salty sea air. The bonus was having both her children back with her under one roof. Erin had even adopted another two adult children into her fold and made a whole lot of new friends. Not the frivolous New York kind of friends either but the genuine type. Friends that jumped right into the muck with you and helped you wade through it no matter how deep, smelly, or messy it was. Erin and her children had been amazed and heartened by the big hearts of the people they'd met at the Cove. It was like a beacon for all the human angels of the world that somehow found their way to it.

The only thing pulling Erin down at the moment was the way her and Zane's relationship had seemed to crash and burn before it even had a chance to blossom. Zane had returned a day ago, sailing into the White Cove Docking bay on The Dorothy Rose, which was one of the most beautiful yachts Erin had ever seen. It had been designed by Zane's niece, Fallon McCaid and had quite a story behind it. When she'd seen Zane in his board shorts and his white pirate shirt emphasizing his tanned arms, Erin thought her heart was going to burst through her chest. He looked so happy as he navigated the large yacht into its birth and had walked down the gangplank in the midst of his family. The McCaids were a really close knit family. Erin could still see the image of Zane laughing at something his oldest great-niece, Blair, was saying as they were piling luggage off the boat.

Erin hadn't stayed around to greet them. She'd taken off to

the office. It had been a cowardly move, but she knew if Zane had seen her, it would've ruined a perfect family moment for him. They'd all gone out for dinner somewhere that night. Michael, Caleb, Lilly, and Kelsey had gone with them. They'd asked Erin to join them, but she'd made an excuse about some work she had to do. Miranda and Jennifer had popped around and after a few glasses of wine Erin had poured her heart out to her two best friends. Erin had heard the McCaids, Caleb, Kelsey, Lilly, and Michael come home quite late that night. Except in passing or from a distance she hadn't really seen Zane. Erin knew she needed to corner him and make him listen to her, but she wasn't ready yet and didn't quite know what to say. Erin sighed and adjusted her large sun hat before looking at her watch. She had another twenty minutes to lounge in the sun before she had to get ready to go into the office.

Erin took a long sip of her fruity cocktail before lying back and closing her eyes when a shadow fell over her.

"Hi," a deep familiar voice had her opening her eyes. "Can we talk?"

"I don't have anything to say to you right now," Erin sighed. "I am on a break for another twenty minutes."

"Please, Erin." His voice held a hint of desperation in it. "I need you to listen to me."

"Fine," Erin sat up and pulled on her beach robe. "You have ten minutes."

"I thought you were on a break for another twenty?" He frowned at her.

"I still need to go and get ready," Erin told him. "Now what's so important that you couldn't phone me or come see me at the office?"

"There was a time, not too long ago, I didn't need to have an excuse to talk to you," he smiled at her sadly.

"That was before I found out who you really were." Erin raised her eyebrows. "This small talk has now cut into almost five minutes of your time, Trent."

"I need you to ask Phillip to reconsider helping me." Trent looked at her. "You know that it's nothing personal when I represent the clients that I do, right?"

"You know, Trent, I have a lot of friends in the legal field." Erin looked at him. "I've faced them down in court many times. Of course I understand that as lawyers we're bound to be on opposite sides of a case at some time or other." Her eyes glittered. "The thing is, we all have a choice what battles we choose to fight. Not only do you make terrible choices, but you feel nothing about twisting things to your client's advantage."

"Is that a nice way of you accusing me of falsifying evidence?" Trent frowned at her.

"Have you?" Erin asked him seriously.

"Not deliberately," Trent told her honestly, "and I can prove it. You know me, Erin."

Trent reached over and took both her hands in his as he looked at her pleadingly.

"I thought I did." Erin shook her head sadly.

"I have all my records, Erin." Trent told her. "I'll give you, Jennifer, Phillip, and Max full access to everything in my office."

"How do we know you haven't already doctored everything?" Erin asked him.

"I'll sign any documents giving you access to all call records, emails, and whatever you need." Trent squeezed her hands. "I refuse to go down with some crooked politician and his best friends."

"Best friends?" Erin frowned. "Who else was involved in the Myers and Parker's scandalous dealings?"

Trent crunched his eyes together and ran his one hand through his hair.

"I'm putting all my trust in you here," Trent told her softly. "There are players involved in this hornet's nest. A hornet's nest your son and daughter kicked over. Players that are a lot more dangerous than the Myers and the Parkers."

"Trent, what are you involved in?" Erin asked Trent worriedly.

"The other night when I was caught in Phillips's office," Trent swallowed, "I wasn't trying to find out what you had on the Myers or the Parkers." He reached into his back pocket. "I was trying to hide this." He handed Erin a flash drive.

"What's this?" Erin's brows creased.

"The missing links Phillip needs to completely close this case," Trent said softly.

"Why didn't you just tell Phillip that before he had you arrested?" Erin asked him.

"Because..." Trent's jaw clenched, "my sister is one of those dangerous people."

"Your sister?" Erin's eyes grew huge. "But she's one of Phillip's customers. We provide security for her company."

"Yeah," Trent nodded. "When Phillip caught me in the office my sister was with him."

"Trent!" Erin put her hand innocently on his leg. "It was your sister that told Phillip that she thought you were after the Myers' and Parker's information."

"She was covering her own tracks," Trent sighed. "Who do you think introduced me to all my upstanding clients?"

"How do I know you're not just trying to set your sister up?" Erin asked Trent. "It's not the first time you've twisted evidence for a client."

"Again, where do you think I got the evidence from?" Trent said impatiently. "Look, Erin. I've come here with no protection, and I've given you the only leverage I have over some awfully bad people."

"Okay," Erin's eyes narrowed. "Come with me. I need to go change and then we can go see Phillip together and find out what you've just given me."

Chapter Thirty-Seven
WHERE YOU GO TROUBLE FOLLOWS

Zane had gotten an ear full from Piper the minute he'd set foot in White Sands Cove. Worse, Piper had managed to catch her sister's and future sister-in-law's relationship with Erin before all four of them had descended upon his doorstep. Maybe they were right, and he'd been a little hasty in his judgement. On the sail back to La Jolla he'd realized his mistake. He should've spoken to Erin before rushing off to Santa Barbara.

Zane had seen Erin walk off and go to her office the day he'd arrived back in White Sands Cove without saying hello. She hadn't come to dinner that evening either. Michael had told him that Erin was currently on the beach getting some sun before going into her office. Zane wanted to find her and ask her if they could perhaps have a sundowner at the Crab Shack and talk. He owed her an apology and an explanation. One thing he knew for sure from not being with her these past few days was that he felt empty without her.

Zane walked down the path from the White Sands Hotel to the beach when he saw a man beat him to Erin. He stopped dead in his tracks when he realized that the man was Erin's ex-fiancé, Trent Wright. Zane felt that icy grip around his heart once again while he stood watching their intimate exchange. He felt numb except for the little prickling sensation of shock zaps targeted at his heart. Zane was about to turn away when he noticed something glint on the hill near the Crab Shack. The hairs on his arms stood on end. He squinted and adjusted his gaze before he froze as he spotted where the glint came from.

Zane pulled out his phone and dialed. His call was answered on the third ring. "Shane, I need you and Amy to scout the hill to the left of the crab shack."

"Amy already picked that up," Shane told him, then nearly scared Zane to death as he came up behind him. "Amy and Lilly were about to come and help you with Erin when we all spotted Trent with Erin."

"How long has the watcher been up there for?" Zane asked Shane.

Before Shane could answer a sound that rang out like the crack of whip exploded from next to them.

"Erin!" Zane shouted and took off towards the beach with Shane hot on his heels.

When they got to Erin and Trent, they found both of them face down on the sand trying to hide beneath Erin's deck chair.

"Are you alright?" Zane slid towards her through the sand on his knees.

"Amy has the sniper," Shane held his phone to his ear. "Erin, you're bleeding." He pointed to the blood on her beach robe.

"What?" Erin said looking stunned. She looked at her beach robe. "I'm not hurt." She frowned and her head moved towards Trent. "Trent!" she shouted.

"I'm fine," Trent rolled over in the sand holding his arm. "The bullet went through my arm." He looked at Erin. "Do you still have the disk?" he asked her softly.

Erin looked at her clenched fist and nodded, feeling the small device still biting into her palm.

"Get it to Phillip right away." Trent's fingers were red with blood as he held his bleeding arm.

"Why is it everywhere you go trouble follows you?" Shane hissed, ripping part of his t-shirt to wrap around Trent's arm. "Can you call Kelsey and an ambulance?" he asked Erin who was still in shock.

"I'll do it," Zane helped Erin to her feet. "You'll be okay." He rubbed the top of her arms as he looked into her eyes.

"No," Trent shook his head, "I can't go to a hospital. You'll have to get Kelsey to stitch me up."

"You know she has to report a bullet wound dipstick!" Zane ignored Trent's wince as he tightened the make-shift bandage. "Let's get you both inside and then you can tell us all why a sniper is trying to take you out."

While Kelsey stitched up the flesh wound on Trent's arm, Phillip and Max arrived at the hotel. Trent explained to all of them what was on the disk Erin had. It was proof of all the shady dealings of some immensely powerful businessmen and politicians. Including his family's business that was now run by Trent's older sister. It also had a whole lot of employee names on Phillip's and Max's agency that were moles.

"No wonder someone wanted you dead." Shane pulled a face. "What are we going to do with him?" He looked at Max and Phillip.

"There's a lot of evidence and roadmaps to where we can find more on this disk." Phillip and Max confirmed. "Why didn't you come forward with this when you asked us for help?"

"That was before I realized just who one of the apex players was," Trent explained to them, wincing as Kelsey sewed him up. "I had no idea I'd just told one of the heads of the multi-headed snake I needed help. Then basically showed them I had incriminating evidence that would bury a lot of powerful people."

"How did you not know your sister was one of the leaders of the pack?" Zane asked Trent. He still didn't trust the man.

"When she tried to frame me for stealing information in Phillip's office," Trent told Zane. "I told her I needed to leave something for Phillip."

"So your sister ratted you out?" Shane grinned.

"What have I ever done to you?" Trent frowned at Shane's animosity towards him.

"I don't like anyone who uses the law as a tool to hurt the innocent and play into the hands of those who think they're above the law," Shane told him. "It's like putting tomato sauce on a perfectly cooked prime steak."

"Everyone deserves a fair trial," Trent defended his profession.

"It's not really fair though when the deck is stacked, and the other side has the money and means to play dirty or wield their powerful contacts as a weapon." Shane raised his eyebrows.

"Regardless of what you think of me or my law practice," Trent told Shane, "I'm no use to this case dead. If you're going to bring these people down, you need someone like me that knows how to play their game."

"I hate to admit this," Erin looked at Phillip, "but Trent's right. The only way to win this is if we know how to play their game. The people on that disk are basically untouchable otherwise and you can bet they'll try to find a way out of this."

"You can't trust this guy." Zane glanced at Erin before looking at Phillip. "How do we know he hasn't been planted here to ensure your case folds?"

"You don't." Trent watched as Kelsey bandaged him up. "Thank you." He smiled at her.

"I think you should put him," Kelsey pointed to Trent, "somewhere he has no contact with the outside world and until the case is wrapped up only a selected few have contact with Trent."

"I like that idea." Zane nodded at Kelsey. "Good thinking, Kelsey."

"I agree with Kelsey," Shane seconded the motion.

"I also think it's a good idea," Max nodded.

"Okay then that's settled." Phillip stood and took the disk. "Amy's taken the sniper in for questioning, and we'll take Trent to a secure facility until the trial is over."

"I'll come with you." Zane offered. "Just in case more trouble follows Trent."

"Shane and I will follow you," Max offered, looking at Shane for confirmation.

"I'll just stay here." Erin gave Phillip a tight smile.

Zane and Erin had hardly made eye contact since he'd helped her at the beach.

"I'll be here with her." Jennifer walked into the room. "We're going to be finishing up the decorations for tomorrow night's stag-hen party."

"Good idea," Max kissed Jennifer on the forehead.

Zane looked up and met Erin's eyes. They stared at each other for a few seconds before Shane helped Trent up and started walking out of Lilly's office at the hotel.

"Let's get you out of here before some more of your friends come calling," Shane said.

"Wait," Trent stopped. "Can I have a word with Erin, alone?" He looked at the others in the room pointedly.

"It's fine." Erin smiled at the looks in all her friends' eyes.

Zane's eyes met hers again and she could see the dark shadow in them.

"Are you okay?" Jennifer asked Erin as they watched the black SUV's pull away from White Sands Cove.

"I just want this all behind us once and for all," Erin sighed. "I felt that bullet zing past my cheek." She turned to look at Jennifer, her eyes were haunted. "Every time I think I can breathe again, and I finally feel myself relaxing I get drawn right back into the past."

"It's over now," Jennifer reassured her. "I think with the information Trent came forward with and his knowledge of the way these people work, you and your kids will never have to look over your shoulders again."

"I hope so Jennifer," Erin smiled at her friend. "I really do. Shall we go and help with the party preparations? I'm really looking forward to the next few days of pre-wedding activities."

"Yes, me too," Jennifer grinned while walking with Erin to the hotel. "Although Maddison is back so you'll find my kids becoming a lot more competitive." Her and Erin laughed. "Even Ray has started to become a little monster competitor."

"Don't worry," Erin assured Jennifer, "Caleb and Kelsey can stand their ground. Kelsey always has to be the best at everything, and Caleb can be a bit of a perfectionist."

"Oh, wait until you see my sisters in action," Ashley McCaid, one of the brides to be and Zane's youngest niece, grinned as she joined the two women going to the hotel.

"Well, this is going to be loads of fun." Jennifer shook her head. "Maybe we need to hire a few bouncers or something just in case."

The three women laughed as they walked into the hall.

"This is beautiful." Jennifer looked around the room.

"Thank you," Lilly greeted them both at the door and handed them each a crisp glass of wine. "Come on in and have some snacks."

"I love a pre-party, party," Ashley sighed. "I don't know how to thank you all for all you've done for us. I feel so guilty for not being here."

"Trust me," Fallon McCaid, another one of the brides-to-be and Zane's oldest niece, came over to join them, "I think it was a lot better that I kept Ashley away. She can never make up her mind about things."

"That's true," Ashley grinned. "I do get a little carried away."

"Fallon, The Dorothy Rose is looking magnificent," Erin complimented her.

"Thank you." Fallon smiled at Erin.

"How are you now that you're sailing again?" Erin took a sip of her wine.

"To be honest I still have times where I feel a panic attack coming on," Fallon told Erin honestly. "Especially if I see any hint of a squall on the horizon."

"But she soldiers through like a champion," Daniel Goddard, Chase's father and Fallon's fiance said proudly as he walked up to them. "How are you, Erin?" He gave Erin a hug.

"I'm well, all things considered," Erin gave Daniel a small smile.

"I heard about your ordeal on the beach," Daniel's voice dropped.

"Zane was right about one thing," Erin gave a small laugh, "wherever Trent Wright goes, trouble follows him."

"He's a very handsome man though." Ashley laughed as her fiancé, Ryan Hurst, gave her a black look coming over to join them.

"Hello, Erin," Ryan greeted Erin before teasing Ashley, "are you eyeing the older men now?"

"Well, when they look like Trent Wright..." Ashley grinned.

"I know," Lilly agreed. "Pity he chose to represent the wrong side."

"I think he's seen the error of his ways," Jennifer stuck up for Trent. "Let's just hope he stays on our side until the trial is over."

"I'm starving," Piper waddled over to them. "Can we eat now?"

"Of course," Lilly grinned. "Tuck in. There are lots of samples of all the food on the wedding menu and six different cakes that will make up the layers of the wedding cakes."

"Oh that sounds so yummy," Piper and Samantha, who were both pregnant, rubbed their hands together. "That oil you gave me for my back, Samantha, is so good," she said to Samantha as the two of them led the way to the food.

Erin stood back and let everyone get their food while she sipped her wine watching all the people in the room enjoying themselves. This is what she wanted all the time. The feeling of belonging with her big extended family. As an only child Erin always wanted siblings so her house was always bursting to noisy capacity during holidays, family days, special occasions, or just drop in to say hi days.

Erin's eyes settled on her daughter holding hands with Michael and laughing as Ray told an animated story about their sailing trip. Caleb stood with his arm possessively around Lilly's shoulders as the two of them chatted with Fallon and Daniel. On the other side of the room the five teenagers sat chatting and laughing as they ate pizza and drank soda. It was so nice to see the younger generation without a device glued to their hands. The only thing that could make this night even more perfect was to be wrapped in the warmth of Zane's arms.

Chapter Thirty-Eight
A TRIPLE STAG-HEN PARTY

Zane still hadn't had a chance to speak to Erin. Zane knew he had to speak to her and clear the air. He owed her an apology for jumping to conclusions not once, but twice. He planned to find Erin at the party later and ask her if they could talk, and hopefully she'd listen to what he had to say. Whatever that was going to be. Zane still hadn't figured out where he'd even start to try to apologize to Erin. He felt like he was sixteen again and trying to navigate the world of dating.

Shane, Zane, Phillip, and Max had spent the previous afternoon until late the previous evening interrogating Trent Wright. If the man wasn't such a shark and if he hadn't been engaged to Erin, Zane might've gotten along with him. Both Shane and Zane had been shocked to find out that Trent had a military background. After walking away from his family's misbegotten fortune, Trent had earned his law degree in the military. Apparently, he'd tried his best to shun his family's not so clean legacy. Pity Trent had caved and given in to his family's pressure.

Trent was safely stashed away where he had no contact with the outside world and none of his enemies, of which the man had a *lot*, could find him. Zane, Max, Shane, and Phillip just hoped those enemies didn't try to come through them to find him. They were ready if they did this time, as Phillip and Max had sent some agents to watch the retreat and keep an eye on Erin and her family. At least the man was now locked away from Erin as well, so Zane wouldn't land up running into what he mistook as intimate moments between Erin and Trent again.

Zane had just finished working on the third wedding trellis Shane had made when a soft wet nose nudged him from behind. He spun around and nearly fell into the trellis with Phantom standing so close to him.

"Hey boy." Zane patted the horse's nose. "I hear you found your forever home right here at White Sands Cove."

Phantom whinnied before pushing Zane with his head.

"Okay, okay," Zane laughed, holding up his hands before fishing a carrot from his work bag. "There you go." He patted the horse's head. "Can I take a quick look to see how the burn is healing?"

Phantom ate the carrot and nudged Zane again knowing that he had other treats in his bag that he carried for the animals.

"You're so greedy today." Zane gave the horse a big grin before fishing out an apple. "Now that you have an apple, do you mind if I take a look at your wound?"

Phantom shook his head, flicking his lush long white mane.

"Good boy," Zane patted the horse gently as he stepped around him to look at the horse's injured side.

Zane sucked in a breath. The scar ran from the top of Phantom's left side along his ribs and covered the top of his back leg. Five months ago, Phantom's previous owners were returning from a horse show with Phantom in his horse box when they were involved in an accident. Phantom was flung from his horse box and skidded across the tarmac. Michael and Ray had witnessed the accident and got out to help. When the vet arrived on scene he didn't think Phantom would make it as his injuries were so bad. But Ray had refused to let the vet even suggest putting Phantom down.

After a few months and many vet bills later, Phantom was making a remarkable recovery, but his owners decided he wasn't useful to them any longer. Ray had begged Max and Jennifer to let her keep treating Phantom at the rehabilitation farm. Seeing the excellent job Ray was doing with the animals she'd taken in they'd agreed to let her continue treating him. The only condition was that Ray had to eventually find Phantom a forever home. Ray had slowly been working on Michael to include Phantom as part of their trial riding horses. When she'd heard that Michael was going to see if Kelsey wanted to adopt Phantom, Ray had been over the moon.

Phantom was so happy at White Sands Cove he'd even made friends with a tortoise, an Egyptian goose, Lunar, and Goose the dog. Phantom's latest friend, Rafferty, could be found hitching a ride on Phantom's back like he was royalty. Zane kept meaning to get a picture of Kelsey's huge cat licking his paws lazily sprawled out on Phantom's back. It was amazing how even the animals seemed happy and content at the Cove. Zane was worried that Goose wasn't going to want to leave when the time came for the McCaids to set sail home.

Zane worried that he too may not want to leave when the time came. Especially now that he'd found Erin and had been offered a job at Phillip and Max's agency. White Sands Cove and La Jolla had stolen his heart in more ways than one. Now that Zane's nephew and nieces were happy and starting their new lives there was no reason to go back to Florida. Even Finn McCaid, Zane's father had found love again and was starting a new life. He was beginning to feel like a bit of a third wheel in his family and was seriously thinking about taking Phillip up on his offer. Michael and Lilly had given him the cabin at White Sands Cove for as long as he needed it.

Zane was so deep in thought he hadn't noticed Phantom helping himself to the snacks in his bag.

"Hey," Zane laughed at the cheeky horse. "You shouldn't take advantage of a man deep in thought."

Phantom nodded his head and looked like he was grinning at Zane.

"Uncle Zane!" Zoe's shout caught his attention. "Come quick, it's Piper."

"Got to go buddy." Zane gave Phantom the last carrot in the bag. "Don't go doing your business around here now okay?" He warned the horse before running off towards Zoe.

"What's up, sweetheart?" Zane caught up with his great-niece.

"I think it may just be Braxton-hicks, but Piper swears she's in labor," Zoe told Zane as they walked into the hotel. "Lilly is sitting with her and everyone else has gone into La Jolla including Kelsey."

"Okay," Zane took off his work bag as he made his way to Lilly's office behind Zoe.

"Uncle Zane's here," Zoe breathed a sigh of relief. "He's going to take you to the hospital."

"I'll come with you." Lilly helped Piper up.

"I'll go get the..." Zane started to walk to the front door of the hotel when Chase ran up the stairs.

"I already got your car for you," Chase handed Zane the keys, not able to hide the look of relief on his face. "I'm so glad I didn't have to drive Piper to the hospital." He looked at Zane wide-eyed.

"It's okay." Zane gave Chase a smile. "Thank you for fetching the car. Do you think you could try to get hold of the rest of the family to tell them we're taking Piper to the hospital?"

"Sure thing." Chase nodded.

"Zoe, could you and Chase just keep an eye on things here for me?" Lilly asked them as she helped Piper.

"Of course," Zoe nodded.

"Come, Pip," Zane helped her into the back of the car, "let's get you to the hospital."

"We need to call Alex," Piper breathed. "I wanted to be here for the party tonight."

"Your sisters and brother will understand," Lilly soothed Piper. "Just breathe and try to relax."

"I don't want to relax," Piper said irritably as Zane drove them to the hospital. "It's way too soon for the baby to be arriving."

"I'm sure everything's going to be okay." Zane glanced at Piper in the mirror.

"A panic attack." Piper sipped her soda water as she explained what had happened to her earlier that day. "Can you believe it?"

"You have been a little stressed out with all the wedding planning and trying to make everything perfect for your siblings' big day." Erin smiled at Piper.

"That's what Dr. Barnes said," Piper sighed. "I never thought I'd ever have kids," she admitted to Erin.

"Why do you say that?" Erin frowned. "When you've been really great with your sister's kids."

"Not sure," Piper shrugged. "I guess I was so busy trying to prove myself in New York that having children never crossed my mind."

"New York has a way of doing that to you." Erin nodded. "It gets under your skin and all of a sudden you're wanting your share of the big apple."

"You're always striving to get one step ahead of your competition even if that competition is your best friend." Piper sighed and shook her head.

"The minute I stepped out the car door, heard the lull of the ocean, and smelled the fresh salty sea air I just felt all that weight of the big city you carry with you melt away," Erin told Piper.

"I know what you mean," Piper smiled. "That's how I felt when I went home after all those years of living in New York."

"Looks like your sisters and brother are having a great time." Lilly came over to join them. "Having the stag and hen parties combined was an awesome idea."

"I'm looking forward to the hike across Pirates Wall tomorrow," Erin said to Lilly. "Have you seen Kelsey?"

"No," Lilly shook her head. "I was also looking for her a little while ago to start the gift opening game."

"I'll go ask Michael," Erin excused herself from Lilly and Piper to make her way over to Michael.

"Hi," Michael called over the music. "Are you having a good time?"

"I am," Erin nodded. "Do you know where Kelsey is?"

"There was an emergency at the hospital that she had to get to," Michael offered Erin another glass of wine.

"No thanks," Erin shook her head. "Oh, okay." She was a little bit surprised Kelsey hadn't mentioned it to her like she usually did before she left for an emergency.

"She said she'd be back as soon as she could," Michael smiled at Erin.

As Erin was walking away from Michael her phone bleeped. She looked at it and was surprised to find out it was from Trent.

"*Can we please talk?*" Trent's message flashed onto her screen.

"*I thought we had said everything there was to say already!*" Erin typed back.

"*You know how I feel about you and always have,*" Trent wrote back. "*Before I'm not able to tell you what I need to tell you, please will you give me just half an hour?*"

"*I'm at a party right now, Trent,*" Erin typed back.

"*Thirty minutes is all I'm asking,*" Trent wrote back.

"*Fine, I'll be there in twenty minutes,*" Erin sighed looking around the room.

There was no sign of Zane. Piper had told Erin after he'd dropped her and Lilly back at the retreat, he had some business to take care of. Erin was really hoping to corner him. She owed him an apology and an explanation. But the party had already been going for two hours with no signs of him showing up. Erin went to get her cabin keys from Lilly's office. As she got to the front desk the hotel's landline phone rang. Erin frowned.

That's strange! Erin thought. The hotel wasn't officially open yet. The opening of the hotel was to coincide with the launch of the annual Crab Shack end of summer games in two weeks' time.

She walked over to the desk and put her mobile phone and club soda down behind the front desk.

"Hello?" Erin answered the phone.

There was no one on the other side. Erin frowned and put the phone down thinking it must've been a wrong number. She was about to leave when the phone rang again. She picked it up.

"Hello?" Erin answered the phone on the desk again.

"Mom?" Kelsey's voice came through the receiver.

"Honey?" Erin frowned, "Why are you calling on this line?"

"I forgot my phone at the party," Kelsey told Erin. "I don't know anyone's number so myself and one of the night nurses have been randomly calling the desk as it was the only number I could find."

"That's the joy of having mobile phones, you think you don't have to learn important numbers," Erin laughed. "Where is it? I'll bring it to you."

"I'm so sorry to drag you away from the fun. I think I left it near where Michael and I were choosing the music." Kelsey explained to Erin. "Have you seen Zane yet?"

"No," Erin shook her head. "He hasn't arrived at the party."

"That's strange." Kelsey sounded a little shocked. "I wonder why?"

"Max and Shane aren't here either." Erin frowned. "I'll be there in twenty minutes."

"Thank you Mom," Kelsey blew a kiss through the phone.

Erin hung up and hurried through to the function room where the stag-hen party was being held. After chatting with Michael, they found Kelsey's phone. Michael offered to take it, but Erin said she'd do it as she had to make a quick stop in La Jolla and the hospital was on her way.

Chapter Thirty-Nine
THE STUBBORNNESS OF GEN XS

Zane had finally managed to get back to the Cove. He should've been at his nieces' and nephew's stag-hen party hours ago. But there'd been a problem when one of Phillip's agents who was working for one of the powerful people Trent was about to put away, tried to poison Trent's food. Zane had quickly gone back to his cabin for a shower and to get changed. His heart beat wildly in his chest as he neared the function room. This was the night that would either make or break Zane and Erin's young relationship.

Zane stood at the door and took a deep breath before walking into the function. He knew without even looking around the room that Erin wasn't there as the place felt hollow. Zane swallowed and his heart sank with disappointment.

"Uncle Zane," Fallon ran up to him to give him a hug. "We've been waiting for you."

"I'm sorry I'm late sweetheart," Zane grinned back. "I see your party is a huge success."

"It was so nice of Lilly and Michael to let some of the guests stay at the hotel before it's even open." Ashley came over to join them. "Hi, Uncle Zane."

"Have any of you seen Erin?" Zane asked them after he'd finished greeting everyone.

"She went to the hospital to take Kelsey her phone," Piper told her uncle. "I'm sure she'll be back soon."

"I just found Erin's phone on my desk." Lilly walked back into the room. Her eyes narrowed as she looked at Zane. "Would you see that she gets it back, please Zane?" She handed Erin's phone to him.

"Sure," Zane nodded his thanks to Lilly. "I'll do that as soon as she gets back."

"We're rooting for you big guy." Fallon patted her uncle on the shoulder before all the women walked off to go have a group dance.

Zane was about to pocket Erin's phone when a message from Trent Wright flashed up on the screen.

"I'm so glad you've decided to give me another chance. I can't wait to talk." Trent wrote.

Once again Zane felt those icy fingers squeeze around his heart as he realized Erin hadn't only gone out to take Kelsey her phone. She was on her way to see Trent. He felt both cold and bruised on the inside, but his feelings were soon replaced by another one — Fear.

"Lilly," Zane called her back over. "When did Erin leave?"

"I don't know," Lilly frowned, "about an hour ago?"

"Thank you," Zane tried to give her a fake smile. He didn't want to alarm anyone at his niece's and nephew's party. "Could you please let the kids know I've been called away?"

"Is there something wrong?" Lilly's frown deepened.

"I hope not," Zane said worriedly. "I don't want anyone here to panic or ruin their fun."

"If you tell me what's going on I promise to keep quiet," Lilly bribed him.

"I think Erin is in danger." Zane showed Lilly Erin's messages on her phone.

"Zane!" Lilly hissed, looking around. "You can't snoop on other people's phones."

"I didn't," Zane told her honestly. "I was about to put it in my pocket when that last message flashed up."

"Zane," Lilly glanced at the message, "you're going to have to let her go speak to Trent. I know it must hurt but ..."

"It's not jealousy Lilly," Zane was only half lying, "Trent doesn't have his phone."

Lilly's eyes grew huge as she stared at Zane and the meaning of what he'd just said sank in.

"Go," Lilly all but pushed him out the door. "I'll cover for you. Keep me updated!" She made Zane promise.

"Thank you for bringing my phone, Mom." Kelsey gave Erin a hug.

"Of course. You need it, especially if you're driving home late." Erin smiled at her daughter. "I see the emergency room is busy tonight."

"There was some pile up on the motorway," Kelsey explained. "It looks like it's going to be a long night." Her pager went off. "Sorry, Mom." She kissed Erin on the cheek and took off.

Erin turned to leave and realized Kelsey hadn't taken her phone. She was about to run after Kelsey when a message from Zane appeared on the screen.

"*Kelsey, is your mother still with you?*" Zane wrote.

Erin frowned and decided to call him.

"Kelsey," Zane breathed. "Is your mother still with you? If she is I need you to keep her at the hospital. Please don't let her go near Trent."

"This is Erin," Erin said frostily. "How did you know I was going to see Trent? Did you find my phone?"

"Yes," Zane admitted. "Lilly found it and gave it to me to give back to you."

"So you read my messages?" Erin said angrily. "You had no right to do that."

"It's not what you think," Zane said defensively. "Erin, I don't have time to explain but please stay there at the hospital. You can't go meet Trent."

"First you violate my privacy and now you're trying to dictate who I can and cannot see?" Anger started to seep through Erin. *How dare he! He'd been ignoring her since he got back to White Sands Cove. He'd taken off and run away without an explanation and now he was trying to tell her who she could and couldn't see?*

"It's not...." Zane didn't get a chance to finish before she hung up on him.

Erin was more determined than ever to go see Trent now. *Who did Zane McCaid think he was?* She stormed down the passage to a nurse's station and asked them where she could find Dr. Carnegie. Erin always felt so proud when she called Kelsey doctor. The nurse recognized Erin as Kelsey's mother and directed her down the hallway to casualty.

Erin's anger had filled her head with hot angry steam by the time she'd stomped her way to casualty. Another nurse who Erin stopped took her to the room where Erin was. Before she could get to Kelsey the door of the room burst open as Kelsey and Dr. Barnes rushed the patient out with Dr. Barnes barking orders to get the man to an operating room.

Kelsey saw Erin and as she turned towards her mother Erin caught a glimpse of the patient and froze. *Oh no!* The feeling of cold chills ran down Erin's spine when pieces of Zane's conversation she'd just had with him ran through her mind.

"Mom," Kelsey ran to her mother. "What are you still doing here?"

"Your phone," Erin gave Kelsey her phone. "When ..." she pointed to the man about to be wheeled into an elevator.

"He was brought in early this evening," Kelsey said softly. "I really can't discuss this with you, Mom. He's under heavy guard at the moment." She took the phone from her mother. "Thanks for this." She pocketed her phone, kissed her mother's forehead, before running to the elevator.

Erin didn't know how long she'd stood staring at the elevator in shock. The recent phone call with Zane playing over and over in her head. She felt numb for a few minutes before tingling stabs of fear started shooting through her when she realized Zane hadn't been trying to control her ...

"Erin," Zane's deep voice snapped her out of her reverie.

Erin turned to see him running towards her. She couldn't remember moving but the next thing she knew she was engulfed in his strong arms.

"Thank God you're still here." Zane hugged her tight and kissed the top of her head. "I was so scared, but Phillip called to say you weren't there and your car was still at the hospital."

Zane was trying to protect her. Even after reading those texts which made it seem like she was going to hear Trent out and maybe give him a second chance, Zane had left everything to save her.

"I'm sorry." Erin looked up at Zane, her eyes misty with unshed tears. "I'm so sorry."

"You have nothing to be sorry about." Zane put her down and stared into her jewel green eyes. "I'm the one that owes you an apology."

"I was so busy trying not to be hurt and angry over you just leaving with no explanation that I didn't even think that Trent had no access to his phone." Erin couldn't believe she'd nearly walked into a trap.

"I was so angry and upset when I saw the messages that I nearly forgot Trent was in a solitary lockup." Zane swallowed. "Then when I realized you were walking into a trap, all I could think of was getting to you before Trent's sister did."

"How did you know it was Trent's sister who sent those texts?" Erin asked.

"She had one of Phillip's agents who worked for her steal Trent's items from the evidence locker," Zane explained. "When her assassination attempt on Trent didn't work out too well her next best leverage would've been you."

"What happened to Trent?" Erin asked. "I saw him get wheeled to the operating room."

"That agent that stole Trent's items tried to poison Trent and when that didn't work, he brazenly let himself into Trent's cell to shut him up," Zane told Erin. "He unfortunately managed to puncture Trent's lung before Trent subdued him."

"Oh no." Erin's eyes were wide. "I..." she looked towards the elevator.

"Would you like to wait and find out how he is?" Zane asked Erin.

"I'll stay," Erin told him. "You go back to the party."

"Not a chance." Zane shook his head. "I'm not letting you out of my sight ever again." He pulled Erin to her and kissed her. "I love you, Erin."

"I love you too, Zane," Erin said softly as Zane pulled her in for another kiss.

They were interrupted by a phone call.

"Hello," Zane cleared his throat answering his phone. "What?" His eyes were big. "We're here at the hospital. I'll meet you at the entrance."

"Zane?" Erin looked at him.

"It seems like my newest niece or nephew is tired of waiting to meet us." Zane's face was a little pale. "Piper's waters broke and they're bringing her in now."

"Didn't she still have just over two weeks left to go?" Erin asked wide eyed.

"Yes," Zane nodded. "I..."

"Let's go." Erin smiled and took his hand. "We'd just be

sitting around here waiting for news of Trent while we can be waiting with our family."

She liked saying our family to Zane. It felt right and she was about to meet the first new member of their big mixed-up family.

"We have a baby boy." Alex came out of Piper's hospital room a few hours later looking dazed and amazed at the same time. "A tiny little baby boy."

Zane grinned once they were told the latest addition to his family was healthy. Craig Wynn might have been born a few weeks early, but he came into the world letting everyone around him know he was there. He had quite a set of lungs on him and wasn't afraid to use them.

"I'm so sorry I ruined your stag-hens." Piper stifled a yawn as she reluctantly let the nurse take baby Craig away from her.

"Are you kidding?" Fallon grinned down at her younger sister. "This was the best stag-hen ever because of the newest edition to our family."

"He's beautiful, my little sister." Hunter leaned down and kissed Piper on the forehead.

"Yes," Ashley sniffed. "He's so tiny but has already made a huge impression on all our hearts."

"We can always have another party," Stephanie told Piper. "It's not every day we get to celebrate the birth of a new little soul into our family."

"Thank you." Piper's eyes looked heavy. "I love you all."

"I think the new mother needs to get her rest," Kelsey gently nudged everyone out of Piper's room. "I'll check on her and little Craig throughout the night," she promised. "Now go home. You can all come back in the morning."

"Please tell Trent we came to see him when he wakes up," Erin squeezed Kelsey's hand.

"I will Mom," Kelsey promised Erin.

"Bye my love," Alex kissed Piper gently on the lips. "I'll see you tomorrow."

The big extended McCaid, Carnegie, and Cooper family ambled tiredly from the hospital. It had been a long day and even longer night that had spread into the early hours of the morning.

Chapter Forty
A TRIPLE WEDDING

The wedding day had arrived. Lilly was more than a little stressed. She'd been asked to step in and take Piper's place as the maid of honor for the McCaid family's triple wedding. The past two days had been a rush of dress fitting, making sure the three brides had everything they needed, and ensuring everything else for the wedding was on track. She was sure she had bags under her eyes as she'd hardly had any sleep over the last two nights.

Lilly looked at herself in the full-length mirror. She loved the soft rose pink shoestring dress that fell softly around her trim figure and showed off her summer tan. Her strawberry blonde hair had been artfully arranged to cascade softly onto her delicate shoulders. The gold strappy heels were just high enough to emphasize her long legs but not too high as Lilly struggled with extremely high heels. She admired the way Erin was so elegant and stable in her ridiculously high heels. If Lilly wore the shoes Erin did, she'd have permanently sprained, if not broken, ankles.

She sighed as she applied a light lip gloss and looked at the time. Lilly had to make one more check of the ball room to ensure that everything was perfect. She also had to make sure

Caleb, who was filming the wedding, remembered to live stream it for Piper and Kelsey who were going to watch it from the hospital. Baby Craig had decided to meet the family early so Piper was still in hospital. Kelsey had taken an extra shift to keep Piper company. With the help of Dr. Barnes, Kelsey had managed to sneak in some snacks and cake for the two of them and the maternity nursing staff on duty.

The previous night Caleb had shown her the pictures he'd taken of the retreat and the setup for the triple wedding. The images were beautiful and somehow captured both the beauty and magical essence of the Cove. Caleb would be starting work at Phillip and Max's security company at the end of summer and had decided to make White Sands Cove his home. Michael and Lilly had wanted to try and find some suitable all year around tenant for the larger cabins. She was so glad it was going to be the Carnegies and maybe Zane.

She took a deep breath before she left the room in the White Sands Cove hotel she'd been using to get dressed. This was her first wedding, and she was really nervous about it. Lilly wanted everything to go off without a hitch and for the three brides to have their perfect day. As she stepped out into the hall of her hotel, she turned to have a look around at the modern and olden day mixed decor. They had tried to rebuild the hotel around the original manor house that once stood in the same spot.

"I hope you're okay with everything we've done here, Great-great-granddad Jacques," Lilly smiled as she spoke to the pictures that hung on the top floor wall.

She smiled looking around at the names of the rooms on the penthouse floor. They were named after Michael and Lilly's grandparents and their heroic sisters, going back to Jacques and Angelique. The rooms on the other three floors were all named after butterflies.

The lift dinged, drawing Lilly's attention to it. Her heart picked up speed when Caleb, wearing a tuxedo, stepped out of it. He looked so handsome. As her face lit up with a big smile Caleb took a few photos of her.

"Beautiful," Caleb breathed, walking over to Lilly, and pulling her to him for a deep kiss. "You look incredible."

"You look awfully handsome in your tuxedo," Lilly smiled up at him.

"You're needed downstairs," Caleb told her. "The whole place looks amazing Lilly."

"I can't take all the credit," Lilly laughed. "I had a lot of help from Piper, Kelsey, your mom, you, Michael, and Zane."

"But none of this would be happening if it wasn't for yours and Michael's dream." Caleb kissed her again before they took the elevator to the function room floor. "Are you ready?"

"Yes," Lilly looked at Caleb nervously. "Here goes my first ever wedding function at White Sands Cove."

"Not just any wedding either." Caleb smiled down proudly at her. "A triple wedding."

Zane was all fingers. It wasn't the first time he'd walked his nieces down the aisle. He really wished his older brother, Craig, and his wife were here though. They'd missed so much of their children's lives having been swept up in a dangerous situation that forced them into witness protection. In order to protect their family, Zane's older brother Craig McCaid and his wife Dorothy-Rose, had to appear dead and lost to their family.

For almost twenty-four years the McCaids had thought Craig and Dorothy were dead. Lost at sea in a boating accident. Until seven months ago when Zane's nephew, Hunter, had been charged with murder. All the McCaids had banded together to help clear Hunter's name, which had led the family to make some amazing discoveries. One of those discoveries led Zane's family to White Sands Cove while another brought Zane's older brother Craig back home. Craig and Dorothy had been in witness protection having been witnesses that put a powerful criminal behind bars. Unfortunately, Dorothy, Craig's wife, had passed away four years earlier. It had been a very emotional reunion the day Craig, who now went by the name Cam Gracie, stepped into his oldest niece's hospital room.

Craig, or rather Cam, was hoping to be able to attend his two daughters and son's wedding. Although the agency was allowing Zane's brother to attend the wedding, they couldn't risk Cam walking his daughters down the aisle. Zane felt like he was stealing a piece of his brother's heart by walking Cam's children down the aisle on this special day.

Zane really had to try and remember that his brother's name was now Cam and that Craig had died twenty-four years ago to save the lives of his family. Craig or rather Cam, was quite a bit older than Zane. There was an eleven year difference in their age. Zane had hero worshipped his older brother. The day the McCaid family were told Cam was lost at sea with his wife, a part of Zane had died. He'd suddenly felt lost because his hero had fallen.

It had taken Zane years to forgive the sea and be able to enjoy sailing again. The only reason he ever set foot on a boat was because of his eldest niece, Fallon. All his brother's children were gifted sailors that loved the sea, but Fallon had the same almost obsessive love of yachts that her father had. Zane had been so scared that the sea would try to claim Fallon too and it almost had, twice.

Zane finally managed to get his bowtie right. He hated tuxedos and swore if he ever got married it would be in a cotton shirt and boardshorts on the beach or aboard a yacht. A knock on his cabin door made him notice that it was time to go across to the hotel. He felt as nervous as his nieces and nephew must be feeling.

"Hi Shane," Zane answered the door. "I'm ready, I just need to get my jacket."

"It's so hot." Shane fiddled with his bowtie. "I feel like someone's trying to strangle me with a pom-pom."

"I'm sure Stephanie appreciates you doing this for her," Zane grinned at the man who'd become his best friend in such a short time.

"I'm honored that she asked me," Shane told Zane. "Your nephew is marrying a remarkable woman."

"I know," Zane nodded. "My two nieces, Ashley and Fallon are also marrying remarkable men."

"Especially Ryan Hurst." Shane whistled. "I own one of his AI's."

"Shane," Zane pulled the door behind him as they left his cabin, "You forget I've been to yours and Amy's mansion in La Jolla." He grinned at Shane. "You have more than one of Ryan's AI devices."

"What can I say?" Shane shrugged. "I'm a technology junkie."

"I see a wedding for you in the near future," Zane teased Shane.

"We'll have to see about that." Shane's eyes narrowed. "Don't get me wrong, I like Caleb, but I'm still trying to figure out if I like him with Lilly or not."

"Oh for pity's sake!" Amy overheard what Shane had said. "Just be happy that your daughter has found a man like Caleb to fall in love with and stop interfering!" she warned him before fixing up Shane's bow tie and jacket. "You look very handsome."

"Of course I do," Shane grinned cheekily. "I really feel like I should be sitting and having a little fatherly chat with Hunter before I give Stephanie away to him."

"Shane," Amy punched him on the arm. "You already grilled Hunter for an hour each day this past week."

"What?" Shane looked at his wife innocently before he noticed the black look Zane was giving him. "Okay," he held up his hands. "I felt like I had an obligation to Stephanie's late father to do so." He shrugged. "I know if I wasn't here when

Lilly got married, I hope that whoever she asked to walk her down the aisle would do the same for me."

"That's actually so sweet and very gallant of you." Zane raised his eyebrows. "I completely understand where you're coming from."

"Thank you," Shane nodded.

"My poor nephew must be so nervous right now." Zane pulled a face. "I also grilled him about being a good husband to Stephanie and taking care of her."

"What's wrong with the two of you?" Amy looked from Shane to Zane, thinking they could be brothers. "Unbelievable. You do realize we live in the twenty-first century? You're both lucky these modern women want you oldies to walk them down the aisle."

Amy threw her hands up in exasperation and stormed off.

"Well looks like we just angered our first female for the day." Shane shook his head.

"Speak for yourself." Zane patted Shane on the shoulder. "I already had my great-niece, Blair, tell me that if I wasn't her uncle, she'd hate me this morning."

"What did you do?" Shane emphasized.

"I wouldn't let her borrow my pick-up truck without Chase being with her." Zane shook his head.

"I've been there with Lilly when she was that age." Shane grinned. "Only Lilly would take it anyway."

"Oh I caught Blair and Paige trying to sneak away in it." Zane laughed as he walked into the hotel.

"Zane?" a familiar voice made Zane turn around. A big smile split his face. "Cra... I mean Cam."

Zane was so happy to see his older brother at the wedding with his fiancé, Laurie Cartwright.

"You look really dashing, little brother," Cam said to Zane. "I'm going to speak to my girls. I have something for them from their mother."

"Dad?" Hunter, Zane's nephew who was one of the grooms that were getting married, walked up to them.

"Hunter," Cam's eyes misted over with tears. "Look at you. I'm so glad I could be here this time," he said softly to his son.

"I'm so glad you could be here too," Hunter greeted Laurie warmly. "I'm glad you could come with my father today." He gave her a hug.

"Have you been to see Piper yet?" Zane asked Cam.

"We went straight to the hospital." Cam had to wipe a tear from his eye. "My grandson Craig is beautiful."

"There you three are," Erin walked swiftly towards Shane, Zane, and Hunter. "Gertie is looking for the three of you."

"Cam," Zane grabbed Erin and pulled her to him, "this is Erin." He looked down at her and caught her eyes with his. "The love of my life."

"I..." Erin was lost in Zane's leaf green eyes and the power of his love for her filling her heart. "You know I feel the same way about you." She smiled before turning to greet Cam and Laurie. "But you'll have to excuse us because Gertie needs to speak to these three."

"You go ahead," Cam told them. "But could I speak to my son before I send him on to you? I have something from his mother."

"Of course." Erin smiled before marching Zane and Shane off to where Gertie was waiting by the trellises for them.

Chapter Forty-One
THE WEDDING CRASHERS

*E*rin watched as Zane walked down the wide red carpeted aisle that stretched out towards the lake at the back of the hotel. Rows of chairs were filled with friends and relatives of the three couples getting married. Zane proudly walked with two of his nieces, Fallon and Ashley, linked to his arms. Shane walked next to them with Zane's nephew's bride to be on his arm. The women looked so beautiful in their wedding gowns.

Waiting and staring in awe at their brides stood three grooms each decked out in their tuxedos. They were a handsome group of men. Gertie, the minister, stood looking so smart dressed in white and gold. Gertie stood in the middle of the three trellis that made the setting look like a fairy tale. Shane and Zane had built them to resemble large arched castle windows. Around each trellis was draped soft lace and delicate pink creeping roses.

Erin sighed and tears filled her eyes. She got so emotional at weddings. But this was extra emotional and extra special. Like her family the McCaids had also gone through hell over the past year. But like Erin's family they had pushed through hell and landed on the shores of La Jolla. The place of golden sunshine, soft white sand, and the magic healing powers of the glistening blue Pacific Ocean.

Zoe offered Erin a tissue. She smiled gratefully at the young woman and took one. By the time the three ceremonies were over Erin had laughed, cried, and cheered along with the rest of the wedding guests. It was the wedding vows that had squeezed at her heart and pumped the tears down her cheeks the most. Especially Fallon and Daniel's.

Fallon the moment I saw you standing in your denim shorts and stained sneakers I knew I was lost. In this past year we've been through a lifetime of adventures together and I hope we get to have a million more. Only without all the danger because that day I nearly lost you I felt my soul slowly dying too. You're my everything. Like Lilly likes to say, you're my heart's forever home, my soulmate.

Erin sniffed and wiped her eyes once again. A strong warm hand wrapped around hers. Erin looked up into Zane's eyes. He pulled her to him and kissed the top of her head.

"Daniel certainly has a way with words," Erin said shakily.

"I taught him everything he knows." Zane wiped a tear from Erin's cheek, making her smile.

"I think Daniel's very scary intimidating mother would disagree with you." Erin laughed and hugged Zane's arm.

"She is quite a scary lady," Zane whispered to Erin. "It was like meeting the queen the first time we were introduced to him. I didn't know whether to bow or curtsey."

"You are so bad," Erin laughed. "But I do know how you must've felt." She shook her head. "I also know her reputation because my parents move in the same circles as Daniel's mother."

Erin and Zane stood while the three newly married couples made their way towards the hotel, followed by a teary Gertie.

*T*he wedding toasts and cake cutting was finally over. Zane stood back watching the wedding celebrations from the back of the room. While he watched Erin be twirled around the floor by her son, Zane's heart expanded in his chest.

"She's lovely," a soft familiar voice said beside him.

Zane smiled. "She really is," he agreed softly.

"I'm happy for you my love," the soft whisper drifted over him. "You've been alone so long, you deserve this."

"Do I?" Zane's eyes glittered with unshed tears. "I should've never let you go inside that shop." His voice was hoarse. "I left you."

"No," the soft voice said, "you didn't. You did exactly what you needed to do. Look at those two lovely teenagers that are here today because you did what you had to do."

"But you're not here," Zane took a sip of his whisky.

"Yes, I am," she said. "I'm always here with you, my love. But it's time for you to let me be that faded memory you take out and smile at fondly. Not the hole in your heart."

"I'll always love you," Zane swallowed. "Erin's not replacing your place in my heart."

"Of course not," she laughed. "She showed you how to open your heart and that there's enough room in that huge heart of yours for everyone."

"Thank you." Zane closed his eyes and saw Ria's startling blue eyes smiling at him.

"Now go to her," he could hear her say. "Remember what you used to say, there's no time like the present to present your intentions and grab every opportunity life throws your way." She blew him a kiss. "Now's your chance to do something for yourself for a change. Seize the day big guy!"

Zane took a deep breath. His eyes settled on Erin and Caleb's dance coming to an end. He downed the last of his drink as Erin laughed up at her son before he walked off. Her head lifted and their eyes met from across the room. Zane felt his heart feel like it was about to burst with love for the tiny woman standing staring back him.

He put his glass down and walked towards her holding her eyes hostage with his. Zane pulled Erin into his arms the moment he stepped up onto the dance floor in front of her. His lips crushed hers as he lifted her up to him.

"I love you," Zane whispered into Erin's ears. "Will you marry me, right here today?"

"Are you serious?" Erin's feet were no longer on the ground making her remember the day they'd met.

"I've never been more serious about anything in my life," Zane's voice was hoarse. "We can speak to Gertie and Jennifer's a judge now so..."

"Yes," Erin grinned and pressed her lips against his. "Yes, I love you, Zane McCaid."

"What?" Lilly gaped at Zane and Erin. "I..." She bit her lip. "Yes...." She squealed excitedly.

"What's going on?" Caleb frowned at the three of them in the corner.

"Your mother and Zane are getting married." Lilly pulled an excited face.

"Mom?" Caleb looked at Erin a little shocked. "When did this come about?"

"Now," Zane told him.

"Oh," Lilly grinned up at Caleb. "They're getting married now."

"What?" Caleb's voice bellowed out as the music stopped and everyone at the wedding turned to look their way.

"Zane and Erin are getting married," Lilly announced on a squeal.

"***D**id Lilly just say my mother and your uncle are getting married?"* Kelsey was sitting on Piper's hospital bed watching the triple wedding Caleb was streaming for them.

"I believe she did," Piper frowned. "If it wasn't for my son, I'd make you bust me out of this hospital right now."

"At least we get to watch it." Kelsey started to dial Caleb. "Let's find out what's going on."

"It's like watching a real-life soap opera." Piper grinned. "My uncle and your mother crashing in on the triple wedding."

"I'm glad for them." Kelsey smiled at Piper. "So, it looks like we're going to be cousins soon."

"Welcome to the crazy McCaid family." Piper gave Kelsey a hug as the tears sprang to her eyes. "Aren't the tears supposed to stop now?"

"No," Kelsey smiled sympathetically at Piper.

"Great," Piper sniffed. "That's just great."

"***T**his is so exciting."* Gertie grinned. "I'm so glad your children's parent trap idea worked."

"Sorry?" Zane frowned. "Parent trap?" He looked over at the suddenly guilty looks of his extended family.

"Do any of you have something to tell us?" Erin asked the guilty faces.

"Uh..." Kelsey said over the phone. "Piper and I have to go, it's Craig's feeding time." She hung up.

"Coward," Caleb looked at his phone.

"I'm waiting." Erin's eyes narrowed.

"We didn't like that you and Uncle Zane had broken up and had a lot of discord between you," Zoe took the floor. "You two make a perfect couple and seeing the two of you together somehow made the world around us all make more sense," she explained. "Being around the two of you is like coming home and smelling fresh baked bread, hearing hearty laughter, and knowing you're home — safe, loved, and happy with two people we trust the most in the world."

"Zoe," Erin's eyes misted over. "Honey." She reached out towards the teenager who surprisingly went and hugged her. "That's beautiful."

"Long story short," Caleb felt a little like a coward having let a fourteen-year-old be the first to step forward. "We could see how the two of you were hurting and Zoe hadn't seen the Parent Trap."

"How do parents split up their twins and then not tell them they have a twin sibling?" Zoe asked the question again.

"It's a movie." Logan threw his hands up in exasperation.

"I wouldn't have liked to be separated from you." Zoe looked at her twin brother.

"You're getting really good at this emotional blackmail thing," Lilly whispered to Zoe, and they did a secret fist bump. "Way to go kiddo."

"I had a good teacher," Zoe whispered back.

"Our parent trapping didn't work," Lilly told them. "Zane came home too early and then Erin got delayed."

"The Braxton hicks." Zane shook his head and pinched the bridge of his nose. "I had to admit I did think it was strange for Piper to act up like that."

"Then Piper really did go into labor," Fallon said on a hysterical giggle.

"Amateurs," Shane grinned. "It takes a pro to pull a parent trap."

All eyes turned to him in shock.

Shane winked and raised his glass before saying. "Are we going to start this fourth wedding or just stand around gaping at me like goldfish?"

"Would you be my best man?" Zane shook his head smiling as Shane.

"I thought you'd never ask," Shane grinned.

"Zoe," Erin looked at the young woman, "would you stand with me as my maid of honor?"

"Seriously?" Zoe looked shocked. "Yes." She nodded.

Gertie couldn't help the big grin on her face. She loved this big extended family. Usually, she'd put the couples she was about to marry through a series of meetings and questions. But if ever she'd seen two people who were meant to be together it was Erin and Zane. Besides, if she didn't marry them the newly appointed Judge Jennifer Guilford was more than happy to step in and marry them.

"Zane and Erin have asked to say their vows." Gertie took the tissue Zoe slipped to her. "Thanks, honey," she whispered.

"Zane," Erin looked up at the tall man towering over her. "The first time I laid eyes on you, you physically lifted me up as if I weighed nothing more than a feather." She smiled as he grinned. "You may have removed me from the room, but my heart stayed behind with you." She raised her hand up and touched his cheek. "It took me all these years to find you and I can't wait to build a future with you," she turned and looked at her family, "and our big, crazy, lovable family."

Two dogs barked from the side.

"You four as well," Erin laughed looking at Goose, Lunar, Rafferty, and Phantom who stood lazily grazing in his field nearby. "I love you, Zane McCaid."

"Erin," Zane smiled down at her, "you opened up a heart that was closed to everyone but my family. You taught me to love and trust again. I didn't even know how big the hole in my heart was until you filled it with your love, kindness, and compassion."

He put his forehead against hers. "I love you."

"I know you didn't have time to get any rings so if there are no objections..." Gertie's voice was hoarse as she dabbed at her eyes.

"Wait," Cam stood up. "I have something for Zane."

All heads turned to Cam as he fished something out of his pocket.

"When I first got married to Dorothy, Mom asked me to make sure that I gave you this when you got married." Cam put the box in Zane's hand.

Zane opened the box and his face fell. His eyes went glassy with moisture.

"Our mother's ring." Zane's head shot around to look at his father, Finn McCaid who smiled at his youngest son and gave him a nod. "I..." He swallowed as Cam gave Zane a hug before sitting down.

"That's beautiful," Erin's voice was just as husky as Zane's.

"Well?" Gertie looked at Zane impatiently.

"Sorry." Zane cleared his throat as he took the ring and slipped it onto Erin's ring finger.

"I now pronounce you husband and wife. You may kiss the bride." Gertie smiled.

Zane pulled Erin to him and kissed her passionately to a roar of cheers.

Chapter Forty-Two
THE CRAB SHACK ANNUAL END OF SUMMER FESTIVAL

THREE YEARS LATER

It was a beautiful day to start off the annual Crab Shack End of Summer Festival. The White Sands Cove Hotel had now officially been open for three years. The retreat was a huge success, and all their rooms, cabins, and adventures were booked up for two years in advance. Lilly, Michael, Ray, and their four new business partners were looking to expand their wedding venue to keep up with all the wedding bookings.

Zane had accepted the position Phillip and Max had offered him at the agency. Erin and Zane had moved into Zane's larger cabin at White Sands Cove after they'd been married. Erin's new hotel venture with Michael's mom and his Aunt Miranda was taking off and they too were looking to expand into the restaurant business. The three women had been speaking to Michael and Lilly about franchising the Crab Shack.

Michael grinned as he got up on the stage to kick off the two-day long festival. His eyes met with Kelsey's and held. Even after three years together his heart still lurched every time he saw her. Kelsey smiled lovingly at Michael and blew him a kiss. His eyes fell to the gold chain around her neck, upon which hung her wedding and engagement ring. His smile grew wider when he watched Kelsey's hand's protectively rub her rounded belly. Michael couldn't believe that in a few months' time he was going to be a father.

"Welcome to the third annual Crab Shack Summer Festival," Michael started talking over the mic. "As you know, we usually kick the summer off with my beautiful wife riding the Phantom horse and hiding the final flag chase flag." He smiled down at Kelsey again. "This year however, Lady Kelsey Cooper is unable to do the honors. In her place my ..."

One of the hotel staff ran up onto the stage and whispered in his ear. Michael nodded and laughed.

"Okay, so it seems Lady Lilly won't be able to ride the Phantom either," Michael turned and grinned. "But we'd like to welcome the new Phantom festival rider, Lady Ray Guilford."

The crowd went wild as seventeen-year-old Ray rode up on Phantom carrying the final flag for the flag race. When the ceremony was finished, and Ray rode off to plant the flag in the designated secret location, Michael and Kelsey went to find Lilly.

"Lilly," Michael and Kelsey walked into her office in the hotel. "What's going on?" His brows furrowed worriedly.

"Come in and close the door," Lilly told Michael.

Kelsey and Michael looked from Caleb to Lilly. They'd gotten married two months after Michael and Kelsey had.

"Are you okay?" Kelsey asked Lilly. "You look very pale."

Lilly looked up at Caleb who grinned down at his wife and took her hand.

"I'm pregnant." Lilly grinned, and tears sprang to her eyes.

"Oh Lilly." Tears didn't spring to Kelsey's eyes these days, they just rolled right out of them at every opportunity they got it seemed. "Congratulations." She went to hug Lilly and Caleb.

"That's awesome." Michael hugged his cousin and shook

Caleb's hand. "I take it this secret meeting is because you haven't told either of your parents yet?"

"No," Caleb shook his head.

"What haven't you told either parents yet?" Shane, followed by his wife, Erin, and Zane, walked into the office.

"You were supposed to close the door." Lilly glared at Michael.

"I did," Michael told Lilly exasperatedly. "I told you to get the door fixed because it springs open."

"What's going on?" Erin looked from Caleb to Lilly.

"I'm pregnant," Lilly said shyly.

Erin, Shane, Amy, and Zane all went dead quiet and stared at Lilly dumbstruck.

"Lilly," Zane broke the silence then went over to give her a big hug then shake Caleb's hand. "Congratulations."

Shane was the next to go over and give his daughter a big hug followed by a thrilled Amy and Erin.

"I'm going to have five new grandchildren in the next year," Erin's eyes were glittering with happiness.

"It's going to be a busy year baby wise for the family," Amy said excitedly.

"Yes, Fallon is due soon, followed by Stephanie, then Ashley, then Kelsey, and not too long after that our little Lilly." Erin turned and grinned at her daughter-in-law.

"Oggy Eri," a little voice called Erin from the door.

"So sorry, Erin," Piper ran after three-year-old Craig. "But you know every time we visit all he wants is you."

"And all Oggy Eri wants is her little Craig," Erin laughed. She bent down to pick up the adorable little boy. Craig looked so much like his great-uncle Zane right down to his leaf green eyes.

Chapter Forty-Three
EPILOGUE
Walk Through the Hills

TWO YEARS LATER

"I can't believe Zoe and Logan are almost nineteen," Erin sighed.

"Yes, they're such intelligent kids. We knew they'd take after their mother Ashley and graduate high-school early," Zane said proudly.

"Ashley said that Logan and Zoe have had a bit of a falling out." Erin frowned worriedly. "They used to be so close."

"I believe it had something to do with Zoe accepting some internship at that new aerospace project when she graduates." Zane shook his head.

"Well, I can't wait to see both of them." Erin smiled up at Zane. "They haven't visited us since Kelsey's daughter was born two years ago."

"Uncle Zane? Aunt Erin?" a deep voice made them both turn and stop dead in their tracks.

Gone was the tall gangly teenager. In his place stood a tall, toned, and extremely good looking man in a well-tailored suit.

"Logan?" Erin and Zane choked.

"It's so good to see you both," Logan was a few inches taller than Zane.

"Hi," Zoe came up behind Logan before stepping around him.

"Zoe," Zane grinned and gave his great-niece a hug. "Look at you, all grown up."

"Hello, Uncle Zane." Zoe leaned down and hugged Erin. "Aunty Erin."

"Hello, Zoe." Logan gave his sister a small smile.

"Logan." Zoe eyed him coolly.

"You're looking beautiful, my dear." Erin suddenly realized what Ashley had meant. You could cut the tension between the twins with a knife. "I love that dress."

"Thank you." Zoe smiled at Erin.

The soft blue sundress gently hugged Zoe's tall trim frame and emphasized her long tanned legs. Her pretty pink painted toes peeked out of white and gold sandals. Her long golden blond hair hung down below her shoulders and her long thick eyelashes framed her big blue eyes. She had grown into an incredibly beautiful young woman, Erin thought.

While they were loading the twins' luggage into Zane's car Logan got a message.

"You didn't tell me Chase and his fiancé were here for the summer." Logan looked up and something flashed in his eyes.

"Oh, yes." Zane smiled. "We invited him and Jayde for the summer as Jayde wants to have their wedding at White Sands Cove." His eyes narrowed. "Is that going to be a problem for the two of you?"

"No." Zoe's face, as usual, was expressionless.

"No problem here." Logan shook his head and shrugged but his eyes told a different story.

"Come on," Zoe dragged her reluctant brother, uncle, and aunt for a hike up the very steep part of Crab Shack Hills. "Do you remember five years ago when we spent our summer looking for the Guilford Jewel?"

"Yes," Zane, Erin, and Logan all muttered together.

"I've been doing extensive research on the boat," Zoe told them, not even a little bit out of breath. "You all really need to exercise more." She frowned as she watched them all sitting down to take a rest.

"Zoe," Logan breathed. "We've been walking uphill for just over an hour."

"Yes," Zane muttered, "and I know I look handsomely youthful and all..."

"Yes, you do my love." Erin gave Zane a kiss. "We're not as young as we used to be." She finished Zane's sentence for him.

"Since when did you become an Olympic hiker?" Logan moaned.

"Since you left me alone at MIT." Zoe glared at her brother.

"Now, you two," Zane decided to nip the argument in the bud, "remember your truce."

"Anyway..." Zoe ignored the warning look in Zane's eyes. "Granddad Cam and I found out why we would never find the yacht."

"You've found the boat haven't you?" Logan looked at his sister.

"Possibly." Zoe's eyes narrowed. "What are they doing here?"

Zane and Erin looked at each other wide-eyed as they noticed the look in Zoe's eyes. Anger. It was the first time they'd seen Zoe look at anyone with such disdain. They both turned around to see who she was looking at to find Chase and his fiancé Jayde walking towards them.

"Hi," Chase greeted them. At twenty-three he was as tall as his father, had strong broad shoulders, a well-toned body, and was ruggedly handsome. He was also interning at his father's company. "You left without us." His eyes glanced over at Zoe.

"I did inform you that we'd be leaving at six am sharp." Zoe looked at Chase blankly. "You weren't at the rendezvous point on time." She shrugged.

"I'm sorry, Chase." Erin apologized to Chase and Jayde. "You know how Zoe likes everything to work like a Swiss watch."

Erin, Chase, and Jayde turned around to find that Logan, Zane, and Zoe had disappeared.

"Where the heck have they gone?" Erin frowned.

"*H*ow on earth did you find this tunnel, Zoe," Zane asked, amazed.

"Sorry we had to sneak you away like that, Uncle Zane," Zoe explained. "Logan and I don't trust Jayde."

"Does this have anything to do with her turning Logan down for Chase?" Zane asked then wished he hadn't when his great-niece and great-nephew stopped and glared at him.

"I never asked, nor did I want to ask Jayde out," Logan informed Zane. "Zoe and I think she said that to drive a wedge between us and Chase."

"Her stories also made Logan's girlfriend break up with him," Zoe said, turning to continue walking through the tunnel.

Zane and Logan followed her with Logan explaining the whole Jayde episode to Zane.

"Oh my God!" Zoe breathed catching both Zane's and Logan's attention as she came to a door with a boat carved onto it. Zoe pulled the key from the chain around her neck.

"How did you find the door to this tunnel and figure out it was in the Crab Shack Hills and not Pirates Wall?" Zane asked Zoe.

"Grandmother's note to us." Zoe's eyes were filled with excitement. "I wish Aunt Erin was here."

"I'll go get Erin and get rid of Chase." Zane smiled at them. "Don't worry, I won't offend him."

"No need," Erin's' voice made all of them jump. "I figured there was something up between the four of you yesterday when Zoe and Logan arrived in La Jolla."

"Thank you." Zoe and Logan said together.

"Zoe was about to tell us how she found this tunnel and the door." Logan brought Erin up to speed on what was going on.

"Logan's key he got from Granddad Cam opened the hidden tunnel door." Zoe held up Logan's key that had a ship on top of it. "The butterfly key with the clue in it that Aunt Fallon found should open this door."

Zoe switched her flashlight to a blue light and shone it on the door. An image of a butterfly with a ship in the middle appeared in invisible ink.

"Okay." Logan's brows drew together.

"Inside the butterfly key was the clue." Zoe dug in the pocket of her shorts and pulled out the note from the key. "On the one side the note is written, '*Guilford Jewel*' *but the* side is written '*walk through the hills*'."

"Walk through the hills," Logan snapped his fingers, "meaning these hills but not over them, through them like we just did."

"Amazing." Zane smiled proudly.

"Are we going to open the damn door or not?" Erin said suddenly impatiently. "Please tell me we are going to find a huge schooner in there packed with treasure." Her eyes shone.

"Not a huge schooner," Zoe said, stepping aside for Zane and Logan to open the door.

"You go first, Zoe." Erin smiled at the young woman. Erin's heart was beating so fast she felt like she was on a game show about to find out if she'd picked the correct box or not.

"Oh my." Zoe breathed. "It is so much more than I expected."

"Okay," Erin almost sent everyone flying as she pushed past; she just had to see what Zoe was looking at. This treasure had eluded them for so long. "Oh..." She sighed.

"No way!" Logan and Zane said together, stepping into the cavern behind Zoe and Erin.

"That's the Guilford Jewel." Zoe smiled. "It's even more beautiful than myself or Granddad Cam ever imagined."

"It's a gold jewel-encrusted statue that was carved by our great-great-grandfather." Zoe smiled. "All the treasure is hidden inside the statue."

"So, the Primus was the ship that brought Jacques and Angelique over to America?" Zane smiled.

"It seems that way." Zoe nodded.

"That's why the picture of the Guilford Jewel never looked quite right." Zane breathed.

"The picture was black and white and taken before the jewels were put on it," Zoe explained to them. "I think it was done like that deliberately to make people think the Guilford Jewel was another large yacht."

"Zoe." Erin smiled up at the young woman. "This is an incredible find and so well pieced together."

The mystery of the Guilford Jewel and missing treasure had finally been solved.

THE SEA BREEZE COTTAGE SERIES

The Sea Breeze Cottage - La Jolla Cove Series

La Jolla, a hilly sea-side coastal town, perched along the rugged shores of the Pacific Ocean forms part of the city of San Diego. Having spent the summers there with her aunt, it was the place Jennifer had called home as a young girl.

It had always been a place filled with the happiest of memories and times for Jennifer. Even as an adult, La Jolla was Jennifer's haven and place to recuperate from the fast-paced world of New York where she had moved to so she could pursue her career after law school.

Now a single mother of three children and a messy divorce behind her, her safe haven is scarred by a tragic accident that rips a hole in her world. Not only does she lose someone she loves dearly, but she unwittingly gets tangled up in a web of betrayal, mystery, and lies.

Go to https://www.amazon.co.uk/gp/kindle/series/B08SK5TMGV to read the series.

THE MCCAID SISTERS SERIES

The McCaid Sisters - A Clearwater Family Series

Fallon and Piper McCaid have not spoken to each other in fifteen years, much to the despair of their younger sister, Ashley. With their brother missing, their grandfather in recovery, and their family home under threat, the sisters are reunited.

The McCaid sisters are forced to put aside their differences to face their fears, unravel a mystery, and confront an unknown enemy.

Stand with them as they battle their demons, fight to protect their family, their home, and salvage their late father's reputation. Journey with them as they get swept away on the high seas of adventure and intrigue while stumbling upon true love and finding the courage to open their hearts to it once again.

Laugh, cry, and fall in love with the McCaid family, broken by loss and tragedy and torn apart by secrets and betrayal. Get lost in a story about the powerful bonds of family and the magic healing ability of love which can drive a person to defeat their worst fears in the face of danger and adversity.

Let the McCaid family show you that love does conquer all and knows no age limit. This timeless love story spans generations as everyone deserves a happily-ever-after.

__Escape into this mystery beach series. You'll fall in love with the McCaid family while you visit the warm white sands of Clearwater beach in Florida's Gulf Coast.__

Go to https://www.amazon.co.uk/gp/kindle/series/B08YWP6RQB to read the series.

A MYSTERY AT SUMMER LODGE SERIES

A Mystery at Summer Lodge - A Coastal Vineyard Series

As Danielle and Nicole Cartwright take on each other's identities they soon come to realize life is not as cushy as they thought it was on the other side.

Join the sisters as they learn how to walk in each other's shoes to come to a realization that they may not be as different as they thought they were.

Embark on an **adrenaline packed journey** through the Amazon jungle with Nicole who is about to find out that her sister is no pampered celebrity chef. Here, Nicole must learn to cook some of the traditional dishes of some of the tribes of the Amazon. But her problems don't only stop at the fact she can't cook. Her sister's TV show is up against a competition show. Nicole must go head to head with the arrogant but gorgeous Zach Goodwin.

Can Nicole manage to pull off impersonating her sister to save

her sister's beloved TV show while trying not to fall in love with a man totally wrong for her?

While Nicole is trying not to burn down the Amazon jungle with her terrible cooking skills, Danielle is roped into pretending to be Nicole. She must quickly learn how to run Summer Enterprises while flawlessly impersonating Nicole because a successful merger depends on it.

Guilted and bribed by her mother to impersonate her sister until after her great-grandmother's ninety-fifth birthday party when the merger will be signed off, Danielle is caught up in a corporate whirlwind of business meetings and galas, and everything she has ever hated about the rich and famous.

If Danielle can pull this off, she would finally be able to elevate Summer Lodge Wines to the prestige it once had.

First, she must solve the mystery of the **curse of the Summer Lodge Winery** which means delving into a vat of hurt and pain.

Escape into this Californian coastal vineyard series. You will fall in love with the Cartwright twins, whilst mysteries are unravelled and love blossoms for all.

Go to https://www.amazon.co.uk/gp/kindle/series/B094D7ZMJN to read the series.

VIP READERS

Thank you so much for purchasing my book. I would love to keep in touch with you and keep you updated.

Every week I send out lovely snippets of all my favorite places I write about in my books. From the beautiful sunsets of La Jolla Cove, San Diego to the white sandy beaches of the Florida Gulf Coast. Both places I visit often from Del Mar, San Diego, where I live.

If you would like to join us, please click on my logo below and pop in your email address. As a thank you I will send you the PREQUEL to 'A Coastal Vineyard' Series, FREE! You are welcome to email me direct at books@amyraffertyauthor.com. I would love to hear from you. I promise to not SPAM you or EVER share your email address with anyone else.

Amy Rafferty
AUTHOR

A Mystery at Summer Lodge - Prequel

Are you ready for romance, mystery, suspense and the power of family feuds and politics? Then it is time to escape to California and spend time with the Cartwright twins.

As Danielle and Nicole Cartwright take on each other's identities they soon come to realize life is not as cushy as they thought it was on the other side.

Join the sisters as they learn how to walk in each other's shoes to come to a realization that they may not be as different as they thought they were.

Embark on an **adrenaline-packed journey** through the Amazon jungle with Nicole who is about to find out that her sister is no pampered celebrity chef. Here, Nicole must learn to cook the traditional dishes of some of the tribes of the Amazon. But her problems don't only stop at the fact she can't cook. Her sister's TV show is up against a competition TV show. Nicole must go head to head with the arrogant but gorgeous Zach Goodwin.

. . .

Can Nicole manage to pull off impersonating her sister to save her sister's beloved TV show while trying not to fall in love with a man totally wrong for her?

While Nicole is trying not to burn down the Amazon jungle with her terrible cooking skills, Danielle is roped into pretending to be Nicole. She must quickly learn how to run Summer Enterprises while flawlessly impersonating Nicole because a successful merger depends on it.

Guilted and bribed by her mother to impersonate her sister until after her great-grandmother's ninety-fifth birthday party when the merger will be signed off, Danielle is caught up in a corporate whirlwind of business meetings, dinners and galas, and everything she has ever hated about the rich and famous.

If Danielle can pull this off, she would finally be able to elevate Summer Lodge Wines to the prestige it once had.

First, she must solve the mystery of the **curse of the Summer Lodge Winery** which means delving into a vat of hurt and pain.

Escape into this Californian coastal vineyard series. You will fall in love with the Cartwright twins, whilst mysteries are unravelled and love blossoms for all.

Go to https://landing.mailerlite.com/webforms/landing/y6w2d2 *for the FREE prequel of 'A Mystery at Summer Lodge"*

ABOUT THE AUTHOR

Amazon #1 Best-Seller, Amy Rafferty is a contemporary romance author of feel-good beach romance reads with heart-warming stories embracing humor and love.

Born in New York, previously a Lawyer, she now lives in San Diego with her beautiful children and cats!

Amy Rafferty
AUTHOR

Aside from writing, publishing and running her home, she spends as much time as she can visiting the beautiful San Diego and Florida beaches where she has family and friends. She calls San Diego her 'Garden of Eden', inspiring her to write clean and wholesome romance novels incorporating mystery, suspense and adventures for her characters as they find a way to open their hearts and let true love in.